Sorrow Lake

To Renee
Best wishes!

Also by Michael J. McCann

The Donaghue and Stainer Crime Novel Series

Blood Passage
Marcie's Murder
The Fregoli Delusion
The Rainy Day Killer

Supernatural Fiction

The Ghost Man

Sorrow Lake

A March and Walker Crime Novel

Michael J. McCann

The Plaid Raccoon Press
2015

Sorrow Lake is a work of fiction. Names, characters, institutions, places and events are either the product of the author's imagination or are used fictitiously. Any resemblance to actual persons, living or dead, events, or locales is entirely coincidental.

ISBN: 978-1-927884-02-7
eBook ISBN: 978-1-927884-03-4

Front cover photograph: Oleg Koslov/iStock
Back cover photograph: Michael J. McCann
Author photo: Tim D. McCann

www.theplaidraccoonpress.com
www.mjmccann.com

To the memory of my father
Hugh McCann
who taught me to love the written word

chapter ONE

His breath visible in the early morning air, Detective Constable Kevin Walker made his way down the hill and across the farmer's field toward the body. There was a crust on the snow from freezing rain that had fallen two days ago, and his boots punched crisp holes as he followed the footprints of the old man who'd spotted something in the middle of his field just after dawn and had come down to investigate.

As he walked, Kevin kept his eyes moving across the snow, alert for anything out of the ordinary. Other than two sets of tracks, one belonging to the farmer and the other to Ontario Provincial Police Constable Bonnie Charles, the first responder to the scene, the surface of the snow was pristine. He reached the little circle of footprints where the farmer had staggered back and retched, he saw the spilled coffee and the cup the old man had dropped in his shock, and then he stopped.

Close enough.

The victim was a man in his fifties. He wore inadequate low-cut boots, grey trousers, and a tweed car coat. No gloves. No hat. The back of his neck was seared where a close-contact gunshot had passed through the base of his skull and out the front of his neck, leaving a frozen bloodstain on the surface of the snow. His face was turned slightly toward Kevin. The eyes were open and lifeless. The mouth was a frozen oval.

Kevin recognized him. He lived in the village, not two blocks from Kevin's house.

He found it difficult to stop looking at the eyes. They had a disturbing cloudiness to them that made him feel uneasy. Kevin had participated in sudden death call outs before and so it wasn't his first body, but it was the first that was an obvious and violent homicide. The blood, the stains on the trousers, and the cloudy, lifeless eyes were upsetting. He forced himself to stand there, taking in all the details, until he no longer felt repulsed.

He heard the sound of tires crunching in the farmer's driveway at the top of the hill and, turning, saw the EMS ambulance arrive. Members of the Sparrow Lake volunteer fire department, they were, like Kevin, residents of Yonge Township, a strip of 128 square kilometres jutting north from the St. Lawrence River between Brockville and Kingston. He watched Constable Charles point the way down the hill, waving her arm to make it clear that they should avoid the farmer's footprints and follow Kevin's down the snowy slope.

As they edged their way toward him, he turned his eyes to the distant line of trees rimming the back of the field. A mixture of evergreen and bare-limbed deciduous, they were white with ice that had formed when the temperature had dropped below freezing again, the night before last. It made a picturesque tableau against the blue morning sky. A crow called out somewhere within the forest. Running his eyes along the tree line, Kevin saw nothing unusual. A second, distant crow answered the first. There was no visible disturbance in the snow between the body and the back of the field.

Somewhere in that stretch, however, would be the expended round that had killed the victim when it ripped through his neck.

He turned and looked at the footprints leading from the road to the body and back to the road again. Two sets coming in and one set returning to the road.

A one-way trip for the victim and a return trip for his killer.

"Another cold morning, Kevin," one of the paramedics called

out, by way of greeting. Behind him, his partner cursed as his boot rolled over a frozen clot of soil beneath the snow.

Kevin held up a hand. “Just you, Philip. Come up beside me.”

The paramedic shifted his equipment bag from one hand to the other and edged forward until he stood next to Kevin. He crouched, resting his bag on the snow, and swore. Behind them, his partner made a coughing sound and turned away. Philip studied the victim for a moment, then stood up and looked at the detective.

“Obviously dead,” Kevin said.

“Obviously dead,” Philip agreed. These two words, quoted from the Ministry of Health’s Deceased Patient Standard, obligated him not to touch the body unless directed to do so by the coroner. He turned to his partner. “Let’s get out of here, Dan. We’ll wait for Dalca in the truck.”

As they hurried back up the hill, they passed Constable Charles, who was talking into her shoulder microphone as she walked down. She took a long look at the body for the second time this morning before making eye contact with Kevin. “The road’s blocked off between Ballycanoe Road and Junetown Road. Everyone’s being advised to approach from the north. We’re setting up the inner perimeters now. You said to use Mr. Lackey’s yard as the command post, right?”

“Yeah.” The old man, Jerry Lackey, kept his yard well-plowed between his house and outbuildings, and it was large enough for a staging area that would accommodate all the respondents to the scene.

Kevin watched Charles depart, issuing instructions into her shoulder mike, then pulled off his gloves and used his smart phone to take a few photographs of the body. He brought out his notebook and drew a rough sketch of the scene, made a few notes, then slipped it back into his jacket pocket, put on his gloves, and trudged back up the hill.

He arrived in the yard just as Detective Sergeant Scott Patterson pulled up in a black-and-white OPP Suburban. Kevin’s immediate supervisor, Patterson commanded the Leeds

County Crime Unit, and it was his call to Kevin that had brought the young detective out to Lackey's farm in such a hurry this morning. A short, stubby redhead in his mid-forties, Patterson was carefully dressed in a full-length black wool topcoat, a black Russian-style fur hat, leather gloves, and rubber galoshes over his dress shoes. Kevin suddenly felt self-conscious in his old blue ski jacket, jeans, and snowmobile boots.

"What have we got?" Patterson demanded.

"Single shot, base of the skull, out through the front of the neck. Bled out. Looks frozen, so he was probably out here all night. Somebody walked him in from the road, shot him, walked back out, and drove away."

"Sounds like an execution. Did you touch anything?"

"No." It might be his first homicide, but Kevin believed he understood what he should and shouldn't do at a crime scene.

"Is it anyone you know?"

Kevin nodded. Patterson was asking him the question not only because Kevin lived ten minutes away from the scene but also because he'd been a member of the now-defunct Sparrow Lake Police Service for seven years before the municipality had contracted out to the OPP. As Kevin himself had emphasized in his application for a transfer to the provincial force two years ago, his personal knowledge of the residents in the area was an asset that had not only served him well in his brief stint as Sparrow Lake's only detective, but should also continue to do so in his new role as a provincial detective constable.

"His name's Hansen," Kevin said. "Bill Hansen. Lives in the village. Runs a car business. Has a wife, Valerie. No, Vivian."

"Kids?"

"Not that I know of."

"What does the witness say?"

"Lackey? I was just about to talk to him. He told the responding officer he was in the kitchen, getting a cup of coffee, when he looked out the window and saw something down here. Came down for a look, then ran back up and called 911."

Patterson turned around as a large white Mercedes cargo van with the OPP logo on the side turned into the driveway.

"Ident," he said.

Two men got out of the van and began unloading equipment. Kevin recognized Identification Sergeant Dave Martin, commander of the East Region Forensic Identification Unit, with one of his identification constables, Serge Landry.

"Talk to the witness," Patterson said. "I'll get these guys started. Where the hell's Dart? I called him right after I called you."

"Well, he lives in Brockville."

"Christ, that's no excuse. So do I. It's only a fifteen-minute drive."

Kevin watched Patterson cross the yard and shake hands with Martin. He listened for a moment to the dogs that had been barking non-stop in Lackey's barn since he'd arrived, then he crossed the yard, knocked on the kitchen door, and let himself into the house.

He exchanged nods with the uniformed officer who stood just inside the door. It was a typical farm house kitchen, large and warm. A fire burned in a box stove in the corner. The appliances were yellow and a long way from being new. A calico cat slept on a side table covered with newspapers, cat food cans, and empty bottles. Jerry Lackey sat at the table with a replacement cup of coffee between his hands. He was a small, wrinkled old fellow dressed in a blue plaid flannel shirt, green work pants, white tube socks, and plaid carpet slippers.

"How are you feeling now, Mr. Lackey?"

"Dunno," Lackey replied in a monotone, "but I stopped throwing up, so I guess I'm okay."

"Up to a few more questions?"

"Sure." Lackey raised his eyes to Kevin. They were red-rimmed and bleak. "Never seen anything like that before in my life. Not a person. Animals, sure. But never a human being."

Kevin removed his gloves and toque, shoving them into his pockets. He pulled off his snowmobile boots and walked across the kitchen in his stocking feet, unzipping his ski jacket. "It's a terrible thing, sir. I understand how you feel. Do you live by yourself here?"

Lackey ran a hand through his uncombed white hair. “Just me and the animals. The wife passed away eight years ago, and the kids are all grown and gone.”

Kevin removed his ski jacket, draped it over the back of a chair, and sat down. “Do you keep any livestock?”

“Just a couple of cows and an old pony. Gives me something to do.”

“How many acres?”

“Two hundred. A lot of it’s bush now. Used to have more in hay, but since I retired it’s started to grow back in. Tamarack and birch sprout like weeds. Next thing you know, there’s ash and maple, and it’s all over.”

Kevin took out his notebook and opened it, giving Lackey a sympathetic look. “I’m sorry about all this. I know it’s very upsetting, but would you mind running through with me what happened? Start when you first noticed something in the field.”

“Okay.” Lackey moved the cup of coffee to one side and clasped his hands together. “I seen him through the window, there, over the sink.” He nodded to the far side of the kitchen, where a curtained window looked down the hill and across the open field alongside Church Road.

“What time was this?”

“About seven thirty, I guess. I used to be an early riser, but not any more.”

“Go on. What happened?”

“Well, like I told the lady officer, I seen something down there at first but didn’t pay too much attention. I was getting water for my coffee pot, and I looked through the window while it was running. It wasn’t too light out yet, and I could just see this dark shape lying on the snow. I’m kind of slow waking up in the morning. Thought maybe it was a deer or something.”

“So you made your coffee?”

Lackey grimaced, upset. “I know I should have gone out right away, but you gotta understand, I was still half asleep. It takes me a while to get going in the morning.”

“That’s not what I meant, Mr. Lackey. Nobody’s blaming you for anything. There was nothing you could have done, anyway.

It was far too late for anyone to have helped him. I'm just trying to get a clear picture of what happened. Please, go on."

"Okay, sorry. I'm trying not to be a baby about it."

"You're doing fine. So you saw the dark shape down there. Did you see anyone or anything else?"

Lackey rubbed his unshaven cheek. "No, just that."

"Then what happened?"

"Well, I brewed a pot of coffee and poured a cup. I was going to go out to the road and get the paper from the box because I like to read it with my coffee, so I had my boots and coat on, ready to go. I always take my coffee with me. Just a little stroll to the road and back. I was walking by the window and looked out again, and I could see it was still lying down there, and this time it looked like a man. I didn't know what to think. So instead of going for the paper I went down across the field and, and, and—"

Kevin let the silence sit between them for several moments while he jotted down a few notes. It gave Lackey time to regain his composure. Then he dotted the last word emphatically, to let the old man know he was ready to move on. "I appreciate this, Mr. Lackey. Very much. It's a great help to us, it'll help us understand what happened. Let's go back a bit, if you don't mind. When was the last time you looked at that field and saw nothing down there?"

Lackey frowned a moment. "I dunno. I suppose yesterday afternoon. I went into the village to gas up my truck. When I came back, there wasn't nothing there."

"What time was that?"

"About four o'clock. Four thirty."

"Would that be the last time you looked there until this morning?"

"As far as I know."

"Okay. Now, last night, did you hear anything unusual on the road? Any vehicles, loud noises, voices, anything at all like that? Maybe your dogs barking at something?"

"Sorry." The old man shook his head, tapping his ear. "Hearing aid. I take it out after I watch TV. Nine o'clock, every night. Don't put it back in until I get up in the morning. Can't hear much of anything without it."

"Did you get up during the night?"

"Couple of times. To take a leak." He glanced self-consciously at the uniformed officer, who was listening to him without expression.

"See any lights on the road?" Kevin asked. "Maybe from a vehicle parked down there, or one passing by? Any flashes of light, anything like that at all?"

"Sorry," Lackey repeated. "I wish I was more help."

"You've been very helpful, Mr. Lackey, and I appreciate it." While still writing in his notebook, eyes down, Kevin asked, "Do you own a firearm, Mr. Lackey?"

"No, not any more. I used to have a couple of hunting rifles, and a shotgun for vermin, but I sold them a while back. I don't do as much around here as I used to. I wish I still had that shotgun, though."

"Oh? Why is that?"

"I sold it too cheap. It was a real good one."

"What about a handgun, Mr. Lackey? Do you own a handgun?"

"Naw, why would I? Wouldn't have a use for it. A waste of money."

"Did you know the victim?"

"No." Lackey pulled over his cup of coffee and stared at it glumly. "Who was he? Nobody's told me."

"Bill Hansen. He lived in Sparrow Lake."

"That so? Oh, wait. That's the guy deals cars, right?"

"That's right. Did you ever do business with him?"

Lackey shook his head. "Not me. Heard about him, though."

"Oh? What did you hear?"

"Just that he's pretty expensive. If I was going to buy another truck, I wouldn't go to him because he buys and sells stuff that's only a year or two old. I heard he wholesales for dealerships and sells other stuff on the side. My kind of new truck is at least fifteen years old and doesn't cost more than a grand."

Kevin smiled. “I hear you. Do you know anyone who did business with him?”

“I don’t run with that kind of crowd.”

“What kind of crowd?”

“People with all kinds of money to spend. People not retired and on a piddly little pension like me.”

“I understand.” Kevin made a quick note. “How well do you know your neighbours, Mr. Lackey?”

“Not hardly at all. I used to know all the families that farmed on this road, but they’re pretty much all passed away, and their kids have sold out and moved to the city. Bunch of commuters along here, now. Young people who work in Brockville or Kingston or Smiths Falls. I never talk to them. Only time I see them is when they’re driving by in their cars. Sometimes they wave. Mostly, they don’t. It’s that kind of world now.”

Kevin stood up and pulled his ski jacket off the back of the chair. “I appreciate your help, Mr. Lackey. We’ll have you provide a written statement later.”

Lackey swallowed a mouthful of coffee. “Sure. No problem.” He frowned at the kitchen window that had started all the trouble.

Outside, Kevin walked down to the end of the driveway. The farm was located about seven kilometres southwest of the village of Sparrow Lake, and eight kilometres north of Mallorytown. Church Road itself was about four kilometres long, running south-north between Junetown Road and Ballycanoe Road. Lackey’s farm was situated about a quarter of the way up from Junetown Road. As Charles had said, the entire road was blocked off, and inner perimeters had been set up to prevent local traffic, what there might be of it, from intruding on the crime scene. On Kevin’s right, to the north, there wasn’t another residence for at least a kilometre, so the inner perimeter was set somewhere between there and here. It was far enough away that he couldn’t see it from where he was standing.

On his left, the road sloped downhill and followed a straight line south. The closest residence, a single-family, ranch-style house, was barely visible across the road, within the trees. The inner perimeter had been set up right at the end of Lackey's field, about thirty metres from the neighbour's driveway—a wooden barricade, an OPP cruiser, and a bored constable.

The road had recently been plowed, but there wasn't much of a snowbank along the shoulder. The ditch was shallow and filled with crusted snow. A page-wire fence ran down the hill along the edge of Lackey's field. The fence posts were grey and weathered, and although a few were canted over at an angle, the rest were in good shape. The entrance to the field, through which the victim and his killer had passed, was about fifty metres from the bottom of the hill. The gate had been missing for a long time.

Crime scene tape fluttered across the road on either side of the entrance, to protect the immediate area in which Martin and Landry needed to work. Constable Charles was in the process of re-tying an end of the tape that had come undone from where it had been secured on the page-wire fence.

Inside the tape, they had set out several series of numbered evidence markers on the road, in the ditch, and through the entrance into the field. Martin was in the process of following the footprints across the field toward the body, placing yellow markers on top of the snow and photographing each print. Landry crouched in the middle of the road, unpacking supplies from a kit box. In their crime scene coveralls and hoods, the identification officers reminded Kevin of animals whose coats turn white in the winter for protective coloration.

Behind him, Kevin heard an approaching vehicle. It was Patterson, coming back from the north perimeter. He stepped out of the way to allow the Suburban room to pull in and park. Detective Constable Craig Dart got out from the passenger side, gave Kevin a look, and started down the hill toward Landry. Patterson joined Kevin at the end of the driveway. "His car wouldn't start, so he had to get a ride. I picked him up at the barricade."

"I thought he looked more pissed than usual."

Patterson sighed. They watched Landry hold up his hand and motion Dart away from his work area. Dart sidestepped, stopped, crossed his arms, and watched as Landry motioned Charles over to him. He passed the end of a tape measure to her and gingerly backed away. He was measuring the distance between parallel tire tread marks, Kevin realized, to get an idea of the wheelbase of the vehicle that had brought the victim to the scene.

Kevin heard the sound of another car behind him. He turned in time to see a black Lexus approaching at top speed. He skipped aside as the car swerved into the driveway, barely missing him.

"*This* fucking idiot," Patterson grumbled.

Dr. Yuri Dalca climbed out of the Lexus, retrieved his bag from the back seat, and slammed the door. "Not even have I had a chance to do my breakfast," he proclaimed loudly to no one in particular, "but now I have to walk all the way through some snow-covered field to look at a body I already know is dead."

"Life's rough," Patterson said, unimpressed. "If you'll follow me, Dr. Dalca?"

The detective sergeant led the way up the driveway and down the hill. Dalca followed, complaining with each step in a loud, accented voice that betrayed his Romanian origin. Kevin brought up the rear. As they approached the body, Dalca minced around Patterson and held up his hand. "Enough for you, right there. Have you already disturbed my body?"

"Nobody's touched it," Patterson snapped.

"A little respect costs nothing." Dalca knelt down beside the corpse. "Frozen stiff. Joke intended. He's been here for a while, probably all night."

Obviously, Kevin thought. Watching Dalca fuss around the body, he mentally reviewed the five questions a coroner must answer when investigating an unexpected death.

Who is the person?—Bill Hansen.

When did he die?—Sometime between four thirty yesterday afternoon and about two o'clock this morning, judging from the frozen condition of the body.

Where did he die?—Right here, given the amount of blood pumped out across the snow by a heart still beating after the fatal shot was fired.

How did he die?—As a result of the aforementioned gunshot wound.

By what means did he die?—Homicide, without question.

"His wife will be so very upset," Dalca said.

Patterson shifted. "You know this man?"

"Of course. He's a patient of mine." Dalca struggled upright and started to put his gloves back on. "There's nothing for me to do here. The freezing of the body is already done, so no point in me trying to figure out time since death. It was what, last night, twenty below, Celsius? Being police, you don't know these things and always expect the impossible, but the progress of rigor mortis, the stiffening of the body, is made slower by cold temperatures, as is the production of insects, gas, and all the other fine things we use to measure time since death. The body fluids freeze when he lies out here like this, in an open field, exposed to the cold winds, and the stiffness we have already is not rigor but simply the freezing of the water in the cells. Look at the blood, there on the snow." He waved his gloved hand. "Frozen as well. Since the middle of the night, obviously. The body must be thawed, very slowly, then we will see the rigor follow its normal course. It could take a full day just to do this. I don't know. The pathologist will tell us."

Having delivered his lecture, he picked up his bag and began to manoeuvre around Patterson and Kevin.

"Hang on a sec." Patterson put a hand on Dalca's sleeve. "You said this man's a patient of yours. Bill Hansen?"

"Yes, of course it's Hansen." Dalca stopped, annoyed at being touched.

Kevin asked, "Is there anything in this man's medical history we need to know about? That might be relevant to the investigation?"

Dalca rolled his eyes at him. "You mean, like drug addiction or alcoholism or STD from too much screwing around? Something like that? Don't waste your time, and don't waste mine, young man. There's nothing in my files to help you answer who did this to him. Which I hope you will go and find out now without frittering away any more of my time." He pulled his sleeve free from Patterson's gloved fingers and moved around Kevin.

"The inspector from CIB is on the way," Patterson said.

"How nice," Dalca called over his shoulder. "I'm going up to my warm car, where I will call my pathologist friend in Kingston to let him know Mr. Hansen is coming. I'll also call the body removal service to pick him up, I'll fill out all my tedious, bureaucratic forms and give you your copies, and then I'm going to go somewhere more pleasant to have my breakfast."

"Don't forget to release the EMS guys," Patterson called after him. "They could use some breakfast, too."

Dalca ignored him, trudging stolidly away.

"I swear to God," Dave Martin said behind them, "that guy's a walking advertisement for scrapping the coroner system in this province and going with professional medical examiners like the rest of the modern world."

Kevin turned. Martin had finally worked his way across the field to the victim. He carefully circled the body, photographing it.

"Don't get me started, Dave." Patterson looked at Kevin. "Stay here. I'm not finished with that son of a bitch, not by a long shot." He shouldered past him and stamped away after the departed coroner.

"First thing," Martin said, slinging his camera over his shoulder and kneeling beside the body, "we need to bag these hands."

Kevin crouched down beside him. "What's in his pockets?"

"Hold your horses." Martin produced two Tyvek hand preservation bags and pointed at the gold ring on the corpse's finger. "Married. Left-handed smoker, too. Nicotine stains." He slipped a bag over the hand, tightened the drawstring, then repeated the process with the other hand. Satisfied that the victim's hands were properly protected, he took out a clear plastic evidence bag and began to search the pockets. He pulled out a wallet and looked at a driver's licence, health card, and several credit cards. "Hansen, William L., 22 Mill Street, Sparrow Lake, Ontario. DOB October 21, 1957. Visa, American

Express, CIBC convenience card. Looks like two hundred and ... ten dollars in cash."

Kevin had his notebook out and was furiously writing it all down.

Martin dropped the wallet into the evidence bag and continued his search, finding a quantity of loose change, a cotton handkerchief, a green after-dinner mint wrapped in cellophane, a small stub of a pencil, several receipts from gas bars and convenience stores—all at least two days old—and a nail clipper.

"No keys?" Kevin asked.

"No keys. And no cellphone, either."

Kevin looked back toward the road. "He didn't drop it, did he? A guy like him would never be without his phone."

"We didn't see it," Martin said.

"Maybe the killer took it and threw it away."

"It's a thought. It might turn up later."

"I don't see a shell casing," Kevin said.

"No," Martin agreed. "If it was a semi-automatic, the shooter may have policed his brass."

"Unless it's under the body."

"You mind if I do my job and you do yours, Detective?"

Kevin smiled, glancing at his watch. He was surprised to see that it was already past nine thirty. "What did you find at the road?"

"Good set of tire tracks," Martin replied, "with a wheelbase that'll probably match a pickup truck, maybe a Dodge Ram. Three sets of boot prints, one size thirteen, one size eleven, and the other size ten, which," he pointed at the boots on the victim's feet, "will match this guy."

"I've always wondered, how do you take print casts like that in the snow when it's this cold?"

"Good question, kid. The secret is an aerosol can of snow print wax. As you may not know, since you're police and don't know jack shit, as Dr. Dickhead nicely pointed out, most casting materials produce heat as they harden, which melts your snow and erodes your details rather distressingly. Snow print wax, on the other hand, does not. In fact, it insulates the print and preserves all those lovely details. Plus, it goes on red, which makes for really good photographs. Then Serge, our resident expert, applies the dental stone for the casting, and he's good to go. Ain't forensics fun?"

After completing a surface examination of the victim's clothing for fibres or trace evidence, Martin carefully turned the body over and took another round of photographs. When he was done with the body, he stood up, motioned Kevin back a few steps, and began to hunt through the crushed snow. After a while he shook his head. "No cartridge case. We'll keep looking, though." He stood up and stared off toward the distant tree line. Then he studied the size thirteen footprints for a moment and chose a pair that represented where the killer likely stood when he fired the shot. Straddling them awkwardly, he raised his hand with his thumb up and index finger extended, and pretended to shoot. "Somewhere out there," he muttered, and slowly moved off in a circuitous route toward where he hoped to find the expended round.

After a while, Landry arrived from the road, pushing a measuring wheel across the snow. "Eighty-one metres, seven centimetres from the first of the victim's footprints to the last one," he told Kevin. "Looks like he got out of the passenger side of the vehicle, by the way, and the shooter got out from the driver's side."

Kevin wrote it down in his notebook.

Landry shielded his eyes with his hand as he stared at Martin in the distance. Then he stood in Martin's footprints, studied the angle at which the body had fallen, raised his hand, and fired his own simulated shot. "He needs to be a lot farther to the left." He headed off toward Martin.

After a while, Kevin glanced at his watch. It was now 10:24 AM. Forty minutes had passed while he'd stood here, watching the Ident officers work, taking notes, refining his sketch of the crime scene. He looked up at the driveway and saw Patterson talking to Dart. It was an animated discussion; Patterson waved his arms about to emphasize whatever point he was making while Dart stared at his boots.

Kevin squinted as crows rose above the farm house, cawing. They swerved and flew off into the distance. Probably the same family group he'd heard before. Above them, a tiny jet pulled a contrail across the blue sky. Martin slowly made his way back across the field to the body while Landry remained behind, bent over, patiently searching for the round in the snow.

Kevin's attention was drawn once more to the road. A vehicle had apparently been allowed to pass through the blockade at Junetown Road and approach the scene from the south. An unmarked grey Crown Victoria, it stopped at the wooden barricade at the far end of Lackey's field. Someone got out of the car, spoke to the uniformed officer, walked around the barricade and approached the scene along the road.

"Who the hell is that?" Martin asked, behind Kevin.

They watched a woman in a navy trench coat, fuzzy hat, and clunky men's winter boots walk up to the entrance of the field. Her hands were shoved into her coat pockets. She stopped to speak to Constable Charles, who nodded and waved her forward. She gave a little wave back and continued across the field.

She looked uncomfortably cold; the trench coat was far too light for a minus 15 degree day. She walked with a slight stoop, her head down, her shoulders hunched. Dark hair protruded from beneath the fuzzy hat. For an instant, Kevin wondered if she was a journalist who'd inadvertently been allowed access. Then he noticed her eyes roving constantly back and forth across the snow in front of her with the trained vigilance of someone experienced in moving through a crime scene.

"Well," he said, "I guess that's CIB."

chapter TWO

Acting Detective Inspector Ellie March hunched her shoulders against the cold wind that whipped across the open field and penetrated her trench coat as though it wasn't there. The warmth of the Crown Vic, which she'd reluctantly left at the barricade after a two-and-a-half-hour drive up Highway 401 from Toronto, was already a distant memory.

Her boots crunched through the crust on top of the snow as she made her way carefully toward the body and the two men who stood watching her. The one in the ski jacket and toque was big and looked very young, while the other, the Ident officer in his white coveralls and hood, was short and middle-aged. The kid looked like a football player in full pads standing next to a referee.

Far beyond them, Ellie saw another white figure edging across the field in a half crouch.

On her left, someone in a long black topcoat hurried down the hill toward her.

"You must be one of Scott's detectives," she said, offering her hand to the big kid. "Detective Inspector Ellie March. Criminal Investigation Branch."

"Detective Constable Kevin Walker." Kevin removed his glove to shake her hand. His paw was so large that his fingers touched the bare skin of her wrist under the cuff of her coat.

"Identification Sergeant Dave Martin," the smaller one said, not offering to shake hands.

Ellie nodded.

Kevin smiled at her. "It's a pleasure to meet you, Detective Inspector March. I've heard a lot about you."

"I'm Ellie, you're Kevin, he's Dave." She pointed at the corpse. "Who's this?"

"William Hansen," Kevin said. "He lived in the village. Sparrow Lake, I mean. It's about ten minutes from here, on County Road 5. Shot in the back of the neck at close range some time last evening."

Ellie took a step to one side and held out her hand to Patterson, who was puffing as he reached them, a little winded. "Scott. Good to see you again. Who found him?"

Patterson shook her hand. "Hi."

"The farmer who lives at the top of the hill found the body," Kevin supplied, giving Patterson a chance to catch his breath. "His name's Jerry Lackey. This is his field. He spotted the body from his kitchen window and came down for a look."

"Caught him off guard, obviously," Ellie said, looking at the coffee cup and vomit stain. "Any chance he shot the guy?"

Kevin shook his head. "I don't think so. He's very upset. He's just some old guy who found a body in his field."

"His boot prints coming down the hill don't match the ones you saw coming in from the road," Martin added. "Not even close."

"What does the coroner say?" Ellie asked.

"He couldn't give us much because of the frozen state of the body," Kevin replied. "We'll have to wait for the autopsy."

"He's the vic's doctor, it turns out," Patterson said, having recovered his wind. "Warrant for the post's been signed, and the pathologist in Kingston has been given the heads-up. Body removal's en route."

"Who are we talking about, here? The coroner, I mean?"

"Dr. Yuri Dalca. A general practitioner in Mallorytown."

"Don't know him." Ellie turned and looked behind her. "So,

a vehicle stops at the side of the road at the opening in the fence, the victim and two other guys get out, one of them walks the victim across the field to this point," she turned back and faced the distant tree line, "the killer stands behind him, fires a shot through the back of his neck, the victim falls face down and, while he bleeds out, the killer walks back to the road—not in any particular hurry, given the spacing of the footprints—gets back into the vehicle, and the two guys drive away." She looked at Kevin. "Did Mr. Lackey see or hear any of that?"

Kevin shook his head. "The last time he looked down here was just before sunset yesterday, at about four thirty or so. There was nothing. He took his hearing aid out at nine and didn't hear or see anything unusual until he spotted the body at sunrise this morning, at about seven thirty."

"Any other witnesses?"

"Not so far," Patterson said. "We're doing a canvass up and down the road as we speak, but most people who live along here commute to jobs in Brockville or Kingston, so we'll have to do a second run this evening."

"What do we know about the victim so far? What's he doing out here in the middle of nowhere getting himself shot?"

"He lived in the village," Kevin repeated. "Ran a car business. Had a wife, Vivian. No kids that I'm aware of. Seemed like a fairly likeable guy."

Ellie raised an eyebrow. "You knew him?"

"To see him around. I live in the village. Sparrow Lake. Just a couple of streets over from him, actually. I'm from Brockville, originally, but I worked for the Sparrow Lake Police Service for nine years before transferring to the force when the municipality disbanded us and contracted out."

"I see."

"Kevin's been with us for a couple of years now," Patterson said.

"Okay." Ellie crouched down next to the body for a closer look at the wound on the back of his neck. "Any priors?"

"No," Patterson said. "Nothing. We ran him and he came up clean."

"Drug use? Gambling? Alcoholism?"

"No indications so far. Not according to Dalca, anyway."

"This is a near-contact wound," Ellie said. "The muzzle was maybe an inch away. There's wider searing around the entrance wound than if it were actual contact, either hard or loose. And see the pear shape?" She looked up at Kevin. "The shot was fired on an upward angle. The shooter was probably shorter than the vic." She looked at Martin. "How tall is this guy?"

"Five-eleven," the Ident sergeant replied. He looked at Kevin. "She's right."

Ellie stood up. "What have we got for physical evidence?"

"Tire tread impressions," Martin said. "Wheelbase measurements suggest a pickup truck. We'll confirm later today."

"And?" she prompted.

"A set of size ten boot prints that match to the vic, a set of size thirteens that came in and went back, and a set of size elevens that stayed with the vehicle at the side of the road. The thirteens were older boots with a distinctive wear pattern. Find them and I can put them here on the feet of your shooter. The second guy, who stayed at the road, wore newer boots that left crisp tread marks." Martin waved his hand above the body. "Not much in terms of trace evidence on the clothing. Some animal hair. Well-distributed, so I'd say it's probably a white cat or dog belonging to the victim."

Ellie had noticed the watch on the victim's wrist. "What about his wallet?"

"Driver's licence, bank card, credit cards, plus $210 in cash."

"So it wasn't robbery," Kevin said.

Patterson shook his head. "More like an execution, to me."

"No cellphone," Kevin added, "and no keys."

Ellie looked up at the sky. "Was there a moon here, last night?"

"Yes. Full moon was three nights ago, so it was waning, but still more than 95 per cent visible. It was clear and cold, down to minus 22."

"So there was visibility."

"Some," Kevin agreed. "Enough to see what he was doing."

"Much traffic along here after dark?"

"Not really. We're well off the beaten path. Most of the late traffic is on County Road 5, which runs between Athens and the 401."

Ellie was silent for a moment, thinking it over. She sighed. "So why did someone bring him all the way out here to the middle of nowhere to execute him? And why did they just leave his body for us to find, instead of taking him down to the St. Lawrence River and making him disappear?"

No one had an answer for that one.

"Hey, Dave!"

They all turned around to look at the distant figure of Serge Landry, who was waving his arm and pointing down at the snow.

"Found it!"

"The round," Martin said to Ellie. "Excuse me."

As he hustled off, Ellie turned to Patterson. "Has notification been made yet?"

Patterson shook his head.

"Who's going to be our primary?"

Patterson's eyes slid over to Kevin.

Ellie pressed her lips together and stared at the detective sergeant for a moment, then looked at Kevin. "How long did you say you've been a detective?"

"Seven years. Five with Sparrow Lake, the last two here. In the crime unit, I mean."

"I take it you've never worked a homicide before."

"No, ma'am."

Ellie gave Patterson another look, then shook her head. "Let's go notify Vivian Hansen, Kevin. You do the driving; I've got some calls to make."

She glanced again at Patterson. "We'll discuss it later."

chapter THREE

Ellie held her free hand up to the warm air blowing out of the dashboard vent of Kevin's Grand Cherokee as she pressed her cellphone against her ear. "I'm freezing half to death, Tony, but thanks for asking."

"Suck it up," replied Superintendent Tony Agosta, director of the Criminal Investigation Branch. "We're getting twenty-two centimetres right now in Orillia. You're only going to see a fraction of that down there. So, how's it look?"

Ellie gave him a quick sketch of the case as she'd found it.

"Keep me posted," Agosta said. "Fisher can be difficult. If you don't get absolutely everything you need, say the word and I'll let the commissioner know we're having problems."

"Hopefully it won't come to that."

"Look, Ellie, before I have Ann process the paperwork to renew your assignment next month, I'd like to know if you actually want it."

"I know, Tony. I'm still thinking about it."

"There are a couple of ways we can do this. There's less than four weeks left, so if you want to go back to your substantive, get the case underway and Whyte can replace you. Or, I can extend you for six months, by which time you'll get a chance to be staffed in the position. If you're going to compete for it."

Kevin slowed to take a curve in the road that looked particularly icy. Ellie shifted the phone to her left hand and held her right palm against the air vent. Her substantive position was as a detective staff sergeant assigned to the CIB in general headquarters in Orillia, an operational position in which she worked with inspectors on major cases throughout the province. Her particular expertise lay in interrogation, and she had participated in several landmark cases during a three-year stretch in the job, including a very emotional child kidnapping and murder in southwest Ontario and a serial homicide investigation in Central Region, before accepting her current acting assignment as a major case manager assigned to East Region.

"I'm not sure what to say. I love the work."

"Your case work's outstanding, Ellie. You were born to do this job."

"I don't know about that, but I *do* love it. I have to admit, though, the travel's starting to wear me down. I'm tired. My kids hate me. My ex and his new wife hate me. Shit, Tony. I've tried everything to stay on good terms with them, but now I think I just need to leave them alone. I need a new life."

"You can always find a place to stay down there," Agosta said. "You don't need to live up here. Maybe that'll help a bit."

"It might." Ellie switched hands again. "Anyway, I'll let you know."

"Just don't take forever, okay? Today's Tuesday; let me know by the end of the week. Wait, Ann's just handed me something. Oh, great. Nothing at all?"

Ellie waited as he talked to Ann Marchant, his executive assistant.

"Ellie, I'm putting you on speaker. Ann's here."

"Hi, Ann."

"Ellie, I'm really sorry," Ann said, "I haven't been able to get you a room anywhere in Brockville. There's a minor hockey tournament and every room in the city's booked. I can't believe it."

"Nothing at all?" Ellie asked.

"I'm sorry. I'll keep trying, but all the main hotels are booked solid. I've even called a couple of B and Bs, and they're filled up, too."

"Well, keep trying. There must be a room somewhere."

"I will. I'm sorry, Ellie."

"Don't be. It's not your fault; it's short notice. I'll talk to you both later." Ellie cut the connection and called the regional office to make arrangements for a victim liaison officer, Constable Janet Olkewicz, to meet them at the Hansen home. She then asked for, and received, Constable Rachel Townsend, who'd done a great job for her before as media liaison officer. She also agreed to meet with Inspector Fisher, the OPP detachment commander, in Smiths Falls at 1:30 PM. She put away her cellphone just as Kevin braked at a reduction in the speed limit. Ahead of them, Ellie saw a sign welcoming them to the village of Sparrow Lake. Kevin suddenly slowed to a crawl and pointed to his left.

"That's his car yard."

Ellie leaned forward to look past him. On the opposite side of the road, she saw a small compound enclosed by a high chain-link security fence. Inside the compound were a mobile office trailer and several parked vehicles. As they passed the big front gate, she saw a sign that said, "Hansen Car Wholesale Ltd."

"A unit should be here shortly," Kevin said. "You can see it's chained and padlocked, but someone might have a key. We definitely don't want them getting in."

He accelerated up a hill into the village. Two short blocks later he pulled up to the curb and killed the engine. They were parked in front of a large, three-storey red brick house with granite cornerstones, white shutters, and a tiny, fenced yard. The front porch featured white gingerbread woodworking and Doric columns. It was a well-kept house, attractive and immaculate.

"I live two blocks over," Kevin said, sounding a little self-conscious. "On Queen Street. It's the last street in town."

"Practically a neighbour. Do you know her?"

"Not really. I never see her around. As far as I know, she spends most of her time in the house."

They got out of the Grand Cherokee and approached the

front porch. Ellie looked at the tiny driveway at the side of the house. Tire marks in the snow suggested that a vehicle had recently been parked there. She wondered if it was the truck that had also stopped at the side of the road at Lackey's field.

Kevin followed her gaze. "Is it possible he was driven there in his own vehicle?"

Ellie shrugged, leading the way up onto the porch. She pounded on the front door. It was a cop's knock, using the edge of her fist rather than her knuckles, something she did out of habit, without thinking about it. The door opened. Ellie looked at a woman in her late fifties, wide-hipped, with dyed auburn hair. She wore a floral print dress and moccasins with little rolls of fleece around the heels. Her eyes and nose were red.

Ellie held up the wallet containing her identification and badge. "Mrs. Hansen? I'm Detective Inspector March with the Ontario Provincial Police. This is Detective Constable Walker. May we come in? There's something we need to talk about."

The woman nodded and backed up, opening the door for them to pass through. They pulled off their boots and unfastened their coats before following her into the front sitting room. Vivian Hansen was silent, and as they sat down, Ellie's internal radar was instantly activated. The woman showed no confusion as to why they were there, and gave every sign of having expected them. She didn't ask what it was all about or what was wrong, but simply waited for them to tell her.

After breaking the news, Ellie watched the woman hide her face in her hands, and although the tears were genuine and the grief heart-felt, Ellie was convinced she'd already known about her husband's death and was trying to conceal it.

Ellie leaned forward. "Did someone already inform you of your husband's passing, Mrs. Hansen?"

Vivian shook her head, sobbing.

Looking around, Ellie spotted a small box of tissues in a knitted cosy sitting on a side table. The cosy resembled a brick house, and the tissue sticking out of the top was supposed to look like smoke coming from a chimney. It was the sort of thing a person would buy at a craft show or yard sale out of politeness.

She got up and brought it over to Vivian, who gratefully pulled out several tissues.

"We understand how terrible this is," Ellie said, "but we'll have to ask you a few questions."

Vivian blew her nose and nodded.

Ellie took out a notebook and pen. She glanced at Kevin, who was sitting on a salon chair that looked too fragile for his big, athletic build. He was leaning forward, his notebook already open. He returned her glance without expression, pen poised, waiting for her to continue.

"When was the last time you saw your husband?" Ellie began.

"Yesterday morning." Vivian pulled out more tissues and dabbed at her nose.

"About what time?"

"About eight, as usual. That's when he always left for work."

"So he leaves the house about eight and goes down to his car yard? The one I just passed, a couple of blocks back?"

"Yes."

"Is that his regular routine?"

"Yes."

"What time does he normally get up?"

"His alarm was always set for seven. He liked to take an hour to get ready for work in the morning."

"Okay, thanks. What about lunch? Does he come home for lunch?"

Vivian shook her head. "He always got something out."

"Dinner? He usually comes home for dinner, though, right?"

"Yes."

"But not last night?"

Vivian shook her head again, staring at the wad of tissues in her hand.

"Is that unusual? Or does he sometimes miss having dinner with you?"

"It was unusual."

"Any phone calls or e-mails from him yesterday, any contact at all after he left in the morning?"

"No."

"Did you try calling him when he didn't show at dinnertime?"

"I never liked to bother him. I thought ... sometimes something came up with a car. Sometimes he had to wait for a late delivery or pickup."

"Does he sometimes do that and not tell you, not call you to let you know he won't be home?"

"Sometimes. I never interfered in his work. I always left his dinner in the fridge."

"All right." Ellie jotted a note and sat back in her chair. "So I take it that when he left to go to work yesterday morning, he drove his own car, is that right?"

"Yes."

"What kind of car does he drive, Mrs. Hansen?"

"A truck. A black one. I don't know what kind."

"He parks it here in the driveway beside the house when he's home?"

"Yes."

"Does he drive other vehicles besides the truck?"

"I guess so. But he loved that truck."

Ellie glanced at Kevin. Although his head was down as he wrote in his notebook, he nodded microscopically, acknowledging that he was following her. The tire tread marks in the driveway could very well match those found at the scene.

"How much do you know about your husband's business?" Ellie continued. "He traded cars, is that right? How does that work?"

"I didn't know anything about it. We never talked about it. He bought cars and sold them to dealerships and other people. That's all I knew about it."

"Can you tell me anything about the people he did business with?"

"No. I didn't know anything about them, not at all."

"How's he been doing? Any financial problems?"

"I don't know. I don't think so. He kept all his bank books in his study upstairs. I never went up there. That was his private place."

"He's never mentioned any money problems, or complained about bills, or said he couldn't afford something?"

"He handled everything, and never said a word about it. We've always had whatever we needed. I don't think there's ever been any problems with money."

"What about family, Mrs. Hansen? Do either of you have relatives in the area?"

Vivian wiped her eyes and shook her head. "I have some cousins in Halifax. I haven't heard from them in years. Bill's family is all gone. He had some nephews in Denmark, I think. We got a Christmas card one year."

"Do you have any children?"

"No."

Ellie waited for a moment, but Vivian had nothing else to say on the subject. "What about friends?" she went on. "Does your husband have any close friends he sees from time to time? Who maybe come over to visit?"

"No. No friends. It was just the two of us."

"Nobody comes over to watch a hockey game with him, or for a barbecue in the summer, anything like that?"

"No. We were alone here."

Ellie looked around the room. There were no framed photographs, and virtually no personal touches to the room, just antique furniture, china figures and collectibles, and a few oil paintings hanging on the walls. The front entranceway and hall had been the same. Ellie's first impression of the home was that Vivian and her husband had indeed lived a rather solitary life. At least, Vivian had. Her husband's contacts must have all been away from home, down at the car yard and in the village and beyond.

"Are you aware of any trouble he might have had recently with anyone? Any arguments or fights?"

"He was a very easy-going person," Vivian replied. "You had to know Bill to understand. He liked people, even though he was very private. *We're* very private. But he was easy to get along with. He never had any trouble with anyone."

Vivian's persistent use of the past tense was not lost on Ellie. She'd done enough notifications in her time to have observed that spouses and other close family members often referred to their loved one in the present tense immediately after having been told they were dead. It took a while to adjust to the fact that their relationship had suddenly become something in the past, rather than the present. Vivian, however, clearly had had some time to make the adjustment. Ellie had been forcing the issue, constantly referring to Bill Hansen in the present tense, but Vivian hadn't once followed suit. She'd obviously been sitting in this house for some time now, crying, thinking about her loss, adjusting to the reality that he was gone forever.

Ellie decided to change tack. "How did he treat you, Mrs. Hansen? How would you describe your relationship with your husband?"

"We were fine. He was a good man. We didn't argue at all."

"Did you ever worry he might be showing interest in other women? Was there ever any sense that he was involved with someone else?"

Vivian laughed shortly. "You must be joking. Bill had no interest in sex, in women. All he thought about, day and night, was cars. He left sex behind a long time ago, believe me. You're wrong if you think he was having an affair with someone."

It was Ellie's experience that almost everyone had an interest in sex at some level or other, but she didn't press it. "Did he have any problems with alcohol or drugs, Mrs. Hansen?"

"*No*."

Ellie could see that her questions were agitating the woman. As she paused, Kevin cleared his throat. "Yesterday morning, Mrs. Hansen, how did your husband seem? How was his mood?"

Vivian blinked. "I don't know. The same as always, I guess."

"Was he happier or sadder than usual? Did he talk about anything out of the ordinary?"

"He was the same as always. Quiet."

"Was he in a hurry to get off to work? Or seem reluctant to leave?"

"No. There wasn't anything different."

"Did he take any phone calls before he left?"

"No."

"Do you own a cat, Mrs. Hansen?" Kevin looked around. "A white cat?"

"Yes."

"Does it stay in the house?"

"Yes. He's probably in the basement. He hides when someone comes to the door."

"That's too bad. I hope we didn't scare him. What's his name?"

"Snowball." It was barely more than a whisper.

Ellie shifted. "Do you or your husband own a firearm, Mrs. Hansen?"

"No. I wouldn't have one in the house."

"What about his cellphone? Any idea where it might be?"

"He always had it with him. In his pocket."

"Are you sure no one told you about your husband's death before we got here?"

She shook her head.

"No one came by to tell you what had happened."

"No, I *told* you that already."

"Do you have any idea at all who might have wanted to do this to him?"

Vivian put her face in her hands and cried.

After the arrival of Janet Olkewicz, the victim liaison officer, Ellie and Kevin excused themselves and stepped outside just as a cruiser was pulling up to the curb ahead of Olkewicz's car. Two uniformed constables got out. Ellie leaned against the passenger door of the Grand Cherokee and watched Kevin explain how he wanted the house and driveway secured for the imminent arrival of the forensics team. She wasn't impressed with the way he'd dressed in response to a call out on a death investigation, but he'd handled himself well inside and knew what needed to be done out here. His directions to the uniformed officers were clear and precise, and his voice was calm and polite. When he was finished, she beckoned him over and asked him to drive her back to the primary scene so that she could pick up her car.

As they passed Hansen's car yard on their way out of the village, they saw a cruiser parked a few yards from the mouth of the entrance. Kevin pulled up behind it. They both got out. The driver's side window went down on the cruiser, and Kevin bent over to talk to the uniformed constable, a young woman, while Ellie strolled up to look at the entrance. It was a fan-shaped expanse of hard-packed, frozen gravel about five metres deep from the lip of the pavement to the closed gate. The constable in the cruiser had set out several small orange cones just off the pavement to protect the entrance from intrusion. Tire marks were clearly visible in the thin crust of snow on top of the gravel. Several sets, by the looks of it. And boot prints, where someone had gotten out, fastened the chain and padlock to secure the gate, and climbed back into the vehicle on the driver's side.

Ellie's eyes drifted down the highway. It was empty and quiet. Crosswinds pushed little eddies of snow across the pavement. Turning back, she saw the constable watching her through the windshield as she talked to Kevin. Shivering, Ellie walked up to them and stood next to Kevin.

"Anyone show any interest in the place since you've been here?" she asked.

"Not so far, ma'am."

Ellie nodded, still looking at the constable. "Anyone slows down to rubberneck or acts like they want to come in here, get their plate number."

"Yes, ma'am."

Back in the Grand Cherokee, Ellie closed her eyes for a moment as Kevin pulled back onto the highway and accelerated south. The sun strobed through the trees, flickering through her closed lids. The Grand Cherokee's winter tires hummed. She thought about Vivian Hansen, replaying the interview in her head.

"I couldn't help overhearing," Kevin began, tentatively.

Ellie opened her eyes and blinked at a wide, snow-covered field on her side of the road. “What?”

“You can’t get a hotel room in Brockville?”

“Everything’s booked. A hockey tournament or something. They’ll keep trying.”

“May I make a suggestion?”

Ellie said nothing, waiting.

“I know a guy who owns a place on the lake. Sparrow Lake. The lake itself. It’s a four-season home. Completely insulated, thermal windows, propane heating, everything. A hundred feet of waterfront.”

Ellie ran a hand through her long, limp hair.

“He’s a buddy of mine, coaches goaltenders for the University of Victoria men’s hockey team, so he’s not around in the winter. I look after it for him. I could call and see if he’d be okay with you using it while you’re here.”

Ellie frowned at a bank of grey clouds edging into the sky from the west. “No,” she said, “that’s all right. They’ll get something lined up for me.”

“He said he’s going to sell it this summer. He bought it as an investment when he got a signing bonus after he was drafted by the Predators, but he was hurt after two years in the minors and had to quit. Never really used it much. It’s a nice place. I’d buy it if I could afford to, but I can’t. You’d have complete privacy, satellite TV and wireless Internet connection, and cell reception’s good all around the lake.”

Ellie thought about it. The novelty of staying in hotel rooms had worn off for her a long time ago, but there was something to be said for the anonymity and autonomy they afforded. Of course, the point was moot since she apparently wasn’t going to find a room in the near future anyway, unless Ann was able to pounce on a miracle cancellation.

“I can show it to you later on,” Kevin said. “You can see what you think. It’s fifteen minutes, tops, from the detachment.”

Ellie held up a hand to shut him up. “We’ll see. We can talk about it later.”

“All right. You’ll like the place. It’s a beautiful lake.”

"Later," Ellie repeated. She shifted in her seat to look at him. "Vivian Hansen already knew her husband was dead. You got that, right? Either someone came around and told her, or she's involved. But she knew."

"Maybe she was just upset. Worried about him not coming home, and her imagination was working overtime. Then we showed up and her worst fears were confirmed."

"No. She already knew he was dead. She'd already started to accept it as fact, to make the mental adjustments. She knew. Either she arranged for her husband to be killed, or someone told her about it. As a threat, maybe. Either way, she knows more than she's telling us."

"You might be right." His tone, however, was doubtful.

Ellie turned away. "You know how this works, Kevin. Start with the people closest to the victim, and work your way out."

chapter FOUR

Kevin swung into the driveway of the tiny bungalow on Queen Street and let himself in through the side door. He pulled off his snowmobile boots, hung up his ski jacket, and ran up the short flight of stairs into the kitchen. Stumbling over a plastic toy dump truck on his way through the hallway into the master bedroom, he unclipped his holstered service weapon and set it down on the bed, followed by his badge in its leather holder. He stripped off his jeans and threw them across the end of the bed, pulled his t-shirt over his head and tossed it aside, and opened his half of the closet.

Five minutes, in and out. Five minutes to repair, hopefully, a less-than-positive first impression. Raking through the hangered clothing, he pulled out a pair of navy cotton trousers, examined them front to back to make sure they were clean, and pulled them on. Next came a white long-sleeved dress shirt that needed ironing but wouldn't get it, followed by a black-and-navy-striped tie. He stripped the belt from his jeans and hastily pulled it through the loops of his trousers. He clipped his gun and badge in place, and transferred his wallet, change, and keys from his jeans to his trouser pockets. He found a navy blazer and put it on. He slid the closet door back in place and hurried out into the kitchen, glancing at his watch.

Four minutes gone.

The house was silent. Janie was at work, and her two children, Brendan and Caitlyn, were at school. The place was a mess. Toys lay everywhere, dirty dishes from breakfast cluttered the counter, and empty water bottles and pop cans had spilled out of the recycling bin across the floor. Paperwork from Janie's hairdressing business in the village covered the kitchen table. A plastic cup with Dalmatians on it had tipped over, and a small pool of orange juice lay dangerously close to Janie's phone bill. Kevin grabbed a handful of paper towels from the roller above the sink and mopped it up. Picking up a red crayon, he printed on the back of the envelope, "Mommy, start paying online. Love, Caitlyn." Then he hurried down the stairs to the side entry.

He hunted through the closet for his OPP-issue outdoor duty jacket with its fur collar and insulated lining. He shrugged into it and bent down to look for his winter service boots among the running shoes, rubber boots, pumps, Crocs, and other assorted footwear. There, at the very back. He pulled them out, struggled into them, and hurried out to the Grand Cherokee. He started the engine and checked his watch again.

Seven minutes gone.

He drove down Queen Street to the end of the block and turned left onto Sarah. He took the first right, drove a block, and turned right onto Mill Street. Vehicles lined the block on both sides. He took the first parking spot he could find and walked up to the Hansen house, where a scenes of crime officer was busy photographing the tire tread marks in the little driveway. Crime scene tape surrounded the house. He spoke to Constable Mark Allore, who had been called in from the community response team to assist. Allore reported that the victim liaison officer, Olkewicz, had taken Vivian Hansen to the Presbyterian minister's home a few blocks over. No one was in the Hansen house at present. Olkewicz had explained to Vivian that they were getting warrants to search the house and place of business, and the woman had provided a set of keys. Allore pulled them out of his pocket and dropped them into Kevin's outstretched hand.

"How's the canvass coming?" Kevin asked.

Allore glanced over Kevin's shoulder. "Looks like they're halfway up the block, this side of the street."

"Why don't you and I take the other side?"

"Sure."

They walked down the sidewalk to the corner, crossed the street, and walked up to the first house on the other side. It was a small white frame structure with a tiny cement front porch. Kevin knocked on the door several times. No one answered. They made notes in their notebooks and walked up to the next place. Same story. They moved on to the third, a large brick house situated almost directly across the street from the Hansens. Kevin rang the doorbell. They heard someone moving around inside. A door closed. Footsteps approached. The front door opened and an elderly woman Kevin knew slightly frowned up at them.

"I'm Detective Constable Walker from the OPP, Miss Kirk," Kevin said, holding up his badge. "This is Constable Allore. Could I have a few moments of your time to ask you a few questions?"

"I know who you are," the old woman replied. "Step inside; you're letting out all the heat."

Kevin and Allore obediently shuffled into the hallway so that she could close the door behind them. They went through a little ballet dance as Kevin and Allore scrunched against the wall and she edged past them again, then she put her hands on her hips and raised her eyebrows.

Kevin opened his notebook. "We're investigating an incident involving your neighbour across the street, William Hansen. Have you noticed anything unusual in the last day or two over there?"

"What happened?"

"Did you see Mr. Hansen yesterday, Miss Kirk?"

"I saw him in the morning. What happened?"

"Well, unfortunately, he's deceased. His body was found this morning on Church Road, down in the township. We're trying to retrace his steps over the last twenty-four hours or so. What time yesterday morning did you see him?"

"Was it foul play?"

"Yes, we believe so, Miss Kirk. What time did you see him?"

"Shortly after eight, as always. Every morning, six days a week, I'm having my tea in the front room when he fires up that noisy truck and drives off. Rattles the front window, it's so loud. Was he shot, stabbed, or bludgeoned?"

"Did you see him again at any time after that?"

"No, I did not. He was shot, am I right?"

"What makes you think that, Miss Kirk? Did you see or hear anything to suggest someone might have shot him?"

"No, of course not. But I didn't teach school for more than forty years because I'm a dummy. I've been watching all the comings and goings over there this morning, so I know something must have happened to him. *And*, I read a report online not long ago that said 39 per cent of rural homicides are committed with a firearm, so it adds up that he was more likely shot than gutted or hit over the head. Who do you think did it?"

"Miss Kirk," Kevin replied, "I'm really not in a position to answer any of these questions at this time. Have mercy on me, okay? I just need to ask you a few basic questions, then I'll let you get back to your tea."

"It's almost lunch time, that's what it is." She turned her head at the sound of furious scratching somewhere in the interior of the house. "I put Chester in the downstairs powder room. If I don't when someone comes to the door, he'll bite them. He's old, but his teeth are still good."

Like yours, Kevin thought. "How well do you know the Hansens, Miss Kirk?"

"Not well at all. She keeps to herself. I see *you* in the drug store and post office all the time, young man, but I've never seen *her* anywhere other than right there, across the street. I understand she's from the Maritimes. Halifax, I think. I've always found people from Nova Scotia a little stuck up and difficult to deal with. He was a real talker. Always standing around on the street corner talking to somebody or other, or in the restaurant having lunch with someone. A schmoozer. Do you think she did it? Forty per cent of rural homicides are committed by a family member, you know."

"I'm not in a position to say, Miss Kirk. Did you ever see Mr. Hansen with anyone unusual?"

"Unusual's a very vague word. I know you're supposed to ask open questions to get me talking, but you really should try to word them better."

Kevin heard Allore make a sound behind him. Something between a cough and a snort.

"If you mean," she went on, "did I ever see him with any rough-looking characters who might be capable of shooting him in cold blood, the answer's yes, absolutely. That describes half the hillbilly farmers in this township, wouldn't you say? But most of them I know on sight, like Ronnie Ross or Gordon Purvis. A few I didn't know, I admit. But he was always talking cars with them, showing them computer printouts, getting forms signed, that kind of thing. He seemed to like doing business in the restaurant more than at his office, if you ask me."

"Did you ever see him with other women, Miss Kirk?"

She shook her head emphatically. "Always men. They're the ones buying and selling cars all the time. Look at me. I've driven the same Toyota Corolla for sixteen years. You don't see me trading and flipping and what not like some of the men around here."

"One further question," Kevin said, scribbling. "Did you see or hear anything out of the ordinary in the street earlier this morning?"

"I presume you mean before you arrived, along with the rest of the circus."

"Yes, ma'am."

"No, it was very quiet."

"What about last night?"

"No." Then she frowned. "No, that's not true. I heard a car stop across the street. I was in bed. I heard it leave again about ten minutes later. I'd almost forgotten that."

"Did you see this car, Miss Kirk? Can you give us a description?"

She shook her head. "My bedroom's at the back of the

house. At first I thought it was Hansen, coming home late. He often does. But it wasn't that noisy truck of his. Then when it left again, I knew it couldn't have been him. I fell asleep right afterward."

"Do you know about what time that was, last night?"

"Almost ten thirty. I go to bed at ten, I read for about twenty minutes or so, then I turn out the light. It takes me a few minutes to get to sleep."

"You'd already turned out your light?"

"Yes, I was nearly asleep."

"So you'd say between ten fifteen and ten thirty?"

She nodded. "Do you think it was important? A clue of some kind?"

"It's all important," Kevin said, closing his notebook. "Thanks for your time, Miss Kirk." He handed her a business card. "If you think of something else, call me right away. Someone will be back to see you later in the day for a written statement, if that's all right."

"It's all right as long as they're a little more forthcoming than you've been."

"It might end up being me again," Kevin said, as Allore opened the door.

"Well, if it is, I hope you use the time between now and then to think up some better answers than you've given me so far."

"I'll try, Miss Kirk."

"See that you do."

Out on the sidewalk, Kevin saw Detective Constable Bishop and a uniformed officer coming out of a house three doors up. He and Allore went up to join them.

"Not getting much," Bishop said, his breath huffing out in a white cloud. "A few people say they knew the vic and maybe spoke to him now and again, but nobody says they were friends. And nobody knows the wife at all, other than maybe to recognize her if they see her. Maybe."

Kevin passed on what Miss Kirk had told him about hearing a vehicle in the street. "Focus on last night between ten and eleven for the rest of the canvass. Maybe someone else saw or heard the same vehicle."

"Will do, Kev. It's all pensionable time, eh?"

"And would you do me a favour? Get her written statement." Kevin glanced back at the brick house involuntarily.

Allore laughed. "She practically ate his lunch for him."

Bishop shook his head at Kevin. "What a chickenshit."

"Yeah," Kevin smiled ruefully. "I know."

chapter FIVE

Ellie sat back in the leather seat across the desk from Leanne Blair, chief superintendent of East Region, and crossed her legs. It was a large corner office on the second floor of the regional headquarters building in Smiths Falls, which was still only a few years old and retained that new-building look and feel. Blair, on the other hand, was beginning to show her age. Her plump face was webbed with creases, her blue eyes looked tired, and her blond hair was beginning to fade to an uncertain straw colour. She was about ten years older than Ellie, and she looked every day of it. Her smile, though, was genuine as she leaned forward and folded her hands on her desk.

"How was your drive down? I understand we caught you on leave."

"I was in Toronto, visiting family."

"Sorry it was cut short. I hope you had a nice time."

Not exactly.

Ellie had driven from Orillia down to Markham on Sunday to make an appearance at her daughter Megan's eleventh birthday party. It was the first time she'd seen her ex-husband's new condominium and, unsurprisingly, it looked like something out of *Architectural Digest*. Gareth was a senior economic advisor for the federal Conservative Party, and the condo was one of several properties he owned. No expense had been spared in its furnishings, and Ellie, despite herself, had felt a little intimidated.

Predictably, Megan refused to see her, and Ellie was forced to stay in the kitchen. Her gift, a new iPad that cost more than Ellie should have spent, lay forgotten on the counter between the espresso machine and the food processor as Gareth and Suzie made an issue of Megan's distress. A cute and preppy tag team, they urged Ellie to stop bothering the children and making things worse for everyone involved. The four of them were going to Cuba for Christmas, Gareth announced, and it would be a very good opportunity for Ellie to make a clean break of it and get on with her own life. They could always bring the lawyers back in to ensure that Ellie kept her distance if she had a problem with the concept, but wouldn't it be better if they just worked it all out between themselves in an amicable fashion? Surely Ellie could see that the best interests of the two girls should come before her own self-centred impulses.

Ellie said a few things that were a little bitter, Suzie began to cry, and Gareth became coldly efficient. He pulled out his cellphone and said, "You need to leave. Now. Or I'm calling the police. *Our* police."

Ellie sighed, looked at the gift sitting on the counter, and walked out.

In the hallway, head down and fists shoved into the pockets of her trench coat, Ellie concentrated on taking long, deep breaths. A chime sounded and the elevator doors opened.

"Oh," a voice said. "It's you."

Ellie moved aside as her older daughter Melanie stepped out of the elevator with another girl her age.

"I can't stay, Mel," Ellie said, holding the elevator door open with one hand. "I just came to wish your sister happy birthday."

"You didn't see her, did you?"

"No, she wasn't up to it."

"I told you she wouldn't talk to her," Melanie said to her friend.

"Uh huh," the friend said.

Ellie let the elevator door close without getting on. "I don't believe we've met. I'm Ellie March."

"I know who you are," the friend said.

"This is Katie," Melanie said. "Suzie's sister."

Ellie stared. "Suzie's *sister*?"

"That's right," Katie said.

"How old are you, Katie?"

"She's sixteen, Ellie," Melanie said.

Ellie raised an eyebrow. "Exactly how old is Suzie, again?"

"She's twenty-four," Melanie said. "You should leave now."

"I think you're right." Ellie stabbed the button to summon the elevator car back to the floor.

"Meg nailed it," Katie said. "I know exactly what she means."

"Yeah," Melanie said.

"What?" Ellie looked from one to the other. "What are you talking about?"

Katie gave her a sardonic look. "Meg says you never smile. She says you're the unhappiest person, like, ever. You make *happy* people feel unhappy. I know exactly what she means."

The two girls abruptly turned their backs on her and let themselves into the condo. Ellie stared at the closed door until the elevator door chimed behind her. Shaking her head, she got in and pressed the button for the ground floor, then repeatedly stabbed the button to shut the doors.

Stab, stab, stab, stab, stab.

Yesterday she'd completed the disastrous trip with a visit to her adoptive parents. Paul and Mary March lived in an assisted-living facility in Richmond Hill, where they'd been for the last eight years after selling their home and business. Paul, whose father had changed the family name from Marchalewicz after emigrating from Poland, had owned the building on Yonge Street in which he'd operated his shoe store for more than four decades. Adopted as an infant, Ellie had grown up in the apartment above the store. She'd continued to live at home while studying for her degree in criminology, but after catching on with the OPP she'd moved out, first to Aylmer, where she attended police college, and then to Caledon East, where she completed her probationary period. She married Gareth, moved forward in her career, and spent less and less time with Paul and Mary.

Ellie had learned about a month ago that Paul had already passed into the intermediate stages of Alzheimer's disease and was about to be moved from assisted living into the long-term care wing of the facility. It had been more than a year, she realized, since she'd visited them. As they had lunch together, Mary explained that Paul now required daily attention that she was no longer able to provide. She was, after all, eighty-four years old herself.

When Ellie asked about the financial arrangements, Mary explained they'd already signed over their powers of attorney to their lawyer, a long-time friend. Ellie would not be burdened with any of the decision-making process. All they wanted from her now was her love and best wishes.

Last night, mulling it over in her motel room before going to bed, Ellie thought about dementia and wondered if she should talk to Mary before the past was completely eradicated from her mind, as well. She'd been debating for some time whether or not to ask about her birth mother. She'd never made an attempt before to look into it, and wouldn't do so without Mary's acquiescence. Mary knew who Ellie's natural mother was, and had let slip to Ellie once, several years ago, that the decision to adopt her had been a mutual agreement worked out among all parties. Excepting Ellie herself, of course.

Sitting on the edge of the bed with her head in her hands, Ellie decided to let it go.

She'd been an adequate adopted daughter, perhaps a good one, but the way she'd fallen out of touch with them over the past few years was, really, inexcusable. On top of that, she'd been a complete disaster as a mother and a wife.

Why look for more family connections to fuck up?

Staring out of Leanne Blair's office window now at the flags flapping in the steady wind on the outskirts of Smiths Falls, Ellie knew in her heart that she would never bother trying to locate her natural parents. She was who she was, and she adamantly believed that her daughters were wrong about her being a black hole that sucked in all the happiness around her. She knew she was content living her life within its current frames of reference. She felt no restlessness, no burning need to know more. She was who she was.

"It was family," she said to Blair, shrugging. "You know how it is."

"I understand. Well, I'm glad to have you on this. Do you know Fisher?"

"Not well." She'd met the Leeds County detachment commander once before, when she'd participated as lead interrogator in the investigation of a serial sexual predator that had resulted in a confession and conviction. She hadn't formed a positive opinion. He came off as unfriendly, draconian, and sexist, all of which were reinforced by the stories that went around about him. Not that Ellie cared much, one way or the other. She wasn't here to get herself on Todd Fisher's Christmas card list.

"He'll be fine," Blair said. "He'll give you whatever you need. Hopefully it won't be as bad as the McRae case."

"We'll see." The case Blair was referring to was one that Ellie had led as case manager just over a year ago. Four people, a couple in their forties and their twenty-something son and daughter, were all shotgunned to death in their home in the Kaladar area. Ellie discovered that the son had had ties to an outlaw motorcycle gang, and had stolen money and drugs from them. Before it was over, the investigation had mobilized more than a hundred officers, including detectives, uniformed constables, and intelligence resources, and culminated with a helicopter pursuit through a heavily-wooded area north of Kaladar, complete with dogs, all-terrain vehicles, and officers on foot, all at a cost to the taxpayers of more than a million dollars.

Blair had supported her every step of the way, and they'd become friends. Since Ellie had very few friends, they were important to her, and she valued the relationship that had developed between them.

"I hear you were caught a little off-guard by the weather, wardrobe-wise."

Ellie rolled her eyes. "It was mild when I left Orillia, believe it or not. They were forecasting above-zero temperatures until tomorrow."

"Never trust Environment Canada," Blair laughed. "They've been cut back so much they couldn't forecast the weather for this afternoon, let alone the day after tomorrow. I'm sure we can line you up with a nice, warm duty jacket before you leave. Give my assistant your size and she'll find one for you while we're in our meeting. Speaking of which, shall we?"

Ellie stood up. She tugged at the creases of her pants and buttoned her jacket over her white blouse. She glanced down at the cheap black pumps she'd carried in with her from the car to put on instead of her clunky boots, and decided they weren't too scuffed. Grabbing her black leather handbag, a cross between a computer bag and a soft-sided briefcase, she followed Blair down the corridor to a conference room on the left. The two men waiting for them at the long cherry wood table stood as they entered. Ellie shook hands with Inspector Todd Fisher, the detachment commander, and Staff Sergeant Rick Tobin, Fisher's operations manager.

Everyone sat down. Ellie pulled her notebook out of her bag and opened it on the table in front of her. "The victim is William Hansen, DOB October 21, 1957, a resident of Sparrow Lake. The body's now in the custody of Dr. Carey Burton of the regional forensic pathology unit at Kingston General Hospital. It's still in a frozen state, and Dr. Burton will have to thaw it out slowly before performing the post-mortem which, as it stands right now, is scheduled for Thursday morning at eleven."

Fisher stared at her, unblinking. A short, neat man with wavy grey hair and thick, jet black eyebrows, he radiated disdain. Tobin, head down, took notes in a notebook open in front of him.

"Cause of death is obvious," Ellie went on, "but time of death is going to be a bit of a challenge. Dr. Burton will look at the overnight temperature for that location and the fact that it was out in the open, exposed to cross-winds. Et cetera. But I wouldn't look to the post-mortem as the primary source of information for our time line for TOD."

"Any witnesses?" Blair asked. "Anybody see or hear anything?"

"It's pretty isolated. The farmer who found the body won't be able to help us on that score, since he's as deaf as a post. We'll see what the area canvass turns up."

Ellie then shifted the discussion to resourcing. Blair immediately repeated her promise that she would have whatever she needed. Fisher looked at Tobin, who acknowledged that detectives would be brought in from other areas to assist the crime unit, and up to four bodies could be made available from the emergency response team as required. Five, if you counted the dog. A regional intelligence co-ordinator would work with the investigative team to facilitate their production orders to banks and phone companies and would analyze the data. The manager of Forensic Identification and Photographic Services at GHQ had promised Blair that Identification Sergeant Dave Martin and company would give top priority to the evidence generated by the case.

Ellie nodded. It was like a pep rally before the big game. She looked at Tobin. "Let's talk about options for primary investigator."

He leaned forward and folded his hands on the table, glancing at Fisher. "We were just discussing that, before the meeting. Patterson feels very strongly that Detective Constable Walker would be the best choice. I understand you and he notified the widow earlier."

Ellie nodded. "But he doesn't have enough experience to handle this kind of investigation, does he? As I understand it, he came over from the local police service two years ago when we picked up the contract with the municipality."

"Yes. It was a staff of seven, excluding civilians, and he was the only one who even applied."

"As I remember it," Leanne Blair said, "the chief retired to Florida, the deputy moved to Edmonton, and the four constables left policing altogether. Walker was the only detective on staff."

Although it might have seemed to an outsider listening in on their conversation that Kevin had transitioned seamlessly from a village cop to a detective in the OPP with little or no effort, he had in fact applied for an appointment at the rank of detective constable through the OPP's rank level determination process. This procedure kicked in when the force picked up a municipal contract and resources wanted to transfer over to the OPP at a rank equivalent to what they'd held in the disbanded service. Walker had been Sparrow Lake's detective for five years. His performance during his tenure with the SLPS was examined, his exemplary evaluations were duly noted, and his training file and test scores relating to core competencies—all off the charts—were taken into account. Once the procedure was complete the commissioner had reviewed the results and signed off on Kevin's appointment at the equivalent rank of detective constable.

"Dart has more job experience," Fisher said, "and a better background."

"But his focus is narcotics," Tobin said, "and he's very single-minded about it. Walker's the one who's been handling violent crime. Granted, it hasn't included a homicide investigation, but that isn't in Dart's résumé yet either."

"Or anyone else's in the crime unit, other than Patterson's," Fisher said. He looked at Ellie. "The alternative is to bring in someone from outside with homicide experience." He turned to Blair. "I have a list of potential candidates. I can reach out to their commanders as soon as we're done here."

Tobin stirred. "Patterson feels strongly that Walker can handle it."

"I see," Ellie said.

"Look," Fisher said, tapping the table with his index finger, "I need to know what kind of case manager you are, March. It's been my experience that a lot of people at CIB are so busy soaking up the GHQ mentality and grooming themselves for commissioner that they've forgotten what it's like to get their hands dirty. Now, the manual gives you the final say on resourcing, including lead detective, but it's my ass on the line here. I'm the one who's accountable. It's my detachment, my staff, and my neck. So I need to know who you are. If you're the girl who's going to sit back and let this case drift while my people sink or swim, then I'm going to have to insist we reach out for more experienced personnel. Understand what I'm saying?"

Ellie glanced at Tobin. She knew the staff sergeant only slightly, but she knew Patterson quite well. They'd spent time together on training courses and at conferences, and she'd developed a healthy respect for his intelligence and judgment. If Scott Patterson wanted Kevin as primary investigator, then he had very good reasons for it.

"What about this Dart?" she asked.

Tobin shrugged. "As I say, he's narcotics. He's been participating in the ongoing JFO down here." Tobin was referring to Project Islander, a joint forces operation between the OPP Drug Enforcement Section, Brockville and Gananoque police services, and the Leeds detachment.

"Any relation to Cecil Dart?"

"His son."

Ellie raised an eyebrow. Chief Superintendent Cecil Dart was commander of the Organized Crime Enforcement Bureau at GHQ, and was cut out of the same cloth as Fisher—bad-tempered, draconian, and known to carry a grudge. If Craig Dart was his son, then it might explain the attitude she'd picked up from the detective at the crime scene while watching him work. Her initial impression was that he was carrying a heavy sense of entitlement.

She looked at Blair, who merely smiled. Ellie understood that by taking Kevin with her to notify Vivian Hansen, she'd done Patterson a favour by giving the young detective constable an early try-out. In her opinion he came across as raw and a little immature, but very intelligent, quick on the uptake, and reasonably self-confident.

"Let's go with Walker," she said. She stared at Fisher. "I'm the kind of *woman* who never hesitates to get her hands dirty. In fact, that's how I prefer to work. But the manual you mentioned stresses that I need to place a very high priority on team management. This is an investigative *team*, Inspector, and I'm their *manager*. So yes, I'm going to be managing this thing, but not by sitting on my ass. Just make sure you're not sitting on your ass when the shit hits the fan and I need something yesterday. Understand what *I'm* saying?"

Fisher, clearly unhappy, looked away without replying.

chapter SIX

The sky had clouded over, and a light snow had begun to fall as Ellie drove south on County Road 29 from Smiths Falls to Brockville. Snow eddied and drifted on the pavement in front of her like smoke, stirred by crosswinds from the open fields on either side of the road.

Ellie liked to drive. It was just as well, since she spent most of her time behind the wheel, moving from case to case within her region and from village to hamlet to farm as each case dictated. It was about a forty-minute drive from regional headquarters in Smiths Falls to the detachment host office in Elizabethtown-Kitley township, just a few minutes north of Brockville, and while it would have been shorter if she'd stuck the bubble light on her dashboard and floored it, she preferred to reduce her speed in weather like this, even though the Crown Vic had snow tires and handled well enough on the road. As a young constable working Traffic she'd once put her cruiser in a ditch during a bad winter storm, and she'd vowed never to let that happen to her again.

So far, so good.

Some people like to listen to music or talk radio while they drive, but Ellie preferred silence. She used the solitary time behind the wheel, particularly when she was working a case, to solve problems and make plans. During the drive down from Toronto this morning, though, her thoughts had been dominated by the girls. She blamed herself for the disintegration of her relationship with them. They were good kids, bright and reasonably well-behaved, and she was fiercely proud of them. But they hated her guts. There was no getting around it. As far as they were concerned, she'd consistently chosen her career—i.e., herself—over them, and they refused to forgive her for it. The time she'd spent in her cruiser as a constable, or on unexpected call outs at crime scenes as a detective, had been time lost, time when the bonds between mother and daughter were supposed to be nurtured and developed. Time she could never get back. Time in which her daughters had turned to their father instead, to their nanny—one of Gareth's many conquests, as she'd later learned—and finally to Suzie.

Now, however, she thankfully had the Hansen investigation to occupy her thoughts. Her mind was doing its thing, compartmentalizing the personal stuff, sorting and prioritizing the professional stuff. Clearing the decks for action.

After leaving Smiths Falls she'd called Crown Attorney Susan Mitchum on the hands-free to touch base and discuss the assignment of an assistant Crown attorney. Paul Beeson, Mitchum told her, would be attached to the case. He would make himself available whenever needed. Ellie then called Patterson to discuss the makeup of the investigative team. He promised to have everyone waiting for her in the conference room when she arrived.

Crosswinds rocked the Crown Vic. Snow slanted across the road in front of her at a sharp angle. She glanced at the sky and marvelled at how quickly the storm had moved in. Hopefully Dave Martin would tell her that the crime scene had been completely processed before the snow had begun to fall. The area search, though, was probably still in progress. It wasn't a heavy snow. Not yet. But the wind had picked up, and it might get worse before it got better.

Finally, her destination appeared ahead on the left. It was a typical OPP detachment building, single-storey brick with a high, peaked roof and flagpoles out the front. The host office was one of three locations in the county, the other two being the Rideau Lakes satellite just west of Smiths Falls and the Thousand Islands satellite in Lansdowne. In all, Todd Fisher's detachment policed a total population of about 35,000 people scattered over a land area of about 2,100 square kilometres. Ellie understood the challenges he faced in a rural jurisdiction where traffic patrol, break-and-enters, and drug enforcement dominated his meagre resource allocation. It wasn't surprising to her, then, that his current detective roster couldn't count a full-blown homicide investigation among their sudden-death call outs. However, Patterson had several under his belt from his days in the Chatham-Kent and Middlesex detachments. His presence would be a big help to his detectives and to her, even though his duties as crime unit supervisor would significantly divide his time.

She pulled into the driveway and parked at the side of the building, in front of someone's office window. On the seat next to her was the duty jacket Blair's secretary had found for her before she'd left Smiths Falls. It had no shoulder patches or other identifying features, just thick, waterproof lining and a warm fur collar. She put it on, grabbed her stuff from the back seat, and went inside. Patterson met her at the reception counter and walked her down a long corridor, past the conference room where the team had already assembled, to a closed door.

"It's all yours for the duration," he said, opening the door. "It's a break-off room for the training room across the hall."

She followed him in. It was small, about ten by ten. She looked at a round table with four plastic chairs, a whiteboard on one wall, a window on another with a view of her Crown Vic right outside it in the parking lot, and a flip chart stand in the corner. Leaning against the wall were extra pads of manila flip chart paper.

"I've got a two-drawer filing cabinet lined up for you," Patterson said, "and a decent office chair. There are voice and data jacks. Do you want a land line in here?"

"A fax machine," Ellie said, "but don't bother with a phone.

I'll work off my cell."

"Okay. I've got a computer for you, too."

"I'll use my laptop. Can you find me a printer?"

Patterson nodded. "I'll give you the password for logging on to the LAN."

"Thanks, Scott." Ellie dumped her laptop and handbag on the table, then took off her jacket and draped it over one of the plastic chairs. She pulled off her boots, set them against the wall, took out her black pumps, dropped them on the floor, and slipped her feet into them. Notebook and pen in hand, she looked at Patterson. "Let's get started."

He led the way to the conference room. Everyone stood as they walked in. Patterson waved them to their seats, introduced Ellie, and walked around the table to a seat down near the end.

A large clock on the wall told Ellie that it was 3:36 PM. Eight hours since the 911 call from Jerry Lackey had been recorded.

She looked at the circle of faces. Some were familiar from the crime scene, others were not. "To begin with," she said, "we'll meet every morning at eight o'clock to share findings and get assignments straight, and again at six whenever feasible. We can cut back to one-a-days as the investigation moves on. Communication, sharing, and teamwork are the most important things we have going for us in the search for the person who shot and killed Mr. William Hansen. We don't compartmentalize information on this team, and we don't hold it back. Understood? We all need to be rowing in the same direction. Furthermore, detectives are expected to carry out their assignments without a lot of micromanagement. You should have already completed major case training, so you're familiar with the roles and responsibilities you'll be assigned this afternoon."

She put her notebook and pen down on the table. "First of all, we're going to be working on a first-name basis, so I'm Ellie. Second, Scott, I see a table back there against the wall, but there's nothing on it. We'll need one of those big coffee urns, from Tim Hortons or whatever, and it has to be full all the time. Plus whatever stuff people like to eat. I'll give you my cost centre number to cover it."

Patterson nodded. His grin was matched by several others around the table.

"Third, although I know some of you, I don't know all of you. Let's get the introductions done now. Just tell me who you are and what you do." She pointed to a middle-aged blond woman sitting on her right. "Let's start with you."

"Detective Constable Monica Sisson," the woman said in a smoke-roughened contralto. "Marine patrol."

"That's full-time dedicated from May to September, isn't it?"

Sisson nodded. "We work between Mallorytown Landing and Butternut Bay. I also do events, like poker runs and festivals. That kind of stuff."

Ellie shifted her eyes to the detective sitting next to Sisson.

"Detective Constable Craig Dart. Narcotics." He stared at her evenly, his jaw tight, his dark eyes unwavering. Challenging. Small and dark-haired, he bore no physical resemblance whatsoever to his stocky, homely father, but Ellie saw immediately that he'd inherited the old man's belligerent personality.

Sitting next to Dart, a tall, slender man with short black hair and blue eyes said, "Detective Constable Tom Carty, Rideau Lakes."

Ellie nodded and raised her eyebrows at Patterson, who was sitting next to Dart.

"Detective Sergeant Scrooge McDuck. I'm supposed to be in charge of this bunch."

Everyone sitting at the table laughed. Ellie said, "Just don't start talking in a fake Scottish burr and we'll be fine."

"Aye, lass, and as long as you keep paying for the coffee, it'll be just grand."

Ellie let the laughter die down before nodding at a slightly overweight man with shaggy brown hair, a thick moustache, and large brown eyes.

"Detective Constable Bill Merkley. RIC."

"Good to meet you," Ellie said. "We'll keep you busy." As regional intelligence co-ordinator, Merkley would carry the load for the team in analyzing Hansen's phone and bank records, along with other data they would be able to secure through production orders and search warrants over the course of the case.

Merkley nodded. “Looking forward to it.”

Ellie moved her eyes to the uniformed officer sitting at the end of the table.

“Sergeant Bob Kerr, ERT.” He was blond and handsome, with a brush moustache and pale blue eyes.

Sitting to Kerr’s right, Martin gave a little wave. “I’m Dave. We meet again.”

“Hi, Dave.”

A stocky fellow with a porcupine brush cut cleared his throat at the far end of the table on Ellie’s left. “Detective Constable John Bishop. Property. You break in somewhere, I’ll catch you.”

“His favourite hangout is the pawn shop on King Street,” Sisson said.

“Yeah, right next to the bar you’re always falling asleep in, Mona,” Bishop shot back.

“People, people,” Patterson said, a little iron in his voice.

Ellie nodded at the tired-looking brunette sitting next to Bishop.

“Detective Constable Janet Olkewicz, victim assistance. I’m also the domestic violence co-ordinator.”

“Glad to have you on board,” Ellie said. She moved her eyes to the woman on Olkewicz’s right.

“Constable Rachel Townsend, media relations.”

“Thanks for coming down, Rachel. Good to be working with you again.”

Townsend nodded. “Likewise.”

Ellie looked at Kevin, who said, “Detective Constable Kevin Walker. Violent Crimes.”

Patterson cleared his throat. “Missing, but definitely in action, is Detective Ben Wiltse, our warrant co-ordinator. He’s hard at work, even as we speak. He has a way with words and wants to be a Crown attorney when he grows up, as I understand it.”

Ellie waited for the chuckles to subside. "You're all familiar with the Campbell Report that came out after the Bernardo case, and the system that resulted from it. Our province is a world leader in the use of this methodology to investigate major crimes, and since you detectives have already done the coursework, you understand why GHQ sends me down from the mother ship to run the show when a homicide occurs in your jurisdiction."

Heads nodded. They were all well aware that after the conviction of serial killer and rapist Paul Bernardo in 1995, a judicial review by Justice Archie Campbell had led to the creation of an automated case management system and accompanying method that would co-ordinate information among the police, forensics experts, the coroner's office, and the provincial government. Its primary purpose was to eliminate the confusion and duplication of effort previously experienced in multi-jurisdiction cases such as Bernardo, but it was also mandatory now in single-jurisdiction major cases such as this one. Using a specialized software system, the method had greatly helped to standardize investigative techniques followed by case managers and detectives.

"I'm not here to push anyone aside and steal the show," Ellie went on. "I never speak to the media, for example. That's why Rachel's here. I don't grandstand, and I don't take credit. This case will be investigated by you, the people on this team, under my direction."

Ellie pulled her chair over and sat down. "Let's start with roles and responsibilities." She opened her notebook and picked up her pen. "Kevin, you're primary. Monica," she looked at Sisson, "you're our file co-ordinator. You two will keep everyone moving, and you'll let me know right away if we need extra help."

"Sounds good to me," Sisson said. She had a tablet in front of her, and had already begun to take notes, using a stylus to write on the screen. They would form the basis of the minutes of this meeting, for which she would be responsible each time the team met.

"We'll get together fifteen minutes before each team meeting to review the register."

"You got it." As the file co-ordinator, Sisson would also maintain a complete list of assignments handed out to each team member. In the absence of direct instruction from either Ellie or Kevin, she'd assign tasks herself and record them in her register. In addition, she'd receive every written report generated by the team and would review them before Kevin and Ellie saw them. In essence, she'd serve as Ellie's whip, maintaining quality and team discipline when it came to assignment completion and report writing.

"Do you know who you want for data input?"

Sisson leaned back in her chair to look down the table at Patterson. "Brenda."

Patterson nodded.

The command triangle mandated by the major case management method was now in place. Ellie occupied the apex as case manager, while Kevin and Sisson would work at the other two corners as primary investigator and file co-ordinator. Ellie was satisfied with Sisson's response to her assignment. Now it was time to put some pressure on the primary.

"Bring us up to date, Kevin."

"A canvass of Church Road has been done," Kevin said, turning a page in the notebook in front of him. "There are only eight residences on the road, including Mr. Lackey's. Of the other seven, we talked to people at three and there was no answer at the remaining four. Commuters, probably. We'll go back early this evening to follow up on them. Of the three residents interviewed, two reported hearing a noise late last evening that may or may not have been a gunshot."

"Oh? That's interesting."

Kevin looked at Dart. "Craig?"

The detective took a moment before responding, his eyes on a spot on the far wall. Then he cleared his throat and looked sideways at Ellie. "A Mrs. Sandra Gibbons, civic number 54 Church Road, reported hearing two quote unquote shots, back to back, at approximately 2030 hours last night. She was standing in the kitchen at the time, quote, getting a beer from the fridge, unquote. Her husband was in the living room watching a movie on TV and didn't hear it."

"That was it?"

"That was it. She took the beer into the living room and went back to watching TV."

"Okay. And the other witness?"

Dart flipped a page in his notebook. "A Mr. Dale McConnell, civic number 69 Church Road, reported hearing a noise at about 2106 hours coming from somewhere down the road. He was outside, behind his house, letting his dog out for a piss. He was very definite that it sounded like a single shot."

"The woman, Gibbons, lives closest to the scene," Kevin said. "Next property over and across the road. It's possible she heard a shot and an echo, and thought it was two shots."

Dart shrugged. "Could be. Makes sense."

"What about the discrepancy in time?" Kevin asked.

Dart looked at him, then turned to Ellie to give his answer. "Gibbons was a little iffy, but the guy, McConnell, was very definite. He looked at his watch while he was putting his coat on to go outside."

"Anyone else who saw or heard anything?" Ellie asked. "Maybe someone who saw a vehicle near the scene around that time?"

"You wish." Dart rolled his pen between his thumb and index finger.

"Okay. Thanks." She looked down the table at Kerr. In major cases like this one, the ERT was usually tapped to provide additional resources, especially to help search for physical evidence, and Kerr had brought a team with him to scour the ditches along Church Road for evidence. "Any luck?"

Kerr shook his head. "Not so far. The road's about four kilometres long. The crime scene's about a kilometre north of Junetown Road. Working on the assumption that the vehicle proceeded north after the shooting, since it parked on the east side of the road and there were no subsequent turnaround tire marks, we began with a sweep north from the crime scene. We've just about completed that stretch, and we've found zero."

"No luck with the dog?"

"No. There's nothing. No gun, no cellphone, no keys. The usual trash, which we dutifully collected as a favour to the township more than anything else, but nothing obviously connected to the case."

"No turnaround tracks in anyone's driveway?"

"There are five entrances into fields and three driveways into households from the crime scene to the end of the road. There were no markings at all in the field entrances, and just a typical set of turnout tracks heading north from one driveway. A household that Detective Constable Dart reported as non-responsive. We found no distinctive k-type turn marks anywhere that you'd expect to see from a vehicle reversing direction. In addition, there's a cemetery on the west side of the road, a kilometre and a half north of Lackey's field, and the gate is shut and snowed in. Plus, there's the decommissioned church right up at the intersection of Ballycanoe Road. It's being renovated and shows no signs of recent activity around it. So, to answer your question, I'm not hopeful. I'll have a follow-up when we've done the southern leg. Do you want us to extend out onto Ballycanoe Road?"

"Yes." Ellie frowned at the far wall. "We need a map. Monica, can you get a detailed map of the area up on the wall for us?"

"Will do."

"Moving on," Kevin said, "we completed a canvass of Mill Street in the village, both blocks, both sides. We also canvassed the block behind the Hansen residence, where anyone might have seen or heard something from the rear of the Hansen house or back yard. We got a lot of generalized comments about the Hansens, all of it suggesting that the victim was a nice guy, worked hard at his business, wasn't known to drink or take drugs or cheat on his wife, and not much beyond that. As for Vivian Hansen, we got very little. She didn't interact with her neighbours at all, to speak of." Kevin paused. "I did, though, get something interesting from the woman across the street." He gave them a synopsis of the information he'd extracted from his interview of Miss Kirk.

"How reliable a witness is she?" Ellie asked.

"Very." Kevin chuckled. "She's a retired school teacher. All I can say is, I'm glad I didn't have her. I'd have flunked for sure."

Bishop grinned, shaking his head.

"This helps our time frame," Ellie said. "If we can confirm that Vivian Hansen was contacted by someone about her husband's murder around ten thirty last night, we can place time of death somewhere before that." She glanced at Dart. "If we work with what the McConnell witness gave us, the shooting happened shortly after nine and the killer showed up to report to the wife ninety minutes later. Which would give him time to dispose of the gun and the vehicle, I suppose, and whatever else he needed to take care of before going to talk to her."

"Do you think the wife's involved?" Dart asked.

"It's a possibility," Ellie said.

"I don't get that feeling," Kevin said, at the same time.

There was a pause. Everyone's eyes were on Ellie.

"Fair enough," she said. "We're going to have to talk to her again, at any rate. Janet, how did it go with her?"

"I called her minister," Olkewicz said, "and spoke to his wife. A Mrs. Hume. Very nice lady. She didn't know Mrs. Hansen all that well, but knew who I was talking about. She attends church every Sunday, apparently, without fail. Mrs. Hume and her husband agreed right away that Mrs. Hansen could come over and stay with them overnight. They live on, uh—"

"Lang Street," Kevin supplied.

"Yes, that's it. I helped her pack a small overnight bag and took her over. I'll check in again in a few hours to see how she's doing."

"What about Victim Services?" Kevin asked, referring to the volunteer organization that provided crisis assistance in situations such as this one.

"I made the offer, but Mrs. Hume said it wasn't necessary. They're willing to keep her there as long as she needs somewhere to stay. She's a little shell-shocked right now."

"Did Mrs. Hansen say anything else about what happened?" Ellie asked. "Or mention a visitor last night?"

Olkewicz shook her head.

"She may need security arrangements," Kevin said.

Olkewicz frowned.

"The issue," Ellie said patiently, "is whether or not she was involved in the murder. She was keeping something from us when Kevin and I did the notification this morning. Either she hired someone to kill her husband and he showed up last night to be paid, or—"

"Either way," Kevin interrupted, "if she's been contacted by the person who killed her husband, she could be in danger herself."

"Whichever," Ellie said, "Kevin's right. Take care of it, Janet. The last thing we want or need is a second victim. Let's err on the side of caution."

"Right away," said Olkewicz, writing in her notebook.

Dave Martin was next, providing an update on the physical evidence collected from the scene. He told them that the expended round was being processed for a possible match in IBIS, the Integrated Ballistics Identification System. It was a 9 mm full metal jacket round that, because it had passed through the soft tissue of the neck without touching bone before landing in snow, had not been damaged very much at all. The cartridge casing, however, had not been recovered. Instead they'd found an indentation in the snow where the casing had landed after ejection from the gun before being picked up by the shooter.

Tire tread images had also been sent for processing through the RCMP's tire tread identification database at the Canadian Police Service Identification Centre. Martin repeated his belief that the vehicle in question was a pickup truck.

Ellie was in the process of discussing their media strategy with Rachel Townsend when Patterson's cellphone buzzed. He stood up and walked to the far corner to take the call. When he was done, he walked back to his place at the table but didn't sit down.

"Well?" Ellie asked.

"The warrants are signed. Wiltse's on his way."

Ellie tapped her hand on the table in front of Kevin. "What's your plan?"

"I'll take the residence," he replied. "Craig, your car's back in action, right?"

Dart nodded. His wife had gotten the battery replaced in the morning and had brought the car out to the detachment an hour ago.

"Okay," Kevin said, "you and JB do the car yard. Merk, follow up on the phone and bank records. Dave, are your teams ready?"

Martin rolled his eyes.

"All right then," Kevin said, getting to his feet. "Let's rock."

chapter SEVEN

While a scenes of crime officer searched the basement of the Hansen home and Kevin and another SOCO covered the main floor, Ellie went upstairs to look around. She wore protective booties on her feet and latex gloves on her hands, but had no intention of collecting evidence. While she'd told Todd Fisher she liked to get her hands dirty, she'd meant it figuratively rather than literally. The forensics team, under Kevin's watchful eye, would take care of the physical side of things. She was here because she wanted to get a sense of the victim and his wife. There were many unanswered questions.

She began in the bathroom at the top of the staircase. It was a nice room, with an enamel claw-foot bathtub in one corner and a shower stall in the other. It looked as though it had been enlarged by removing a wall to expand into a small bedroom next to it. An antique dresser had been added that held towels, extra bars of soap, and other bathroom supplies. In front of the yellow-curtained window was a settee with scrolled arms and old-fashioned upholstery, perhaps for sitting on while trimming your toenails or admiring the view of the back yard. It gave the room a relaxed, homey feeling.

The medicine cabinet above the sink held a variety of products, male and female, and several prescription bottles—

anti-depressants and sleep aids for Vivian Hansen; stomach acid reducers, nicotine patches, and blood pressure pills for Bill Hansen. All were prescribed by Dr. Yuri Dalca and filled at a major chain drugstore in Brockville. Ellie wondered who did the shopping in the family. A background check on Vivian had not turned up a driver's licence in her name. Had her husband done all the shopping and prescription filling when he was in Brockville, or had she gotten him to drive her into town to do it while he waited?

She left the bathroom and entered the master bedroom. There were two twin-sized beds in the room, neatly made and covered with white duvets. Between the beds was an occasional table that held a lamp and nothing else. There was a bedside table on the outside of each bed, with matching lamps and pull-out drawers. Ellie walking around the left side of the bed and pulled out the drawer. It contained a small pad of notepaper and pen, a half-consumed roll of cough drops, and a romance paperback novel. There was nothing written on the pad. She closed the drawer and looked at a framed black-and-white photograph of a man and woman standing arm-in-arm in front of a house. It was an old picture; judging by the clothing they wore, taken in the 1940s or 1950s. Vivian's parents? She looked around and saw no other photographs in the room. The only other framed item was a print of a Van Gogh painting of sunflowers, hanging just inside the door.

Ellie walked around to the little table on the other side of the bed. The drawer contained spare change, a foil packet of nicotine patches, a bolt with the nut threaded partway up, a pocket knife, a blister pack of watch batteries with only one battery left, and a cigar clipper. The victim's side of the bed. She sniffed the air in the room, and could not detect the odour of tobacco smoke. He'd been trying to quit, but had clearly not smoked in the bedroom during the night. Out of consideration for his wife?

Ellie opened the left-hand sliding door of the closet and looked at dresses, blouses, and nightgowns. After a quick glance at the shoes on the floor, she tried the other side and found polo shirts, long- and short-sleeve dress shirts, polyester trousers, several sports jackets—all off-the-rack from discount chains—and a cheap green suit.

There was a dresser with a mirror and a highboy cluttered with odds and ends that belonged to the victim. She looked at neatly folded t-shirts, underwear, socks, a few pairs of blue jeans, and not much else.

The SOCO would go over everything with a fine-toothed comb, including the undersides of the drawers and the floorboards inside the closet. She stepped back and ran her eyes around the room. It was neat, tidy, and almost impersonal.

Out in the hall, Ellie opened the louvered door of a linen closet and saw only carefully folded sheets, towels, and pillow cases.

In the guest room, she looked at a wall of bookshelves filled with dolls. There were dolls with bisque heads and delicately-made clothing, wax dolls with glass eyes, and an extensive collection of Barbie dolls, many in their original boxes. Along the other wall, on the other side of the neatly made bed, was a row of plastic storage drawers on wheels. The drawers were filled with doll parts, doll clothing and accessories, and doll-collecting magazines.

Vivian Hansen had a hobby, after all.

Ellie slowly climbed the stairs to the third floor, her nostrils detecting a whiff of stale cigar smoke as she ascended. Here, then, was Bill's study. There was a big walnut desk and office chair, a four-drawer metal filing cabinet, an armchair, and a pedestal lamp. A telephone, desktop computer, and inkjet printer sat on the desk. Against the wall was a large bookshelf filled with plastic magazine holders. Ellie peered at a collection of back issues of *Car and Driver*, *Road & Track*, *Auto Trader*, and *Motor Trend*. Another shelf held dozens of metal die-cast cars. The rest of the floor was given over to storage, mostly old furniture, boxes of Christmas decorations, a record player and a small collection of vinyl long-play albums, knick knacks, and boxes filled with more car magazines, many of them dating back to the 1950s and 1960s.

She went back to the desk. There was dust visible on the

telephone and the computer keyboard, suggesting they hadn't been used in a while. There was, however, an ash tray filled with cigar butts and ash, and a desktop air purifier. Next to the ash tray was an empty whisky tumbler which, when she bent down and put her nose over it, smelled of alcohol. Beside the glass was a car magazine, open to an article about the 2013 Range Rover. Recent reading, apparently. The desk drawers were filled with miscellaneous office supplies and giveaways from car shows and dealerships—key chains, buttons, pins, bumper stickers, pens, and other items. There were no bank books; Ellie suspected that Bill handled everything online and that Vivian was out of date with modern banking practices.

The bottom drawer held a half-empty bottle of Jim Beam bourbon.

While the rest of the house appeared to be under the control of Vivian and her rigid, unrelenting loneliness, the attic office must have been the victim's refuge at home, a place to relax and cheat on his attempt to quit smoking with a cigar and a glass of booze. His office in the trailer at the car yard, then, must have been where all the action took place.

Downstairs, she found Kevin opening cupboard doors in the kitchen. She described the victim's third-floor lair and said she was heading over to the car yard.

"All right." Kevin closed the cupboard door and eased his hip against the counter. "So far, there's nothing. There must be something here, *something* that explains why someone would take this guy out into a field after dark and put a bullet through his neck."

"Keep looking. If it's here, it'll turn up."

Ellie understood his frustration. She thought about it while driving from the house to the car yard. If Vivian Hansen had shot her husband to escape her life with him, why had she not just taken off afterward? Made arrangements for the man she'd hired to take her to Kingston or Ottawa, where she could catch a bus or a train to a new life? What would there be in that house to hold her there, without her husband?

While walking through Vivian's home, Ellie had been

watching for signs of spousal abuse. Vivian's withdrawal from external social contact could be considered an indicator, as was her husband's complete control of their finances. The extreme neatness of the home might be another sign, if Hansen had tended to become upset when he found something untidy or out of place. On the other hand, Vivian might be agoraphobic and withdrawn by nature, uncomfortable handling financial responsibilities and obsessive about cleanliness and neatness, without her husband having applied any abusive pressure whatsoever to bring out those traits.

The fact that she collected dolls was potentially important, because it was a hobby that could be expensive to pursue. Judging by the dolls on those shelves, Hansen certainly hadn't refused to allow her to spend money on herself.

At this early stage, Ellie had to consider all possible options. Once they'd gone through the telephone and bank records, something might turn up to indicate that Vivian had made some sort of arrangement to have her husband killed, or there might be absolutely no evidence whatsoever to support this hypothesis. Time would tell.

She parked on the shoulder of the road behind a line of police vehicles and got out. It was nearly five o'clock, and the sun had set. The car yard was a large, bright rectangle jumping out at her from a dark landscape. Someone had turned on the big spotlights attached to the poles at each corner of the compound, and Dave Martin's team had set up additional 1800-watt lights on tripods.

She showed her identification and badge to the constable at the perimeter and signed the log. Lifting the yellow tape, she followed the trail of green cones through the open gate into the yard. It had been plowed several days ago, leaving behind only a thin crust of ice and snow on the paved surface. The compound was probably about sixty square metres in size, and the chain-link security fence enclosing it was in excellent condition. Immediately within the gate, on the right, was a dumpster with its lid up. Inside, she saw several garbage bags crusted with snow and ice. Parked on the far side of the dumpster was a red

Ford F-150 truck with a snow plow on the front, likely used by Hansen to keep the yard clear. Looking around, Ellie counted six vehicles in addition to the F-150. None of them bore licence plates. She wasn't an expert on cars, but she recognized a Range Rover, a Lexus, and a BMW.

The office trailer was a common one, about ten metres by three in size, with grey vinyl siding and a makeshift set of stairs built from unpainted pressure-treated wood. Hydro and telephone lines ran to a stack on one side. A satellite dish perched on the roof.

Dave Martin emerged from the trailer and walked across the lot to her. "It's okay to walk around anywhere outside now. We've lifted the tire tracks and boot prints already."

Ellie nodded, having noticed patches of red snow print wax all over the place.

"Got the victim's boot prints," he went on. "Fairly recent, and the shooter's."

"Christ. You're sure?"

"I'll try not to be insulted by that question. I told you before, find me those boots and I'll put them at the crime scene. Now I can put them here, too."

"That's great."

"Also we got a couple sets we haven't seen before, including a female's. Stiletto-type heels, size six. I called Wainwright at the Hansen house and he took a look around. No boots of that style anywhere to be seen. So I called Olkewicz, who happens to be with Mrs. Hansen at the moment. The boots the missus wore over to the minister's house are low-cut, flat-soled, and size eight."

"So, some other female. What about tires?"

"We've got impressions matching the F-150 with the plow over there, the Range Rover, and the BMW. Then, there was an auto transport rig in here a few days ago. Its tracks are overlaid by three other sets, all new to us, and the tires we've already seen at the house and on Church Road, which might belong to the victim's Ram."

"Tell me about the office trailer."

"Typical small business set-up. Office area inside the door on the left, with a desk, swivel chair, filing cabinet, bookshelf, key cabinet. Small kitchenette straight on, a bathroom about the size of a phone booth, more filing cabinets, then down at the far end a personal area with a recliner and TV, more files in boxes, and a little closet with miscellaneous items of clothing."

Dart came out of the trailer, glanced at her, and waited on the tiny step until Bishop emerged behind him. The two detectives sauntered across the yard to the BMW.

"Computer?" Ellie asked.

"Laptop. Internet connectivity through the satellite dish. It'll be a while before we finish the fingerprinting, but we started with the office and we're boxing the files now, as per Walker's instructions. A lot of vehicle files, client files, even some employee files. He wants the team to go through them tonight."

"All right."

"We've also dusted the key cabinet and the fobs." Martin turned around. "The boys are anxious to take a look at the cars. Hey fellas, how about you let Serge and me do that, okay?"

Dart had used a key fob to unlock the BMW and, after opening the driver's side door, had reached in and pressed the trunk release button. He straightened and raised his hands in a gesture of impatience. Bishop, beside him, looked at the ground.

At that moment, Serge Landry walked back through the gate, having just gone out to the forensics van for another camera. Martin pointed. Landry nodded and changed direction toward the BMW. Martin and Ellie followed.

"It's okay," Martin said quietly to Ellie. "Serge already printed the door handles."

"You guys have been busy."

"You know it. But there was nothing. Glove smears. Which you'd expect, since it's cold as hell out here."

Ellie stopped in front of the two detectives. "Let Ident do their work."

Bishop nodded. Dart shrugged and mooched off to take a look at the Range Rover.

Landry raised the trunk lid on the BMW, and they all leaned over for a look. It was empty and very clean.

"Looks like it's been detailed," Bishop said. "The whole car. It's as clean as a friggin' whistle."

Martin looked around. "You know, these vehicles are not all that easy to find. The Shelby GT500 over there, for example, retailed new for fifty-five grand last year and had a limited production run. Hansen would be able to turn it around real fast and make a nice profit."

"Hey," Dart called out, "this one has stuff in it."

"Hands off," Ellie ordered.

"I've got it," Martin said. He took a key fob out of his coat pocket and handed it to Landry. "Serge, you do the honours."

They followed Landry over to the Range Rover. Ellie looked in the front passenger window at comfortable seats, a touch-screen entertainment centre, and a backup camera screen. She moved to the back passenger window and saw that the second row of seats had been lowered. The rear contained some kind of cargo.

"This thing must be worth a fortune," Dart said.

"You got that right," Martin said, nudging Ellie aside.

Landry used the key fob to pop the hatch. He took several photographs, then carefully peeled back the tarp. Ellie counted eight small cardboard boxes sealed with packing tape. Martin pulled down a box, and Landry photographed it. Martin produced a box cutter from his coveralls and carefully slit the packing tape. He opened the lid and removed a small zip-lock plastic bag containing what looked like frozen, flattened maple sugar with a slightly greenish tint.

"Hash oil," she said, staring at the bag.

"Butane honey oil," Martin agreed, turning the bag around. "Also known as butane hash oil. Frozen. Easy to transport this way, especially in winter. At the other end, they crush it back into powder and thaw it before they sell it in its regular form. It was probably supposed to be on the road by now." He looked in the box. "There are maybe, uh, fifty bags in here. About ten grams a bag, give or take, equals five hundred grams in a box.

Half a kilo. At forty bucks a gram, you're looking at twenty grand worth of BHO in a box. Times eight boxes is one hundred and sixty thousand bucks."

"Add in the value of the Range Rover," Landry said, "and you're well over two hundred grand."

Ellie stared at the boxes. "Now this is starting to make a little more sense."

chapter EIGHT

Kevin was coming out of the washroom just as Bishop was going in.

"Where the hell's the food, Kev?" Bishop was already unzipping his fly as he made a beeline for the urinal. "I'm starving."

"Should be here shortly."

"This broad's something else, eh?"

Kevin turned around. "Who, Ellie?"

Bishop snorted, relieving himself. "What a hard-assed know-it-all. 'Let Ident do their work.' Like I'm a fucking rookie wearing a clown suit and towing a monkey on a leash. Just what we need, our very own palace princess."

"She's all right."

"Now we're plowing through all these files like we're friggin' desk clerks." He shook himself off and zipped himself up. "It's simple," he said, heading for the sink. "Let Dart find out who the vic was dealing with, and boom. There's your killer."

"It's never that simple, JB. We have to cover all the bases. I'm the one who wants to work these files now, tonight."

Bishop grabbed a handful of paper towels. "Jesus, Kev." His phone buzzed. He took it out and looked at the call display. "My wife. I gotta take this."

Kevin left the washroom and walked down the hall into the conference room. He looked at the big clock on the wall and saw that it was 8:22 PM. He poured a coffee and flipped up the lids on the doughnut boxes. Nothing but stains on the cardboard and a few crumbs. At the far end of the room, Tom Carty sorted through piles of Hansen's client and vehicle files. Constable Mark Allore, brought in to assist the team, stood at the flip chart from Ellie's makeshift office, writing down names and addresses as Carty fed them to him. At this end, Dart was poring over Hansen's employee files as Ellie watched over his shoulder. Behind them, Monica Sisson had started a link chart on a big whiteboard on wheels, confiscated from the training room. Next to her, Brenda pounded on the keyboard of a computer that had been brought in and connected to the local area network.

Kevin stood beside Ellie as she bent over and tapped a file folder.

"There he is," she said.

Dart pulled the file out of the pile and opened it. "Steve Barron. It says his address is 14 Valley Park Court, Lyn. I know that place." He glanced over his shoulder at Ellie. "It's a trailer park."

"DOB?" Sisson demanded from the whiteboard, hand on her hip.

"Hang on a sec." Dart consulted the form. "Uh, June 6, 1986."

Sisson wrote it down on the board.

"Looks like he started driving for Hansen in 2012," Dart said. "There are tax forms in here for 2012 and 2013. Hmm. Here's his criminal background check. Came back clear."

Kevin looked at the whiteboard. Sisson had written down three names linked to Hansen in a column labelled "employees"—Steve Barron, Ken Price, and David Ryan. Price had an address in Athens, and Ryan lived in Delta. What made Barron special was that the victim had written, on a Grand & Toy calendar pad on his desk, "Steve" and "Sudbury" in today's square. As a result, they were working on the assumption that Barron had been slated to deliver the Range Rover, with its cargo of BHO, to Sudbury today.

"Here we go," Carty called out from the other end of the table. He came down to Kevin with an open file in his hands. "The Range Rover was purchased through an online auction site in September. The consignee was a finance company in Etobicoke. He only paid fifteen grand for it."

"Unbelievable," Dart muttered.

"It was shipped to Sparrow Lake by Kilkenny Car Transport and signed for by Hansen on September 29." Carty flipped pages. "Faxes back and forth. Looks like he sold it to Otto's Used Autos on Toller Road in Sudbury on October 8." He flipped another page. "Here we are. Delivery date to Sudbury listed as December 9."

"Today." Kevin took the file and walked it over to Brenda. "Run it for us, okay?"

"Okey doke. On the pile." Brenda pointed at an in-box next to her keyboard. It was already filled with manila folders.

Dart smacked his hand down on Barron's open file. "We need to nail this guy. Right now, before he bugs out."

"We know he drove for Hansen," Kevin said, looking at Ellie, "and we've got evidence indicating he was supposed to drive for him today, plus evidence the Rover was scheduled for delivery today. Victim to Barron to vehicle to BHO. That gives us reasonable grounds for an arrest on conspiracy to traffic. We start with that, bring him in, and take it from there."

"Call Wiltse," Ellie said. "Get him on it."

Kevin stepped away, pulling out his cellphone. As their designated search warrant co-ordinator, Wiltse's job involved writing what was known as an Information to Obtain a Search Warrant, or an ITO. Essentially an application for a warrant, the ITO presented to the judge all the information forming the basis of their reasonable grounds to believe that the search would produce evidence related to the criminal offence under investigation, at the specified location. Because it was specialized work, and because it was important to have all the relevant information from the investigation in the ITO at the time of the application for the warrant, Wiltse remained separate from the actual investigative work itself. This precaution ensured that the ITO was objective and constituted a "full, frank and fair" disclosure of everything known to the investigating officers at that time. In other words, the detectives either had reasonable grounds at that point or they did not, and Wiltse's responsibility was to speak up when it was apparent to him that they did not.

As Kevin punched in Wiltse's number and listened to it ring, he heard Dart say something about talking to his contacts in the drug unit for whatever intelligence they might have on Barron. When Wiltse finally answered, Kevin told him he was needed immediately to write ITOs for arrest and search warrants on a suspect.

"I don't have a ride," Wiltse said. "My wife's got the van. I'm watching the kids."

"Can you reach her?"

"Yeah, but it's her book club night and she's the designated driver."

"If I send someone to pick you up, can you let her know and arrange for someone to look after the kids until she gets back? We need to move on this right now."

"Yeah, I guess so."

Kevin turned around; Dart was already on his feet, grabbing his coat off the back of his chair.

"Do it," Kevin said. "Craig's on the way."

Kevin ended the call and put away his phone. Bishop came into the room and sat down in front of another pile of file folders from Hansen's office. Carty, who'd been huddling with Brenda at the computer, picked up the stack of files in her out-box and showed them to Kevin. "All the cars in the yard right now came back clean, including the Rover. We'll start working our way back through his past inventory to see if we get any hits, but so far they're all legitimate transactions."

Ellie sat down in a chair pushed up against the wall. Kevin sat down next to her.

"How's Wiltse's working relationship with Beeson?" Ellie asked, referring to the assistant Crown attorney. Wiltse's job also involved liaison with the Crown attorney's office when they needed to verify that they had sufficient reasonable grounds to support a warrant application. He also requested advice and guidance from the Crown attorney's office on other legal questions relating to suspects and any other aspects of their evidence-gathering process.

"The guy's an asshole," Kevin said, "but Wiltse gets along with everyone. It'll be all right."

"Okay." Ellie rested her head against the wall and closed her eyes. "Backtrack through this for a minute, Kevin. How did our victim go from a load of BHO in a Range Rover to a field on a back road with a bullet through his neck?"

"Someone drove him out there in his own truck. Two guys."

"To execute him, apparently. Why? What's the motive?"

"It wasn't that drug shipment specifically," Kevin said, "otherwise it wouldn't still be sitting there. Something to do with distribution arrangements, maybe. An argument over money? Maybe Hansen hadn't paid Barron for past deliveries, and he decided to do something about it. Or the producer of the BHO was getting stiffed. But why leave the shipment in the Rover, if that was the case? It's weird that it was just sitting there."

"Agreed." Ellie was silent for a moment. "Look," she finally said, very quietly, "I understand it's your first time through this kind of thing. You're doing well. If you have any questions, just ask. I'm here to help."

"Okay," Kevin replied. "Thanks."

"Don't be so focused on making an impression with senior people that you make a mistake that could be avoided just by asking about it first. In something like this, there are no dumb questions. It's very important to talk things through. All the time. Don't be afraid to think out loud."

"All right." His cellphone buzzed. He took it out, checked the number, and answered it. He listened for a moment, then grinned. "Be right there."

He stood up, putting the phone back in his pocket. "JB. Come with me."

Sighing, Bishop pushed away from the table. He followed Kevin down the hall and out into the front reception area. The civilian personnel who normally worked out here had gone home for the night and the overhead lights were turned off, but emergency lighting provided enough illumination for them to navigate the desks and front counter.

Standing outside the front door was a tiny man holding a big insulated bag containing half a dozen boxed pizzas.

Bishop clapped his hands together. "Yeah, man!"

Kevin unlocked the door. "Come on in, Birdie."

The little man stepped inside to escape the blowing snow.

Bishop watched him unzip the bag to remove the pizzas and impatiently grabbed the top box, lifting the lid. "Canadian!" He pulled out a slice, took a big bite, and headed back through the reception area with the box.

Kevin took the other pizzas, set them on the counter, and dug out his wallet. Willie Bird worked part time as a delivery man for the Silver Kettle restaurant in Sparrow Lake. Kevin was a regular customer and, although pizzerias in Brockville were closer, he preferred to give his business to the Silver Kettle. Besides, the pizzas were fantastic. On top of that, Birdie was a confidential informant to whom Kevin reached out from time to time.

"Messy night out there, Kev," Birdie said. He wore a Minnesota North Stars jacket that was as old as Kevin, and a John Deere baseball cap that looked as though it had been run over by one of their tractors several times. He stood about five feet three inches and weighed about 115 pounds soaking wet. He wiped his enormous nose with a handkerchief and pulled out a leather wallet attached to his belt by a chain. Kevin handed him the money for the pizzas. It was cash Ellie had insisted he take to pay for the food.

"Yeah, sorry to bring you out."

"No problem." Birdie slipped Kevin's cash into the wallet and put it away. It was understood that the extra was part of his tip. "Working late?"

"You could say that."

"Heard about Billy Hansen on the radio." Birdie looked over his shoulder at his beat-up Sunfire, parked close to the door.

Snow cut in front of the headlights on a forty-degree angle. "Terrible thing."

"Heard any talk about what happened?"

"Nope." Birdie shifted from foot to foot. He was a fidget, a guy who found it impossible to remain still. "Nobody's got a clue."

"You knew him pretty well, didn't you?"

"Oh, sure. I suppose. Delivered to him all the time at the yard. Took him out an order yesterday, matter of fact."

"You're kidding. When was that?"

"Oh, lemme see." Birdie tipped back his head, eyes closed. He took off his cap, revealing thinning grey hair, and resettled it on his head with fussy little tugs. The tip of the bill came about even with the knot on Kevin's tie. "Seven o'clock. About then. The heart attack special. Bacon cheeseburger, home-cooked fries, big bottle of Coke." He opened his eyes again and looked up at Kevin. "But I guess it wasn't no heart attack, was it?"

"Anybody with him?"

"Nope."

"How'd he seem?"

"A little wound up. He's usually good for a little small talk, but he just paid me and shut the door. No tip."

"What's the word on him, Birdie? Was he clean?"

The little man shrugged, shoving his hands into his jacket pockets. "Heard maybe some of his cars were dicey, a while back. Before your time. Your old friend was looking at him, so I heard."

Kevin hesitated. "You mean Chuck Waddell?"

"The same. Guess nothing come of it, though. Maybe Billy got scared off and stopped messing with the hot stuff. Anyway, he was pretty straight as far as dealing with people. Never heard no-one complain he'd cheated them on a car they bought from him."

"What about other stuff?"

Birdie frowned. "You mean like drugs?" He popped his lips disdainfully. "Never heard nothing like that. He was a drinker, though."

"What about the guys who drove for him?"

"Been a few, over the years. Not exactly steady work."

"What about the ones driving right now?"

Birdie shrugged. "I dunno. One guy's up in Athens. Price. Used to drive a cab in Brockville. There's a loser. Ryan, in Delta, drives for Green, the transport company. Asshole."

"Oh?"

"Thinks his shit don't stink like the rest of us."

"What about Steve Barron?"

"Don't know him real well. Not from around here."

"Where's he from?"

"North. Sudbury, somewhere like that. Mean bastard."

"Oh?"

"Done a few deliveries to his place, you know, in the trailer court? His girlfriend always calls in the orders. Guess she can't cook worth a shit. Little mousy thing, never says a word. Acts scared of her own shadow. Nice looking, though, if you go for that type. One time, she didn't have enough when she come to the door. Got mixed up on the phone and thought it was less. She had to ask him for it. He come to the door with a big roll in his hand, peeled off a fifty and told me to get lost. Just like that. Mean fucker. Acts like a biker."

"Oh?"

"Don't know it for sure. Just the impression he gives."

"Does he hang with anybody around here?"

Birdie shrugged. "A few guys. Seen Lennie Ross's truck there once or twice."

Kevin had his wallet back out. He gave Birdie two more twenties. "Forgot your tip."

"Thanks, Kev." The bills disappeared into Birdie's pocket.

"Drive safely. Let me know if you hear anything else."

Birdie tugged the bill of his cap once more. "Don't stay up too late, kid."

"I'll try not to." Kevin watched the little man push back out into the storm, then he locked the door, grabbed the pizzas, and returned to the conference room. The box that Bishop had taken with him sat empty on the side table next to the coffee urn. Kevin closed the lid and put the other boxes down on top of it. "We've got another Canadian, a Hawaiian, and two deluxe. Help yourselves."

"What about plates?" Monica Sisson demanded, coming over. "And utensils? Paper napkins?"

Kevin bit his lip.

"Men. Just useless." She walked out, heading for the kitchenette.

Kevin stepped back to avoid the line that was forming in front of the pizza. "Just had a word with a CI about our case."

Bishop, at the head of the line, rolled his eyes and snorted, guessing that Kevin was referring to the delivery guy. He opened the top box. Deluxe. He closed it again, shuffled it to the bottom, and looked at the next one. Canadian. He grabbed two slices and moved aside.

"What'd he have to say?" Ellie asked from the end of the line.

"Heard that Hansen might have been involved in moving stolen cars, but that was a while ago. Maybe ten years or so. Sparrow Lake looked at him at the time, the guy who was detective before me, but I guess nothing came of it. And nothing connecting him to narcotics, either."

Sisson nudged Kevin from behind and pushed by him, setting out a stack of paper plates, a handful of plastic knives and forks, and a package of paper napkins. Then she headed back to the kitchenette for another load.

"Who wants Hawaiian?" Brenda asked, carrying an open box.

Allore put up his hand. She put a slice of the pizza on his paper plate.

"Keep it coming."

Brenda rolled her eyes and gave him a second piece.

Sisson pushed in front of Kevin again with a tray of soft drink cans. "This is the last of them. Did everyone pay the kitty this week? I gotta make a run tomorrow."

"He thought maybe Barron has OMG connections," Kevin said. If Hansen's driver was somehow linked to an outlaw motorcycle gang, it would open up their investigation rather significantly.

"A biker?" Bishop asked while he chewed. "Really? Fuckin' A."

"Don't talk with your mouth full," Sisson said, helping herself to pizza. "It's disgusting."

Bishop, leaning forward to grab a can of pop, opened his mouth to show her masticated pizza.

"Christ." Sisson turned away, shaking her head.

"Not sure," Kevin said, "but he says he handles himself like one."

"So does my husband," Sisson said, "but he sells boats for a living."

"Yeah, to cigarette runners," Bishop snorted.

"Piss off, Bishop. My point is, looking like a tough guy doesn't mean he's OMG."

Ellie had finally made it to the pizza. She helped herself to the last piece of Canadian, sliding it onto a plate. She raised an eyebrow at Kevin.

"We'd better find out, then."

chapter NINE

Snow angled through the headlights of the Crown Vic as Ellie followed Kevin's Grand Cherokee down Lake Road, a winding, narrow tunnel through cedar trees and scrub brush, on her way to catch a few hours' sleep. On a good day, Kevin had promised, the cottage was only fifteen minutes from the detachment. On a stormy night such as this one, however, it had taken twenty minutes so far, and Ellie was starting to feel exhausted. Hopefully, it wasn't much farther.

Kevin had called his friend in Victoria, who'd given the okay for her to stay at his place. Ellie insisted on paying for it out of her accommodation allowance at the prescribed daily rate, which was fine with him. She could clear it with GHQ in the morning, but right now she needed to put her head on a pillow and close her eyes for a few hours.

Ahead, Kevin's brake lights flared, and the right-hand turn signal on the Grand Cherokee began to flash. Where the hell was this place? Would she be able to find her way back out again in the morning? She caught a glimpse of a road sign that said "Tamarack Lane" as she eased around the corner. The trees thinned as the lane ran about half a kilometre through open fields, then crowded the road again as she went up a short rise and down the other side, around a corner, and saw the first of the cottages in her headlights. They passed three driveways, all empty and snow-filled, before Kevin's brake lights flared again and he turned off. She followed and found herself pulling into a small parking area marked off with a wall of snow-covered flat stones. Kevin was waiting for her as she stopped beside the Grand Cherokee and got out.

"Here it is," he said. "You're going to like it."

Ellie popped the trunk on the Crown Vic and grabbed her overnight bag. All she cared about was that it would be warm, dry, and quiet, wasn't inhabited by vermin, and had some kind of decent bed she could sleep on. The rest was irrelevant at the moment.

As Kevin led the way down a stone-framed walkway to the cottage, Ellie's eyes were drawn to the place next door, about thirty metres away. It looked enormous, like a hunting lodge or something, and every light in the place appeared to be on. She was about to say something to Kevin about it when she noticed a tiny flare of light on the back deck, illuminating the profile of a bony face. Someone was standing outside over there, smoking a cigarette.

Kevin unlocked the door, switched on the lights, and led the way inside. "Kitchen," he said, pointing to the right, "and dining room." He kicked off his boots and put the key down on a kitchen island surrounded by high wooden stools. "The thermostat's right over here."

Ellie removed her boots and followed him across the kitchen to an archway leading into the living room area.

"I keep it at 15 degrees for Gerry, to save on propane, so it's a little chilly. I'll turn it up to 20, and you can adjust it to suit yourself later."

As he fiddled with the controls, Ellie wandered through the doorway. It was a nice place, modestly furnished, but very comfortable. On the right were large picture windows and sliding French doors without curtains, like a wall of blackness. She saw herself standing there in stocking feet, coat unzipped, fuzzy hat still on her head, overnight bag in her hand.

"Do you like it?" Kevin asked, behind her.

Ellie took off her hat and stuffed it into her coat pocket. "It's very nice."

"It'll warm up pretty quickly." He walked over to a propane stove in the corner and held out his hand to make sure that heat was coming from it. It looked like an old-fashioned Franklin wood stove with flames flickering behind fake logs. It gave the room a rustic, homey atmosphere that Ellie found appealing.

"Master bedroom is there," Kevin pointed behind them, "bathroom here, a guest room over there, and the laundry room. You can go out onto the deck. I keep it cleared of snow, although I guess I'll have to do it again tomorrow. That's the tour, basically. There's bedding in an armoire in the guest room, pillows, towels for the bathroom, all that stuff. You're all set. Oh, and there are a few things in the fridge. Couple cans of Coke, and I think some beer. You can pick up some groceries tomorrow."

"This is great," Ellie said. "Thank you."

"You're welcome." He pointed at the French doors. "The lake froze over, thanks to the cold November we had, but the ice will be soft right now because of the mild snap a few days ago. Best to stay off it."

"I don't go out on frozen lakes. Trust me on that one."

Kevin smiled. "Think you can find your way back okay in the morning?"

Ellie nodded. "We're on Tamarack. I turn left onto Lake Road, then left onto Bradley Road, then right onto 29."

Kevin smiled. "That'll do it."

"I noticed someone outside, next door."

"Your neighbour. His name's Ridge Ballantyne. He lives down here year-round. There are half a dozen or so who stay on the lake all the time. His place is incredible. Wait till you see it in daylight. He's a retired rock musician."

"Really. Ballantyne?" The name wasn't familiar to her.

"Yeah. He's got a recording studio in there, and apparently he does session work and other contract stuff. Commercials or something."

"Interesting. Well, I'll be in at seven and we'll meet at eight."

Kevin smiled awkwardly and held out his hand. "It's been an honour to meet you, Ellie. I'm very glad to be able to work with you."

Ellie shifted her bag and shook his hand.

When he was gone and she was alone, she threw her bag on the bed in the master bedroom and went outside for the rest of her things, which also went on the bed. She checked the fridge. Sure enough, there were three bottles of Sleeman in there. She uncapped one and drank deeply. Beer in hand, duty jacket still on over her blazer, she grabbed her boots, walked them over to the French doors, put them on, then slid the door open and stepped outside onto the deck. She took a pack of cigarettes and a disposable lighter out of her pocket and lit a cigarette. She inhaled deeply and blew the smoke out into the night.

She allowed herself one cigarette a day, always at night before she went to bed. She preferred Jack Daniels to the beer, and allowed herself one drink with the cigarette, but for now the beer would do.

The snow, she suddenly realized, had stopped falling. She moved her boot on the deck and thought that perhaps three centimetres had come down. Not that much, after all.

She looked at the cottage next door. Lodge, studio, whatever it was. Lights still blazed behind every window. She could see the edge of the deck where Ballantyne had stood, smoking a cigarette as she was right now, but he was gone. Her keen ears, however, detected a very faint bass pulsation. Music.

She drank all but a very small amount of the beer, then set the bottle down on the snow-covered barbecue. She finished her cigarette, dropped it into the beer bottle, and went back inside.

She hung up her overcoat and left her boots by the kitchen door, then used the washroom and came back out into the living room. It was a nice place. Very comfortable. She went into the bedroom, removed her gun and spare magazine, and locked them away in their case, which she'd brought in from the car. She wandered back out into the living room again. She sat down in a recliner chair next to the propane stove, leaned back so that her feet went up, and closed her eyes.

They'd pick up Steve Barron early in the morning and sweat him. Ellie was certain he'd known what was in the Rover. She was anxious to learn if he was the one who'd visited Vivian Hansen late last night to inform her of her husband's murder. If so—

She fell asleep.

chapter TEN

It was well after midnight when Kevin finally slipped into bed.

After showing Ellie to the cottage, he'd returned to the detachment office to continue working through the files with Merkley and Bishop. They'd put together a list of Hansen's vehicle transactions going back several years, and the vehicle identification numbers would be run to see whether any of them had been reported stolen. Kevin had his doubts, since it would have been rather dumb on Hansen's part to have kept records of hot cars in his files, but it was a box that had to be checked off on the list of things to do, and so that's what they were doing. Meanwhile, a list had also been compiled of the people with whom Hansen had done business in those transactions, and starting tomorrow they'd begin to work the telephones, calling each name on the list to explore Hansen's relationship with them and to probe for possible leads.

Janie stirred beside him and muttered something. Kevin was exhausted, and he was trying not to wake her up, but she rolled over and put a hand on his arm.

"That you, Kev?"

"Sorry I woke you. Go back to sleep."

She put her cheek against his bare bicep. "Did you get

something to eat? There's leftovers in the fridge."

"I'm good. We had pizza."

"I thought you were working."

"I was. We ate at the office. There's a million things to do."

She ran her hand over his bare chest. "We only had one person come in today. Just a cut, not a perm."

"Christmas parties are coming. It'll pick up."

"It better. I'm having trouble paying the bills. I had to tell Lacey I couldn't use her any more."

"It'll get better."

"I hope so. Cute note you left."

"Glad you liked it."

"Are we going to the arena Friday night? Everyone's expecting us."

Kevin's eyes were closed. His brain fought through the fog to answer her. "Maybe. Have to see."

"If you can't, I'll go anyway."

Kevin startled himself snoring. He must have dozed off.

Janie pinched his nipple. "You weren't even listening to me."

"Ouch. Sorry. Tired, I guess."

She slipped her hand under the waistband of his track pants. "I know how to fix that."

"I should get some sleep," he said. "I have to get up at six." It sounded feeble, even to him. He reached for her.

"I was waiting for you, big boy."

Kevin smiled in the dark. "I know."

chapter ELEVEN

Pee-pee-pee-pee-pee-pee-pee-pee-pee-pee-pee-pee-pee-pee-pee-pee-pee.

Ellie opened her eyes, annoyed. It took her a moment to realize that the persistent sound she was hearing was coming from the alarm on her wrist watch. She fumbled around, pressing buttons, until it quit. It took her another moment to figure out where she was—asleep in a recliner next to a warm propane stove.

The cottage.

Sparrow Lake.

The Hansen case.

She'd never made it to bed, obviously.

She squinted at the watch again: 6:01 AM. Time to get rolling. She went into the bedroom, pulled her last change of fresh clothing out of her overnight bag, and went into the bathroom. When she came out, showered and dressed once again in her navy pantsuit and her last clean blouse, she felt better. She searched the kitchen cabinets for coffee, found a small can of ground arabica roast, and turned on the coffee maker. As it percolated, she wandered over to the large picture windows to look outside. Dawn was still about forty-five minutes away, and all that she could see out there, beyond the deck, were shadows.

Within that darkness, though, beneath a thin, grey crust of ice, was the lake.

She was reminded of a routine she used to follow in the mornings, when she'd first transferred up to Orillia, after her split with Gareth. She'd joined a beginner's group learning tai chi in the evenings at the high school, more for something to do than anything else, and had discovered that she liked it. She followed it with another, more advanced, course on qigong, a related discipline that focused on breathing and meditation. Afterward, she'd developed her own hybrid routine that didn't take very long to complete but left her feeling relaxed and refreshed. The routine had included the visualization of a koi pool she'd seen at the zoo when she was a kid. She would recall the colours and lazy movement of the fish, picturing them in her mind as she progressed through the routine. For several years, it had helped her prepare to face the stress of her job each day.

As she poured a cup of coffee and sweetened it with a teaspoon of honey from a container in the fridge, she tried unsuccessfully to remember why she'd stopped doing it. Being near water for the first time in a while, though, had reminded her of the koi, and the koi had reminded her of the routine.

She remembered having felt good, back then.

The girls were wrong, really.

She wasn't an unhappy person. She just wasn't very happy right now. That was all.

There was a difference.

She drained her coffee cup and set it aside. In front of the windows looking out onto the darkness, she took off her jacket and slacks. Draping them over a kitchen chair, she spread her bare feet and put her hands over her abdomen, breathing deeply and slowly. She then brought her hands up over her shoulders, brought her arms together until her elbows touched, and bent forward slightly, head bowing, flexing her spine. Back and forth several times, then she brought her arms to her sides, palms out, and began spiralling movements with them, palms in, palms out, combined with a slow rolling motion of her head, back and forth. At that point she could see the koi in her mind's eye, and as she followed their lazy movement through the glassy water, skimming close to the surface, she passed through the rest of the routine, remembering each step as though she'd last done it only yesterday.

When it was finished, she put her slacks back on and went into the bedroom for her gun case and kit. She took them out to the kitchen table and sat down to begin the last portion of her old routine. The first thing out of the kit was a gun mat, which she smoothed out in front of her. On its cloth face was an exploded diagram of her service weapon, the SIG Sauer P229. She set out a small bottle of cleaning solution and another containing lubricant, a tube of gun grease, a polymer rod and a pick, a toothbrush, and a pile of small cloth patches. Then she unlocked the gun case and took out her weapon.

She dropped out the magazine and ejected the round from the chamber. She disassembled the gun and arranged the parts neatly on the mat. She cleaned each part carefully, applied grease to the rails on the frame and inside the slide, then re-assembled the weapon. She racked the slide several times and ran through a quick function check to make sure the trigger was resetting properly, then used a towel with gun oil on it to wipe down the exterior of the gun. She replaced the magazine, racked a round into the chamber, uncocked the hammer, and dropped the magazine back out again. She picked up the round she'd ejected from the chamber at the beginning of the cleaning process, fitted it into the magazine, and snapped the magazine back into place.

The gun was now ready for use, should it ever come to that. So far in her career it hadn't, as she'd never fired her weapon in the line of duty, but she was a firm believer in being prepared for any contingency. She put it into the holster on her hip and dropped the spare magazine into the pocket of her jacket on the back of the chair. She repacked everything, took the kit and the gun case back into the bedroom, and put them in the bottom drawer of the dresser. She went into the bathroom, washed her hands, and walked back out into the living room.

The picture windows and sliding French door were still

black, but had modulated into charcoal patches here and there. She looked at her watch. The sun wouldn't rise for about another forty minutes.

Her day, however, was now nicely underway.

chapter TWELVE

Every morning after a vigorous workout with his weights in the basement, Kevin liked to jog through the village before showering and getting dressed for work. He usually ran in regular Reebok running shoes, but this morning he threw them into the back of the closet in favour of another pair that had more of a tread to them. Last night's storm had left behind four centimetres of dry, powdery snow, and he wanted something on his feet that would grip the pavement with more certainty.

He ran up to Main Street and followed it all the way through the village. The streets were completely deserted at this early hour. The air was fresh and crisp in his lungs. Overhead, the sky was a mix of blue patches and scrubby clouds moving from west to east in strong high winds.

He worked his way up and down the side streets until he reached Sarah Street, where he turned right. One block from home, he saw Chuck Waddell come out of the house on the corner. Picking up a broom, Waddell began to sweep off his front verandah. As Kevin reached the end of Waddell's sidewalk, he stopped and, jogging in place, said hello.

Waddell smiled and came down the sidewalk to greet him. He wore a black leather jacket over a grey turtle-neck sweater, jeans, and Kodiak boots. He leaned on the broom and looked at Kevin with sharp, dark eyes. He was a small man, barely five nine and 150 pounds, but he had a charismatic presence that commanded attention. The hair on his bony, round skull was thin and grey, and his white, neatly-trimmed Van Dyke beard still carried patches of black at the philtrum and just below the lower lip. The spray of freckles across his round forehead and high cheekbones were spreading into liver spots betraying his age, but he still moved with the assurance and flexibility of a younger man.

"Caught a big case, I hear," he said.

"Yeah." Kevin stopped jogging in place, out of politeness. Waddell was the kind of man who made eye contact and held it, and it would be annoying for him to have to follow Kevin's eyes up and down while they talked. "I guess you heard about it on the news."

"And around. Any leads?"

"One or two. Can I ask you a question, Chuck?"

"Sure. Fire away."

"I heard that you took a look at Hansen a long time ago for hot cars. Did anything ever come of that?"

Waddell stared at him for a moment, lips compressed. He'd spent twenty-three years on the Sparrow Lake police department, the last twenty of them as the municipality's only detective, and he'd been Kevin's mentor, grooming him as his replacement before retiring to start his own business as a security consultant. Kevin had found him to be patient and tolerant, but not overly friendly. He'd always made it clear to Kevin that there was a distance between them in experience, knowledge, and skills that Kevin could never overcome.

"Smoke, but no fire," Waddell finally replied. "A CI mentioned something about being able to sell Hansen stolen vehicles for twenty cents on the dollar. Supposedly he was flipping them to a chop shop in Cornwall, or on the island, or something. I nosed around, talked to Hansen, but nothing came of it." He shifted his weight on the broom. "You think it's connected to that?"

"Not likely. What about other stuff? Drugs?"

Waddell's eyebrows went up. "You think he was into that?"

"Looks that way." Kevin hesitated, then decided not to ask Waddell to keep the information to himself. It went without saying that their conversations had always been confidential.

"I'm surprised. Very surprised. Any leads on his connections?"

"Not yet. We're still in the early stages. We found a shipment in a Range Rover scheduled for delivery to Sudbury yesterday."

For a moment, Waddell's face went completely blank. His pupils suddenly dilated. Watching him, Kevin remembered a scientific study he'd read that suggested sudden pupil dilation could be connected to surprise during the reception of negative feedback. It was the kind of thing that constantly rattled around in Kevin's brain, part of the storehouse of assorted bits of information he liked to squirrel away for a rainy day. It was easy to understand that Waddell would be surprised and disappointed to hear that Bill Hansen had hidden drugs in one of his vehicles.

"I'd never have taken him for a distributor," Waddell said. "Still, it makes sense when you think of it. Moving all those vehicles around, all over the place, it would have given him a built-in network. It should have occurred to me before."

"It's not the sort of thing that would have occurred to any of us, Chuck."

"I guess not. Of course, Sudbury's a known hub for distribution in northern Ontario. There've been a couple of JFOs up there in the last few years, remember? Maybe Hansen was connected to gang bangers up there."

Kevin considered it. "Could be. Do you know anything about the guys Hansen had driving for him? Price, Ryan, or Barron?"

Waddell shook his head. "Been out of things too long, kid. I don't keep up with the locals much anymore. No money in that, now, is there?" He laughed.

Kevin smiled. "Guess not. Speaking of which, how's your business going?"

"Great. Just inked a new contract with the real estate association in Kingston to come in and give talks to their members and provide advice and guidance on home security.

Gets our business cards into the hands of almost every home buyer in the city, if we play it right."

"How many guys you got working for you now?"

"Two, at the moment. A guy in Kingston and a guy who helps me with stuff around here. He's staying at my place on the lake right now. Why? Looking for a new career?"

Kevin laughed. "Not just yet. Although, if I screw up on this case, I might be looking for some place to hide."

Waddell's expression grew serious. "I hear you got a girl down from Orillia to manage the case."

"Yeah, that's right."

"Never send a girl to do a man's job. I heard some talk about her, that she's good at taking credit for other people's work."

Kevin frowned. "News to me."

Waddell reached out and patted Kevin on the shoulder. "That's all right, kid. You always did try to see the best in everybody, even while you were shoving them into the back seat of a cruiser. Just don't turn your back on her. Don't trust anybody. Isn't that what I keep telling you?"

"Yeah, it is, Chuck."

"Well, maybe it's about time you started listening."

chapter THIRTEEN

Craig Dart walked into the tiny interview room and closed the door behind him. He tossed a file folder down on the desk and dropped into the chair. Steve Barron sat at the end of the desk, knees splayed, arms folded across his chest, a tight smile on his face. Dart glanced up at the camera in the corner of the ceiling. The others were watching the audio-visual feed in the room next door. He'd just come from there, where he'd waited while Barron made his phone call. March had made some noise about how he should handle the interrogation, but he'd tuned her out after a while. He preferred to do things his own way.

"So, where were we?" Dart asked, leaning forward.

"The lawyer said he was going to talk to you. Did he call you?"

"Yeah," Dart admitted. "I explained to him that we had your ass in a sling."

"Bullshit. He said he'd be down in an hour and have me out by lunch. So stick it up your ass."

Dart sighed. Twenty-eight, blond and good-looking, Barron was taller and more muscular than Dart. He was also completely self-confident. Getting hauled out of bed at seven in the morning didn't seem to have bothered him in the slightest. He'd thrown on jeans and a t-shirt, a leather jacket and cowboy boots, listened to his rights, submitted to the cuffs, and had calmly gotten into the back seat of the cruiser, the smug little smile never once leaving his face.

The lawyer, from a Kingston firm, had been equally insufferable. "What's the story with Mr. Barron?" he'd asked in a low, confident baritone meant to intimidate. "You folks aren't serious about this conspiracy charge, are you? Isn't that tactic getting a little tired?"

Dart had gotten off the phone as quickly as possible and endured the little chat with March and Walker. Now it was time to try a full-court press on Barron to break through his arrogance and wrap up a confession.

"Whatever," he said. "They always tell you to say nothing. But *I'm* telling you, it's in your best interest to answer questions right now. You drove cars for William Hansen, correct?"

Barron shrugged.

Dart opened the file folder, took out a piece of paper, and slapped it down on the corner of the desk where Barron could see it. "Here's a copy of your employee record from Hansen's files. See?" He pointed. "There's your driver's licence number. That's you. You drove cars for Hansen."

"So if you know that, what are you asking me for?"

"How long have you been driving for him?"

Barron nodded at the piece of paper. "There's a date right there. Guess it's been since then."

"How'd you get the job?"

"Some guy set it up for me."

"Who?"

"That's for me to know and you not to find out, dickwad."

"Someone in Sudbury? Maybe your cousin, what's his name?" Dart pretended to hunt through the file. "Here it is. Marc? Current address 1542 McArthur Boulevard, unit 2. Did he get you this gig with Hansen?"

Shrug.

Dart rolled his chair back a few inches. "You were scheduled to drive up to Sudbury yesterday, weren't you?"

Shrug.

"Where were you supposed to deliver?"

Shrug.

"What vehicle were you bringing back on the return trip?"

Nothing.

"Do you supply the BHO as well?"

Snort.

This time it was Dart who shrugged. "We're executing a search warrant on your girlfriend's trailer as we speak. We're tearing it to pieces, and we're going to be asking her a lot of hard questions. She's going to see her home dismantled, and she's going to be treated as a co-conspirator. Not that you seem to care, but she doesn't strike me as the biker girl type. We'll break her down pretty fast."

The smug little smile was gone. "Back off her, man."

"Not going to happen. We've got nearly a quarter million in illegal drugs and we've got you, the guy who was scheduled to deliver them. Your girlfriend's also going to be looking at a conspiracy to traffic charge. Do you know what the sentence is for that? Her life's ruined now, thanks to you."

Barron leaned against the edge of the desk and pointed a finger at him. "I won't say it again. Back the fuck off her. She doesn't know anything about it."

"About what? The drugs you've been running? Why don't you tell me about it, tough guy? Where does the BHO come from?"

"Look, I don't know nothing about BHO or none of that shit. I drive a car for Hansen wherever he needs it to go, and I drive another one back. That's it."

"You expect me to believe you don't take a little look in those boxes in the trunk now and then, maybe help yourself to a little sample? You look like a stoner to me."

"Fuck you, man. I've got nothing to do with drugs. My record's clean."

"Not any more, it isn't. When did you last see Hansen?"

"I don't know. Two or three days ago."

"Is that the last time you talked to him?"

Shrug.

"What about e-mail, texts, Facebook? Talk to him through any of those?"

"Got a text from him day before yesterday. To confirm the delivery. I said I'd be there. That's it."

"You got this on Monday?"

"Didn't I just say that?"

"What time, smartass?"

"I don't fucking know. Eight o'clock or something that night."

"What'd you do then?"

"What do you mean, what'd I do? I answered back, said okay, I'd be there."

"Did you drive over to talk to him?"

"Why the hell would I do that?"

"What did you do the rest of Monday night?"

"Same thing I was doing before he texted me, man."

"Which was what?"

Barron sighed. "Look, it was Brianna's birthday. I took her into town. We had dinner and then we caught a movie."

"What movie was it?"

"Christ, I don't know what it was called. Some chick flick. Fucking awful, but she thought it was great."

"What time did it start?"

Barron shrugged. "A little after eight."

"So where were you when Bill Hansen sent you the text?"

"In the parking lot, man. We just got there. I answered him back, and then we went in."

"Did you stay for the whole movie or leave early?"

"The whole damned movie, man. Right to the end."

"Meaning you left the theatre at what time?"

"I don't know. Nine thirty? Ten? You figure it out, Einstein."

"Sounds like something you're making up, Barron. I'll bet you can't prove any of it."

Barron shrugged again. "Your Gestapo buddies have probably searched my car by now. Won't be too hard for them to find the movie stubs and the restaurant receipt now, will it? Or do they need help finding their ass in the dark with both hands?"

Dart pretended to write something in the file, then asked, "How well do you know Vivian Hansen?"

"Who?"

"Mrs. Hansen. The wife."

Shrug. "Never met the woman."

"You never went over to the Hansen house to talk to her when he wasn't there?"

"Why the hell would I do that, man? What the fuck's the matter with you? You saw what I'm living with. Why the hell would I chase after some old fart's tired-out wife?"

"A witness saw you outside her house Monday night, after her husband was killed. Did you go there so she could pay you for offing her husband?"

"You're completely full of shit, man."

"Is that a yes? You went there to get paid for killing her husband?"

"It's a no, asshole."

"You went there to tell her you'd just killed her husband, didn't you, dickhead? And if she didn't keep her mouth shut you told her you'd kill her, too. Didn't you?"

"I didn't kill Hansen. End of fucking story."

"I say you did. And before you know it, we'll have all the hard evidence we need to prove it in court and send you away for the rest of your life. You really need to make this easier on your girlfriend, tough guy. You're going down for murder, but she doesn't have to."

"You're full of shit, and you're a fucking liar. You ain't got any fucking witness saying I was at Hansen's place because I wasn't there, so there's nothing to talk about." He curled his lip. "Now get out of my fucking face. I ain't saying another word."

"You'll tell me everything, before we're through."

Barron folded his arms, leaned back, and sneered.

Dart badgered him for another five minutes without success, then closed up the file folder and left the room.

chapter FOURTEEN

Ellie met Dart in the corridor and motioned him into the next room, where Patterson and Kevin were waiting. Making an effort to keep the frustration out of his voice, Patterson explained that Barron would have his bail hearing on the conspiracy to traffic charge later in the afternoon. Upon being granted bail, he would be released.

"That's bullshit." Dart crossed his arms, the file folder sticking out from under his elbow.

"Come on," Patterson said, "get with it. Beeson's willing to work with us on the BHO and, depending on what we get from Barron's phone records and trailer, we might be able to get a wire on his phone going forward, but strictly on the drug stuff at this point, understand? There's zero connecting him to the murder, and you weren't exactly going to squeeze a confession out of him in there."

"I'm just getting started. The girlfriend's obvious leverage, and when I convince him that talking to us about the murder will keep her out of jail, he'll break."

"I'm not seeing it," Ellie said. "He may be a link in the chain, but he's not the link we need right now."

Dart stared at Patterson. "Tell me you're not going along with her on this."

Patterson stared back, his jaw stiff.

Dart broke eye contact first, rolling his eyes at the ceiling. "Unbelievable."

"Look," Kevin said, "he's a courier with a clean record who's now been compromised. He's going to jump around. We'll give him some rope and watch where he goes with it."

"He's a biker. He'll go to them. That's obviously how he connected up with the lawyer so quickly."

"Which is why," Kevin said, "I want you to run with this on the drug side. We're meeting with the team in five minutes and we'll go over it then, but I want you to hear it now, from me. Work your contacts, run down the Sudbury connection, and get a sense of whether this was a drug-related hit by a contract killer from the outside. Okay?"

"We've got a guy sitting right in there—"

"Who's not giving us jack shit and is going to walk, as of this afternoon," Patterson finished. "Now get onside, and get your ass down to the conference room."

They watched him storm off down the corridor.

Ellie shook her head. "I thought you said he was good in the room."

"I'm sorry," Patterson replied, frustrated. "He knows better than that. He was over-anxious, pressing for the big score right away."

"It was amateurish."

"He was trying to impress you."

"I don't think so. Either he's forgotten his training, or it didn't take in the first place. Either way, he sits on the bench for any future interrogations, as far as I'm concerned." Shaking her head, she went down to her little office, grabbed her handbag, and headed for the washroom. On her way out, she met Kevin, who was coming out of the men's room. Together they walked down the corridor to the conference room. At the door, Kevin stepped aside so that she could pass through ahead of him.

"That damned bitch—" In mid-rant, waving his arms at Merkley, Dart saw Ellie and shut his mouth, turning away to stare at the whiteboard.

Ellie stopped dead, just inside the door. Kevin barely managed to avoid running into her from behind.

Merkley, sitting at the conference table, found something interesting under his fingernails. Carty shook his head, looking down. Sisson and her data clerk, Brenda, stood frozen just inside the door, their eyes riveted on Ellie.

She walked to the head of the conference table and put down her handbag. She opened it and removed her notebook and pen.

The conference phone console in the middle of the table popped loudly. "Hello, are you there?"

"Yes, Janet," Ellie said, sitting down, "we're just getting started. Sorry for the delay." She glanced at the clock and saw it was 8:28 AM. "Rachel, are you there, too?"

"I'm here, Ellie," Rachel Townsend said. "We're in my office. Dave Martin's here, too."

"Can you all hear me okay?"

"We hear you fine, Ellie."

"All right, let's get going." Ellie opened her notebook and turned the pages. "Everyone, if you could find a seat? Craig? Sit down, please."

Monica Sisson and Brenda were still frozen in shock. Kevin touched Sisson lightly on the elbow. She exhaled and walked around the table to her seat, Brenda following behind like a timid spaniel. Kevin sat down in the same place he'd occupied last night, on Ellie's left. Dart circled the table and dropped into the seat on her right, his angry eyes fastened on Kevin.

"Rachel, Janet, and Dave," Ellie began, "I'm here with Kevin Walker, Tom Carty, Bill Merkley, Craig Dart, Monica Sisson, and Brenda Milton. John Bishop and Mark Allore are executing the search warrant at the Barron residence, so we'll hear from them later. I want to start with you, Rachel."

Townsend spent the next ten minutes running over the radio and television coverage the homicide had received during the last twenty-four hours. Radio reports had first begun at noon yesterday, continuing after that throughout the day. Television had picked up the story shortly after lunch time. Crews from

Kingston and Ottawa appeared early in the afternoon to shoot ERT officers as they combed the ditches along Ballycanoe Road. As agreed, she'd provided a news release including the throwaway line that "the ongoing police investigation is being conducted by members of the Leeds County Crime Unit under the direction of Detective Inspector Ellie March of the Criminal Investigation Branch." She also made a brief on-camera statement that both television outlets had included in their late-night broadcasts, and had forwarded case information to Crime Stoppers, who would be featuring it in upcoming media spots. At this point they'd released only the victim's name, the fact that he lived in Sparrow Lake, his occupation, and where the shooting had occurred.

"Let's give them a little more today," Ellie said, looking at Kevin.

"Let's give them Hansen's truck," he said promptly. "Tell them it's missing and we're trying to find it. That it may have been stolen by the persons responsible."

"Persons, plural?" Townsend asked.

"Yes," Ellie said. "Go with the truck, and let's let them know we're looking for two people connected to this."

"What about the Barron arrest?"

"No," Ellie said. "Arrange for a separate release on that, without connecting it to Hansen. At this point we need to hold back on publicizing the drug angle, to give us time to run down some leads."

Dart snorted. Carty gave him a disparaging look, while everyone else ignored him.

"You'll remain the only person to speak to the media at any time about this case, Rachel. Make sure the reporters understand that. We don't want our cellphones clogging up with useless calls we can't answer while we're trying to communicate with each other."

"Understood."

"Janet, did the media look for a statement from Mrs. Hansen?"

"Yes, they made a token effort, but Reverend Hume and his

wife have done a good job of keeping things quiet, and no one's found out she's there."

"What's Mrs. Hansen saying?"

"She's not really talking much. She's very withdrawn at this point."

"Any signs she's been the victim of domestic abuse?"

"None at all, physically. Mentally, it's a little too early to say. We've arranged for her to see her doctor."

"When?"

"At two this afternoon, in Brockville."

"Bring her here afterward," Ellie said, glancing at Kevin. "We need to talk to her again."

Kevin nodded.

"Inspector," Carty said, holding up his pen, "may I ask a question?"

"Sure, Tom. Ask away."

"Am I to understand that Barron's a dead end as a suspect? Are we looking at the wife instead?"

"No, Barron's still in play. We'll see if the searches of his home, financial records, and phone records give us any concrete evidence to work with, but until that time we have to pursue all other lines of inquiry as well. Right? Barron remains a person of interest in our homicide case, but that's all he is until evidence suggests otherwise. Make sense?"

"With all due respect," Dart said, his voice heavy with sarcasm, "he's good for a confession any time now."

"You're dreaming in Technicolor," Kevin interjected. "He's not going to talk. But like Ellie says, we're not dropping him, just looking at all the other possibilities, too."

Dart shook his head and lifted his eyes to the ceiling.

"Dave," Ellie said, turning her attention back to the phone console, "where's the lab at right now with our physical evidence?"

There was a brief pause. "Sorry," Martin finally said, "I was just swallowing a mouthful of muffin. Rachel made them. They're fantastic, by the way. Um, let's start with tires. The vehicle at the scene, which also parked in the driveway of the Hansen house and in the car yard, in the vacant spot next to the plow, had four nearly new twenty-two-inch Cooper Zeon XST A performance tires. Rather pricey, at least for my budget. They fit the 2013 Dodge Ram 1500 truck, which is also a match to our wheelbase measurements. Insert wild assumption here."

"Hansen's truck," Kevin said. "He was driven out to Church Road in his own vehicle, which was then stolen."

"So yes, going to the media with his truck is a move in the right direction," Martin agreed. "It's definitely important to find it."

Martin then began to run through the various tire tread marks that had been found in Hansen's car yard. In addition to the tracks that had been matched to vehicles still in the yard, he said, there were four other sets of tracks that didn't match known vehicles. As he listed the specifications for these marks and the wheelbase measurements corresponding to them, Sisson scribbled furiously on her tablet, trying to keep up.

"Hang on," she finally said, "I'm not getting all this."

"Everything will be in my report," Martin said.

Kevin stood up and walked to the whiteboard. Picking up a marker, he said, "Let's see if we've got this straight. We have four unknown vehicles that drove in the car yard within twenty-four hours of Hansen's disappearance some time Monday. Correct?"

"Correct."

Kevin wrote "Vehicles – Car Yard" on the board and drew a line under it. "One was a twenty-one-inch Michelin Latitude Sport?"

"Yes. Now, this is a rather rare tire, usually found on high-end SUVs and crossovers like the Audi Q7 and the Porsche Cayenne. That sort of thing. Plus, it's a summer tire. This vehicle was parked in the empty space on the far side of the Lexus. It was delivered by the auto transport rig I said had been in there a few days ago, but it was driven out after that."

"If it's on summer tires," Carty said, "it can't have gone very far."

"A fairly safe assumption."

“Probably sold to a local,” Kevin said. “Tom, have you found a Q7 or Cayenne in Hansen’s files?”

Carty shook his head. “I’ve been working my way through his dealership clients and making a list to start calling this afternoon. The files with individual names were private sales, and I’ll get to them next.”

“Fair enough. Dave, there were also eighteen-inch Michelins?”

“Correct. The LTX M/S2, which is a fairly common tire for light trucks and SUVs. This vehicle parked near the steps to the office trailer, and the tires show moderate wear.”

“Someone visiting,” Kevin said, writing it down on the whiteboard.

“Could be. The third set belonged to a vehicle that parked in front of the dumpster and circled around in the yard when it left. These were Goodyear Wranglers, the MT/R with Kevlar, LT265/70R17/E, expensive tires often used off-road, so maybe belonging to a farmer or something. Measurements suggest another light truck, maybe a GMC Sierra. These tires were nearly new.”

Kevin wrote this down on the whiteboard. “And what was the fourth set, again?”

“Our last mystery tires parked right near the trailer steps. They were the fourteen-inch 195/70 R14 Goodyear Nordic winter tires. Very worn. These tires would fit a lot of sub-compact cars that you wouldn’t expect a guy like Hansen to deal in, so definitely a visitor.”

“Would they fit a Pontiac Sunfire?” Kevin asked. “About ten years old? Dark purple?”

Martin laughed. “Okay, yeah, I suppose.”

“That’d be Birdie, the delivery guy from the local restaurant. Hansen apparently phoned in an order Monday that was delivered around seven o’clock.”

“No longer a mystery tire,” Martin joked.

Kevin put the marker down and took a step back. “So, we’ve still got to locate a rare twenty-one-inch summer tire that probably fits a Cayenne or Audi sold by the victim just before his death, a visitor in a light truck like a GMC Sierra who parked in front of the dumpster, and another visitor in a light truck or SUV who parked in front of the trailer." He looked at Sisson. "Okay?"

She glanced up from her tablet and nodded gratefully.

"Anything else related to tire tread marks, Dave?" Kevin asked.

"No, that's everything. As I say, you'll get my report right away. The next piece of news concerns our bullet. Our IBIS query was non-resultant. No matches."

"Shit," Sisson said.

"Don't forget, though," Martin went on, "all this means is that it wasn't used for something in the past that got it into the system. If you find a gun and we can match it to the round we found at the scene, that's rock-solid physical evidence the Crown attorney will love."

Sisson, eyes on her tablet, reddened. She nodded.

"What about footprints?" Kevin asked.

"You may not be aware of it," Martin replied, "but our boy Serge Landry is a CFE. A certified footwear examiner. Which means he's golden not only in evidence collection but also courtroom testimony, another plus for your Crown attorney. He's been busy with the tire treads, since he's also our expert in that field, but he'll be running our collection of boot prints against a bunch of different databases to see what they can give us. I can tell you one thing right off, though. I understand the suspect you arrested this morning, Steve Barron, is strictly a cowboy boots man."

"That's what he was wearing this morning," Kevin said.

"Yeah, well, my guy at Barron's residence tells me that's all they found, other than sneakers and sandals in a bedroom closet. All size eleven, by the way. We haven't collected any prints at any of our scenes that would match cowboy boots. Food for thought."

"He probably got rid of them," Dart muttered.

"What's that?" Martin asked. "I didn't catch that."

"He may have gotten rid of them," Kevin said. "What else do

you have for us right now?"

Martin explained that they were still collecting fingerprints from the vast array of items taken during their searches. They planned to begin running them later in the day. The garbage collected from the ditches along Church Road and Ballycanoe Road was being examined, but none of it looked promising. DNA samples from the bathrooms in the trailer and Hansen house, along with fibre and hair samples, were being processed for shipment to CFS, the Centre of Forensic Sciences in Toronto.

"As you know, they work on priority," Martin said. "If you believe it's urgent, I can request that our analyses be moved up to the front of the line."

"Stand by on that," Ellie said. She saw Kevin raise his eyebrows at her, but said nothing else. She was thinking of her follow-up interview with Vivian Hansen this afternoon. She was determined to find out what the woman was holding back. If Vivian was in danger, they would then have justification for requesting a rush job on the DNA in order to prevent possible further violence.

When Martin was finished, Bill Merkley gave an update on the processing of the production orders for Hansen's bank and telephone records. The order for Hansen's financial records gave the bank a deadline of thirty days in which to comply, but Merkley explained that he'd worked with them before and was expecting to get the highlights over the phone this afternoon, with hard copies of everything to follow. As for the telephone records, he explained that the phone companies liked to complain and threaten to demand compensation for their efforts, but he'd see what he could do. It *was* a homicide investigation, after all.

Ellie then suggested that Kevin wrap things up with a quick summary of assignments. Checking his notes, he reminded Rachel Townsend to include Hansen's truck in her next press release, along with the fact that they were looking to question two men in connection to the shooting. Martin would begin sending his reports to Sisson for inclusion in the case file. Carty would begin calling the dealerships this afternoon, and Merkley would work the bank and phone companies.

Kevin then made a special effort to bring Dart out of his sulk and back into the fold. “Talk to Bishop right away,” he told him. “Find out if they’ve found anything in Barron’s trailer or from the girlfriend. Then reach out to your colleagues on the drug unit to see if they know of anything connecting Barron to organized crime in Sudbury. Maybe they can tell you if Hansen’s been on their radar.”

Dart nodded without speaking.

Ellie ended the conference call, and the others around the table stood up, gathering their things. She watched Kevin hurry around the table to Sisson.

“Let’s sit down and go over all this, Mona,” he said. “You’re about to get swamped.”

“I’m gonna need more help.”

“I know. We’ll get Brenda and go over it. We can bring in more support staff.”

Ellie joined them. “Whatever you need, ask for it.”

“It’s coming at me from all sides,” Sisson said. “I didn’t realize there would be so much stuff to take care of. And we didn’t even have our meeting to go over the assignment register.”

“I know,” Ellie said. “That’s all right. You can handle this. Put together a little team and delegate to them. Anything you’re not sure about, ask Kevin or me. We’ll get through it together.”

“Okay.” Her voice trembled slightly, but she was trying to smile.

At the door, Ellie touched Kevin’s arm and drew him back. The conference room was now empty except for the two of them. “Are you okay to sit down with her and go over everything?”

“Sure, I’ve got it. No problem.”

“All right. I’m going out for about an hour. When I get back, we’ll chase down those other two drivers.”

Kevin looked at her.

Ellie sighed. “Walmart. I need underwear and frozen dinners, okay?”

chapter FIFTEEN

Kevin glanced at Ellie, who was sitting in the passenger seat of his Grand Cherokee. She'd been quiet after leaving the detachment, reading e-mail on her phone, and he'd let the silence sit between them as they drove northwest on County Road 29. Their first stop would be Athens, where Ken Price lived with his mother. How would she want to play it? Kevin preferred to take the lead, but wanted to clear it with her first. Was she still upset with Dart? She might not trust any of them at this point.

Turning onto County Road 42, which would take them directly to Athens, he watched her in his peripheral vision. She put the phone into her coat pocket and leaned back. Then she sighed and moved her handbag from her lap into the back seat.

The rear of the Grand Cherokee was piled high with bags from her shopping blitz. They'd moved them from the trunk of the Crown Vic before setting out, along with a case of beer and a discreet paper bag from the liquor store. The plan was to drive by the lake after interviewing Price and Ryan and drop everything off at the cottage. Ellie had said it was the only chance she'd get for the next while to stock up on supplies, so she'd decided to add the little side trip to their itinerary.

She was staring out the side window, her elbow on the centre console, her chin in her left hand. She was in her early forties, he guessed. Tall, slender, a little gawky. Her ring finger was bare. Her nails were closely trimmed. She wore no cosmetics at all and her hair, although neatly combed, was straight and unattractive. Her cheekbones were high and prominent. Her eyebrows were unplucked. The eyes beneath them were narrow and sober. He'd yet to see her smile. Even when she joked, revealing an active sense of humour, her wide, pursed lips didn't participate. She was a very strange and intense person who didn't seem to care what anyone thought about her. She'd talked on the phone in front of him about her kids, saying they hated her and that she needed a new life, without giving a damn that he was listening.

She puzzled and intrigued him.

"I'm sorry Dart's being such a dickhead," he said, experimentally.

"Don't worry about it."

"I don't want you to think we're a bunch of misogynists, or that we're hostile toward people from GHQ, because that's not the case at all."

"I can count on the fingers of one hand," she said, "the number of times I've heard a cop use the word 'misogynist' in a sentence."

Aware that she was ragging him, Kevin felt his face grow warm. "Sorry, I didn't mean to be offensive in any way."

They passed an impressive-looking farm property on her side of the highway. She stared at the large stone house, two freshly painted barns, a silo, and other well-kept outbuildings. "You're still green. You haven't been completely assimilated into the culture yet. Two years, you said?"

"Yeah."

"Hold on to your objectivity as long as you can. It'll make you a better cop."

They passed a snow-covered farmer's field that was as bare as a lunar landscape. Crosswinds chuffed against the car, as though testing its weight.

"Take the lead with Price," she said. "His record's clean, so play him straight. We'll see where it goes."

"All right."

As they approached Elbe Road on the right, he asked, "Have you been around here before?"

"Yeah, once, I think. On the way to Brockville."

"This area used to be known as Rear of Yonge and Escott Township, but now it's part of the municipality of Athens. Athens was called Farmersville until the late 1880s. You probably knew that already."

"No, can't say that I did. Interesting, though."

"Ben Wiltse, our warrants co-ordinator, can trace his family history all the way back to the original settlers of this area. The Wiltses emigrated from Holland to the States in the 1600s, at the same time as the English Puritans. His ancestor, Captain Benoni Wiltse, was a United Empire Loyalist who came up here from Albany during the Revolutionary War."

"Ben's a genealogist, is he?"

"Actually, no," Kevin replied, embarrassed. "I was the one who told him about it. I read a lot of local history, and I did some research for him on his family tree." He slowed as they rode around a long curve in the road. "That's Wiltsetown Road, on the left. There's a two-hundred-year-old cemetery down there where his ancestors are buried."

Chin still resting in her hand, she turned her eyes to look at him. "You're a reader, are you?"

"Yeah."

"Just history?"

"Oh no, all kinds of stuff."

"I thought you were a jock of some kind."

"I used to be. I played junior hockey and thought about getting drafted, but ended up outgrowing the sport. Physically, I mean. I got too big and slow. I play in a men's hockey league, just to stay in touch with the game."

"You must work out, too."

He nodded. "I follow a weight training program. A general fitness routine, nothing too drastic. Plus I run. What about you?"

"Tai chi. When I'm not slacking off."

"Tai chi's good. Balance, flexibility, breathing."

Ellie said nothing, looking out the side window at a cluster of buildings set back from the road.

"That's a long-term care facility," Kevin said. "It used to be a poor house. A house of industry for the poor and unfortunate, as they called it. Terrible. Apparently there's a cemetery in back with more than a hundred unmarked graves."

"Cheerful stuff, Kevin."

"Sorry." He glanced over at her. "What about your family history? March is an English surname, isn't it?"

"It was originally Marchalewicz, which is Polish. They were my adoptive parents. I don't know who my birth parents were, so family history's not something I'm really into."

"Sorry."

"It must be weird," she said after a moment, "knowing your ancestors back through hundreds of years. Knowing where they're buried. It'd make me feel claustrophobic."

"Oh? How so?"

"I don't know. All those strangers contributing to your DNA, whether you like it or not. I'd rather not know that kind of stuff. I'd rather get up in the morning and enjoy the illusion that I'm a free agent."

"You believe in fate? Predestination?"

"I'd just rather not dwell on it."

They passed farms directly across from each other, silos and barns crowding the highway, then the speed limit dropped to fifty and they arrived at the village of Athens. Kevin turned right, left, and stopped in front of a tiny single-storey house that looked no larger than a shack, its white vinyl siding stained and cracked. A ten-year-old black Impala sat in the driveway, marks still visible on the roof from where the taxi light had been.

Kevin walked through a narrow trail in the snow and tried the screen door. It was locked. He pounded on the aluminum frame, making a sound that was more rattle than thump. The inner door was cheap and flimsy, the kind of door normally found in a bedroom. It had been painted green at one time. Someone had tried to spruce it up with a coat of white, but the result looked worse than the green probably had. Kevin pounded again.

The inner door opened a crack and an old woman looked out at him. "What do you want?"

"Ontario Provincial Police, ma'am. We're looking for Kenneth Price. Is he here?"

"What do want him for?"

"We need to talk to him, ma'am. He may be able to help us with something."

The door closed. Kevin glanced back at Ellie. Her face was a careful blank.

The door opened again and a tall, gangly man looked out at them. "What is it?"

"Are you Kenneth Price?"

"Who's asking?"

Kevin held up his badge. "Detective Constable Walker, OPP. This is Detective Inspector March. Can we come in for a minute? We need to ask you a few questions."

"What about?"

"It's very important, Mr. Price. Can we come in for a few minutes?"

"I guess it's okay." Price reached through the crack and unlocked the screen door.

Kevin opened it and they stepped inside as Price backed away. They stood in a narrow, cluttered hallway. In his late forties, Price was as tall as Kevin but thinner. His short hair was grey. He wore a stained white t-shirt with a Toronto Maple Leafs logo on it, grey track pants, and black carpet slippers on his enormous feet. He breathed noisily through dentures that didn't properly fit in his mouth.

He closed the inner door behind them. "You can sit down if you want."

Kevin looked through an archway into a living room that was filled with junk. An old woman, presumably Price's mother, sat in a recliner next to a television set that had probably stopped working in the 1970s. Price picked his way across the room and sat down on a chesterfield next to a plate with a half-eaten sandwich.

Kevin found a spot to stand next to a china cabinet filled with dishes and knick knacks. Ellie moved a stack of magazines from an old kitchen chair and sat down. She took out her notebook and pen, crossing her legs.

"This is my mother," Price said.

The old woman stared at Ellie as though she'd just emerged from an alien spaceship.

"Hello, Mrs. Price," Kevin said politely, taking out his notebook and pen. "Mr. Price, can I call you Ken?"

"I guess so."

"Ken, you worked for William Hansen of Sparrow Lake as a driver, is that right?"

Price clicked his dentures. "Yeah. I heard he got killed yesterday."

"When was the last time you saw him?"

Price looked at his mother. "When did I go to Cornwall, Mom? The last time, I mean."

"Thursday," Mrs. Price said.

"Thursday," Price repeated.

"Last Thursday, December the fourth?" Kevin asked.

Price nodded.

"Were you driving for Hansen that day?"

"Yeah. I took an Escalade down to the Toyota place and brought back a Lexus."

"I see. How often did you drive cars for Hansen?"

"Sometimes. I need the work. Brockville Taxi let me go, so I take all kinds of driving jobs. Whatever I can find." He looked at his mother. "We need the money."

"Once a week, then?"

Price shook his head. "Not that much. A couple times a month."

"How did you know when he wanted you to deliver a car?"

"He called me." Price glanced at his mother again. "On my cellphone."

"When? The day before?"

"Usually the night before. After supper."

"How much did he pay you for a delivery, Ken?"

"Two hundred. Plus he gave me twenty for my lunch. But

I'm not allowed to eat or drink in the cars. I have to put a plastic drop sheet on the seat before I get in, too."

"Is there ever anything in the cars or trucks that you deliver, Ken? Maybe a few boxes or bags in the trunk or back seat?"

"No. Just the cars." Price frowned. "I'd have to get paid more if I was delivering stuff besides the cars. You know, like a handling fee. But Mr. Hansen just wanted me to deliver cars. Not any other stuff."

"Did you look? To see if there was anything else in the cars?"

"Oh, yeah. I look them all over to make sure everything's all right before I drive them. I don't want to get blamed if there's anything wrong or something's missing. I even make sure the spare tire and jack are there. I'm real careful that way."

"And there was never any cargo at all?"

"Nope."

"Tell us about last Thursday. What time did you leave Sparrow Lake with the Escalade?"

"Early. A little after eight."

"How did Hansen seem to you then?"

"I don't know. Okay, I guess."

"He didn't seem stressed or upset about anything?"

"No."

"Explain to me how it usually worked, Ken. When you got to the car yard in Sparrow Lake, was Hansen already there?"

"Yeah. If the gate's open, I know he's there, so I go in and get the keys from him, then leave with the car."

"You go into the trailer to get the keys?"

Price nodded. "He reminds me which one it is, he gives me a big envelope with all the papers for it, and I get the keys from the board and the dealer plate from the cabinet, and I go out and open the trunk, check everything, put on the dealer plate, close the trunk, and get in. I check the gas, but it's always full so I don't have to stop along the way. I drive all the way there without stopping."

"What happens when you get to the dealership?"

"I park at the back and walk around to the front. I go in and ask for Mr. Collins. He's the manager. I give him the papers, we sign some of them, then he gives me an envelope and the keys for the car I have to drive back. I go out and check the new car and put the dealer plate on it. I forgot to mention I take Mr. Hansen's plate off the old car so I can put it on the new one. Then I drive the new car from the dealership back to Mr. Hansen's. Sometimes I have to stop for gas. You have to watch because the dealers are cheap and they don't bother gassing up for you first."

"How do you pay for the gas?"

"I put it on my card. Then I show Mr. Hansen the receipt and he gives me cash for it."

Kevin took a moment to catch up on his notes.

"Ken," Ellie said, "tell us about Monday. Did you see or talk to Hansen?"

"No, not since last Thursday when I got back from Cornwall, like I said."

"What did you do on Monday? The day before yesterday?"

"Not much. Watched TV, mostly."

Kevin looked at the television set dubiously.

"I have a TV in my room."

"Did you go out Monday evening?"

"No." He looked at his mother.

"He don't go out after dark," Mrs. Price said. "I won't allow it."

"What can you tell us about the other drivers who worked for Hansen, Ken?" Ellie asked. "Do you know them very well?"

"Not really. Ryan drives a truck for a company in Brockville. He's not very friendly. The other guy, I forget his name. He's worse than Ryan."

"Steve Barron?"

"Yeah. I steer clear of him."

"Why is that?"

"I don't like the looks of him."

"How did you get the job with Hansen, Ken?" Kevin asked.

"There was an ad in the paper. In the Rip and Tear."

Ellie looked blank.

"The Brockville *Recorder and Times*," Kevin explained. "What about the other two? How did they hook up with Hansen?"

"Ryan answered the same ad I did. The other guy was already driving for him. I heard he had connections with some people around."

"Around here?"

"Here, and up north somewhere."

Ellie sat forward. "Have you ever met Mrs. Hansen? Hansen's wife?"

"Yeah. I guess so."

"Oh? When was that?"

"I don't know, a year ago, I guess. I went to see Mr. Hansen at his house. He wasn't there, so I talked to Mrs. Hansen."

"What about, Ken? Why did you go to Hansen's house?"

Price glanced at his mother. "I went to ask for a raise. We need the money, but he wasn't there. I asked Mrs. Hansen, but she said to talk to him. So I asked him later. He said no."

"Cheap bastard," muttered Mrs. Price.

"Ken, do you own a gun?"

Price shook his head, staring at Ellie.

"Mrs. Price? Do you own a gun? If we came back and searched the house for a gun, would we find one?"

"You won't find no damn gun here," Mrs. Price said, emphatically. "We don't have nothing to do with them. They're dangerous."

Ellie put her notebook away and stood up. "Thanks very much for your time."

Out in the hallway, she looked at a boot tray that held a pair of women's winter boots, a pair of women's rubber garden boots, and two pairs of men's sneakers. "Where are your winter boots, Ken?"

"There." Price pointed at the boot tray.

Ellie frowned. "Which ones?"

Price nudged a pair of battered white Adidas with the toe of his slipper. "Them, mostly. Or the ones next to them." The other pair were Reeboks, also white, also old and scuffed.

"What size do you wear?"

"I dunno. Mom, what size are my shoes?"

"Sixteen," Mrs. Price called out from the living room.

Kevin picked up one of the Adidas and found a tag stitched on the inside of the tongue. "Sixteen," he confirmed.

Out in the Grand Cherokee, Ellie belted herself in with a sigh. "That was depressing."

Kevin started the engine. "He didn't have anything to do with it."

"Mmm. Let's find Ryan and then get something to eat. My blood sugar's starting to take a nosedive."

Fifteen minutes later they pulled into the driveway of a bungalow on a side street on the outskirts of Delta, a small village just down the highway from Athens. A woman was strapping a baby into a carrier in the van in front of them. She frowned as they got out of the Grand Cherokee.

"OPP," Ellie said, holding up the wallet containing her badge and identification. "Is this where David Ryan lives?"

The woman slid the door shut on the van. "Yeah. What do you want?"

"Is he at home right now? We need to talk to him."

"He's on the road. He won't be back until tomorrow."

Ellie put away her wallet. "On the road? Where?"

"Oh, let's see," the woman said, her tone sarcastic, "if he's due home tomorrow, he's probably in Ohio today."

"He's working, I take it?"

"Yes, he's working. What's this all about?"

"He drives for Green Transport, is that right?"

"That's right." Her stare shifted to Kevin, who stared back.

"Does he work for William Hansen as well?"

"He hasn't driven for that cheap bastard for more than a month. Not since Green gave him this run."

"When did he leave on this trip he's on now?" Ellie asked.

"Last Friday."

"He's been gone since then?"

"Look, lady, he does the Gulf Coast run. Mississippi, Louisiana, Texas, then all the way back up again. He's gone six days out of every seven. Check with Green if you don't believe me." The baby in the van began to cry. "Jesus Christ. Are we done here?"

"Thanks for your help," Ellie said.

They piled back into the Grand Cherokee. Kevin backed down the driveway and out onto the street. The van barrelled out, narrowly avoiding his front bumper, and roared away.

Kevin waited for a moment, looking at the house.

"Forget it," Ellie said. "He's not there. He's on the road, like she said. He probably appreciates the peace and quiet."

"I guess you're right."

Ellie reached out and pulled on the sleeve of his jacket. "Hey."

Kevin looked at her, surprised.

"Food," she said. "Now."

chapter SIXTEEN

Ellie checked her e-mail again as Kevin drove from Delta back to Athens and turned south onto County Road 5. Dave Martin had sent a number of reports to Monica Sisson, copying Ellie on each one, and she spent a few minutes glancing through them to reassure herself that there was nothing new since the morning. When she felt the Grand Cherokee slow, she looked up and was surprised to see that they'd already reached Sparrow Lake. She put the cellphone away.

"I'm starved. How's the rest of the menu at that pizza place you ordered from last night?"

"You liked that, did you?"

"Oh, yeah."

"Then you'll love their sandwiches."

They found a parking spot on Main Street in front of the Silver Kettle and went inside. The place was a dive. A boom-box radio mounted high on a shelf along one wall blared out racket from the local country music station. The linoleum on the floor was faded and cracked, the wood panelling on the walls looked as though it had come from a hunting camp torn down in the sixties, and the tables and chairs were battered and mismatched. There was, however, no place to sit, because it was filled with customers, all of them watching as they made their way to the counter at the back.

Ellie followed Kevin past a thin woman in a peach-coloured dress who was taking orders at a table occupied by four males in their early twenties. The server turned and patted Kevin on the arm. "Uh oh, it's the law. How you doing, kid?"

"Fine, Edna. It's quiet in here today."

"Ha ha. It's never quiet in this dump. Who's your friend?"

"This is Ellie," he said. "We're working together."

Edna nodded. "Terrible, what happened to Billy." She looked at Ellie. "He was a nice guy. I hope you find whoever did it and put him away for good."

"That's the plan," Ellie said.

At the counter, she looked around in vain for a menu board. There were four stools in front of her, all occupied by men, all close to retirement age, all talking at once. On the other side of the counter was the kitchen area, an open space that was a complete contrast to the dining area. It was spotless, tidy, and modern-looking. There were two people working, a young kid in his late teens and a fat man in his fifties. Ellie watched as the man built a sandwich with meat from the grill and vegetables from stainless steel pans. His hands moved with the confidence of long experience. He produced a big knife out of thin air, sliced the sandwich diagonally, and wrapped it in wax paper. The boy picked it up, put it in a paper bag, and set it down next to the cash register with its order slip.

"That's Skinny Jimmy," Kevin said in her ear, nodding toward the fat man. "He doesn't talk to anybody."

"Okay." Ellie spotted a pile of take-out menus on the counter and reached between two men to grab one. The guy on the right turned to look over his shoulder at her. His ski jacket made a crinkling sound as he twisted on the stool. Ellie stared back until the guy turned away again, then opened the menu. It was hand-made, probably typed up on a computer and printed out on a cheap inkjet printer, then folded accordion-style, like a brochure. The front of the menu was dedicated to pizza—deluxe, Canadian, Hawaiian, meat-lover's, and so on. She turned it over. The first section on the back side listed the usual restaurant fare, including hotdogs, hamburgers, chili, and spaghetti. Then came the sandwiches—curried chicken salad, grilled tasso and cheese, grilled vegetable and garlic, California hoagie, club, BLT, ABT. The list covered an entire fold.

"Looks good, doesn't it?" Kevin said. "Anything strike your fancy?"

"I don't even know what tasso is."

"It's smoked pork, Louisiana style. Very peppery."

"What the hell's an ABT?"

"I'm getting one of those for Janie. It's her favourite. Grilled avocado, bacon, and tomato."

"Good lord."

"I'm having the curried chicken salad. You might want to try the club. It's incredible. He smokes the turkey himself. Or you could have it with smoked trout and chipotle mayonnaise, if you ask for it."

"Maybe next time."

"What can I get you folks?" Edna asked, coming up behind them, order pad ready.

"An ABT and a curried chicken salad sandwich," Kevin said. He looked at Ellie.

"Just a regular club." She folded the menu in half and put it into her coat pocket.

"Nothing's regular around here, honey, but you're gonna love it, just the same." Edna gave the order to the kid, who kept track of the slips by clipping them to a string hanging above the prep station.

As Kevin started up a conversation with a man and woman at a table on the left, Ellie wandered off to an empty chair against the far wall. She sat down and eased her head back. She closed her eyes for a moment, listening to the noise of the place, a mixture of conversation, the radio, and kitchen sounds.

"That's where the drivers sit."

Ellie opened her eyes. The kid was standing at a metal prep table, arranging take-out bags in a line. "Pardon?"

"That's where the drivers sit when they're waiting to pick up a delivery," the kid repeated. "But I guess it's okay, cuz he's on the road right now."

"How many delivery guys do you have?" Ellie asked.

"Three. Birdie, James, and me. I do weekends."

Ellie looked around. "Busy place."

The kid nodded. "Uncle Jimmy's a fantastic cook. Actually, he's a chef."

Ellie looked at Skinny Jimmy, who was anything but thin. His bald, egg-shaped head sat on top of a pear-shaped torso with no apparent neck in between. His arms and legs were short and stubby. He looked like a prison cook. The smells coming from his immaculate workplace, however, lent credence to the kid's claim. "He's your uncle?"

"Peter! Jesus!" Skinny Jimmy's yell penetrated the din, causing the kid to disappear back around the corner into the kitchen as though jet propelled.

Ellie closed her eyes again and rested her head against the wall.

Conversation abruptly stopped in the restaurant, replaced by the voice of a newscaster coming from the radio on the wall in the dining area.

"—ongoing murder investigation in Yonge Township continued today as Ontario Provincial Police announced they're looking for a truck belonging to the victim, fifty-six-year-old William Hansen of Sparrow Lake. Police say the black 2013 Dodge Ram pickup truck, Ontario dealer licence plate number DDJ 462, is missing and may have been stolen by two men police say may be connected to the Hansen shooting, which occurred sometime late Monday evening. Anyone with information about the vehicle or the two men are asked to call the OPP at 1-888-310-1122 or Crime Stoppers at 1-800-222-TIPS. In other news, a Brockville teen—"

Edna turned down the radio. The only sound in the place came from the kitchen, where food sizzled and Skinny Jimmy scooped something off the grill onto a plate.

Ellie stood up.

"Has anyone seen Bill's truck lately?" Kevin asked loudly, looking around.

“Not for a while,” a man replied.

“I saw him last weekend,” someone said. “Sunday afternoon.”

“Anyone else?”

Silence.

Kevin reached into the inside pocket of his coat. “I’m going to leave some business cards by the cash register. If anyone knows anything and wants to tell me about it, they can give me a call.”

Edna stuck out her hand. “Gimme.”

Kevin started to peel off a card, but she shook her head. “No, them all.”

Kevin handed them over.

Edna went from table to table, passing out the cards to everyone in the dining area. “These guys have to be caught. We don’t want killers running around loose in our community. Help Detective Walker.”

Everyone took a card from her.

chapter SEVENTEEN

Skinny Jimmy jumped their orders in the queue, and very shortly they were back outside. Following Kevin down the sidewalk, Ellie opened her take-out bag and stuck her nose in. It smelled delicious. She folded it up again, not sure she could wait until they got to the cottage.

"I'll just drop this off with Janie," Kevin said, "and we'll get going."

"That was interesting."

"Yeah. They all know me around here."

"Apparently."

Kevin opened the front door of the Skissors Hair Salon and moved aside, motioning her in. Ellie walked into a small waiting area with six plastic chairs and a coffee table piled with magazines. A young brunette with cerise streaks in her hair looked up from behind the cash register. "Oh, hi, Kev. She's in back."

"Thanks." Kevin led the way through an archway into the salon. "I'll introduce you," he said over his shoulder.

It was a small, narrow place with bright overhead lights, maple laminate flooring, and mirrors on the walls. There were four chairs, all empty.

They went into a back room where Ellie looked at hair dryers and sinks for washing and rinsing. A toilet flushed.

A door opened, and a tiny young woman in her late twenties walked out, drying her hands with a chunk of paper towel. Her black t-shirt and black denim jeans showed off a slim, compact figure, and her shoulder-length black hair, cut in a stacked bob style that framed her pretty face, was streaked with copper. She looked up, saw Kevin, and grinned.

"Big boy! Is that my lunch?"

"An ABT from the Silver Kettle." Kevin handed her the bag and bent down so she could kiss him. He started to straighten up but she grabbed his forearm and prolonged the kiss. When he was finally able to come up for air, he said, "This is Ellie."

Janie blinked, noticing her for the first time. "Oh, hi."

"Nice to meet you," Ellie said.

Janie squeezed his wrist. "What did you get? Curried chicken, again?"

"Yeah." Kevin held up his bag.

She kissed him again, on the arm.

"It looks quiet," he said.

"We had two appointments this morning," Janie said, rubbing the spot she'd kissed. "There'll probably be walk-ins this afternoon."

Ellie said, "I'll wait out front."

"We can't stay," Kevin said, flicking hair from Janie's cheek. "We have another stop to make."

"Are you going to catch the guy?"

"Of course we are."

"I'll wait out front," Ellie repeated. "Nice to meet you, Janie."

She walked out through the salon and went outside. As the minutes ticked along, she amused herself by watching the cars and trucks passing in the street. People walked in and out of the restaurant, the drug store, and the hardware store. On the other side of the street she could see a florist, a couple of vacant storefronts, and, down at the end of the block on this side, a second-hand store.

For no real reason, Ellie decided that she liked the place.

Kevin came out, apologetic. "Sorry about that." He led the way back to the Grand Cherokee. "I eat lunch with her whenever I can."

"Don't worry about it. She's cute."

A man in a black leather jacket stepped out of the second-hand store and came up the sidewalk toward them, a small cardboard box tucked under his arm. Ellie saw his eyes pass quickly over them, hesitating briefly on her before settling on Kevin. The man grinned, shifted the box, and stopped. "Twice in one day!"

"Antique collecting again?" Kevin asked, looking at the box.

"Yeah. She had a pair of those old-fashioned skates, the kind you used to put on the bottom of your boots. I've been looking at them for a while, and finally decided to get them. How's the case going?"

"Oh, it's going." Kevin moved his hand in Ellie's direction. "This is Detective Inspector March. Ellie, this is Chuck Waddell. He was the Sparrow Lake detective before me."

Waddell shifted his grin to her. "What's a nice girl like you doing in a place like this?"

"Chuck's retired now," Kevin said. "He operates a security consulting firm."

"Oh?" Ellie tilted her head. "What kind of security consulting?"

"We're full service, believe me. Hardware, software, and wetware. Alarm systems, employee background checks, you name it."

"Pretty competitive field. Making any money at it?"

"You have no idea." Waddell whacked Kevin on the arm with his free hand. "I'm trying to get this kid to come work for me again, but he's got this loyalty thing going right now for the big police machine. I'll get you some day, though," he grinned at Kevin. "Won't I?"

"We'll see. Ellie's staying in Gerry Staley's cottage at the lake while she's here."

"Is that right? Mine's on the north side of the lake, up near the eastern end. Beautiful spot. You'll like it there."

"I'm sure I will."

Waddell shifted the box, looking at Kevin. "Heard the news report at noon that you guys are looking for Bill's truck."

"Yeah, we are. Have you seen it around lately?"

"You can bet it's long gone." Waddell glanced at Ellie, as though to gauge her reaction. "Like I said this morning, Kev, if Bill was moving drugs, especially to Sudbury, it had to be through bikers. They probably sent a hitter down to whack him, and the guy must be back up there by now."

"Could be," Kevin said.

"That's where I'd be looking, if I was you. Well, gotta go." He nodded at Ellie, punched Kevin on the arm, and strode away.

As Ellie walked around the Grand Cherokee and stood by the passenger door, waiting for Kevin to unlock it, she glanced behind her at the second-hand shop.

A middle-aged woman stood in the window, watching her. She held Ellie's gaze for only a moment, then backed away, out of sight.

chapter EIGHTEEN

Ellie brought out her cellphone once again to check her e-mail as Kevin drove south from the village toward Lake Road. According to a message from Sisson, Bishop's search of Barron's trailer had turned up nothing useful connected to the murder. His interrogation of Brianna, Barron's girlfriend, was also unhelpful. She'd admitted to owning the small quantity of hash found in the trailer, along with a couple of bongs and other assorted paraphernalia, but she knew nothing at all about Hansen or his death.

The search of Barron's car had yielded ticket stubs and a restaurant receipt for Monday evening, as he'd told Dart it would. Someone was following up in town to verify with eyewitnesses at both businesses, but it looked as though Barron's alibi was solid.

Ellie replied with instructions for Bishop to verify that David Ryan had been out of the country since last Thursday while driving for Green Transport. She copied Kevin on the message, then put the phone away.

"I don't remember anything about drugs or Sudbury in the media release," she said.

Kevin grimaced. "Sorry. I was talking to Chuck this morning, before work." He glanced at her. "According to my CI, Chuck had looked at Hansen for dealing hot cars several years ago. I asked him about it this morning, and he said nothing came of it. So I asked about the drug angle, and he said he'd never looked at Hansen for that. I thought there might have been some kind of file on Hansen that was destroyed when the department disbanded."

Ellie said nothing.

"Chuck's trustworthy," Kevin said. "He was my mentor when I was a constable here. He taught me a lot. When I became detective and he retired, he came in from time to time, just to talk, see how I was doing. I'd run a few things by him, and he'd give me advice. Sometimes it was ground he'd already covered, so he'd give me a heads-up on it. He's a good guy."

"From now on, Kevin, ask questions but don't answer his, okay? I don't care what he was before, he's a civilian now, and we don't share case information with civilians who are under no obligation to keep it confidential. Understood?"

"Understood. Sorry."

Ellie watched the road as they turned onto Tamarack Lane. It was her first time seeing the place in daylight. The open fields on either side of the road had been planted with corn that had grown poorly and was never harvested. The spindly yellow stocks jutted up through the snow. Beyond the fields they entered the tree line. Cedars loomed close on either side. There was almost no shoulder on either side of the road, which rose and fell. Large rocks filled the spaces between the trees, pink and grey boulders bulging out of the snow.

"I told Sisson that Bishop needs to check out David Ryan's alibi," Ellie said, "to make sure he's been out of the country since last Thursday."

"Okay. Thanks." Kevin slowed, rounding a corner. They passed the three driveways Ellie had seen last night in the dark. Now she could see cottages down at the edge of the lake, through the trees. The driveways were unplowed, blocked with snow. Kevin swung into the little parking area walled in with flat stones and shut off the engine.

Ellie carried in her groceries and other purchases, with

Kevin's help, then they sat in front of the sliding doors and ate their sandwiches. Kevin raised his bottle of water at the view. "Do you like it here?"

"It's nice."

"The locals sometimes call it Sorrow Lake. When they're referring to the lake and not the village."

"Why's that?"

Kevin smiled tentatively. "It has a bit of a history."

"Local history, and you know all about it. Why am I not surprised?"

"Back in the sixties there was a bad boating accident. Some guy was giving a ride to a bunch of kids from around the lake and stayed out too late. It was already dark when he ran into a dock at full speed. Killed all the kids and himself."

"That's terrible."

"Then in the seventies there was a big murder-suicide. At a cottage on the other side of the lake. An American from Pennsylvania shot his five kids, his wife, and himself. After that, people started calling it Sorrow Lake."

Ellie put the last bite of her sandwich in her mouth.

"Twenty years ago," Kevin continued, "a retired couple living in a winterized cottage up at the east end of the lake were killed by looters after a January blizzard. It was a couple of young guys who were hitting all the cottages along the way. Because of the snow, they thought the place was deserted. Didn't notice the car parked on the other side of the cottage.

"You're a cheerful guy," Ellie said.

"Sorry. You asked. Hopefully it won't keep you up at night now, listening for prowlers."

"Not a chance of that."

Ellie got up to put the frozen food away while Kevin used the washroom. When he came back out, they put on their coats and boots and left the cottage. As she was locking the door, Kevin said, "There's your neighbour."

She turned around. Smoking a cigarette on the deck of the lodge next door was a man wearing a navy pea jacket and a black watch cap. He stood at the railing, staring out across the frozen lake.

"Want to meet him?" Kevin asked.

Ellie looked at her watch and saw that it was 1:18 PM. She'd been thinking ahead to the interview with Vivian Hansen, which would take place around 2:30 or so. Between now and then she wanted to sit down with Monica Sisson to review the reports and see how she was making out with things, but they weren't in a particular rush right at the moment.

"Sure." She followed Kevin across the snow to a walkway running alongside the lodge. It was a beautiful log structure that must have cost a fortune to build. They passed a window through which Ellie could see a long wooden table and chairs, a sideboard, and a chandelier made from a wagon wheel. As they went up the stairs to the deck, the man kept his back to them, staring across the lake, hands shoved into his pockets, smoke curling from the cigarette between his lips.

"Hello, Mr. Ballantyne," Kevin said.

The man didn't move.

As Kevin stepped up beside him, the man jumped. Ash fell from the cigarette onto the front of his jacket. A hand came out of his pocket to remove earbuds as he turned to stare at them.

"Bloody hell! I didn't know anyone was there."

"Sorry, Mr. Ballantyne," Kevin said, embarrassed. "I didn't realize you were listening to music. We thought we'd just come over to say hello. We're on our way back to Brockville."

"That's all right. At least I've still got a strong heart." He looked at Ellie. "Moved in next door, have you?"

"Yes. I'm Ellie March." Seeing that his right hand now held his cigarette, she didn't offer hers.

"Ridgeway Ballantyne. But since we're to be neighbours, you can call me Ridge."

"Nice to meet you." She looked at his weathered face, the grey hair sticking out from under the watch cap, and the white in his short beard, and decided that he was well past retirement age. "You have a beautiful place."

"Thank you. Sorry I nearly jumped out of my skin. I'm working, and my mind was elsewhere."

"Working?"

He showed her one of the earbuds. "Music. I recorded some stuff last night, and I was just giving it a listen to see what's to be done with it." He shook his head. "Back to the drawing board, I'm afraid."

"Kevin mentioned you're a musician."

"I am."

"From Scotland?"

Ridge sketched a little bow. " A working class Glaswegian by birth and upbringing. Are you police too, like Kevin?"

"Yes."

"Well, as I've told him, I won't hold it against you."

"If you're working," Ellie said, "we should let you get back to it. It's nice meeting you."

"Likewise. Come over for a glass anytime. It'll be nice to have some company down here. It gets a little too quiet sometimes."

"I wouldn't want to disturb you if you're working."

"Pfft. Ring the doorbell at the side. If I'm in the studio, it flashes a light. I won't mind the interruption, believe me." He stuck the cigarette back into the corner of his mouth and leaned toward her. "It's only a bloody advert, after all."

Ellie nodded. "All right, I will. I'm not sure when, but I will."

"I'll look forward to it." Ridge slipped the earbuds back into his ears and turned away to stare out once again across the whiteness of Sorrow Lake.

chapter NINETEEN

After dropping Ellie off at the detachment, Kevin turned around and went back up County Road 29 to the Glen Buell intersection, where he turned west onto Temperance Lake Road. Passing the Brockville Ontario Speedway, which was closed for the season, he drove for a few kilometres and then slowed as he passed a house in a clearing on the north side of the road. He was looking for a small pickup truck, and when he didn't see it, he kept going. After about half a kilometre he slowed again and turned down a very narrow lane that was nearly hidden by thick balsam and cedar. Following fresh wheel tracks in the snow, he eventually reached a small clearing. The pickup truck was parked in front of a shed, next to a wood splitter and an enormous pile of sawn chunks of wood. Kevin stopped and got out.

Somewhere behind the shed he could hear the high-pitched whine of a chainsaw. He walked around and saw Josh Palmer lopping limbs off a fallen tree. Josh wore a protective headset over his baseball cap to block out the noise of the saw. Kevin followed Josh's tracks about halfway across the field and then circled around until he was in Josh's peripheral vision. He waved an arm. Josh saw him, finished his cut, and straightened, shutting off the saw.

"Thought I'd find you out here," Kevin said.

Josh put the saw down on an upright chunk of wood and slipped the headset off his ears. He took off his gloves and tucked them in an armpit, then removed his sunglasses and put them into the pocket of his jeans jacket. Taking out a pack of cigarettes, he lit one and exhaled smoke at the sky.

Kevin rested his foot on another chunk of wood and clapped his gloves together. "Cold day to be out cutting firewood."

Josh pushed a thin stream of smoke through his lips. "Gotta be done."

"I guess so. How's your mom?"

"Good. Still sober. One year, four months, and three days."

"How about you?"

"Still good."

"Glad to hear it." Kevin leaned forward, arm across his thigh. "I saw Jill in Brockville last week. She looks fine."

"Haven't talked to her for a while." Josh wiped the sweat from his forehead with the sleeve of his jacket. His yellow safety boots were old and scuffed, and the steel toes showed through tears in the leather. His jeans were stained with oil and grease. His young face was lean and unshaven, the bristles light brown, and his hands were red and nicked from manual labour.

During the winter of 2010, not long after he'd made detective with Sparrow Lake, Kevin was driving along Temperance Lake Road one winter evening when he came across the pickup truck in the ditch. Josh was behind the wheel, drunk and ranting. His lip was split and there was a scuff on his left cheek, but Kevin could see no other injury. It took nearly twenty minutes for Kevin to convince the kid to get out from behind the wheel, but finally he had him sitting on the snowbank, hugging his knees, reluctantly telling his story.

Josh's father, Cameron Palmer, had attacked Josh's mother that evening. When Josh, eighteen at the time, tried to defend her, his father beat him as well. Palmer then stormed out of the house and drove off in his car. Mrs. Palmer disappeared upstairs. It was apparently something that happened on a regular basis. After finishing off his father's bottle, Josh decided to find his father and kill him. He got a few hundred metres down the road, lost control of the truck, and ended up in the ditch.

When the boy had calmed down, Kevin got him back to the house. Josh's sister Jill helped steer him upstairs and into bed, where he fell asleep almost immediately. Kevin went to the farm next door and talked to the neighbour, who brought out his tractor and helped Kevin get the truck out of the ditch. Back at the Palmer house, Jill didn't want to explain what was going on, but when Kevin showed her his badge, she began to cry. The old man was not only beating his wife but abusing Jill as well. Josh had tried on several occasions to do something about it, but Palmer was too big and strong for him. Josh had turned to drugs—weed, hash, and sometimes mushrooms. Meth was probably just a buy away. Jill was petrified that something terrible would happen, that someone would end up dead.

When Kevin talked about having Palmer charged, Jill shook her head. She wouldn't co-operate, and neither would her mother. Their lives would become a worse hell than they already were. Palmer was sadistic, had no inhibitions, and would punish them horribly if they tried to come forward. She shouldn't even be talking to Kevin now, she said repeatedly. He might find out and punish her for it.

Kevin gave her his card and told her to hide it somewhere her father wouldn't find it. "Call me," he said, "any time, day or night, and I'll be here. I'm only ten minutes away."

The following August, the call came on a Sunday afternoon. Palmer had gone crazy, and Jill was desperately afraid he'd kill her mother this time. Josh was away, and there was no one to stop her father. When Kevin arrived, Jill was waiting for him in the yard. "They're in the shed! Hurry, he's killing her."

Kevin ran through the yard to the shed. Dogs in pens outside the shed barked madly. Inside, Mrs. Palmer was on her hands and knees on the dirt floor of the shed, weeping as Palmer beat her with a broomstick. There was blood and vomit everywhere. Kevin shouted, and Palmer turned on him.

Palmer was a big man, but Kevin was bigger, twenty years younger, and sober. It was no match. Kevin took the broomstick away from him and cuffed Palmer's hands behind his back before the man knew what was happening. There was a prolonged struggle as Kevin took him back through the yard to his car, during which he found it necessary to deliver a few short, crisp blows while dodging Palmer's boots and knees.

Palmer was convicted of domestic assault and assault on a peace officer. The maximum penalty for each charge was five years in prison, and after Jill's testimony, Palmer received consecutive, rather than concurrent, sentences. He was still in prison, but would soon be eligible for parole. Everyone was afraid of what would happen when he got out.

After graduating from high school, Jill found a job in Brockville as a receptionist at an insurance broker's office. She was living in an apartment above a Chinese restaurant. Josh worked part time at a lumber yard outside Brockville and sold firewood on the side. With Kevin's help he got off drugs and alcohol, and from what Kevin could tell, had managed to stay off. Kevin stopped in to check on him from time to time. He'd also begun to use Josh as another confidential informant.

Josh knew everyone in the area, and although he was a quiet young man he kept his eyes and ears open. Kevin's arrangement was different than the one he had with Willie Bird. Birdie was a businessman who sold information for cash, but Josh was a worrier. He knew what could go on behind the walls of houses on country roads like this one, and when something came to his attention, he felt strongly that action needed to be taken to stop it. He'd never forgiven himself for not having been home when his father was arrested, and he believed that he owed Kevin a special debt.

"You heard what happened to Bill Hansen," Kevin began.

Josh nodded, pushing back his baseball cap to get at more of the sweat on his forehead. "Bit of a shocker."

"Heard anyone bad mouthing him lately?"

"Not at all."

"He was found down on Church Road, just below Ballycanoe. Know anybody down there who might have had some bad business with him?"

Josh studied the tip of his cigarette, thinking about it.

"Not many people on that road. None that I know of, anyway. Sorry."

"No problem. Let me switch gears for a minute. We came across a shipment of BHO around here the other day, about half a kilo's worth. We're not sure if it was just in transit or if it was produced locally."

"BHO?" Josh flicked ash and shook his head. "It's all the rage these days." He squinted at Kevin. "It's not that hard to make, if that's what you're asking. A lot of times, these guys just use their skuff. To get rid of it. Know what I mean? Leaves, trimmed stuff, that sort of shit. The idea is to extract THC from what you might otherwise throw away."

"Good business practice, I guess."

Josh showed him a very brief smile, throwing his cigarette into the snow. "Yeah, it's definitely about the money."

"So somebody with a grow op around here might have decided to get into BHO as a side line to make extra cash."

Josh shrugged.

"The narcotics guys have been chasing the Turgeons all over the countryside for years," Kevin said, "trying to find their grows. Were they in business again this year?"

"They're small time now, Kev. It was mostly the older brother, Jock, but he went out to BC last year. Pete scaled way back. Hardly brings in enough for his own use, let alone to make money off of it. People don't buy from them any more."

"What about the guy who had the medical grow? O'Brien?"

"No, he got out of it. As soon as they started the big commercial op in the Falls, he quit. He's into strawberries now."

Kevin frowned, guessing it was slang for something.

Josh laughed. "No, man. Real strawberries. Christ."

"Okay, okay. Who else? Can you still buy weed from Lennie Ross?"

Josh's grin faded. He took his gloves from his armpit and put them back on. "The Rosses are a different story. Mean fuckers. I steer clear of them."

Kevin nodded. He straightened up and looked around, shading his eyes. "If somebody was making BHO around here, what the hell would I be looking for? I don't know much about it. Are we talking a lot of equipment and precursor stuff? Something like a meth lab?"

Josh looked at his chainsaw, but didn't pick it up. "Depends on how big they're trying to go with it. Some guys just use a plastic tube or metal pipe and pass the butane through that. Makes a small amount they can sell or use themselves, whatever."

"But if they're doing bigger lots? Half a kilo at a time?"

"Then you're looking for a setup with pots, pumps, and canisters of gas. You could do it in a back shed with ventilation, although a lot of these guys do it outside because they're scared it'll blow up on them."

"Oh? It's dangerous?"

"It is if they don't know their ass from a hole in the ground. If they're stupid or trying to make it on the fly, they could fill the pot or tube with too much gas and it'll explode from the pressure. Or they could smoke while the butane's venting and ignite the fumes, or some other brainless stunt like that." He shook his head. "Anybody who understands how a refrigerator works can do this on a large scale. They get some of those big paint pressure pots, two-and-a-half gallon or whatever, hoses, a few refurbished refrigerant pumps, and tanks of butane, maybe the ten-inch ones like you see on a barbecue, or maybe the bigger, commercial-sized ones. Depends on what scale they're doing it in, eh?" Josh looked at him. "The butane has to come from somewhere, Kev. You could always check around with distributors in the area."

"So somebody with a lot of skuff on hand might turn to BHO to use it up."

Josh put his sunglasses back on. He'd already answered that one.

Kevin took his foot down off the chunk of wood. "Thanks. Appreciate it."

Josh nodded, slipping his ear protectors back on.

It wasn't until Kevin was getting back into his Grand Cherokee that he finally heard the chainsaw start up again.

chapter TWENTY

Back at the detachment, Ellie sat down with Monica Sisson to review her progress. Patterson had brought in another clerical support person, a young man named Jonathan Smart, who was busily opening files for the hard copies of all the reports, witness statements, and other documents being generated by the team. Sisson had finally gotten a handle on the assignment register, and had made a good start on a detailed chronology of the investigation while Brenda was entering data and maintaining all the case files in the software database. Sisson was much calmer now that she had the extra help, and her rough-edged humour was beginning to reappear.

Once they'd gone over everything, Ellie turned the page in her notebook and leaned back. "Monica, you've read the civilian statements and the officer notebook entries from yesterday after the area canvasses. I haven't had a chance to go through them all yet, so let me ask you a question."

"Shoot. And call me Mona; everybody else does."

"Okay, Mona. Did the witnesses have much to say about the relationship between the victim and his wife?"

Sisson thought for a moment. "Not that I noticed. No one said they'd seen them arguing or fighting."

"Anything in the detectives' notes?"

Sisson shook her head. "Whenever they asked the questions, you know, 'Did the Hansens get along?' 'Did you ever see them argue?' or that sort of thing, it always came back negative. Do you think there was domestic violence going on?"

"I don't know. It's something you have to look at. I'm just not seeing any evidence of it yet, that's all."

"There'd be something in her medical records, you can bet, if he was abusing her."

"At this point we need a warrant, or her consent." Neither of which was going to happen right now.

There was a knock on the door frame. She looked up at Merkley, who was standing in the doorway with a notebook in his hand.

"Got a sec?"

"What's up?"

"I just got off the phone with my bank contact. We're looking at three accounts, all with the same bank. I'm not finding anything anywhere else in either name, so I'm reasonably confident this is it."

"Okay."

"One is a joint chequing account in both their names, one's a business account in the name of Hansen Car Wholesale Limited, and the third's a chequing account just in William Hansen's name."

"Okay."

"A couple of things stand out. First, his business account. He was registered as a motor vehicle wholesaler under the Ontario *Motor Vehicle Dealers Act*. Technically, that class of dealer is only permitted to trade with other registered motor vehicle dealers, or sell through car auctions. So transactions we see in his business account involve him buying from and selling to other registered dealers, and trading vehicles through auction services. So when I get the actual data for this account, I'll have to match transactions in it to his dealership files to see if there's anything that doesn't check out."

"Okay."

"Then there's the personal account in his name only.

There are regular deposits and withdrawals in large amounts, sometimes up to forty or fifty grand. So the assumption here is that he was using his access to find cars at really low prices, buy them as a personal transaction, then flip them to customers for a profit. Again, I'll need to match all this stuff to the files from his office to see if anything doesn't fit."

"To see if he was dumb enough to bank his drug money," Sisson said, "in the same place he was banking his car money."

"Exactly. Not that I'm hopeful. I doubt he was stupid enough to move drug cash through bank accounts with his name on them. Anyway, we have to be sure. Criminals are often a lot dumber than we think."

"What about the joint account?" Ellie asked.

"Boring, thank God. Every week he paid himself a salary from the business account, regular as clockwork. And there are direct withdrawals to pay bills and stuff. Looks like he used a debit card to pay for gas, groceries, and that sort of thing."

"No big payoffs to hired killers," Sisson said.

"Nope."

Ellie bit her lip. Although Merkley's analysis of Hansen's transactions might well uncover evidence related to his drug distribution, it appeared as though there was nothing at all, once again, to suggest that Vivian Hansen had paid someone to kill her husband.

"How in the hell would she have gotten her hands on that kind of money?" she asked, more to herself than to the others.

Merkley shrugged. "There are ways."

Ellie sighed, not seeing it. "What about phone records?"

"Still to come. By which time, I'm going to be swamped just trying to analyze his car transactions. And with the production orders on Steve Barron. It's a good job I'm an insomniac."

"Let's get an analyst in here," Ellie said, "to take on some of the workload."

"Sure."

"Anyone in particular I should ask for?"

"Um, Sally Gordon. She's good."

Ellie wrote the name down in her notebook.

chapter TWENTY-ONE

Rather than question Vivian Hansen one-on-one in the interview room while the others watched the audio-video feed, Ellie played a hunch and decided to have Olkewicz bring her down to her little office across from the training room.

Her objective for the interview was to reach a decision as to whether to continue investigating Vivian as a suspect in her husband's murder or to consider her the victim of a family tragedy and concentrate everyone's time and energy elsewhere. Her gut sense told her that if she confined Vivian in a small, cramped room and pressed her, the woman would shut down and they'd end up getting nowhere. After some thought, she called Olkewicz, who was waiting for Vivian at the doctor's office, and explained what she wanted to do. The victim liaison officer agreed that while Vivian seemed to be doing a little better today, her state of mind was still quite fragile, and that a more informal approach, in a larger room, might be a good idea.

"Would it help, Janet, if you sat in? Since you've been spending time with her?"

"Maybe," Olkewicz replied slowly. "She's responsive enough to me. She understands I'm trying to help her."

"Okay," Ellie said, "that's how we'll start off. As though it's a meeting. We'll include Kevin. He radiates sympathy. But if she reacts the wrong way, I'll clear the room and try a different approach."

Ellie enlisted Brenda's help to prepare for their arrival. They attached a video camera and microphone to Ellie's laptop and set it up so that it was connected to the network server. Brenda brought four chairs across from the training room. They were more comfortable than the plastic moulded things Ellie was currently inflicting on her visitors. They gathered up all the files, reports, releases, and other miscellaneous stuff that covered the big round table Ellie was using for a work surface and stacked them in a neat pile on top of the filing cabinet.

When Olkewicz and Vivian arrived, Ellie and Kevin met them in the corridor outside her office. Kevin collected coats and put them in the training room while Ellie asked if anyone would like coffee or tea. When Vivian hesitated, Olkewicz cheerfully declared that she would love a cup of coffee, black, one sugar. Vivian timidly agreed to try a cup of tea with milk, no sugar. Kevin went off to get them while Ellie seated everyone, directing Vivian to the chair facing the camera on her laptop.

"Before we begin, Mrs. Hansen," Ellie said, sitting down, "I just want to let you know that our meeting will be video- and audio-recorded." She pointed at the camera. "In important cases like this, when someone comes in to talk to us, we want to make sure we have a record of what's said, to avoid any misunderstandings on either side. I'll also mention right up front that you're here voluntarily, at our request, and that you can leave at any time. Okay?"

Vivian nodded.

"Janet mentioned that you had a chance to speak to a lawyer this morning."

"Yes, he called at the house where I'm staying."

"That's fine," Ellie said. "If for any reason you'd feel more comfortable talking to him again, just let me know. Is that something you want to do?"

"No, I don't think so."

"All right. If you change your mind at any time, let me know." Ellie looked over her shoulder as Kevin walked in with a tray.

He served Vivian her cup of tea, winked at Olkewicz as he gave her her coffee, put a bottle of water next to Ellie's elbow, closed the door, and sat down next to Ellie.

"Thanks," Vivian said, not touching the tea.

"I understand this is a difficult time for you," Ellie began, "and we appreciate your coming in. We have a better understanding of what happened than we did on Tuesday, when we first talked, but there are still a few things we hope you can help us with."

"I'll try."

"Good. I appreciate it." Ellie leaned back. "You've had a bit of time to think about things, so maybe now your memory's a little more clear. You said that the last time you saw your husband was at about eight o'clock Monday morning when he left for work, and that you didn't see or hear from him again. Is that right? Was that the last contact you had with him?"

"Yes. That's right."

"I understand that your husband drove a black 2013 Dodge Ram truck. Did he ever lend it out to anyone? Let someone else drive it for whatever reason?"

Vivian shook her head. "No. Never. He didn't like anyone else driving it. He hated it when he took it in for servicing and they moved the seat or the mirrors. He was very fussy about his truck."

"Okay. You and your husband have a joint bank account, but are you aware of any other accounts your husband might have kept in his own name?"

"He had an account for the business. Hansen Car Wholesale Limited."

"Right. Any others that you know of?"

"No."

"Did he have a safety deposit box? At your bank or any other bank?"

"I don't think so. No."

"Did you ever see him with large amounts of cash, Mrs. Hansen?"

She frowned. "He liked to have several hundred dollars in his wallet, and there's a cookie jar in the kitchen where we keep money in case I need it for something. Is that what you mean?"

"How much money would be in the cookie jar?"

"Maybe three or four hundred. He called it an emergency fund for me."

"Okay. But nothing more than that? Maybe a thousand or several thousand in cash?"

"No. He wouldn't feel comfortable with that much on him, and he didn't work in cash. He accepted certified cheques and bank drafts, I think, but not cash like that."

"Okay, that's fine." Ellie removed the cap from her bottle of water and took a sip. Olkewicz picked up her cup of coffee and tried it. Vivian looked at her cup of tea, put her finger through the handle, hesitated, and lifted it to her lips. Ellie was satisfied that they'd made a good beginning. Vivian was reasonably responsive and seemed clear-headed enough. She was obviously depressed and anxious, but was apparently working through it.

"May I call you Vivian? I'm Ellie. Janet. Kevin. I like to be on a first-name basis with people; it feels more comfortable. Is that all right with you?"

"Yes. That's all right."

"Vivian, do you know a man named Ken Price?"

"Who?"

"Price. Ken Price. He was one of your husband's drivers."

Vivian's eyes suddenly widened. "Him. Oh, yes. I met him once."

"When was that?"

"Maybe a year ago. Last winter. He came around the house, looking for Bill, but he wasn't home. What an odd man."

"What did he want?"

"He said he wanted to ask Bill for more money. A raise, I mean. I said I didn't have anything to do with Bill's business, that he'd have to ask Bill himself. He stood there in the doorway and pleaded with me. I didn't want to let him in because he looked like the kind of person who'd never leave. He said he lived with his mother and all they had was her pension and whatever he could make driving for Bill. He was a taxi driver in Brockville, but they fired him for having liquor in the cab. He came right out and told me that. I said there was nothing I could do, that he'd have to take it up with Bill."

"Did you ever see him again?"

"No, thank goodness." Vivian took another sip of tea.

Ellie had brought Vivian through an initial phase of questioning to assess her behaviour and truthfulness, and the woman had done well enough. Now it was time to get down to business.

"You have a very lovely home, Vivian."

"Thank you."

"You keep it incredibly neat and tidy. I wish I was that good a housekeeper."

Vivian politely drank a little more tea.

"Is that the way your husband wanted the house to be? Everything clean and in its place? Was he particular, that way?"

"I suppose so."

"Did he get upset with you if he found something out of place, or if something had spilled on the floor, or if there was dust you hadn't cleaned?"

Vivian hesitated, frowning. "No. Not especially."

"He didn't get angry with you if things weren't just the way he wanted them?"

Vivian glanced at Kevin before replying. "No."

Ellie could see that she was clearly puzzled by this line of questioning. "Did he prefer that you stay in the house all the time? Did he discourage you from going out shopping or having friends?"

"No, of course not. Why would you think that?"

"Did he ever hit you, Vivian?"

"No! Of course not!"

"Did he yell and scream at you? Get angry with you often?"

"Never!" Vivian put down her tea, looking at Kevin. "Why is she asking these things about Bill?"

"If there's anything you need to tell us about your relationship with him," Kevin said, "this is a very good time to do it."

"Have you lost your mind? You knew Bill. He wasn't like

that at all."

Ellie leaned forward. "Was he controlling or short-tempered or cruel to you?"

"Of course not! Bill was the kindest, gentlest man I ever knew. He got me through some very rough patches when we were first married, and he always helped me when I needed it. He was polite and sweet."

"What kind of rough patches?"

Vivian looked at her hands. "Before we were married, I ... there was a car accident. My roommate was driving, and I was with her. A boy came out from behind a tree on a bicycle and she hit him. He was killed."

Ellie waited.

"She wasn't charged, it wasn't her fault, but she took it hard. A month later ... she killed herself. I found her when I came home from work."

"Were you in a relationship with Bill at that point?"

"No. He was a friend of my roommate's boyfriend. He took me to the funeral, and after that we started seeing each other. He knew I suffered from depression, and he was worried it would get worse. He got me through it."

A tear rolled down her cheek, but there was iron in her voice when she said to Ellie, "If you think Bill was abusive, you don't know what you're talking about."

Olkewicz took out a packet of tissues from her handbag and gave one to Vivian.

Ellie watched her dab at her eyes. It had the ring of truth to it, but they weren't finished yet. "Vivian, there's something that concerns me. I don't think you were completely truthful with me and Kevin when we talked to you yesterday morning. I want to give you a chance now to clear things up with us."

"I don't understand."

"I asked you twice yesterday whether someone had come around to the house before we got there to tell you that Bill was dead, and you said that no one had. That wasn't true, was it?"

Vivian's lips compressed.

"I understand completely that you were upset. I understand

why you acted that way, Vivian, but now you've had some time to get over the shock. We need you to tell us about Monday night. Who came to see you Monday night to tell you about Bill?"

Vivian shook her head.

"There's no point in staying quiet about it. We have a witness who saw someone at your house on Monday night between ten and ten thirty. Who was it?"

"Nosy old witch," Vivian murmured, looking away.

Ellie leaned forward. "Pardon?"

Silence.

"Vivian, did you pay someone to kill your husband?"

Her eyes flew back to Ellie in shock. "What? No! Are you insane?"

"Then tell me the truth. Who came to your house Monday night?"

Vivian's lips were pressed so tightly together they were white.

"This man, he threatened you, didn't he?"

Silence.

"I believe you, Vivian, when you tell me that Bill was good to you. I can see you're telling the truth about that. But you need to tell me about this person who came to your house Monday night. Who was he?"

"I don't know."

"You mean, you don't know who he was?"

"No."

"You never met him before?"

"No."

"Do you know his name?"

"No."

"What did he say to you?"

Vivian closed her eyes. "I'd rather ... not talk about it."

Ellie gave her a moment, but only a short one, before repeating, in a gentler tone, "What'd he say to you?"

Vivian whispered, "I'm afraid."

"I understand," Ellie said. "Janet's job is to make sure nothing happens to you. My job, and Kevin's, is to find this man who visited you Monday night. Please, Vivian. Tell us what happened. What did he say to you?"

"That Bill was dead. And I'd be dead, too, if I said anything about it."

"Did he tell you he did it? That he was the one who shot Bill?"

She nodded, her eyes still closed. "He laughed. He said Bill wouldn't shut up. He said he gave him a chance to shut his mouth. Bill wouldn't. So he shot him."

"Why did he tell you, Vivian? Why was he there?"

"To see how much I knew. About the business."

"To find out if you knew about a connection between him and Bill's business?"

"Yes. I said I didn't know. I didn't have anything to do with it."

"Did he say what this business was all about?"

"No. He said Bill was in it up to his neck and should have been smart enough to go along for the ride and make some money, but Bill had to be a smartass about it. He said they knew Bill was giving the money away, to charities and that, instead of keeping it. He said they weren't stupid. He said they knew Bill wanted out, but it wasn't going to happen. He insisted Bill must have given me some of the money, too. I said he didn't. Whatever the money was, I didn't know anything about it. I don't know if he meant the money in the cookie jar, but it sounded like a lot more money than just a few hundred dollars." She opened her eyes and looked at Ellie. "It sounded like what you were asking me about."

"And he threatened to kill you, too?"

Vivian nodded. "If I talked to the police."

"And you'd never seen him before in your life?"

Vivian shook her head.

"Have you seen him again, since Monday night?"

"No."

Ellie leaned back. She put her elbow on the arm of the chair and rested her chin in her hand, index finger extended, tapping her temple. She looked at Kevin. His expression was neutral, but his eyes were riveted on her.

"What did this man look like?" she asked. "Can you describe him to us?"

"Very mean looking. Nasty."

"About how old would he be? Was he Bill's age?"

She shook her head. "Younger."

"How young? In his thirties or forties?"

"In his forties."

"What colour was his hair?"

"Black. But he was going bald." She took a deep breath and exhaled. "And there were some white hairs."

"What race was he, Vivian? White? African-American? Or something else?"

"He was white."

"Was he tall? Short? Fat? Thin?"

"Short. Not much taller than me. Stocky."

"Okay. That's good, Vivian. Did you see any tattoos or scars, anything like that?"

"No. He had his coat and scarf on the whole time."

"What did his voice sound like? Deep, or high-pitched?"

"Sort of high-pitched."

Ellie walked her through it again, pressing for more detail. Vivian described having answered a pounding on the door at about twenty minutes after ten. He pushed his way inside and walked around the downstairs, looking to see if anyone else was there. Then he forced her to sit down in the living room and proceeded to describe how he'd taken her husband for a ride in the country to convince him to shut his mouth about his involvement in "a little business venture" of his. He didn't say what the business venture involved. Bill had refused to co-operate, saying he was going to go to the police unless the man let him quit, but the man jeered at the idea and told Bill he was in too deep. Finally, the man stopped the truck and forced Hansen to walk at gunpoint across a field. When Hansen still insisted he would go to the police unless he let him walk away, the man shot him. As an example to everyone else, he told Vivian. So that everyone else would know to keep their mouths shut, or the same thing would happen to them. Before leaving the house, the man told her that when everything had died down, she was to sell off Hansen's business and transfer the money to a bank account number he would give her when the time was right. If she failed to comply, she'd end up face-down in the same field as her husband.

She didn't see him leave. She stayed where she was, in the living room, when he left. She didn't see his car. When Kevin asked if the man had touched anything in the house, maybe picked up an ornament to look at it while they talked, she shook her head. He wore leather gloves the whole time, she said, and just kept shaking his fist at her.

"Can you stay with Reverend Hume and his wife for another day?" Ellie asked.

Vivian was silent for several moments before nodding.

Ellie then asked if she'd be willing to sit down with a police sketch artist to provide a description of the man, so that they could produce a composite drawing to release to the public. When Vivian balked, afraid he'd come back and hurt her, Ellie promised to step up security around her and, if necessary, temporarily relocate her to ensure her safety. Reluctantly, Vivian agreed to meet with the artist.

Olkewicz then took her back to the village. Ellie and Kevin went into the conference room for coffee. Someone, probably Sisson, had made a food run, and when Ellie flipped up the lid on a box of doughnuts she found two still left, one with sprinkles and one dusted with cinnamon. She pointed.

"Ladies first," Kevin said.

Ellie took the cinnamon one and dropped into one of the chairs lined up against the wall. She closed her eyes, leaned her head back, and took a bite of the doughnut. She washed it down with coffee. It tasted wonderful. She heard Kevin sit down next to her.

"I believe her," he said. "Don't you?"

"Yeah. But what we believe doesn't matter. Without hard evidence, it's just another story. We need Wiltse to get Ident back into that house with their vacuum cleaners and all the rest of it. If this guy's going bald, maybe he shed a few hairs on her rug for us to find. We find DNA in that living room that can't be accounted for any other way, we've got something solid to build on."

"My gut instinct says she's telling the truth."

"Gut instinct never put anyone in a prison cell, Kevin." She tapped her temple with a finger. "This is where all the work gets done. Feelings are fine; we all have them. You should never ignore them. But if you're going to do this job, and do it well, you'll have to learn to file them away and use that intelligence of yours to build a case based on evidence that the Crown attorney will kiss you on the lips for. Know what I'm saying?"

"Yeah."

Ellie finished the doughnut and rubbed her fingertips together to get rid of the crumbs and cinnamon. Massaging her temple, she asked, "Did her description remind you of anyone?"

"No. Maybe he's from out of town after all."

"Maybe."

"But I don't spend nearly as much time in the township as I used to. It's a fairly big county, Ellie."

"Point taken." She pulled out her cellphone and speed-dialled Dave Martin. Setting the phone to speaker, she held it up between herself and Kevin as she sipped coffee with her free hand.

"Speak of the devil," Martin said. "I was just about to give you folks a call."

Ellie explained what they needed from a return visit to the Hansen home. This time they could confine themselves to the main level, but all the floor surfaces and tables needed to be processed, with a particular emphasis on hairs, fibres, or other trace material. She told Martin they now believed there was an urgent need to have CFS process their case material on a priority basis in order to prevent harm to Vivian Hansen, and she would provide written justification for the request.

When it was Martin's turn, he reported that the processing of latent fingerprints collected at the house and car yard had been completed. "You'll be particularly interested in a print we lifted from the Range Rover's key fob, because it gave us a hit. A specimen by the name of Leonard Robert Ross, DOB June 15, 1984, last known address 460 Caintown Road, Yonge Township. Has a record for impaired driving, possession of cannabis, and, interestingly, careless use of a firearm."

"Lennie Ross," Kevin said.

Ellie turned. "You know him?"

"We're acquainted."

chapter TWENTY-TWO

That evening, Ellie left the detachment building with her laptop filled with reports to read. In the parking lot, she glanced up at the night sky and was relieved to see faint stars overhead. Although the wind was cold, the sky was staying clear, which hopefully meant there would be no more snow overnight. She made a mental note to check the forecast online before going to bed.

Sound and movement startled her as she rounded the end of the Crown Vic. A shadow shifted behind another car farther down from her, but as her hand flew under her jacket reflexively to grip the stock of her SIG Sauer, Craig Dart stepped into the light from a window, cellphone pressed to his ear.

Ellie took a deep breath. As Dart stared at the phone in his hand and shoved it into his coat pocket, she could see he was angry. She walked across the frozen gravel toward him. "Something wrong, Craig?"

He shook his head in disgust. "Everything's fine. Wonderful."

Ellie stopped, noticing for the first time that the hood on Dart's car was up. "Won't start again?"

Dart said nothing, looking at his watch.

It was a crappy little eight-year-old Hyundai hatchback

that had apparently given Dart trouble ever since he'd bought it second hand four years ago. Patterson had described to her Dart's constant preoccupation with money and his worries about debt. Dart's wife Norma was a bookkeeper who hadn't worked since the birth of their second daughter, who was now three years old. They carried a large mortgage on their house, their older daughter was heavily into figure skating, a surprisingly expensive sport, and Norma's father in Barrie was a disabled veteran who needed the extra money they sent him every month just to get by. Not all Dart's stress, Patterson had explained, came from trying to get out from underneath his father's constant disapproval. A lot of it was a result of trying to make ends meet on a constable's salary while never seeming to catch a break when it came to unexpected expenses.

Ellie walked around to the front of the car and peered in under the hood. "If I knew anything about cars, I'd try to help you get it going. Do you need a boost?"

"No." Dart folded his arms, staring at the road.

"Did you call CAA?"

Dart shook his head. "A tow truck's coming."

"You should get CAA. It's worth it."

"I can't *afford* CAA, Ellie."

She stood next to him, staring out at the road. "Is it the battery again?"

Dart grunted.

"I thought it was new."

"It is. It's probably the alternator."

"Uh oh." A very expensive repair job, as Ellie understood it. One that his bank account likely couldn't handle without additional credit.

A truck of some kind passed on the highway at full speed, its red tail lights disappearing into the darkness. "That was a good report you gave us tonight, Craig. It's important to follow up on it."

Headlights appeared from the other direction and passed the detachment without slowing. Dart stared after them in silence.

Earlier in the evening, he'd kicked off their team meeting

with copies of a report he'd prepared on Steve Barron and his biker connections in Sudbury. Between 2010 and 2012 Barron shared a Sudbury duplex with his cousin Marc. Six years older, Marc Barron had a record featuring two arrests for assault, one of which had resulted in a conviction, and a DUI.

"As you can see on page two," he said, "the cousin's a known former hang-around of the Hells Angels who went underground seven years ago when Sudbury arrested three senior members and the chapter went through a shake-up. According to our intel, if you turn to the next page, he's been linked to another club who've opened a chapter up there."

"The Iron Horses," Kevin said, reading.

"They're known to have recently gotten into narcotics distribution in the north, although on a much lesser scale than the Angels."

"I understand that Sudbury's a hub for northern distribution," Kevin said.

"That's right," Merkley agreed. "The money they can make in the north is ten times what they'd get down here. But we don't have a lot of intel on them right now. They're extremely secretive, and we're still trying to cultivate a confidential informant on the inside who can give us a better idea of what they're up to."

"So we're operating on the assumption," Dart said, jumping back in, "that Hansen made a connection to them via the Barrons and has been using his business to transport product up there, bringing back payment in an exchange vehicle."

The disagreements had come when the discussion turned to the question of where Hansen's product was coming from. Dart had directed their attention to another page in his report where he'd explained that Jamaica was still considered a primary source country for cannabis resin. Intelligence indicated it either came through Pearson International Airport in Toronto or Pierre Elliott Trudeau International Airport in Montreal, or across the land border at various points along the St. Lawrence corridor.

Kevin then suggested that they might want to consider a local producer. He began to describe his earlier conversation with one of his confidential informants, but Dart dismissively cut him off.

“There’s absolutely no intel suggesting BHO production in that township, Walker.”

“How would you know? How many informants does the drug unit have in Yonge Township? When was the last time the eradication program even came near there?”

“Yeah, right. A 120-square-kilometre scrap of rock with next to no agriculture to begin with, and your big player’s some medical grow guy who’s already gone out of business—”

“A local source isn’t outside the realm of possibility,” Merkley interjected. “God knows, they sprout up like weeds all over the place.” No one laughed at his joke. “Admittedly, we tend to focus on the river corridor, the border crossings, and Gananoque and Brockville. You have to understand, Kevin. Intelligence works on priorities. Top-down, objective-driven, with focused information collection. Dart’s right. Outside of Mallorytown Landing, because it’s a customs reporting station on the river, the rest of the township just isn’t on the radar because nothing so far has put it there. Since you’ve been boots on the ground, maybe we should have had this conversation a while ago. Do you have something for us, something suggesting a local grower who might be producing the BHO in question?”

It was obvious to Ellie that Kevin didn’t want to step on Dart’s toes. Dart was their drug enforcement detective, and the last thing Kevin wanted to do was make it personal. Challenging Dart on his own turf wouldn’t exactly be a constructive team-building exercise at this early stage of the investigation. On the other hand, if he had information, he needed to get it out onto the table.

“There are two families in the township who probably had grow ops this year,” he said. “One of them, the Turgeons, have apparently scaled back to next to nothing and would be a low-percentage possibility. The others are the Rosses. Their name has come up several times so far.”

“In what way?” Merkley asked.

“The witness who lives across the street from the Hansens

told me she'd seen the victim doing business with Ronnie Ross, the father, in town. A CI told me he's seen Lennie Ross's car at Steve Barron's trailer before, and another CI confirmed not only that the Rosses are still growing and selling weed but that they're dangerous to deal with."

Merkley frowned at Dart. "Name mean anything to you?"

Dart shook his head.

"I'm not saying he's the one," Kevin said, a pained expression on his face. "I'm trying to explain that Lennie Ross is involved just as much as Steve Barron. Another link in the chain that we need to look at more closely."

"Your theory is that Ross produced the BHO we found in the Range Rover," Merkley said, "wholesaled it to Hansen, who distributed it to a connection of Barron's? Based on a CI telling you he's seen Ross's car at Barron's trailer?"

Kevin shook his head. "No, based on the fact that Ident found Lennie Ross's fingerprint on the Range Rover key fob."

Bishop, who'd been silently following the debate so far, sat forward and grinned at Carty. "*Hell*-o!"

Having made his point that they had another option to consider, Kevin went on to describe the interview with Vivian Hansen and her admission that she'd had a late-night visitor on Monday. He told them that Wiltse was busy with new warrants to get Ident back into the Hansen house and trailer in search of physical evidence left behind by this unknown subject, and he explained their decision to ask CFS for priority processing of their findings. He then reported on their interviews of Ken Price and Dave Ryan's wife. Bishop confirmed that Ryan had crossed the border last Friday and was still in the United States, ruling him out as a possible suspect.

After Merkley walked them through what he'd told Ellie earlier about Hansen's financial records, the meeting had ended with Dart's carefully-prepared report on Steve Barron trumped by Lennie Ross's fingerprint. His theory of an outside shooter was superseded by the strong possibility that a local producer was their primary suspect. He'd begun the day with a failed interrogation, had vented his active dislike of Ellie in front of everyone, and now was standing outside with her in the freezing darkness, waiting for a tow truck to take him and his worthless car to a garage where his bank account would take another hit that it couldn't sustain.

A tow truck coming from the direction of Brockville slowed at the entrance to the parking lot and turned in.

"Looks like this is you," Ellie said.

Dart remained silent, moving slowly forward.

Ellie walked away, disappointed by his sullen refusal to accept her olive branch. She wanted to kick his ass and tell him to grow up, but instead she bit her lip, swallowed the words, and got into the Crown Vic.

chapter TWENTY-THREE

In the laundry room, next to the apartment-sized washer and dryer, Ellie found a set of wooden TV tray tables. She set up one on each side of the recliner, one for her deluxe pizza from the Silver Kettle, now half gone, and the other for her bottle of beer, cellphone, and cigarettes. Tipped back in the recliner, feet up, she was reading Carty's reports on her laptop while she ate.

Each report detailed a telephone interview he'd conducted with car dealerships Bill Hansen had done business with in the last ten years. Carty had methodically plowed through the list he'd compiled from Hansen's files and had spoken to someone at each business on the list except for the last, Wright Honda in Kingston. Since Ellie and Kevin were due in Kingston tomorrow to attend Hansen's autopsy, she'd told Carty they'd stop in there themselves after the post to finish off the list.

Carty was a good writer. While most law enforcement officers—Bishop, for example—tended to write reports in a crabbed, overly formal style that was difficult to read and easy to parody, Carty used plain language and simple sentences to communicate his information. It matched what she'd observed of his precise, military style and calm professionalism.

Hansen had done business with a total of thirty-nine dealerships in the past decade, but only twelve in the last two years. The farthest west was in Orangeville, the farthest north was in Sudbury, and the farthest east was in Cornwall. After speaking to six or seven of them, Carty had recognized a common theme—Hansen's business on the wholesale side had been slowly shrinking as dealerships pulled away from him. A general manager at a Ford dealership in Peterborough bluntly told Carty he'd heard that Hansen was cloning VINs. For him, as well as a few other dealers the man knew, it was the kiss of death as far as Hansen was concerned.

The process involved taking the unique vehicle information number, or VIN, from a legitimate car and printing it on a blank replica of a VIN plate. This fake plate would replace the VIN in a stolen car. When accompanied by falsified paperwork, it gave the car a superficially clean history. Often thieves would circulate through parking lots at shopping malls or other public places, looking for high-end vehicles of a make and model that matched cars on their shopping list. Using a cellphone, they'd quickly lean over the windshield and photograph the dashboard VIN plates in these cars to capture the numbers for their cloning process.

No one had actually reported receiving a stolen vehicle from Hansen, though. The owner of the Cornwall Toyota dealer told Carty the rumours were "pure horseshit." His theory was that someone was trying to sabotage Hansen's business, although he had no possible candidates in mind.

Carty was tracking down a list of registered wholesalers in eastern Ontario. Once he had it, he would cross-check it against all the other lists the team was putting together. It was more legwork, more of the necessary, if mind-numbing, drudgery that was part of any investigation.

Her cellphone vibrated. She picked it up and checked the number, but didn't recognize it. A glance at her watch told her that it was just a few minutes past ten thirty. "Detective Inspector March."

"Ellie, this is your next-door neighbour calling."

"Mr. Ballantyne?" Surprised, she lowered the lid on the laptop. "How did you get this number?"

Ridge chuckled. "Well, now, you're the detective, aren't you? How do you think I got it?"

"From Kevin."

"Right in one. Am I interrupting anything critical?"

The laptop beeped as it went into hibernation mode.

"No, I'm just reading. Is there something I can do for you?"

"I saw your lights and wondered if you'd care to have a glass with me. I'm taking a break and was just about to open a bottle of single malt when it crossed my mind you might have a burning curiosity, being a police officer and all, about what the inside of this place of mine looks like. If you're not busy."

Ellie hesitated. "I wouldn't want to disturb you."

"This bottle I mention is a Glenrothes, the 1994 vintage which, I have to admit, is my favourite. Let me read you the tasting notes: 'fruity, toffee, marshmallows, lemon citrus.' I got it from a friend of mine this summer on my seventieth birthday. As in seven-zero, seven decades, born an extremely long time ago, pretty damned old and used up now. Isolated, lonely, harmless. If you catch my general drift."

Ellie looked at her reflection, bright against the black glass of the sliding French doors. "You're sure it's not too late?"

"My dear woman, you forget. I'm a musician. My day starts at about half-past noon and ends at four in the morning. This is my equivalent to your mid-afternoon break. If police detectives take breaks, that is."

"Occasionally." Her phone suddenly blipped. "I've got another call. Wait one." She pressed buttons on the phone and put it back to her ear. "Detective Inspector March."

"Ellie, it's Dave Martin. We're all done at the Hansen house."

"How'd it go?"

"Fine. We did a thorough vacuuming and brought the living room carpet with us for good measure. If our guy shed a hair from his balding pate, we'll find it. Talk to you tomorrow."

"Great, Dave. Thanks." She ended the call and switched back to Ridge. "Sorry about that."

"Have you caught your bad guy? Should I give you a rain

check?"

"No, nothing so dramatic. I'll be over in five minutes."

Ridge was waiting for her at the side door. She pulled off her boots as he hung up her coat, then followed him into the kitchen. "There's the whisky," he said, waving at a long expanse of shiny stone countertop. "I also have red and white wine. And there's beer in the refrigerator, if you prefer that."

"I'd love a glass of red wine, thank you. You have a beautiful place, Mr. Ballantyne."

"Thank you. Call me Ridge."

As he removed the cork from the bottle of wine and chose a glass from an overhead rack, Ellie looked around. It was an enormous kitchen by her standards, with brushed metal appliances and maple cabinets. It was the sort of place featured in magazines. Rather like Gareth's condo, she thought.

"Do you like to cook?" he asked, handing her the glass.

"No." She sipped the wine; it was delicious.

"I suppose you wouldn't have the time, for one thing." He ran a small glass of amber liquid under his nose. "They say that as long as your sense of smell is still functioning, you haven't yet started down the slippery slope of Alzheimer's disease." His nostrils flared. "Yes, there's the toffee, I daresay." He raised the glass. "Here's to neighbours." He sipped and nodded. "Always very nice."

He led her out of the kitchen, past the dining room with the wooden table and wagon wheel chandelier she'd seen from outside this afternoon, into the great room where large black windows faced the lake. "No view right now, of course, but it's lovely in the daytime."

Ellie felt herself drawn to the large stone fireplace in which a fire burned energetically.

Ridge pointed over her head. "Upstairs is the master bedroom, two bedrooms, and a loft where we sometimes like to jam when we're brainstorming. I have a couple of friends in the Merrickville area who come down once or twice a week. We call ourselves The Happy Teazle. After the plant, you know?" He rolled his eyes at her. "It's all in fun."

Ellie pointed at an acoustic guitar on a stand. "This is yours?"

"One of several," Ridge said. He smiled. "Would you like to see the studio?"

"I'd love to." Sipping her wine, Ellie followed him into a short hallway. The walls were lined with framed posters of rock concerts from the 1960s and 1970s. She paused before an illustration of a young man with an afro haircut, sideburns, and a Nehru jacket with an elaborate paisley design. In typical psychedelic lettering, the poster advertised a three-day appearance at the Fillmore Auditorium in San Francisco by Pink Floyd, the Amazing String Players, and Blue Cheer. "This is very striking. You collect these?"

Ridge smiled. "As a matter of fact, I was there."

"At this concert?"

Ridge tapped his finger lightly on the glass. "Pink Floyd headlined the show, of course. This was actually our first North American appearance." His finger moved down and tapped again. "We were scared to death. Imagine, the Fillmore. Four working-class kids from Glasgow."

"The Amazing String Players? You were in this band?"

"John Woods and I got together in '62, in Glasgow. Called ourselves The Amazing Lepers. Kind of daft, but it got us a bit of attention when we needed it." He moved down the hall to a framed photograph of five young people sitting at a cloth-covered table in an outdoor setting, with trees and a grassy hill in the background. "That's yours truly," he said, pointing to a clean-shaven young man in the foreground with shoulder-length black hair and a tentative smile. He moved his finger to a muscular, long-haired blond in a blue tank top. "That's John. This is Amy Jacobs, next to him. She joined us in '65. Played the harp. Beautiful instrument, but a bit of a challenge to travel with. We changed our name when she came on board. We brought in Eric to play drums," he tapped the other young man in the picture, "then got ourselves discovered. Bob Parsons signed us to Elektra, and suddenly the world was ours for the taking."

Ellie pointed at the other young woman in the picture, a shy-looking brunette wearing a white dress embroidered with red and blue flowers. "Who's this?"

Ridge sighed. "Nancy. She wrote lyrics for us, back then. She and I were ... together."

"She's beautiful."

"She was." Ridge sampled his whisky. "Unfortunately, like a lot of us back then, she didn't make it."

Ellie frowned.

"We broke up in '73, she and I. We were in LA at the time, and she'd pretty much lost control. She died of an overdose on February 14, 1974. Valentine's Day. It was a knife through my heart, I can tell you that."

"I'm sorry," Ellie said. She stared at the photo. With long, wavy hair, clear skin, slender, bare arms, and a shy smile, Nancy looked young, happy, and innocent.

"This picture was taken in Scotland, a month before we started that first tour in '67. She saved my life, though. I really believe it."

"Oh?"

"When she died. I'd only experimented up to then. Just a toker, really. I didn't like the hard stuff and pretty much stayed away from it. But the pressure was getting to all of us, John was into heroin already, and I was looking for something else too, I admit. But when she died, the *way* she died, so horribly, that was my wake-up call. I swore off all of it, went easy on the booze, and got back to the music. Which was, after all, supposed to be the reason we were there in the first place, wasn't it? Not for the lifestyle, not for the money. For the music."

"That must have been very difficult for you."

"It was incredibly difficult. But you know what? Something absolutely unexpected happened to me." He moved down to a multi-coloured poster advertising an evening concert in Central Park, New York City, on August 1974 with Led Zeppelin, Three Dog Night, Lynyrd Skynyrd, and The Amazing String Players. "This was our first gig after releasing *Heartbeat Echoes*. We played the entire album for them that night. The audience was completely blitzed, and we went on right before Zeppelin, so nobody, absolutely nobody was listening to us, but that was our best performance ever, by far. All the material was mine. I started writing it a week after Nancy's funeral, we recorded it in late July, and the album came out three days before this gig. It was our *Close to the Edge*, our signature album, where everything inexplicably just came together for us. We'd left the psychedelic folk stuff behind with the previous album, *Rolling Hills*, since even John was getting bored with it and wanted to go back to something simpler. Back to the traditional sound we'd started out with." He sighed. "I was very much in love with Nancy, as only a young man can be, but we'd let everything else get in the way, she and I. We'd grown apart." He touched the corner of the frame, then downed the rest of his whisky and beckoned. "Never mind all that. Come and look at the studio."

It was a very sophisticated and expensive-looking set-up. The live room contained a baby grand piano, an array of acoustic and electric guitars on stands, a drum kit, digital keyboards, microphones, and amplifiers. The control room was an impressive display of sound boards, computers, and other esoteric-looking equipment. Ellie listened as he explained the purpose and function of each device, demonstrating with short excerpts from his current project, which was a public service advertisement for a provincial mental health association. Ellie thought the music was very good, almost haunting in its beauty, but Ridge expressed only dissatisfaction. Then he abruptly picked up his glass, said "I need a little more of this," and led the way back out to the kitchen.

Ellie accepted a refill of the red wine and they took their drinks back into the great room, where they settled into chairs close to the fireplace.

"How do you like it down here on the lake?"

Ellie shrugged. "I haven't seen much of it so far, but it seems like a nice, quiet place."

"It is. The hockey player who owns your cottage has some noisy parties in the summer, but he doesn't come around very often. Otherwise, everyone's very quiet. It's a private lake, spring-fed, and the people who own the properties around the shoreline behave responsibly. We have an association that looks after things, deals with the ministry on whatever issues come up, and all that fine stuff. I don't get directly involved, that's not my thing, but I'm appreciative of the efforts of the others."

"Are there many people down here, this time of year?"

"No. There's myself, a retired couple down at the far end who are originally from Delaware, and that's pretty much it. There's the place that's owned by Kevin's former colleague, Waddell. He's got some guy staying there right now who works for him, as I understand it. Burrows, I think his name is. Then there's you."

Ellie sipped her wine. "Do you know Chuck Waddell?"

"Some. Have you met him? A blustery, aggressive bag of wind, if you ask me. Kevin thinks the world of him, but I could certainly do without having made his bloody acquaintance, and that's a fact."

"I've met the man."

"He was a prison guard with the federal correctional service, apparently, before he became a police officer. He was on the Kingston police for a few years and then moved up here to the village. Brought that mean-spirited, big hoose mentality with him." He laughed at Ellie's frown. "Sorry. My Glaswegian slang's flaring up again. Jail. Prison mentality."

"Ah." Ellie considered her wine. "Kevin tells me Waddell mentored him while he was on the local police force."

"Mmm." Ridge watched the fire for a moment. "I came up here in 2000. There was a run-down little cottage here when I bought the property. I had it torn down to build this lovely, lovely palace. I bought in late summer and construction went on right through the fall. I was teaching at Queen's at the time and would come up whenever I had a free day, to meet with the contractor. You know, to see how it was going, stick my nose in, change my mind about this or that. Every blessed time I set foot on this lot, that damned Waddell showed up in his police car, like some American sheriff from the deep south, to ask me all kinds of questions about my business, my intentions up here, and all the rest of it. I moved in the first week of November, and on the second day he came to the door and invited himself in, looked around, and had the gall to ask if I had any illegal substances on the property. I'm afraid I wasn't very polite in inviting him to leave."

Ellie waited.

Ridge held up his glass. "I have a wee drink, now and again. I smoke mentholated cigarettes, and I take medication for hypertension, cholesterol, and migraines. But I left the dope behind forty years ago, as I mentioned, and I haven't touched it since, nor anything else that's illegal in this country." He shook his head. "Forgive me if I'm a wee bit defensive on the subject."

"Would I be correct in guessing, then, that you're unaware of anyone who *is* involved in drug distribution around here?"

"You'd be quite correct."

They listened to the sound of the fire in the fireplace. Ellie drained her glass, sensing it was time to leave. She'd taken a liking to Ridgeway Ballantyne, and hoped she hadn't put him off by slipping in that last, work-related, question. She stood up. "I should get back. Thanks for the tour and the wine."

Ridge continued to stare at the fire for a moment. Then he jerked, noticed that she was on her feet, and shot out of the chair. "Got it," he said, flashing a sudden grin.

"I'm sorry?"

He laughed, touching her arm. "I apologize. I just figured out what's wrong with that piece. It just played itself through, in my head, the way it's *supposed* to be. What a terrible host I am. You have to leave?"

"Yes, I still have things to do before bedtime."

"Come back again. Tomorrow, if you can. Whenever you like." He showed her back to the entry, watched her slip on her boots and coat, and opened the door.

"Good night," Ellie said.

As the door closed behind her, she looked back through the window and saw him run a hand through his hair, count a beat with his finger, and hurry off toward the studio.

chapter TWENTY-FOUR

Kevin leaned against the back fender of the Crown Vic and concentrated on taking long breaths. In through the nostrils and out through the mouth. In and out. In and out. In and out.

The cold wind whipping off the water felt good. Realizing his overcoat was still unfastened, he zipped it up with unsteady fingers. Lake Ontario was not yet frozen over, and the water was choppy with whitecaps. The windmills in the distance on Wolfe Island turned steadily. Traffic on King Street buzzed and growled behind him. Kevin fumbled in his pocket for his toque.

When they'd arrived at the Kingston General Hospital campus, Ellie had discovered, to their chagrin, that the underground parking garage serving both KGH and Queen's University was full. There were no empty spots at all on Stuart Street. She cruised around, found nothing, and they ended up down in a staff parking lot on the waterfront next to the steam plant. Grouchy, Ellie threw a police placard onto the dashboard and they made the long trek back up Lower University Avenue to the lab building where the autopsy of Bill Hansen was being performed.

It was Kevin's first exposure to a post-mortem examination, and he'd started out well enough. Identification Constable Bill Jamieson, who'd accompanied the body from the scene Tuesday morning, was already present, along with another constable whose name Kevin couldn't remember. They'd overseen the external examination before Ellie and Kevin arrived and had taken photographs as the clothing was removed and bagged and the body was cleaned. It was then taken for a CT scan and x-rays, and when it returned it was weighed and measured, more photographs were taken, and the internal examination began.

The forensic pathologist, Dr. Carey Burton, was friendly and kind. In his early forties, he was short and heavy-set, but he moved with the grace and poise of a dancer. He and his assistant calmly worked over the body while Jamieson took more photographs, following Dr. Burton's directions. Biological samples were drawn and secured with a CFS seal. Kevin frowned at the powerful odours rising from the body, and stared as the heart was removed, bringing blood with it. He glanced at Ellie and Patterson, who were following each movement without expression.

He listened as Dr. Burton directed that the esophagus and duodenum be tied off, and the significance of those actions didn't strike him until the stomach was removed and handed to an assistant. Kevin realized that the organ still contained remnants of Bill Hansen's last meal, the dinner order from the Silver Kettle Restaurant that Birdie had delivered to the car yard around seven o'clock Monday evening.

The heart attack special—a bacon cheeseburger, Skinny Jimmy's special home-cooked fries, and a Coke.

He turned away, his gorge suddenly rising.

The rest was a blur. Somehow he managed to get out of the morgue, shed his protective garments, put on his boots and coat, and get out of the building before throwing up. The next thing he knew, he was back in the steam plant parking lot, bent over the rear fender of the Crown Vic, unable to stop retching.

Finally, he managed to stand upright and regain control of his body. He felt ashamed and embarrassed. He'd been fine at the crime scene. He'd managed to deal with the unpleasantness of confronting Bill Hansen's dead body lying frozen in the snow, blood everywhere, eyes glazed over. But the dissection of a man he'd actually known had been different. So very different. The revulsion had caught him by surprise. The stomach—

With an effort, he forced his thoughts to Hansen himself, the man, as he'd known him in life. He'd actually only spoken to him three times. As a rookie constable he'd pulled Hansen over for speeding on a Sunday afternoon in August 2003. Hansen was behind the wheel of a candy-apple red 1976 Corvette Stingray that he'd just bought in an auction, he explained sheepishly as Kevin wrote out the ticket. He'd been anxious to see what it could do.

"Well," Kevin told him, "you were doing 124 in an 80, so I guess it runs okay."

"That's just scratching the surface," Hansen had replied, taking back his licence, "but I'll never know for sure, now." He waved the licence. "I don't want to lose this."

The second time he'd talked to Hansen was five years later, in the Silver Kettle. Hansen was waiting for an order and Kevin had gone in to pick up a sandwich for lunch. They exchanged small talk, and Kevin asked his opinion of the Grand Cherokee. He needed a new car, and had spotted one at a dealership in Smiths Falls.

"People seem to like them," Hansen said. "Is it the diesel V-6?"

"Yeah."

Hansen nodded. "Better than the gasoline V-6, which gives pretty poor mileage per gallon. The diesel's about 30 per cent better, actually. The engine's made by Mercedes, so there's quality there. It's a good SUV that handles well, so you'll probably like it."

The last time he'd seen Bill Hansen was about three months ago, in mid-September. Kevin had been walking along the sidewalk on Main Street when Hansen stepped out of Lois Shipman's second-hand store and walked right past him without looking up. His expression, Kevin recalled, had been odd. Almost a mixture of anger and fear. Kevin spoke to him, but Hansen kept on going without giving any sign that he'd heard.

Wiping his mouth on his sleeve now, his stomach under

control, Kevin saw Ellie coming down the sidewalk, head lowered, hands shoved into the pockets of her overcoat, kicking chunks of icy snow left behind by the sidewalk plow. She hurried across the intersection into the parking lot and brought out her key fob, unlocking the Crown Vic.

"Sorry it was locked. You must be freezing." She opened the driver's side door and got in.

The fact of the matter was that Kevin hadn't even tried to get into the car. The thought that he was locked out in the cold hadn't crossed his mind. His focus had been entirely elsewhere. He slowly got into the car and belted himself in.

"How are you feeling?" Ellie asked.

"Better. Sorry I screwed up."

Ellie snorted, starting the engine and cranking up the heat. "Forget about it. You lasted a lot longer than a lot of other people at their first one. Most don't make it past the Y-cut."

"Next time I'll be okay. It just caught me off guard, that's all."

"I know. And it didn't help that you knew the guy."

"No, that didn't help." He glanced at her. "I suppose Scott's pissed at me."

"Would it make you feel any better if I told you he and Jamieson laughed their asses off as soon as you were out the door?"

"I don't know. I don't think so."

"Well, nobody's pissed at you, so don't worry about it. And you get brownie points for not puking on the floor. Pathologists hate it when cops do that. Trust me."

"Yeah. Great."

She patted his arm. "You look better now. The cold air put some colour back into your face." She fastened her seat belt. "You left just as it was getting interesting. You said that the delivery guy, Willie, dropped off Hansen's meal at seven, right?"

"Yes."

"Dr. Burton says the stomach contents give us a decent shot at narrowing TOD. According to him, food generally clears the stomach four hours after consumption. At death, the food stops moving. So, given the amount that was still in there, he figures the meal was ingested about two and a half hours, max, before he was killed. So we can look at a window between nine and ten. We were figuring nine thirty, so it looks like we're right on track. Are you okay to talk about this?"

"Sure. I'm fine."

"The shot severed the carotid artery. He bled to death while he was lying there in the snow. Which takes a little while. At least he would have been unconscious." She frowned. "But there were no other signs of violence. No bruising, no cuts or scrapes, no puncture marks, nothing like that at all. They didn't have to force him to go with them, whoever they were. He went along more or less voluntarily. There was no smell of alcohol or anything else unusual. That's why they tolerate the stench when they're doing post-mortems, because sometimes they smell something important. We'll see what the lab says, but it doesn't look like he was either drunk or drugged."

She put the transmission into reverse and looked over her shoulder. "Everything else was pretty routine," she said, backing out of the parking space. "The main piece of information we're going to come away with is a pretty reliable time of death."

She shifted into drive and rolled up to the parking lot exit. Leaning forward, she grabbed the placard from the dashboard and threw it onto the back seat. When there was a break in the traffic, she turned left onto King. "The dealership's on Bath Road. You okay to check them out with me?"

"Yes."

"You still sound a little off."

"I'm humiliated. Mortified. A little off, yeah."

"You'll get over it. We all do."

They were heading north on Portsmouth Avenue when Kevin's phone vibrated. It was Bishop.

"Two things," the stout detective said without preamble. "We found the dealer in Brockville who supplied the butane to old man Ross this fall. They deal with them on a regular basis for welding stuff, but this was Ross's first butane purchase. It was part of a larger order."

"Good," Kevin said. "Well done."

"You okay? You sound a little hoarse."

"I'm fine. What else?"

"We talked to the kid who made the delivery. He admits to buying weed from the Rosses whenever he's out there. That gets us in and puts all their asses in the room where we can ask them some very pointed questions."

"When?"

"Soon. This afternoon. It's gonna be a party, Kev. Try not to miss it."

"Thanks." Kevin ended the call and explained to Ellie what was happening.

"You said before that you know Lennie Ross."

"Yeah, we have some history."

Ellie pulled into the left-hand lane and stopped at a red light. "Tell me about it."

Kevin glanced at the price of gas at the Shell station across the road. It was two cents more per litre than where he filled up, north of Brockville. "We played hockey against each other when I was in Junior B. I played defence for Brockville and Lennie was a right winger for Athens. We got into a few scraps."

"Oh?" The advance green light came on, and Ellie accelerated around the corner onto Bath Road.

"We were both eighteen. That turned out to be my last year in competitive hockey, because I was already the biggest guy on the ice and not fast enough to make the move up to major junior. In my earlier days, at the bantam and midget levels, I was kind of a rough player. One Saturday morning a kid got hurt by accident trying to take a run at me. It changed my attitude toward the game. So in Junior B, I took it easy and concentrated on playing good defence. Unfortunately, though, our games with Athens were different. We played them eight times and they weren't very good that year. Lennie sat at the end of their bench and played with the fourth line when their coach wanted to stir things up. He was a dirty player and a fighter. Right away I realized I had to do something to protect our better players. As I say, we ended up getting into a few fights. He was a mean prick and could handle himself, but he couldn't match me for size and strength. I ended up pounding him every time. It never slowed him down, though. We must have had ten fights that season. By the end of the year we had an understanding of sorts. He took it easier on our players, and he stopped hitting me from behind and trying to take out my knees."

"All the fun I've missed over the years, disliking sports."

"Yeah, well, it didn't exactly turn us into best buddies."

"Oh?"

Kevin pointed as they passed through the intersection of Bath and Queen Mary Road. "There it is, up ahead on the right."

Ellie shifted into the right-hand lane.

"When I worked traffic," Kevin said, "I wrote him up a couple of times for speeding. And the DUI on his record was mine, too."

Ellie slowed and turned into the lot of the Honda dealership. One of the salesmen was out in the yard, cleaning snow off the cars. He glanced over his shoulder and gave them a little wave. He looked frozen and unhappy.

The general manager's name was Grant Devine. Tall and skinny, prematurely balding with a sand-coloured Van Dyke beard, he met them on the showroom floor and politely examined their badges and identification before admitting he'd done business with Bill Hansen in the past. Not for several years, though. When Ellie invited him to explain further, he led them into his office.

They sat down at a little table in the corner. The walls were covered with posters of Honda cars and trucks, framed diplomas and certificates testifying to Devine's education and experience, and a photograph of a group of men on a tropical beach somewhere. Devine closed the door and, without a glance at Kevin, offered Ellie a beverage—coffee, tea, or bottled water? When she declined, he sat down across from her and folded his hands on the table with a professional smile. "How may I help you today?"

"How well did you know Mr. Hansen?" Ellie asked.

"So-so. I was the one who did the buying and selling with him, I suppose for about a six-year period. A lot of it was over the phone or by e-mail, but he stopped in about once every two months or so. We'd talk."

"How did he strike you, Mr. Devine? How did he come across? Honest? Dishonest?"

"I thought he was fine. Seemed like a fairly nice guy. Loved to talk cars. I'd have to throw him out of my office, practically, or I'd lose most of the afternoon listening to him. That kind of guy."

Ellie nodded. Kevin watched her write something down in her notebook. His was in the Crown Vic. Another slip-up.

"How long have you worked here, Mr. Devine?" Ellie continued.

"I've been here sixteen years. I started in our service department, became service manager, moved over to sales manager, then up to general manager. And please, call me Grant."

"All right, Grant. I'm Ellie."

The smile he showed her, Kevin noticed, was less professional than the previous one had been. "How long have you been with the OPP, Ellie?"

"Seems like forever. So, you were hands-on with all the financial transactions between the dealership and Mr. Hansen?"

"For most of them, yes."

"How did they go?"

"Never a problem. We mostly bought from him, so there wasn't anything really to go wrong, but occasionally he'd buy from us, stock we couldn't move and needed to get rid of. We usually send them to an auction service, but Bill would ask about certain vehicles when he was here, and buy them if we were clearing them out. Most of the time, he bought them through his personal account, if I remember correctly. Wholesalers don't generally work that way, but I suspect he was turning them around for a mark-up of some sort. I never asked. What's it like, investigating murders? You must have an exciting life."

Ellie looked up from her notebook and blinked at him. "It's fine, thanks. Why did you stop doing business with him?"

"Actually, it was a phone call from one of our district managers. He said he'd heard a rumour that Bill was cloning VINs. We had to back-check everything we'd bought from him. It was a royal pain, and everybody around here was pretty unhappy about it. We didn't find anything that wasn't kosher, but we sent all the information in and waited to see what would happen. The word came down that we were in the clear, but we were to cut him off. No more trading with him, period."

"How long ago was that?"

"Let's see, I guess about seven years ago."

"Can you give me the name and contact information of that district manager?"

"I'd love to, Ellie, but I don't know if it'll help you at all. He passed away last year."

"I'll take the number of his replacement."

Devine produced his cellphone and navigated through the directory, then read off the current district manager's name, address, and phone number. After putting his phone away, he touched the baby fuzz on the top of his skull self-consciously. "May I ask you a question?"

Still writing, Ellie nodded. "Sure."

"I see you're not wearing any rings. Is that just because you're working, or are you single?"

Trying valiantly to suppress a smile, Kevin watched Ellie stop writing and slowly look up at Devine.

"I beg your pardon?"

Flushing bright red from his shirt collar to the top of his skull, Devine covered his mouth with his hand. "I'm very sorry if I stepped out of line. I never ... it's just ... I'm divorced, and you seem really smart and all that, and I thought ... well, I guess I didn't think. This isn't like me, at all."

Ellie shook her head, slowly. "So, let me see if I understand this correctly. Your district manager heard a rumour that Hansen was dealing in stolen vehicles, but you'd never seen any indication of that in any of your personal dealings with him? Is that correct?"

"Um, yes, that's right."

"None of the vehicles you bought from him ever came up as stolen?"

"No."

"Were you the one who told him the dealership wouldn't do business with him any more?"

"Yes." Devine looked distinctly unhappy.

"How'd that go?"

"Actually, not as bad as I thought it would. It was like he expected it. Which he probably did. I talked to a good friend of mine who's with the Ford dealership in Belleville, and he told me they'd already cut ties with him. The rumour must have been going around all over the place."

"All right." Ellie took out a business card and put it on the table in front of him. "If I give you this, can I expect you to call me if you think of anything else connected to Bill Hansen, but not on some silly excuse to ask me any other personal questions?"

Devine picked up the card and put it into his shirt pocket. "I'll try not to. I mean, if I think of anything, I'll call you. About Bill."

Kevin left his card on the table without a word. It sat there, ignored, as Devine opened the door to show them out.

In the car, Kevin watched Ellie start up the engine and check her mirrors. He waited until they were out on the street before saying, "He likes you because you're smart."

"Be quiet." Her tone was flat, but as she put on her sunglasses Kevin could see amusement creasing the corners of her eyes.

chapter TWENTY-FIVE

They bought sandwiches and Cokes in a Subway restaurant and went back out to the car. Kevin devoured his quickly, surprised to find that he had an appetite. Ellie fiddled with the temperature controls as she ate, trying to coax more heat from the air vent, and as he crumpled his left-over paper into a ball and shoved it into the plastic bag, she glanced at him.

"Feeling better now?"

Kevin nodded, draining his can of Coke.

"You have to have a short memory for that kind of stuff," she said.

"I know. It's not easy, though."

"Of course it's not." Ellie took his garbage from him, added it to hers, and tossed it into the back seat. "That's why you and I are doing this job, and not your next-door neighbour."

She drove north on Gardiners Road to the overpass at the 401 that was dedicated to the memory of John Flagg, an OPP senior constable killed in the line of duty in 2003. As she merged into the eastbound lanes, Kevin looked over at her.

"What made you choose this for a career, Ellie?"

She shrugged, eyes on the highway. "Something I always wanted to do."

"Me too." He waited for a moment. "Why a cop? Why not something else?"

She moved into the left-hand lane to pass a slow-moving tanker truck. "My parents had a shoe store. When I was eleven, some guy came in and robbed them. I was in the store that day, and I was terrified. I hated being that scared, and I promised myself afterward I'd never feel that way again. By the time I was in high school, I knew that going into law enforcement was the best way to deal with it."

A kilometre went by while he thought about it.

"What about you?" she asked. "What made you become a cop?"

"My father."

"He was a cop?"

"He's a drunk," Kevin replied shortly. As they passed the Joyceville exit, he sighed. "His name's Johnnie, appropriately."

"Oh, right. Johnnie Walker."

"His favourite." Kevin shifted, staring out the window. "We don't talk. I haven't seen him in about thirteen years, I guess."

"He's in Brockville?"

Kevin nodded. "In the same house where I grew up. He was a foreman at the detergent factory when I was a kid, a real big shot in his own mind. Heavy drinker, always had a girlfriend working on the shop floor, wasn't home a lot. My mother got stomach cancer when I was fourteen and he stayed away, shacked up with his latest, until she died. No discussion, no argument, no nothing. He just stopped coming home."

"I'm sorry to hear that," Ellie said.

"It took her three years to go. I was an only child, so I took care of everything. The housework, shopping, looking after her. I got a part-time job in the evenings to earn a little extra for us to get by. I'd just started Grade Twelve when she died, and I hadn't seen him the entire time. Then all of a sudden there he was at the funeral. He drove me home, went into the living room, turned on the TV, and that was that. It was his house again."

The car was quiet. Ellie passed a tractor trailer and eased back into the right-hand lane.

"I finished that school year with him, then I got my student loan and moved to Kingston to do my police foundations program at St. Lawrence. I never saw him again. But, to answer your question, I went into law enforcement because I wanted to be the kind of man who's responsible. Know what I mean? Unlike him, I wanted to be someone people could look to for help and depend on to do whatever had to be done, no matter how hard it was."

"A guy with a strong sense of justice who wants to get out there and right wrongs, save the innocent, and bust the guilty."

He stiffened, thinking she was making fun of him, until her tone of voice registered. She was asking, not ridiculing.

"Not the man with the cape, if that's what you mean."

"A lot of different people go into the job for a lot of different reasons, Kevin. A lot of guys your age love the adrenaline rush, they love making the busts and pushing people around. They like being on the edge, where it's dangerous."

Kevin thought immediately of Bishop, who fit that profile. "I'm not like that. I'm not on a power trip. That's not why I'm here."

"Okay." Ellie watched the road for a while. "I'm surprised you didn't go to university. Being a thinker and a reader."

"I couldn't afford it."

They drove in silence for several kilometres, until Ellie nodded at his side of the highway. "Rough country along here."

Kevin looked out the window. They were passing a long stretch where the work crews many years ago had cleared a path for the highway by removing tons of rock from outcroppings and knolls. In some spots the rock cuts bore large icicles where water had flowed down between the crevices during the recent warm spell before freezing into long, thick, vertical ridges.

"Remnants of the Frontenac Arch," Kevin said quietly.

"What's that?"

"Just something I read about."

"Well, now, don't leave me hanging. Talk to me."

Kevin shifted. "Actually, there are tours you can take if you're interested in geology. About a billion years ago, this entire area was a gigantic mountain range. It's referred to as the Frontenac Arch. It gradually eroded down until half a billion years ago the region was flooded by a shallow sea that deposited a sedimentary cover of sandstone, shale, and limestone on top of the igneous rock left over from the Arch."

"I'm glad I asked."

"It's fascinating, when you think about it. This place is basically made up of layers, one on top of the other. A layer of granite from the Arch, which they call the basement rock, a layer of younger soft rocks from the Paleozoic period on top of that, a lot of which has eroded away, leaving knobs sticking up—many of which form the Thousand Islands, by the way—and then during the Ice Age thirteen thousand years ago, this whole area was covered by a glacier that created another layer. Apparently it was a couple of kilometres thick at one point. It deposited gravel and sand as it churned along, and it polished down the granite knobs a little more, and then when it melted, it left a gigantic freshwater lake, Lake Iroquois. So this area went from a giant mountain range to a sea, then to land, then to a lake."

"You're right. It *is* fascinating."

"Go ahead, poke fun. I don't care. And that's hardly the end of the story. When the glacier melted and shrank, the saltwater Champlain Sea rolled in, flooding this whole area again from the east. That left another layer of sediment with all kinds of marine life and minerals only found in the ocean, completely messing up the fossil picture around here. When that finally drained back out, about six thousand years ago, we ended up with our present configuration with the St. Lawrence River , Lake Ontario, and all the smaller lakes, including Sorrow Lake. Along with a confusing mixture of freshwater and ocean fossils."

"I see," Ellie said, politely.

"If you think about it, six thousand years is not a lot of time, compared to what was here a billion years ago, like the rock in those cuts we just passed."

Ellie thought about it, watching the highway.

"It's just something that interests me," Kevin said, trying not to sound defensive. "We take things around us for granted. If people don't actually see something happen in front of them, it doesn't mean very much to them. They spend all their time caught up in what's on the surface of things without having a clue what lies beneath, and without caring, really. Canadians are stereotyped as being preoccupied with topography, especially when it comes to our culture, but I don't think that's the case at all. Not any more. Nobody today gives a second thought to their physical environment. If it's not trending on Twitter or a touch away on Instagram, they haven't a damned clue."

He paused for breath, then shook his head. "If people driving up the hill into Sparrow Lake realized that it was a leftover knob from a gigantic mountain range a billion years old, they might be a little less inclined to get bogged down in all the stupid, shallow crap that screws up their daily lives. It might give them something to think about that's bigger and more meaningful than their own petty little problems."

Ellie glanced over at him. "You don't really believe that, do you?"

Kevin laughed self-consciously. "No. I'm an optimist, but I'm not an idiot. People are people."

"Damned right they are. And thank God, otherwise we'd be out of a job."

Kevin laughed again.

A few kilometres later, when the image of Bill Hansen's detached stomach invaded his head once more and he saw it gripped tightly at each end by the gloved hands of the pathologist's assistant, so as not to spill its contents, he found it no longer had the power to upset him. Next time, he vowed, he'd make it all the way through.

His cellphone vibrated just as they were easing onto the off-ramp at the Mallorytown exit. It was Bishop.

"This is it, Kev. We're up. ETA at the Ross farm is five minutes. What's your twenty?"

"Mallorytown," Kevin replied. "We're on our way." He ended the call and looked at Ellie. "The raid on the Ross farm."

Ellie glanced over. "This better get us something more than just drugs, Kevin."

"I know," he replied, frowning out the window at the landscape he no longer saw.

chapter TWENTY-SIX

Ellie slowed at a bend in the road. The pavement dipped and the Crown Vic bounced, fishtailing slightly.

"Slow down," Kevin cautioned. "This is it, on the right."

Ellie feathered the brakes, reducing speed, and turned onto Caintown Road. They passed a small Presbyterian church and cemetery. She kept both hands on the wheel, concentrating on the road, which was down to a single lane as a result of its narrowness and the snowbanks on either side. She slowed for the dips and curves, and finally they saw the Ross farm ahead on the left. They passed a rocky, snow-covered pasture, a rusted, doorless metal shed housing an old tractor, and suddenly there was nowhere else to go. Vehicles were everywhere, blocking the road and the driveway leading up to the farm. Ellie parked behind an ERT van, and they got out.

Bishop met them halfway up the driveway. "Dart's here somewhere, with his boys. They've got the two brothers, Lennie and Dougie, but they haven't found the old man yet. That shed over there," he pointed to a pre-fabricated metal outbuilding with large open doors, "is jackpot city. There's a drying room, a curing room filled with jars of bud, and even a little greenhouse in back where they've got some winter plants on the go. Even better for us, though, is a room with the whole BHO production set-up. Butane cylinders, pressure pots, pumps, a little freezer with product still in it, the works. They're telling me there's a real good chance they can positively connect the stuff we found in Hansen's vehicle to this stuff here. Something about impurities and the level of THC. Whatever, eh? You were right, Kev. These guys were the vic's suppliers. Fucking A!"

They walked into the yard, which had been plowed out from the house to the barn and surrounding outbuildings. It was filled with police vehicles, including the Drug Enforcement Unit's mobile response vehicle and the ERT canine unit's Suburban. Uniformed officers wearing protective gear ran into the barn just as Kevin reached the back porch of the house. Dart stepped out, caught sight of him, and came over.

"We're still looking for the old man. Surveillance said he was here all morning, and his truck's over there. Give us a little room; we're bringing the brothers out now."

Kevin took a few steps back as the screen door banged open and Lennie Ross, in handcuffs, staggered out onto the back porch in the grasp of a uniformed officer. His mouth was bloody and his eyes were wild.

Bishop chuckled. "He was considerate enough to put up a little fight."

As Lennie was being led across the yard, another officer emerged onto the porch with Dougie Ross. The older brother, who lived with his wife and three children across the road, spotted Kevin and began to struggle. "You know I don't have anything to do with this, Walker. Tell them! Tell them they're making a mistake!"

Kevin didn't respond. His eyes had been drawn to a pair of bulkhead doors at the back of the house that led down to a root cellar. One of the doors opened, and the father, Robbie Ross, emerged with a shotgun held loosely in one hand.

Kevin moved forward to intercept him. "We have a warrant for your arrest, Mr. Ross, and a warrant to search your property. Put down the gun. Let's do this without any trouble."

Ross was short and squat, in his sixties, and his white hair and mutton chop sideburns were wild and uncombed. He held the shotgun above the trigger guard, the muzzle pointed down at the snow.

"Didn't you people see the sign at my gate?" he yelled. "I own this land, and the government's not welcome on it! Back the hell off, right now!"

"I'm afraid we can't do that today, Mr. Ross," Kevin replied, now only a few metres away. "Please put the shotgun down on the ground."

"I told you nothing good would come of all this, Dad!" Dougie called out from the porch as Kevin reached the old man. "I told you to give it up and get rid of it!"

As Ross turned to answer his son, Kevin deftly plucked the shotgun out of his hand.

Uniformed officers rushed in and wrestled the old man to the ground. Kevin handed the shotgun to one of them and calmly walked away.

chapter TWENTY-SEVEN

On Friday night, Kevin got into a fight despite his best efforts to avoid it.

After supper, to please Janie more than anything else, he tossed his hockey equipment into the back of her van and they all drove into Brockville. Janie dropped Caitlyn and Brendan off at her mother's house, then they went on to the arena, where Kevin was scheduled to hit the ice at eight o'clock. He played for the Bruins, a team in a local men's league that included several other OPP officers on its roster. Their opponent this week was the Stars, dominated by Brockville cops. It was fast, aggressive hockey, and the games were always hard fought. Kevin enjoyed the competition, and he was grateful for an excuse to spend an evening away from the case.

Janie watched from a glassed-in area at the north end of the rink with the other wives and girlfriends. They drank beer from plastic cups, gossiped shamelessly, and showed little interest in what was going on down at ice level. Janie's best friend, Kate Donnelly, was here because her husband, Bill Donnelly, was captain of the Bruins. A former right winger with the Kingston Frontenacs, Donnelly had been drafted in the late rounds ten years ago by the Vancouver Canucks but was cut after breaking his ankle in training camp. Now an OPP traffic sergeant working out of Prescott, Donnelly was their best player and a good friend of Kevin. Kate disliked hockey and wanted to talk about their mutual friend, Liz Crook, who was not at the arena tonight. They discussed Liz's attraction to a local lawyer and debated the probability that she and her husband, a police constable in Gananoque, would separate before spring.

Down on the ice, with the score 3-2 in favour of the Bruins in the second period, Jerry Waite, a Brockville cop playing for the Stars, took a clearing pass from a teammate in the Stars' defensive zone and led a rush across centre ice. He cut diagonally through the neutral zone and tried to skate around Kevin, who delivered a crisp hip check at the blue line while skating backwards. Waite hit the boards with a resounding crash and went down. Bill Donnelly reached the puck first and nudged it to his goalie, who trapped it under his big glove, stopping play. Kevin suddenly found himself with his hands full as Waite, back on his skates, charged straight at him. Other players moved to intervene.

"Wow," Kate said, "that guy looks pissed."

Janie sipped her beer, unconcerned. She knew Waite and his wife, Sarah. Waite was older, shorter, and quite a bit lighter than Kevin, and although he had a reputation as an ass-kicking hotshot on the Brockville force, he posed absolutely no threat to Kevin. Janie glanced over at Sarah, who was watching the game with her friends. Sarah grinned and made an obscene up-and-down motion with her fist. Janie laughed, nodding.

The teams lined up for the faceoff in the Bruins zone. No penalties had been assessed, so both Kevin and Waite remained on the ice. When the puck was dropped, a Bruins player immediately cleared it out across the blue line. Waite paid no attention, charging Kevin and dropping his stick and gloves.

Kevin stood his ground, shedding his own gloves. He grabbed the sleeves of Waite's jersey just above the elbows. He had no interest in fighting and hoped that Waite would expend his energy trying to wrestle Kevin off his skates, which he was certainly not strong enough to do. Unexpectedly, though, Waite tore his right arm free of Kevin's grasp and stripped off Kevin's helmet. Before Kevin could latch onto Waite's arm again, the Brockville cop delivered a roundhouse punch that caught Kevin on the left ear.

Annoyed, Kevin belted Waite on the side of the helmet with his open left hand. The force of the blow took Waite off his skates and they fell to the ice together, Kevin on top.

As they stepped into their respective penalty boxes after order had been restored, Waite smashed the butt of his stick against the glass between them several times. Kevin sat down and glared back. Waite screamed a few obscenities at him and broke his stick on the floor of the penalty box.

After the game, everyone headed for a popular Irish-style pub on Parkedale Avenue. Standing at the bar with Janie, Kevin ordered a glass of wine for her and a tonic water for himself. Although he longed for a beer, he was their designated driver for the evening and would abstain. As he paid for their drinks, Waite came up beside him and slapped him on the shoulder.

"What the fuck did you hit me with, you bastard?" He slid onto the stool next to Kevin.

Janie patted Kevin's arm. "Stay out of trouble." She took her wine over to their table with Kate and Bill.

"Which time?" Kevin asked, sitting down next to Waite.

"True enough. You knocked me down twice, you prick." Waite drained his glass and smacked it down on the bar.

Kevin smiled. "What are you drinking?"

"Bass."

Kevin motioned to the bartender. When Waite was sipping from a fresh glass and Kevin was waving away his change, Rob Jensen sat down next to Waite. Pointing his bottle of beer at Kevin, he asked, "Am I going to have to separate you two again?" A regional intelligence officer with the Canada Border Services Agency, Jensen had refereed tonight's game.

"Naw, we're good," Waite said. "It was a clean check, I admit it. I just wanted to see if I could take him down."

Jensen clapped him on the shoulder. "We need to change your medication, Jerry." To Kevin he said, "I hear you guys made a clean bust yesterday."

"That's right."

"The Rosses. I don't know them. How long have they been around?"

Kevin shrugged, poking at the slice of lime in his tonic water. "Apparently they've had a grow op going for several years."

"I heard that the BHO is a new thing for them," Waite said. "Right?"

"Probably. Anyway, they weren't on the drug team's radar before this."

"I also heard you got torn a new one for pulling a hero stunt."

Kevin grimaced. The incident commander in charge of the raid had delivered a prolonged tongue-lashing to him for having jeopardized the safety of everyone on site by taking matters into his own hands and disarming Ronnie Ross. Once he'd finally run out of things to yell, Patterson had drawn Kevin aside to deliver his own stinging lecture. Kevin was keeping his fingers crossed that it would remain a verbal reprimand and not make it into writing. At any rate, it was a subject he preferred not to discuss.

Waite asked, "How's your big murder case coming?"

"It's coming."

"I've heard of that chick who's your case manager." He shook his head. "Another Dickless Tracy."

"I hear she's very good," Jensen disagreed. "Very experienced."

"The right kind of experience can be real good," Waite grinned.

"Fuck off," Kevin told him mildly. He said to Jensen, "She *is* very good."

"She had the McRae case up near Kaladar a few years ago. A real tough one."

Waite frowned. "That was her?"

Jensen ignored him. "She was also the interrogator who brought down Edward James Patton."

"*That* was her?"

Leaning his elbow on the bar, Jensen looked around Waite

to stare at Kevin with deceptively sleepy eyes. "Pay attention to her and you might learn something."

Kevin nodded, not really surprised that Jensen knew as much about Ellie as he did. Collecting information was an obsession with most intelligence officers he'd met. Inside knowledge was their stock in trade, no matter what it had to do with.

Waite was still frowning. "Any connection between the two cases? The drug bust and the shooting?"

Kevin saw Jensen's eyes crease at the corners as the intelligence officer suppressed a smile. Waite had asked the question for him.

"Not that we can say at this time," Kevin replied carefully.

"He can't say, Jerry," Jensen said. "Strictly need-to-know."

"And I need to go," Waite replied, sliding off his stool and heading for the men's room.

Jensen switched stools and hunched over the bar next to Kevin. "I talked to your RIC, Merkley. He was sounding me out about cross-border BHO sourcing these days. I told him I like the local angle better, from what I've been seeing and hearing."

"Thanks," Kevin said.

"No problem. Your colleague, Dart. He's too noisy. I know his old man's the head honcho in OC enforcement for you guys and all that, but he needs to settle down and not make so many waves."

Kevin wiped beads of moisture off the side of his glass with his thumb.

Leaning closer, Jensen said, "If I hear anything that helps your case, I'll let Merk know."

"Thanks," Kevin said again. "I appreciate it."

He clapped Kevin on the shoulder. "Keep the faith, Kev. The connection's probably there. You're just not seeing the whole picture yet."

Jensen slid off the stool. "And I meant what I said about March. Pay attention to what she does and how she does it. You'll be a better detective for it."

"Thanks. I will."

Left alone at the bar, his attempt to get away from the

case now thoroughly defeated, Kevin stared at his tonic water and thought about what Jensen had said. There was no doubt yesterday's raid had solidified the connection between the Ross family and Bill Hansen's distribution of butane honey oil. Unfortunately, though, Kevin and Bishop had failed miserably last night in their attempt to connect Lennie or his father to Hansen's murder. Kevin shook his head in frustration.

How was it that he could try so damned hard, and still screw up?

chapter TWENTY-EIGHT

Ronnie and Lennie had both refused to answer all questions until they'd spoken to a lawyer. The raid produced a wealth of physical evidence supporting the drug charges and also turned up several firearms that were improperly stored, leading to additional charges, but tests on the handguns had already come back negative on a match to the round that had killed Bill Hansen. In fact, no physical evidence at all was found that could put the Rosses at Lackey's farm on Monday night or firmly connect them to a conspiracy to kill Hansen.

After the calls to the lawyer, Kevin and Bishop began with the father. Divorced for fifteen years, Ronnie was a bitter, angry man with a penchant for violence, but he'd spent Monday evening in Brockville in a tavern on King Street with a couple of old cronies, and he left when the place closed at one in the morning. Follow-up interviews this morning with the two friends and staff at the tavern had confirmed his alibi.

When Kevin shifted to questions about wholesaling product to Bill Hansen, Ronnie refused to play along. He claimed not to know anything about Hansen's business, legal or illegal, and stubbornly refused to discuss what happened to his product after it left his driveway. When Bishop insisted that lab tests would be able to link Ronnie's product to the BHO found in the Range

Rover in Hansen's car yard, Ross showed him a contemptuous smile and merely shrugged. When Kevin applied pressure, explaining that Ross's money, vehicles, and other possessions would be seized as offence-related property, Ronnie leaned back and said, "Take your best shot, kid."

Their interrogation of Lennie had a slightly different outcome, although no less frustrating for Kevin. Back in the interview room after having consulted the lawyer, he ignored Bishop and sneered at Kevin defiantly. Asked about having sold an illegal drug to the kid who delivered the butane to their farm, Lennie denied it. When told that the kid had admitted buying weed and hash oil from Lennie on a regular basis, about once a month, and was going to be an excellent witness for the Crown, Lennie said the kid was a fucking liar. Questioned about his connection to Bill Hansen, he claimed to know nothing about the victim other than what he'd heard around town. He'd never had any dealings with him, he insisted, and had never been up to Hansen's car yard.

"Not buying it, Lennie," Kevin said. "Want to hear the best part? Our lab found your fingerprint on the key fob of the Range Rover filled with Ross honey oil. Proves you were the last guy to touch it, when you loaded the shipment for Bill Hansen."

"Bullshit," Lennie retorted. "Your lab fucked up, and my lawyer's gonna prove it."

After repeated questioning about his whereabouts on the night Hansen was murdered, he finally told Kevin he'd been in Athens with a woman he occasionally liked to visit. They'd ordered a pizza from a local restaurant, watched TV, and then went to bed. He got home some time before noon the next day. He refused to provide her name and telephone number.

"You used to hang around the one with the dress shop," Kevin said carelessly. "I forget her name. The one who's separated from her husband. Is that who you were with?"

"None of your fucking business, Walker."

"Sheila. That's it. Sheila Weems, or something like that."

"I don't know what the hell you're talking about."

"She could help you out of a tight spot, Lennie. What's her

number again?"

"Screw you."

Bishop opened a file folder and showed Lennie a crime scene photo of Hansen's body, followed by shots of the hash oil extraction set-up in the Ross's shed and photos of the BHO-filled boxes in the back of the Range Rover. Next came a picture of a tire tread mark, which Bishop explained was found in Hansen's car yard and matched the tire on Lennie's 2013 GMC Sierra. Finally, as though revealing the last card in a winning hand, he set out a blow-up of Lennie's fingerprint, which they'd found on the Range Rover's key fob. He'd obviously left it there, Bishop said, when he was loading the BHO into the Rover. "Probably had to take your glove off to get it out of Hansen's key cabinet, eh, Lennie? Dumb but cute. That's you."

Tapping the photo, he explained how it would all be used in court to connect Lennie to the victim. It was a rock-solid, lead-pipe cinch. The work of an officially certified, highly-respected lab with a record of zero errors, compared to Lennie's record with its various convictions and assorted pathetic screw-ups.

"Slam dunk, Lennie." Bishop bared his teeth in a fake grin. "Nothing but net."

"Was he holding back on the money, Lennie?" Kevin put in. "Or were you asking for more?"

Lennie studied his knuckles for a moment. "No."

"Did you tell him you'd rough him up unless he paid you extra, on the side, that your dad wouldn't know about?"

"No. No way. I wouldn't do that."

Bishop snorted. "You wouldn't go behind your old man's back to squeeze Hansen for a bigger payday?"

Lennie chewed the inside of his cheek. "He'd fucking kill me."

"Oh?" Bishop raised his eyebrows theatrically. "Interesting choice of words. Did he kill Hansen?"

Lennie sighed. "It's a fucking expression, man. He still gets a fucking charge out of trying to beat on me, the damned old bastard, but he wouldn't kill nobody. He's not fucking stupid."

"So it must have been you, then." Bishop leaned back in

apparent satisfaction with the way it had all gone. “We got those two guns from your house, Lennie. I’m betting the one we found in your room is gonna match the bullet that went through Bill Hansen’s neck. That’ll give us everything we need to put you away for the rest of your useless life. You get that, don’t you? You see how it’s going to go down?”

Lennie’s tough-guy veneer fell away like an old skin. He admitted to Kevin that he’d spend Monday night with Sheila Weems, and he gave them her address and phone number. He admitted to having delivered the BHO to Hansen early Monday evening before driving to Athens, but saw no one else there other than Bill, who was in apparent good health, and he had no idea who might have killed him. No idea whatsoever.

At that point, he began to cry. The interrogation was over. Lennie was unable to say another word.

They were no further ahead in finding out who’d pulled the trigger on Bill Hansen than they’d been before.

Kevin sipped his tonic water and jumped as Waite slapped him on the back.

“All right, Walker! I’m ready for my next fucking brewskie. Order up.”

Forcing a smile, Kevin excused himself and left the bar to join Janie at their table. He figured Waite had gotten all the free beer a clean hip check was worth.

chapter TWENTY-NINE

Ellie got up on Saturday morning feeling tired and out of sorts. She'd been up late last night, spending most of the evening at the detachment and another two hours afterward reading reports at the cottage. When she'd finally gone to bed, she'd stared at the ceiling for a very long time before finally surrendering to sleep.

As she made a pot of coffee, her thoughts picked up right where they'd left off the night before. The Rosses had been arraigned, had received their bail hearing, and were back home. As far as her homicide investigation was concerned, the entire exercise had consumed valuable time without yielding a solid suspect. Ronnie Ross was solidly alibied while Lennie Ross's female friend, Sheila Weems, had confirmed Lennie's story.

Meanwhile, the composite sketch of the unknown man described by Vivian Hansen had appeared on television news broadcasts and in all the newspapers. They'd received a number of calls to the hotline in response, and detectives had spent long hours following up on those calls, but every potential lead had quickly turned into a dead end. The sketch was too vague to be of any practical help.

As Ellie stood in the shower, her exercises finished, she reluctantly admitted that the investigation was spinning its wheels. What she'd originally seen as the first break in the case, the discovery of the hash oil in Bill Hansen's Range Rover, had ultimately taken on a life of its own and was leading them, like a stoned Pied Piper, farther and farther away from their victim.

As she rinsed the shampoo out of her hair, she thought again about something that had been bothering her off and on all week. Why was the BHO sitting there in the Rover for them to find in the first place? If Hansen had been killed by someone who knew it was there, ready to be delivered in the morning, wouldn't that person have taken Hansen's keys, let themselves into his compound, and removed the drugs from the Rover to prevent the police from making a connection between Hansen and their operation? The person who killed him had taken his keys, sure enough, so wasn't it logical to assume that whoever killed him didn't know the BHO was sitting there?

Absent-mindedly shampooing her hair a second time, she considered what this meant. Either he was killed by someone not connected to the drugs at all, or he was killed by someone connected to the drugs at a level where they weren't familiar with Hansen's schedule or routine. Rinsing her hair, she ransacked her memory for anything she'd read in the case file so far that would suggest a suspect unconnected to the drugs. Vivian was the only family member, and Ellie had all but ruled her out. Hansen had had no close friends, and no one among his acquaintances in the area had presented a motive strong enough to draw her attention. The three drivers were a bust. As far as business connections were concerned, she'd read Carty's reports and agreed with his assessment that the few dealerships still doing business with Hansen presented no real leads, and the ones who'd cut ties with him had done so merely as a result of the rumours concerning his stock and not because of any actual conflict with him. Carty had promised to brief everyone on his findings related to Hansen's personal customers today. Would there be a suspect among that bunch? Someone who'd bought a bum BMW and went over the edge, driving Hansen in his own truck out into the countryside to shoot him in the back of the neck as payback for having cheated them on a lemon, all while enlisting the help of a second person to do so?

Standing on the bath mat, dripping everywhere, she realized she hadn't shut off the water in the shower.

She reached in, turned it off, and pursed her lips at a sudden thought.

What she needed to do, goddamn it, was reconstruct Bill Hansen's time line for last Monday. The final day of his life. Hour by hour. Minute by minute, if necessary.

Somewhere in the last twelve to fourteen hours of Hansen's life they would find the event that would connect him to his killer.

His *two* killers—shooter and accomplice.

Towelling herself off, she bared her teeth. They hadn't parachuted into Hansen's life out of a clear blue sky five minutes before killing him, dammit. They'd been there longer than that.

They must have left a trail.

Rebuild the time line.

Find the bastards.

She threw the towel over the shower curtain rod, grabbed her cellphone from the lid of the toilet, and called Kevin.

chapter THIRTY

"All right," Ellie said, looking around the conference room at the circle of faces, "thanks for giving up your Saturday for the cause. We're going to go back to square one and rework the time line. I want to know how Bill Hansen spent every minute of his last day on earth. Mona," she pointed at Sisson, who was standing by the whiteboard, "is going to be our note-taker. Bill," she nodded at Merkley, "you and Sally can start by giving us an update on the data you've got."

The regional intelligence co-ordinator cleared his throat. "Yesterday morning I received the spreadsheets from the bank and phone companies. Sally and I spent the day entering everything into i2 and preparing analytical reports." He indicated a thin young blond woman who tugged at a cuff of her long-sleeved pink cardigan sweater and smiled at the group. An intelligence analyst, Sally Gordon had reported for work yesterday morning. "We've added e-mail and Internet browser data from Hansen's laptop and home computer, but there hasn't been time yet to include the information Tom's been gathering from the hard-copy files."

Carty lifted a shoulder. "It's coming."

"Understood."

Ellie glanced at the clock on the wall and said, "Okay, it's

8:06 AM. Vivian Hansen told us her husband left the house right around this time Monday morning. Bill and Sally, did our victim have any outside contacts that morning before leaving the house?"

Merkley looked at Sally. She shrugged, deferring to him. "In short, no," he said. "No incoming or outgoing calls or texts on either the house land line or his cellphone. No Internet activity on the computer upstairs in the home."

"So he got up, showered and shaved, had breakfast, and began another normal Bill Hansen day," Ellie said.

No one contradicted her, so she folded her arms and looked at the whiteboard. "Okay, Vivian Hansen told us her husband's alarm was set for seven, that he took about an hour to get ready to leave for work each morning. So start our time line with 7:00 AM., Mona. 'Alarm goes off.' "

Sisson wrote it down, using a black dry erase marker.

"And 8:00 AM," Kevin said, " 'leaves the house.' "

Sisson wrote it down.

"How long would it take him to drive to the car yard?" Ellie asked.

"Three minutes," Kevin said. "Five at the most."

"What's his next known activity, people? What does the data tell us?"

Merkley tapped his finger on the touchpad of his laptop. "He logged onto his Internet service provider at 8:12 AM using the laptop in the office trailer."

"So, he's sitting at his desk by 8:12. Then what?"

"Between 8:12 and 8:16 he read and deleted twelve e-mails," Merkley said, "all of them junk mail or spam. From 8:16 to 8:28 he browsed the Internet, looking at various news sites. Then at 8:28 he got to work, logging onto a car auction website using his user ID and password. From then until 11:45, he spent time there and at two other auction websites as well, plus he queried car records through CARFAX, where he had logon privileges, and the Canadian Black Book website. There was a dormant period between 10:06 and 10:14—"

"Pee break," Bishop crowed.

Merkley smiled. "Could be, and another where he spent six minutes on the page of a car being auctioned, which was longer than usual."

Kevin sat forward. "Phone call?"

"Yes," Sally Gordon said suddenly. She stared at her tablet. "We're talking about 10:29, correct?"

"That's right," Merkley said.

"He called Wilson Motors in Westport on his cellphone. The call lasted five minutes, forty-two seconds."

For the next ninety minutes they hashed through Bill Hansen's morning, cross-referencing information from every source available to them, not only electronic records but paper documents in Hansen's files, entries on the big calendar in his desk, even scribbled notes on the notepad beside his coffee cup. As Ellie had hoped, the detectives were engaged and enthusiastic, challenging each other, clapping when a puzzle was solved and an answer found.

Dart was the only exception. He sat at the far end of the table, arms folded, legs crossed, and didn't contribute to the discussion. He inadvertently made eye contact with Ellie at one point and quickly looked away.

At ten o'clock they took a break, and when they reconvened, Ellie stood at the whiteboard and walked them through what Sisson had recorded. Hansen had spent most of the morning shopping online for three specific cars, which he'd scribbled down on the notepad on his desk after receiving inquiries over the phone for them. He placed several calls and received others, he sent a few e-mails and received others, he checked cars and placed bids, and he used his accounts with CBB and CARFAX to perform due diligence on his three prospective purchases. There were no anomalies at all during this time, no strange calls or odd website visits. At 11:55 AM, he logged off the CBB website and closed his browser.

Ellie walked back to her chair and sat down. "What happened next, folks?"

"He used his debit card at 12:22 PM to pay for something at a Subway restaurant in Brockville," Merkley said. "The one on

Stewart Boulevard."

"No, wait." Sally Gordon frowned at her tablet. "He made a phone call first. Here it is. At 12:12 he called a local phone number. A four-second call." She recited the number to them.

"Holy freakin' shit," Sisson blurted.

Sally looked up, startled. "Sorry, did I say something wrong?"

"That's our number," Bishop said, stunned.

"I don't understand."

"It's our number," Kevin said. "He called here. The detachment."

Sisson hurried over to the computer in the corner of the room and sat down. As she searched the archives for the digital recording of the call, they debated why Hansen would have called the police the day he was murdered.

"Maybe he felt threatened," Carty offered. "Maybe someone came around to see him, and he thought about getting protection for himself."

"Could be he wanted out of the game," Bishop said. "He was going to turn himself in, then changed his mind."

"Here it is," Sisson said, switching on the set of external speakers plugged into the computer.

They waited expectantly, then heard the call being answered by their civilian receptionist. There was a pause, then a male voice said, "Um, sorry. Called the wrong number." The call ended.

Ellie broke the silence that followed by asking Kevin, "Was that him? Do you recognize the voice?"

"I think so. I didn't talk to him very often, but I think it was him."

"He sounded stressed," Merkley said.

"Under duress?" Carty asked.

Merkley shrugged. "Who knows, but he sounded like a guy who changed his mind about calling the police about something."

"But he didn't call 911, he called the general office number," Bishop pointed out. He looked at Kevin. "Think he was trying to get you? You're the only one he'd know here."

"No idea," Kevin replied. "People usually just call my cell."

"Maybe he didn't have the number."

"Okay," Sisson announced from the corner of the room, "I've got an even better one for you."

"What?" Kevin swivelled his chair around to face her.

"I was thinking about the time line, right? He gets off his laptop at 11:46 and drives into town to get a sub at the Subway on Stewart. Which is this road, right? He has to drive right past here to get there. So I'm wondering, okay, where did he call from? It takes about twenty-five minutes for him to drive from Sparrow Lake into town, but the call was made only sixteen minutes after he logged off, right?"

"Somebody's paying attention," Bishop quipped.

Sisson rolled her eyes. "Stuff it, Bishop. So I got a hunch, and I checked the video surveillance footage for our parking lot, and guess what I found? A big black pickup truck with his licence plate on it."

"You're kidding," Kevin said.

"I kid you not. He was parked right outside—in our parking lot—when he called us."

chapter THIRTY-ONE

When the team took a short break for lunch, Craig Dart slipped out of the building and drove down to Butternut Bay. He followed the Thousand Islands Parkway along the river to a small marina. He parked next to a Gananoque Police Service cruiser and got out. Other than his car and the cruiser, and two cars around the side belonging to staff, the lot was empty. He turned up his collar against the bitter wind blowing off the St. Lawrence River and walked across the lot to the entrance of the restaurant. The marina offered forty boat slips, a fuel dock, and a locked compound where shrink-wrapped boats sat on cradles waiting out the winter. It was closed for the season but the restaurant remained open. Its clientele consisted mostly of cops, who liked being able to sit and talk shop in relative privacy while enjoying unusually good food.

Trent Barrie was waiting for him at a table near the big picture window with a view of the river. He was already eating when Dart pulled out the chair across from him and sat down. "You were late, so I ordered."

"Don't worry about it." Dart looked up as a server appeared with a menu. "Reuben sandwich and an iced tea." The server nodded and headed for the kitchen.

"You should try the chicken caesar salad," Barrie said, wiping his mouth. "It's really good."

"Whatever." Dart took off his jacket and twisted around to drape it over the back of his chair.

"How's your paperwork coming?" As another member of the regional drug unit, Barrie had participated in the Ross raid on Thursday, and they both had reports to write as a result.

"Barely made a dent."

"I hear that." Barrie tossed his napkin down on the table and ran a hand over his closely-trimmed, rust-coloured hair. Despite the cold weather, he wore a short-sleeved uniform shirt that showed off his muscular arms and thick neck. He was vain and cocky, and Dart was aware that Barrie had cultivated him as a friend because he knew who his father was and had vague aspirations of swinging over to the OPP if he found his way blocked up the Gananoque ladder. Dart didn't really care. He liked the guy, and didn't really give a damn beyond that.

"What the hell was that guy of yours thinking," Barrie said, "walking up and grabbing the old man's shotgun? I thought the IC was going to have a shit haemorrhage."

"Fucking hillbilly." Dart leaned back as the server placed a large glass of iced tea in front of him. When he was gone, Dart took a long drink and shook his head. "If he had brains he'd be dangerous."

"Isn't he the primary on your murder case?"

Dart made a disgusted sound.

"So how's that happen? He's only been with you guys what, a couple years?"

"He's Patterson's pet cat. Don't ask me why, because I haven't a fucking clue."

When Dart's sandwich arrived, they ate in silence for a few minutes until Barrie set down his fork. "So how's it going with March? Does she know what she's doing?"

"She's supposed to be some kind of shit-hot interrogator. I don't see it."

"She seemed okay to me." Barrie had seen Ellie at the Ross farm, and had spoken to her briefly to introduce himself. "Not much to look at, but she seems pretty smart."

"She's making it up as she goes along. We're getting nowhere."

"I thought you said the shooter was a heavy hitter from up north. Sent down to eliminate the competition."

Dart looked through the window at the choppy surface of the river. "That's what I thought at first, but I'm working on another theory now."

Barrie waited, and when Dart continued to stare out at the water, he said, "What? Do you really think it was a supply line fuck-over that the Rosses couldn't let slide?"

"Both their alibis held up." Dart brought his eyes back to Barrie. "What I can't get is why they let Walker act as primary. It's like he's got something on Patterson and he's holding it over his head. I just don't get it."

"I don't know, Craig. He seems pretty smart."

"He's an embarrassment."

Barrie finished his glass of Coke with a loud sucking sound. "The guy I didn't like up there was the other detective, the one who retired. Waddell."

Dart looked at him. "Why not?"

"Slimy, slimy fuck. From Corrections. Prison guard. Then did a stint with the KPS. Heard he was called onto the carpet a few times because of citizen complaints. Kingston told him to continue his career elsewhere, so he went up to Sparrow Lake."

"Sounds like a winner."

"Kept in contact with a few ex-cons, as I heard it. Let a few of them live with him after they got out, and I hear he's even hired a couple."

"Oh?"

"He runs a security company now and the ex-cons do most of the leg work for him."

"I've heard Walker mention him a couple times." Dart thought about a conversation he'd overheard yesterday between Patterson and March. "Apparently he was even bouncing stuff off him about the case. If you're telling me this guy's got ties to known criminals, then I'm concerned."

Barrie spread his hands. "Hey, I'm not implying anything.

I'm just telling you what I heard."

Dart paid for their meals, which he knew Barrie expected despite his protestations, and they walked out into the parking lot. The wind from the river cut at him like a cold knife. He turned up his collar and unlocked his car, then leaned over the roof and rapped on it with his knuckles.

"Here's a thought. How about you ask around about those ex-cons Waddell's got working for him? Let me know what you come up with."

Barrie grinned. "Looking for an angle on Walker?"

"No, no. Not at all. Just following up on a hunch."

"Yeah, right." Barrie opened the cruiser door and winked. "Let me see what I can find out for you."

"I appreciate it, Trent."

"Hey, what are friends for?"

chapter THIRTY-TWO

As intrigued as Ellie was by the discovery that Bill Hansen had called the detachment while sitting in his car in the parking lot outside, she knew it wasn't what she'd been looking for from the time line. When lunch was delivered, she prompted Kevin to push the team back to work while they ate.

They ran through Bill Hansen's Monday afternoon. He'd returned to his trailer and resumed accessing web pages through his ISP at 1:06 PM. He surfed a few news and sports sites, then returned to his car auction websites at 1:25 and spent the afternoon much as he'd spent the morning—calling clients on his cellphone, placing bids on vehicles that attracted his attention, and conducting due diligence on them through his online accounts. At 4:25 PM this activity came to a halt, and he sat on the logout page of CARFAX for thirty-four minutes without moving.

"Something happened," Sally Gordon said.

"Phone call?" Kevin asked.

"No."

"Somebody drove into the yard," Carty said.

"Could be." Kevin stood up to pace back and forth behind the table. "What's the next call he makes?"

"It was at 4:57," Sally said. She recited the telephone

number.

"That's Wilson Motors again," Carty said immediately. He flipped a page in his notebook. "They bought the BMW from him, the one still in the yard."

"Is this when Hansen took delivery of it? Between 4:25 and 4:59?"

Carty pulled out a file folder from a stack near his elbow and hunted through it until he found the piece of paper he wanted. "Here's the bill of lading. It has Monday's date on it. No time, but this could be when it was delivered, yes."

"Then he calls the dealership at 4:57 to let them know it's in."

"Looks like. It was supposed to go out on Friday," Carty added.

"Fate intervened," Sisson said from the whiteboard.

"What's next?" Kevin asked. "What does he do after the BMW gets there?"

"After he calls Wilson Motors," Merkley replied, "he goes back online."

"To do what?"

"Surf, basically. Auto Trader, Automobilemag, Car and Driver, CBC, The Sports Network."

"At 5:35 he calls a local number," Sally Gordon said. She read it out loud.

"The Silver Kettle," Kevin said. "Ordering something to eat. Which was delivered to him around 6:30."

"Then it's quiet until 6:38," Sally said, "when he receives a call from another local number. This one's registered to a George Clayton, 3704 Upper Oak Leaf Road, Athens."

"Clayton," Carty mused. He flipped pages in his notebook. "That's a private client, I think. Hang on." He turned another page. "Here. Jeanne Clayton. Same address and phone number. She bought a 2014 Audi Q7."

"The missing vehicle that was parked next to the Lexus?" Kevin asked. "With the summer tires?"

"Could be," Carty said.

Kevin looked at Ellie. "She called him to ask about her SUV.

She must have picked it up Monday, some time after 6:38."

"If so," Ellie said, "she may have been the last person to see him alive before his killers got to him."

chapter THIRTY-THREE

Kevin drove northwest on County Road 29 with Dart in the passenger seat, inscrutable behind his sunglasses and unsmiling face. The weather had cleared and the sun was shining, but the gusting wind and patches of ice on the pavement forced Kevin to pay attention to his driving rather than to Dart, whose dislike of him seemed to radiate from every pore. He eased into the left-hand turn lane at the intersection of County Road 42 and rolled to a stop, waiting for oncoming traffic to pass. The Grand Cherokee rocked slightly as a tractor trailer blew past, then the way was clear and Kevin made the turn.

"Why would the vic call you, Walker?" Dart asked suddenly.

"I don't know. Maybe he wasn't calling me. Maybe he just wanted to talk to someone at the detachment. Anyone."

"You're the only one he knew. He had to be calling you. You guys were neighbours, right?"

"He lived in the village, yeah, but I didn't know him all that well."

"Ever buy a car from him? Maybe this one?"

Instead of replying, Kevin gave him a long stare. He'd long since grown used to Dart's unfriendliness, but he definitely didn't like his tone now.

"Careful of your lane integrity, Walker."

Kevin had drifted into the centre of the road. He eased back into the right-hand lane in time to avoid a white van with a ladder on the roof. "What are you getting at, Craig?"

"Nothing. By the way, what's the name of the detective you replaced in SLPS?"

"Chuck Waddell. Why?"

"Right, that's it. He's still hanging around, isn't he?"

"Lives just down the street from me."

"Right. Did you talk to him for background on the vic?"

"I talked to him." Kevin glanced in the rear-view mirror as a subcompact car rapidly approached from behind, swung into the oncoming lane, and passed without signalling. The car swerved in front of him and disappeared up the road in a cloud of flying snow.

"And?"

"As a matter of fact, he supports your theory that Hansen was shot by outside hitters. He figures the only way we'll find these two guys is through intel."

Dart shook his head. "What do you know."

"Where are you with that, Craig?"

"Nowhere. They've started surveillance on Marc Barron and the dealer who was supposed to buy the Range Rover, but that sort of thing takes time."

Kevin puzzled over Dart's apparent lack of enthusiasm for his own theory.

"Waddell runs a security company now, doesn't he?" Dart asked.

"That's right."

"I heard he has a couple of guys working for him. Know them at all?"

"No, I don't. Why?"

"I don't know. Has he offered you a job yet?"

Kevin waited a moment before answering. "I wouldn't be interested."

"Don't be too hasty. It could be good money, you never know. You should think about it."

Kevin simmered as they passed through Athens and took the left-hand turn onto Upper Oak Leaf Road. Civic number 3704 appeared quickly on the right, at the end of a long driveway leading up to a well-kept Gothic Revival-style stone house. A white board fence ran along the driveway. Beyond it, several odd-looking animals peered at them from the open door of a wooden shed.

"What the hell are they?" Dart asked, leaning forward. "Llamas?"

"Alpacas." Kevin turned into the yard and parked next to a light brown Audi Q7 SUV. Across the yard he could see a nearly-new red pickup truck with a plow on the front. He got out of the car and looked at the licence plate on the Audi.

"There it is," he said to Dart, who came up next to him and peered through the driver's window.

"Was there ever any doubt?"

They walked up onto the deck at the rear of the house. Kevin opened the aluminum screen door and knocked. After a moment, the inner door was opened by a tall, silver-haired woman. "Yes?"

"Are you Jeanne Clayton?"

"Yes. Are you here about the cria?"

Kevin held up his badge. "I'm not sure what that is, ma'am. I'm Detective Constable Walker of the OPP, and this is Detective Constable Dart. We'd like to ask you a few questions."

"Oh, I'm sorry. I thought you were the man who was buying the cria." She smiled at Kevin's blank look. "A baby male alpaca. Do you need to come in?"

"Yes, ma'am," Kevin said.

She stepped back and they shuffled into a large kitchen, standing on a large brown carpet as she closed the door behind them. "We can sit at the table. Please remove your boots. You can leave them right there on the carpet. It's made from one hundred per cent alpaca yarn. I hand-wove it myself. Isn't it lovely?"

Kevin agreed that it was. He shed his boots and sat down at the kitchen table, an antique that must have been very expensive to buy. As Dart pulled out the chair next to him, Kevin took out his notebook and pen. “Is that your vehicle outside in the yard, Mrs. Clayton? The brown Audi?”

“Yes it is. Actually, it’s cardamom beige. Can I get you gentlemen something? Tea or coffee?”

“I’ll have a coffee,” Dart said. “Black, two sugar.”

“Nothing for me, thanks,” Kevin replied.

Jeanne took a coffee mug from a glass-faced cupboard and put it on a single-cup coffee maker. “How does Metropolitan blend sound? Or would you rather have a latté?”

“The first one’s good,” Dart replied.

She removed a disc from its box, put it into the machine, and pressed a button. “What’s this all about?”

“We’re investigating the murder of Bill Hansen,” Kevin said. “Did you buy your Audi from him?”

“Yes. That’s right, he was killed this past week, wasn’t he?” She stirred sugar into Dart’s coffee, put it in front of him, and sat down at the table across from Kevin.

“When did you pick up the car?”

“At the beginning of the week.” She plucked a hair from the sleeve of her blue denim blouse. “I was a little put out. It sat there and he didn’t call to arrange for delivery. My husband saw it on his way home from work. That’s when I called.”

“That was Monday?”

“Yes.”

“At what time?”

“Well, I called him just before dinner. Around six thirty. Then I picked up the car after dinner. I suppose it was about eight o’clock.”

“How’d you get to Hansen’s?” Dart asked.

Jeanne sighed. She crossed her legs and smoothed her denim skirt over her shin. “Oh, George dropped me off on his way to his meeting.”

Kevin glanced at Dart. “Did he drive right into Hansen’s yard to let you out, Mrs. Clayton?”

“Oh, heavens, no. That would have cost a few extra seconds of his precious time. He let me get out on the side of the road, like a hitch-hiker. I had to walk in from there, thank you."

"What does your husband do for a living?"

"He's a partner with Odette, King and Cameron in Brockville. Commercial law. 'Boring as bat shit,' as my daughter likes to say."

"Tell us what happened when you got there."

"Well, I don't know." She tilted her head and studied the tin ceiling above them. "I walked in from the road, it was freezing, and I knocked on the door. I had to wait for a minute while the other person came out before I could talk to Bill. In fact, I had to move down, right off the steps, to get out of his way. Not a very polite person at all."

Dart shifted. "This other individual, who was he?"

"I have no idea. Some person or other. I'd never seen him before, and I don't know who he was. I'm not interested in knowing, either."

"This could be important," Kevin said. "Tell us how it happened, step by step. You knocked on the door."

"I knocked on the door and waited. When the door opened, I looked in but it wasn't Bill opening the door, it was this other man. He had his back to me, talking to Bill, so I just had to stand there while they argued."

"What were they arguing about?"

"I don't know. Something about 'you should have known better' and 'take care of this and then you're going to have to explain it to him.' Bill was trying to calm him down. I suppose someone was unhappy with their car. It didn't surprise me that he was reading him the riot act. I was in a similar mood."

"Then what happened?"

"Well, as I say, I had to back down off the steps to let him by. He sat in the car parked in front of the trailer. I went inside and signed for my Audi."

"The guy didn't leave?" Dart asked. "He sat in his car while you were inside with Hansen?"

"That's what I'm saying. How's your coffee. Need a refill?"

"No, it's fine. How was Hansen when he talked to you? Angry? Scared?"

"His stress level was very high. You'd expect as much after dealing with one dissatisfied customer and having to cope with another, right on his heels. He was very apologetic, fell all over himself explaining why he hadn't called sooner to arrange for delivery. In fact, he offered me a two hundred dollar credit on my next purchase from him, as a peace offering. I told him it wasn't necessary. Frankly, I don't think I would have bought from him again. The Audi's fine. Lovely, in fact. I just found him rather too unreliable as a business person."

"So you signed the paperwork," Kevin said, "and Hansen gave you the keys?"

"Yes."

"Did he say anything at all about the other man?"

"Nothing. Not a word."

"Did he say or do anything else that struck you as odd or out of character?"

Jeanne raised her eyebrows and thought about it. "No. Nothing, really."

"Then you left the trailer?"

"Yes. I got into the Audi and it started right away. That was one thing I wanted to be sure of, and the other was the gas. The tank was full, so he'd remembered that much, at least. I tested everything. The wipers, the radio, the heater, the air conditioning, everything. There were no problems, so I drove out. Oh, yes, I forgot. He told me the tires were summer tires, that he hadn't been able to get his hands on winter tires in time. That was his excuse for waiting for so long and not calling. He told me to be very careful driving home. So I was."

"And the other man stayed in his car the whole time?" Dart asked.

Jeanne nodded. "With the engine running, polluting the atmosphere. Is he important for some reason?"

"What kind of vehicle was it?"

"I don't know. It looked like a Jeep. That style."

"What colour?"

"It was after dark, so I can't really say. Beige, grey, something like that."

"Did you see the licence number?"

"No, sorry."

"You're sure you've never seen him before?" Dart pressed.

Jeanne gave him a look. "I'm not a person who likes to chew her cabbage twice. If I'd seen him before, I would have told you, wouldn't I?"

"Can you describe him?" Kevin asked.

"Certainly. My height, which is five nine, round, balding head, dark hair, what there was of it, dark eyes. Wide nose, fleshy lips, big ear lobes. He wore one of those ludicrous puffy ski jackets that make people look like the Michelin Man. It was blue. He had on jeans and brown boots like those hiking shoes people wear. Black leather gloves. His voice was rather high-pitched. His breath was bad. It was impossible to miss it in the cold air when he pushed by me and got into his car. Diabetic ketoacidosis."

"I beg your pardon?"

"It's a condition that people with Type 1 diabetes sometimes get, a build-up of ketones in the blood. It can make their breath smell pungent, like nail polish remover. Unmistakable. My father had it. It's an odour you don't forget."

Kevin was writing furiously, but he stopped and took out a copy of Vivian Hansen's composite sketch he had folded into his notebook. He smoothed out the creases and passed it over. "Did he look like this?"

Jeanne studied it for a moment. "Not really. I saw this picture on the news, didn't I?"

"It was in the papers and on TV."

"I suppose there's a bit of a likeness, but it's very vague. The nose and lips are close, but the eyes and the shape of the head are off. Who gave you this description?"

"Would you be willing to sit with our sketch artist and provide a description of the man you saw? To give us a better drawing?"

"Of course. You're not suggesting, are you, that the man I saw was the one who shot Bill? Could that be possible?"

"We're not sure at this point, but we'd definitely like to talk to him."

"Oh, my God." Jeanne closed her eyes and rubbed her forehead.

Kevin pushed back his chair. "Are you all right, Mrs. Clayton?"

She nodded, eyes closed. "I was six inches away from a murderer. Can you believe it? Just wait until I tell Linda."

"Linda?"

"My BFF." She opened her eyes and stared at Kevin. "She'll be insanely jealous."

chapter THIRTY-FOUR

Ellie stood in the snow at the edge of Sorrow Lake, cigarette in her bare hand, glass in her other, mittened, hand. The moon had climbed above the trees, a third-quarter moon, and in its pale glow she could barely see the carpet of ice on the surface of the lake. The opposite shore was a dark, bristling smudge. She sipped her Jack Daniels and drew on the cigarette. It was somewhere around ten thirty at night, and she was tired.

Unfortunately, their sketch artist had not been available to meet with Jeanne Clayton today after her interview with Kevin and Dart, but a time had been set up for tomorrow morning. Ellie hoped they would be able to produce a more accurate drawing of the man who was now their primary person of interest.

There was some progress, though. By process of elimination, they knew which set of tires from Hansen's car yard most likely belonged to the man Jeanne Clayton had seen. Of the four sets of tire tread marks Dave Martin had collected, one had been matched to delivery man Willie Bird's Sunfire, another to Lennie Ross's GMC Sierra, and a third to Clayton's Audi Q7. They were now focusing on the fourth set, Michelin eighteen-inch LTX M/S2 tires with moderate wear which, if Clayton was right, were sitting on a Jeep.

She heard a door close next door, but didn't look over. A

lighter clicked several times. Footsteps moved across the frozen deck and stopped.

She looked up at the moon, which was yellowish in colour. She could hear a train whistle somewhere in the distance. It was a faint, drawn-out sound, accompanied by the low thunder of the train's engine. When it faded away into nothing, the lake settled back into dark silence.

She drained her glass and bent down to scoop up a bit of snow into it. She dropped in her cigarette butt and, turning her back on the lake, walked slowly up toward the cottage. She saw Ridge Ballantyne leaning over the railing of his deck. He raised his cigarette in greeting. She clumped across the snow to his deck stairs and went up.

"I didn't want to disturb you," he said. "You looked lost in thought."

Ellie leaned on the railing next to him. "Just winding down."

"How's the case coming? Or shouldn't I ask?"

"It's coming." She glanced at him. "It's okay to ask. I may not answer, that's all."

He chuckled.

"It's so quiet here," Ellie said.

"Too quiet?"

"Not for me. I don't miss the city. I grew up surrounded by concrete and pavement. I like this a lot better."

"Sorrow Lake certainly has its appeal. I wouldn't live anywhere else. As long as I have a choice, of course."

Ellie felt in her coat pocket for her other mitten. Her hand encountered a piece of paper. She took it out and unfolded it. It was a copy of the news release with the composite sketch provided by Vivian Hansen.

Ridge peered over her shoulder. "What's that? The fellow you're looking for?"

"Yes. We ran the sketch in the newspapers and on TV. Hasn't helped so far."

"I never watch the news. Too damned demoralizing. Let's have a look." He took it from her and walked over to the corner of the deck. Standing directly under the floodlight, he put on a pair of reading glasses and studied the sketch. He removed his glasses and came back to her, paper extended.

"Doesn't look like anyone I've ever seen before. Frankly, it doesn't look much like a human being at all. More like something that might have escaped from Area 51."

Ellie took the paper and folded it back up, shoving it into her pocket. "Oh well. Thanks for looking."

"I sometimes wonder why the police bother with sketches. To me, they never look like anyone you might actually recognize in real life, walking down the pavement."

"It's a problem," Ellie admitted. She leaned over the railing. "There was a study done—in fact it was in Scotland—in which participants studied a photograph for several minutes and then gave a description of the face to a forensic artist. The recognition rate for their sketches was less than 3 per cent."

"That's bloody awful."

"Then there was another study where forensic artists were given photographs of famous celebrities, like Tom Cruise and Ronald Reagan, faces everyone knows, and they used the best available forensic software to produce computerized composite drawings. The results were completely unrecognizable. It's an inexact science, I guess you could say, whether you use computers or human sketch artists."

"Once more, I wonder why you'd bother."

Ellie sighed, staring across the lake. "True." She shrugged. "Then of course there's always Muppet Man."

"Who?"

She watched a thin finger of cloud reach out across the moon. "A recent case down in the southern United States. A couple of women gave police a description of a man they said had robbed them, and the composite drawing was so bad, people said it looked exactly like some character from the Muppets. Everyone made fun of it on the Internet. It was a huge joke."

"Not surprisingly."

"Yeah. The hell of it is, though, they brought in a guy after that, on completely different charges, and one of the officers looked at him and thought, 'shit, this guy looks just like Muppet Man.' So they brought the women back in, they made a positive ID, and the guy ended up being convicted. So you never know. Sometimes these things actually work."

"So let me understand this, then. If I see some fellow who looks exactly like an alien from outer space wanting to give me a rectal examination, I should give you a ring straight off, is that it?"

"Just on general principles, Ridge, I'd say that would probably be a good idea."

chapter THIRTY-FIVE

The following afternoon, Craig Dart drove slowly along Sunset Lane on the north shore of Sparrow Lake, looking for civic number 29, the cottage belonging to Chuck Waddell. He was driving his wife's vehicle, a ten-year-old Mazda, because his own car was still in the shop having the alternator replaced. It was a very expensive repair, and they would have to use their line of credit to pay for it. He might be a chief superintendent's son, but he was still struggling to make ends meet on a constable's salary that never seemed to go far enough to cover all their needs. Sometimes, Dart thought, without bad luck he wouldn't have any luck at all. Today, though, he was trying to convince himself that the secret to success was to generate his own good luck.

He tapped the accelerator to climb a rise on the narrow lane and felt the back end fishtail on the icy surface. The Mazda's all-season tires didn't have much tread left, and Dart was a little nervous taking it down this back road in these conditions. At the top of the rise he slowed to a crawl as the lane curved close to the lake shore. He passed a snowed-in cottage on the right and caught a glimpse of a blue sign with the civic number 23. He was getting close. He glanced at the clock on the dashboard: 1:34 PM. Hopefully Waddell's tenant would be home when Dart arrived.

Trent Barrie had come through with flying colours. The package he'd e-mailed Dart last night had contained information on Chuck Waddell and his business, CW Security, Limited. The company apparently had a small client list but was doing well for itself through alarm system sales and "consultation services," whatever that meant. Dart wondered if it was being used as a front to launder cash. On top of that, Barrie included information on Waddell's two employees, and the first package Dart looked at rang all the bells.

John Michael (Mickey) Burrows, DOB January 21, 1966, born and raised in Scarborough, was a loser who'd served time for assault, sexual assault, and armed robbery. He was forty-eight years old, stood five feet, nine inches tall, and weighed 190 pounds. His mug shots looked remarkably like the new composite drawing produced by Jeanne Clayton and the sketch artist this morning—round head, bald on top with thick black hair shot through with grey on the sides, and thick, black eyebrows. Dark complexion, no visible scars or tattoos.

He still had a year of parole to complete on his latest conviction, the armed robbery offence in which he'd held up a gas bar in Belleville. His initial address on release had been an apartment building in Kingston, but a year ago he'd advised his parole supervisor of a change of address to the location Dart was now looking for on the shoreline of Sparrow Lake—29 Sunset Lane, Yonge Township, Ontario. The change of address notification had been accompanied by a letter from Burrows's employer, Chuck Waddell, explaining that the purpose of the move was to permit Mr. Burrows to carry out job-related duties closer to his employer's residence.

It didn't take a genius to connect the dots. Waddell was a bent ex-cop. He'd probably gone over a long time ago, perhaps while still with Corrections, before switching to Kingston Police. He'd likely been the kind of cop who always had his hand out, expecting a cut in exchange for looking the other way. He'd obviously carried his love of grift into retirement, using his business as a way to get behind the security systems and firewalls of clients whenever it suited his purpose. His other employee, a loser by the name of Thomas Edward Ratliff, a.k.a. Tommy the Rat, had a record for identity theft, credit card forgery, and unauthorized use of a computer. He was undoubtedly the one with the skills, while Burrows was the one with the muscle.

The enforcer.

The killer.

After receiving the information last night, Dart had given it a lot of thought, trying to fit all the pieces together. Among them was the fact that Kevin Walker didn't bother to hide his friendship, or whatever it was, with Chuck Waddell. Waddell had been his mentor with SLPS, and had turned over his detective job to Walker when he'd retired. Walker had all but admitted that Waddell had approached him about a job with his company. Was it possible that Walker was just as bent as Waddell? Had the veteran not only coached the rookie on departmental policy and procedure but also in the fine art of shaking down citizens and cutting in on dope smuggling and stolen car operations?

Would Walker be the next one Craig Dart would bring down?

Dart fiddled with the temperature controls, trying to coax more heat from the Mazda's vents. When a fresh news release had been issued this morning along with the new composite sketch, March and Walker had sent the detectives out on the road with it to conduct door-to-door canvasses hoping to identify the man. Dart immediately volunteered to cover the lake, and no one objected. He was paired with Constable Mark Allore, but quickly convinced him it would be more efficient to split up and cover the distance in half the time. Allore would take the south shore of the lake while Dart covered the north. Dart planned simply to walk up to the door of Waddell's cottage, using the news release and canvass as his pretext to initiate contact, then miraculously "recognize" Burrows from the sketch and make a warrantless arrest. Because he knew what to expect and Burrows didn't, it should go smoothly. Then he could call Allore for backup and take it from there.

Dart skidded to a stop just past an unplowed driveway which, according to the blue civic number sign, was 31 Sunset

Lane. Somehow he'd managed to pass the driveway of Waddell's cottage without realizing it. He shifted into reverse and backed up into the driveway of 31, then shifted into drive to retrace his steps to number 29.

The Mazda's tires spun ineffectually. He gunned the engine. The tires whined and the car sank lower.

He was stuck.

Dart cursed. He shifted back and forth from reverse to drive, trying to rock the car out of the snow, but it didn't work. The wheels spun in place, and he didn't move an inch.

Shoving the gear shift into park, he got out. The front tires had dug deep ruts below the surface of the snow, and the back tires were barely visible. He dropped down onto his hands and knees for a look. Snow was packed tightly under the frame all the way around. It had piled up underneath when he'd driven backwards into the driveway, and now the damned car was wedged solidly in place. He stood up, swearing. He stalked around to the back and opened the trunk, but saw nothing he could use to dig himself out. The car would have to be towed out. Maybe somebody around here had a tractor and a big chain and could pull him out.

He started walking down the lane the way he'd come. First things first—arrest the shooter, then call Allore for backup, then get Norma's useless piece of shit car unstuck.

As he plodded along, he rehearsed his pretext. *Hi, I'm with the OPP. We're investigating the death of a local man and going door-to-door asking everyone if they've seen anyone unusual in the area. Mind if I step inside for a moment?* As soon as Burrows's back was turned, he'd bring out the cuffs and have him in custody before he could react.

He reached the entrance to the previous cottage and immediately understood how he'd missed it. The driveway had been plowed out, and the snow was piled up directly in front of the civic number, making it invisible from behind the wheel of the low-slung Mazda. The previous number, if he remembered correctly, had been 23. He'd been expecting to see a 27 before reaching 29, and that's what had fooled him.

Whatever—this was it.

He started down the driveway, adrenaline flowing through his veins. He visualized each step in the contact as he expected it to unfold. First, Burrows would open the door. Dart would deliver his pretext and ask to come in. Burrows would hold the door open and turn away to give Dart room to enter. Dart would whip out the cuffs, grab Burrows's wrist in a half-Nelson grip, force the arm up as he kicked the back of Burrows's knee, bringing him down, then the cuffs would go on and that would be it.

The cottage, when he reached it, was unspectacular. It was a small structure covered in white vinyl, with a black shingle roof. Smoke curled from the chimney, and Dart could smell the pungent aroma of a wood fire. He followed a shovelled path down the slope, passing a small spur in which a grey Jeep Wrangler was parked. It looked to Dart just like the vehicle Jeanne Clayton had described, the one in which Burrows had waited while she picked up her Audi. He passed a stack of chopped firewood, a snowmobile, and a shovel stuck in a pile of snow. Reaching the cottage, he walked up the steps and across the deck to the door, taking off his gloves.

He knocked on the door while slipping the new press release out of his coat pocket. Through the uncurtained window of the door, which was darkened by Dart's reflection and the rest of the sunlit world behind him, he could vaguely see a linoleum floor, a case of beer filled with empties, and a step-on kitchen waste basket. He saw no movement and heard no sound. He knocked again.

Silence rang in his ears. It reminded him of how isolated the place was, and how alone he was at the moment. He shifted nervously, his boots squeaking on the frozen cedar boards of the deck. He'd kept Barrie's information to himself because he didn't trust Walker. On top of that, March's decision to use Walker as the primary on the case, a move recommended and supported by Patterson, made their judgment questionable, as far as Dart was concerned. He wasn't about to take his hot new lead to her either, then, or share it with Patterson, who was cozy with her. Dart's plan was to arrest Burrows, transport him to Smiths Falls, and present him to Todd Fisher as a fait accompli. Dart knew the detachment commander didn't have any more love or respect for March than he did, and he was certain Fisher would support Dart's decision not to follow chain of command in this particular instance, given all the uncertainties within the investigative team.

Footsteps sounded inside. A shadow loomed in the glass. The door opened a crack.

"What is it?"

"Good afternoon, sir." Dart held up the news release so that the blank side was facing the man, "I'm with the OPP. We're investigating the death of a local man and going door-to-door to ask everyone on the lake if they've seen anyone unusual in the past week or so. May I step inside for a moment?"

"Haven't seen anyone." The door began to close.

Dart put the toe of his boot forward, blocking the door. "It'll just take a moment of your time, sir. A reward's being posted for any information leading to a conviction, and you could be eligible if there's anything you tell me that leads to an arrest."

"What'd you say this was about?"

"The murder of a local man. He was shot last week. This is a sketch of someone we want to talk to. If you could just take a look, I'd appreciate it."

"There's a reward, you say?"

"It's being posted this morning. The news release on it should be going out later today."

The door opened wider. Mickey Burrows kept his hand on the inside doorknob as he looked Dart up and down. He wore a green plaid shirt, jeans, and high-top sneakers. His lip curled in a crooked sneer. "Let me see some ID."

"Sure, of course." Dart dug into the inside pocket of his coat and showed Burrows his badge. The reek of the man's breath was unmistakable. Burrows was definitely the one Jeanne Clayton had seen at Hansen's trailer on Monday night.

"I haven't got my glasses on," Burrows said. "What's it say your name is?"

"Uh, Dart. Detective Constable Craig Dart. May I come in for a moment, sir?"

"Sure. Let me get my glasses, so I can read about this reward."

It was happening just as Dart had visualized it, with Burrows turning away and the door wide open, and then it wasn't like it at all. Just as Dart started forward through the door, Burrows closed it on him. The edge of the door banged against Dart's leg, bringing him up short. His cheek bumped hard. Instinctively, he reached down for the door knob to push it back open again. As he did so, stepping into the cottage, he discovered that Burrows was already standing in front of him. The business end of a shotgun stopped him in his tracks, an inch from the bridge of his nose.

"Here's your reward, pig," Burrows said calmly. "Come and get it."

chapter THIRTY-SIX

Kevin had divided the township into quarters, with Bishop leading the canvassing team in the southwest quadrant, including Mallorytown and the river shore up to Brown's Bay, Carty taking everything southeast from Caintown to Yonge Mills and Butternut Bay, Dart and Allore covering the northeast corner and Sorrow Lake, and he and Ellie leading a team canvassing the village.

Their first stop was to see Vivian Hansen, who'd returned to her house yesterday. She agreed that the sketch looked much more like the man who'd visited her on Monday night than the drawing her own description had produced. When Kevin asked whether or not she remembered any unusual odour coming from the man, she suddenly recalled how bad his breath had smelled. Pungent, like nail polish.

While officers fanned out along the streets to work door-to-door, Kevin played a hunch and took a copy of the release into the Silver Kettle. The lunch rush was over and the place was quiet. Skinny Jimmy and his nephew Peter were cleaning up the kitchen while Edna wiped tables in the front. She straightened when Kevin walked in, then put down her dishcloth and wiped her hands on her apron when she saw Ellie behind him.

"Our newest customer," she smiled at Ellie. "How'd you like

your order?"

"Terrific. I'm hooked." She shrugged at Kevin's look. "The curried chicken salad. With the crackling."

"Glad you liked it," Edna said. "Birdie thought you were kind of lonely out there, all by yourself. Wanted to talk to him, he said."

"I asked him a few questions, but he didn't seem to know any of the answers. I hope I didn't make him late on his other deliveries."

"Not at all."

Kevin hid a smile, understanding that Ellie had tried to question Birdie, knowing he was Kevin's confidential informant, and had gotten nowhere with him. Willie Bird was extremely cautious and very selective in terms of what he said and to whom he said it. He didn't know Ellie, and he wouldn't trust her yet.

"We have a new sketch of the guy we're looking for." Kevin passed her a copy of the release. "If you wouldn't mind putting it up in your window, we'd appreciate it."

"Sure." Edna frowned at the drawing. "I know this guy, though."

"You do?"

"Yeah. I don't know his name, but I know who he is. He works for Chuck Waddell." She looked up at Kevin. "You've met him, haven't you?"

Feeling Ellie's eyes on him, Kevin shook his head. "I've never met Chuck's employees. You've seen him around the village?"

"Sure, a couple of times. He's been in here for pizza. Unfriendly son of a bitch."

"Any idea where we can find him?"

Edna looked at him oddly. "He's living in Chuck's cottage on Sorrow Lake, Kev. I thought you knew that."

Kevin grimaced, closing his eyes. "Oh, shit. Dart."

chapter THIRTY-SEVEN

"That looks a lot like me," Burrows said, prodding Dart in the neck with the muzzle of the shotgun. "Where'd you get it, dickhead?"

Dart coughed, his Adam's apple taking the force of the blow. His hands were up and his head was back as he tried to lean away from the weapon. "Artist," he managed.

"Well, I figured that much. Turn around, stupid, and keep your hands up."

Dart shuffled around. Burrows shoved the door open with his free hand and jabbed Dart in the back with the shotgun.

"Out. Now."

Dart obediently stepped out onto the deck. He looked hopefully up the shovelled path toward the road, but there was no one coming to rescue him. He could hear a vehicle somewhere in the distance but it sounded very far away, perhaps on Temperance Lake Road. Might as well be on the moon, for all the good it would do him.

He was totally, completely screwed.

Burrows prodded again. "Move. Nice and easy."

Dart slowly went down the stairs, hands in the air. His cellphone was in his left coat pocket, and if he could just—

"Now," Burrows said, interrupting his train of thought,

"we're going to have a little fun."

"What?" Dart started to look over his shoulder. "I—"

"Shut up, pig. Stand still and listen. I'm going to give you a sporting chance to make it. Ain't that nice of me?"

"Yes, I—"

"Shut up. Start running. I'll give you a five-second head start. Then I'll see if I can blow your fucking head off with this thing. Sound good?"

"Listen, sir, I think—"

"One," Burrows said, "two—"

Dart bolted up the shovelled path. The shotgun went off, spraying pellets ahead of him. Dart skidded to a stop, lost his balance, and fell on his back. As he rolled over, struggling to regain his wind, Burrows laughed.

"Not that way, you stupid fucking pig. The other way. Across the lake. It's your only chance to make it. Find the road on the other side. Move!"

Dart got to his knees, gasping.

"I'll start counting again, just because I'm such a nice guy. One, two—"

Dart staggered to his feet and plunged down toward the lake. There was a metre drop over a hand-made rock wall that he didn't see and he lost his balance at the bottom, falling awkwardly. Behind him, Burrows yelled, "Three! Four!"

Dart struggled to his feet, pain searing through his right ankle. He ran out onto the ice. He skidded on a bare patch but kept his balance, lurching forward.

"Five!" Burrows called out. The shotgun went off. The blast echoed around the lake.

Dart heard the flat, hissing sound of pellets nearby and felt a painless little tap on the back of his neck. He kept running, out across Sorrow Lake, trying to make it to the other side.

He reached a broad band of ice that was grey, rather than white. The shotgun went off again. Blast and echo. He kept running, his injured ankle sending shocks of pain up his leg.

The ice suddenly collapsed under him.

Down he went, into freezing water and jagged ice shards.

He pumped his legs, still trying to run, but felt nothing beneath his feet.

Then he sank below the surface into icy darkness.

chapter THIRTY-EIGHT

The car Dart had heard was not, in fact, a random traveller on Temperance Lake Road but Ellie's Crown Vic, lurching down Sunset Lane toward the cottage. Kevin knew which cottage belonged to Waddell and had directed her there while calling for backup.

As Ellie turned into the driveway, she heard the sound of a shotgun down at the edge of the lake, behind the cottage. She reached for the radio and reported shots fired as Kevin freed himself from his seat belt and tumbled out the door.

Ellie followed, weapon drawn. She hurried down the shovelled path toward the cottage as the shotgun boomed out again and a man's laughter echoed back to her.

Kevin rounded the deck and pointed his weapon.

"Police! Freeze, mister! Drop the gun, right now!"

Ellie ran past Kevin and circled down toward the lake, her attention on the man with the shotgun. She immediately recognized the resemblance to Jeanne Clayton's sketch—it was their unknown suspect. The shotgun shifted back and forth between them as Kevin moved steadily toward him. Ellie aimed at his centre mass and shouted, "Drop the weapon! Right now!"

She was aware that someone behind her was running away,

across the lake, but she kept her focus on the man with the shotgun as Kevin bore down on him, gun up. When he was only a few paces away, the man contemptuously threw the shotgun down into the snow and pointed across the lake, laughing.

"He's gone! Didn't you see him? Your buddy just fell in!" As Kevin reached him, the man suddenly posed like a boxer, fists raised, one foot forward. He threw a jab that missed. Kevin briskly punched him with his free hand, dropping him like a shot steer.

Ellie swung around. There was no one on the lake. There was, however, a large hole about sixty metres from shore. As she stared, a hand reached up and sank down again.

"Jesus Christ!" Kevin yelled. "Dart!"

Ellie pointed at their suspect. "Secure him." Holstering her gun, she looked around frantically for rope, a pole, something she could use, but saw nothing. Her eyes fastened on the shotgun, lying in the snow. She grabbed it and ran down to the shore, unloading the weapon on the fly. She saw the metre-high drop just in time, made it down without incident, and started across the ice.

She'd had the training as a constable and knew that the first rule of rescuing someone who'd fallen through ice was to resist running onto the ice yourself. *If it wasn't strong enough to hold them, it won't be strong enough to hold you.* She thought about the wisdom of this basic rule as she ran. The idea was not to create additional victims and make matters worse. Instead, you were supposed to follow five basic steps—preach, reach, throw, row, go. Preach meant encouraging the victim to stay afloat, but since Dart was underwater and couldn't hear anyone, that step was useless. Next, you were supposed to reach out to the victim, but how you were supposed to do that without going out on the ice yourself had always baffled her. Throw and row were fine if you had a rope to throw or a boat to row and open water to row it in, but the absurdity of these two steps made it obvious that the only one of the five steps worth following was the last one—go!

She reached a broad stretch of grey ice and, recognizing its thinness, slid to a stop. She was still about four metres from the edge of the hole Dart had made, and there was no sign of him. She got down on her hands and knees, wishing for the millionth time that she was petite instead of five-ten and 130 pounds. She stretched out on the ice. It groaned beneath her, but didn't crack.

So far, so good.

She began to belly crawl forward, shotgun extended in front of her, as though moving under barbed wire on an obstacle course. The ice groaned again, and she stopped.

A fist punched up through the thin ice a metre from her head.

"Christ!" She shrank back in shock as the ice splintered and cracked around her. Frantically, she wriggled backward.

Dart's face appeared in the hole, mouth gasping for air, eye staring blindly at the sky. His hand clutched at the edge of the hole.

She shoved the barrel of the shotgun into his palm. His hand instantly closed around it, and she felt the gun being pulled down. She tugged, and he frantically pulled back, yanking it out of her grasp. It clattered on the ice across the hole.

Dart kept his wits about him, though. Ellie watched him let go of the barrel and search for a better grip, his fingers fluttering down toward the middle of the weapon. She stretched out full-length, perilously close to the edge, and pushed the shotgun so that it straddled the hole, each end on thicker ice.

Dart pulled his face up out of the water.

"Hold on!" Ellie shouted. "I'm here. Stay calm! Give me a moment to widen the hole and we'll pull you out."

Dart gasped something unintelligible.

Ellie slithered around and pounded on the ice with her fist. It fractured and sagged, but didn't fall in. She reached underneath her and freed her gun from her holster. Holding it out, she dropped the magazine, cleared the chamber, and turned it around in her hand. Using it as a club, she bludgeoned the ice until it gave way in chunks, widening the hole. She kept at it until the hole seemed wide enough to accommodate Dart's shoulders. She flung the gun behind her and reached out her hand.

"Grab on! I'll pull you out!"

One hand still on the shotgun, Dart brought his other arm up through the opening and grabbed her wrist.

"Unh! Unh! Unh!" He pulled on her. His head bobbed up, his shoulders clearing the water for a moment, then he went back down again.

Ellie tried hauling him up, but even though he was a small man, he was still too big for her to manage on her own. She inched forward, coming as close to the opening as she dared. Her elbows now rested on the edge of the broken ice. "Climb up on me, Craig. Like a ladder. Grab my coat and pull yourself up. Both hands. Let go of the gun."

Dart hesitated, then obeyed, releasing the gun and grabbing the sleeve of her coat. He reached with the other hand, thrusting himself up, and got a grip on her shoulder. She dug her toes into the ice to try to stop from being pulled forward into the water herself.

Dart suddenly surged upward and flopped onto her back, his thigh forcing her head down into the icy water, his elbows striking her back, his hands grappling at her calves. She forced her head up and gasped for air as he surged again, up out of the water. He rolled off her back, away from the hole. Ellie raised herself up, looking over her shoulder, and saw him lying a few metres away in a fetal position, gasping and coughing.

The ice began to sag beneath her.

She jack-knifed, spun on her side, and rolled away just as the ice caved in where her body had been an instant before.

As she lay there next to Dart, her face numb and her breath ragged, she thought she could hear the distant sound of sirens.

chapter THIRTY-NINE

The coffee from the machine outside the hospital cafeteria tasted bad, but it was hot and sweet, and Ellie drank it gratefully as she followed Patterson down the corridor to the elevator. Despite her protests, she'd been transported to Brockville General along with Dart and examined in Emergency before being released, cold and exhausted but unaffected by her first close and personal encounter with Sorrow Lake. Dart, on the other hand, had been diagnosed with hypothermia and would stay in hospital for at least the rest of the weekend.

As they rode in the elevator up to Dart's floor, Patterson said, "His wife's with him right now. Norma's her name. Nice kid."

"Have you talked to him yet?"

"Briefly. Then she came in and I let them have some time. I came down to rescue you from Doctor Love."

"He was completely professional."

"I noticed he got you out of your clothes in record time."

Ellie rolled her eyes and didn't deign to reply. The doctor had been friendly and courteous. That he'd repeatedly expressed concern for her well-being, was her age and good-looking—reminding her of George Clooney—and had made a note of her cellphone number before letting her go should not, in her opinion, be held against him.

"The doctor says he just has moderate hypothermia," Patterson went on, "and they've pretty much been able to bring his body temperature back up to normal. They've got him on an IV and they're running a whole bunch of tests, but he's awake. His throat's messed up from the freezing water, but he can talk. More or less."

"That's good."

Norma was sitting on the edge of Dart's bed when they entered the room. She released her husband's hand and stood when she saw Ellie.

"This is Detective Inspector March," Patterson said, but Norma had already passed him without a look, throwing her arms around Ellie.

"Thank you so much," she whispered, hugging her tightly.

"You're welcome," Ellie replied, awkwardly holding out her coffee to keep it from spilling.

Norma released her and stood back. "You have to talk business. I'll be downstairs. Craig, I'll be back in a few minutes."

Dart said nothing, watching her leave the room. Then his eyes passed over Ellie as he turned his head to stare out the window on the other side of the bed.

"I saw the information you had on Waddell and Burrows," Patterson said. "Did you ask Barrie for it, or did he just happen to send it in case you were interested?"

Dart licked his lips as the machinery monitoring his heart rate and core temperature made quiet, rhythmic sounds.

"Allore told us you insisted on splitting up," Patterson pressed. "What kind of dumb-assed move was that? Why didn't you pass this information on to Walker or Inspector March, or even to me? Why keep it to yourself and bring this lovely shit storm down on all of us?"

Dart slowly turned his head back to them and whispered, "Don't trust Walker."

"Why the hell not? That guy's never said a single word against you, Dart. What the hell's the problem?"

"Closer to Waddell than us," Dart murmured, glancing at

Ellie. "Offered him a job. Walker..." he swallowed painfully, "fed him info on the case. You know he did."

"Are you suggesting Walker conspired with Waddell? That he's complicit?"

Dart didn't reply. He looked at Patterson with obvious bitterness.

"Excuse me," someone said behind them.

Ellie turned to look at a middle-aged man in a wrinkled blue suit standing in the doorway. She recognized his face from general headquarters in Orillia, but didn't know his name. "Yes?"

"I'm Detective Staff Sergeant Miles Greene, Detective Inspector March. Chief Superintendent Dart is here to see his son."

"I see." She looked at Patterson. "We'll do this later."

Patterson nodded and moved up the side of Dart's bed. "I want everything. No more games. Understood?"

Dart stared back, his lower lip trembling.

As they left the room and walked back down the corridor to the elevators, they passed a glassed-in room behind the nurses' station where Ellie saw Cecil Dart conferring with his son's doctor. The doctor was pointing at something on a clipboard in his hand, his back to them. Dart looked up, saw Ellie, and stared at her for a moment before returning his attention to the doctor.

Ellie drained her coffee cup, threw it into a trash can behind the counter, and joined Patterson on the elevator.

Downstairs, Inspector Fisher and his operations manager, Staff Sergeant Tobin, were waiting for them in the front atrium corridor. The detachment commander led them over to an empty seating area and immediately went after Ellie.

"How the hell could you let this happen? What were you thinking, sending a constable all by himself to arrest an armed and dangerous suspect?"

"That's not how it was, sir—" Patterson began.

Ellie held up her hand. "I agree with your concern completely, Inspector, but Detective Constable Dart had information he chose to keep to himself rather than share with his primary or his sergeant. In a situation like that, where someone chooses to act outside the investigative team—"

"Oh, pardon me, missy," Fisher snapped. "I thought you were the team manager who didn't sit on her ass all day dreaming of becoming commissioner while *my* people were busting their hump out there working a homicide investigation. Where the hell were you while Dart was off gathering this so-called outside information, which turned out to be the key to solving the case?"

Before Ellie could reply, Tobin touched Fisher on the arm and motioned with his chin, looking over the detachment commander's shoulder.

They all turned around. Chief Superintendent Leanne Blair was hurrying through the atrium toward them.

"Oh Christ," Fisher muttered, obviously not pleased to see his boss arrive just as he was getting wound up.

After assuring Leanne that she was fine, Ellie slipped off with the excuse that she wanted to get another cup of coffee to warm up her insides, leaving Fisher to brief Leanne. It was a regional meeting and a regional concern at the moment, and Ellie felt like an outsider. She also felt like a failure. She slumped past the ambulatory care unit and stood in front of the coffee machine outside the cafeteria, taking her wallet out of her jacket pocket. Fisher had had every right to read her the riot act, as unfair as it might seem on the surface. Dart had been her team member and her responsibility. She'd known he felt disconnected from the team and out of step—but dammit, how could she have anticipated that he would stumble onto their unknown suspect a step ahead of the rest of them? That he would ditch Allore and go solo to play the hero? She wasn't telepathic, was she? Was she supposed to be able to read minds now?

She pushed coins into the coffee machine and punched buttons without really looking at them. Yes, Ellie, she told herself. You *are* supposed to be telepathic. You're supposed to be perfect. The margin for error in this line of work is slim, at best. Forget the pity party. Drink your coffee, shut the hell up, and face the music.

"Ellie?"

She turned around. Patterson waved at her from the big swinging doors leading back into the atrium.

Time to regain control of this thing, she told herself. She threw the coffee into the garbage without having tasted it.

Patterson said quietly, "Old man Dart wants to talk to you."

Oh *great*, she thought. Blindfold, Ellie? Cigarette?

Cecil Dart was discussing his son's condition with Leanne Blair as Ellie and Patterson joined the little circle in the seating area. Everyone had remained on their feet despite the fact that the chairs and couches were all unoccupied and looked very comfortable.

"His pulse and respiration are up," Dart was saying, "but he got a little water in his lungs, so they need to watch for signs of damage and monitor for pneumonia. They're pretty sure he'll be all right, though."

"Thank goodness for that." Leanne massaged her forehead, her stress level obviously still very high.

"They found two pellets just under the skin in the back of his neck," Dart continued, "so technically he was not only shot at, but shot in fact." He stopped talking and turned around, realizing that Ellie was behind him. His homely face was lined with fatigue after what must have been a very tiring helicopter ride from Orillia on short notice, but his bloodshot eyes burned with fierce energy as he grabbed her hand and shook it. "Detective Inspector March." He pulled her into an awkward embrace and his free hand clapped her twice on the back before he released her and took a step back. "Thank you for saving Craig's life."

"You're welcome." It was not lost on Ellie that Dart's wife and his father had expressed their gratitude for what she'd done, but Dart himself had not.

"He owes you an apology for being an asshole," Dart went on. "He admitted to me that he withheld important information and acted on his own without authorization, and for that he'll have his ass kicked as soon as he's back on his feet. But I'm very glad that you and the other detective figured out what was going on when you did."

"Yes, sir."

Dart turned to Leanne. "I won't allow Craig's behaviour to cast a shadow on March's work. According to what you told me en route, you were going to brief Agosta. Has that happened?"

"It has," Leanne said. She'd called Ellie's supervisor in Orillia immediately after being informed of the incident.

"And he's on side with what we've discussed?"

"He is."

Dart turned to Ellie. "Although you're the case manager, March, we want you to put on your interrogator's hat and go into the room to get a confession from your suspect and his co-conspirator. *I* want you to take that son of a bitch apart, as a personal favour to me. Do you have a problem with that?"

"Of course not, sir."

"It's your show, Ellie," Leanne said. "Do what you have to do."

Ellie looked at Fisher, who was staring at the floor, biting his lip. She looked at Tobin, who was studying her with the detached interest of an entomologist examining a bug on the end of a pin. Patterson lifted an encouraging eyebrow.

"I don't think Craig should be treated harshly in this," she said to his father. "He was doing what he thought was right."

"Oh, for God's sake, March." Dart narrowed his eyes at her. "That's bullshit and you know it, but I appreciate the sentiment." He clapped her on the arm. "It'll play out as it's supposed to. Right now Craig wants to make sergeant more than anything else in the world, but this little stunt is going to make that road a longer one than it was yesterday. He's still got a lot to learn. Right now, let's focus on closing your case. How's that sound?"

"It sounds fine, sir."

Dart grunted. "Glad to hear it."

chapter FORTY

The woodlots north of Sparrow Lake were cross-hatched with countless forced roads, private lanes, and snowmobile trails. Some of them had seen occasional use during the winter, while others were snowed in and inaccessible to Kevin's Grand Cherokee as he crept along, part of the massive search underway for Bill Hansen's truck and any other evidence Mickey Burrows may have left behind while covering his tracks.

Patterson, Merkley, and a few others believed that Burrows must have disposed of the truck a long way from here, perhaps in Kingston or Sudbury, but Kevin had a hunch they were giving him much more credit for brains than he deserved. Dave Martin had already matched the boots Burrows was wearing at the time of his arrest to the size thirteens that had left their distinctive tread marks in Lackey's field and at Hansen's car yard. If Burrows was dumb and lazy enough not to have thrown them away to protect himself from being caught with incriminating physical evidence, then he was probably also dumb and lazy enough to have stashed Hansen's truck somewhere nearby in the deluded belief that no one would bother to look for it.

Kevin drove slowly along a private lane that had been kept open all winter, probably for weekend hunting and snowmobiling. He slowed at a page wire gate on the right that was chained and padlocked. The trail on the other side was narrow and snowed in. It probably hadn't been used all winter. He glanced at his gas gauge, saw that he was down to a quarter of a tank, and was about to continue on when his cellphone vibrated.

He shifted into park, checked the call display, and saw that it was Bishop. "What's up, JB?"

"We nearly got stuck twice so far, Kev. This is for shits. How're you doing?"

"Nothing yet, but there's been some kind of traffic along here in the past while. I'm going to keep going a bit farther."

Bishop paused for a moment, then said, "Look, Kev. I don't know if you're hearing the buzz that's going around right now."

Kevin frowned. "Buzz? What about?"

"I've talked to a couple of guys this afternoon. It's that fucking Dart."

"I don't understand."

"I like you, Kev. I think you're a straight-up guy. That's why I'm giving you a heads-up. That bastard's telling people you were in on this."

For a moment, Kevin was confused. "In on this? What do you mean?"

"That you're on this Waddell guy's payroll, same as our shooter and the other doofus in Kingston, What's-His-Name. The computer guy. The Rat."

Kevin stared out the windshield at nothing, his stomach suddenly churning. The sense of betrayal and wrongful accusation was like a sudden blockage in his throat. He couldn't swallow, couldn't breathe, couldn't talk.

"Kev, it's bullshit. Nobody's buying what that dickhead's trying to sell, trust me."

"I talked to Chuck about the case," Kevin managed.

"That don't mean nothing, Kev. You just didn't know, that's all."

"I asked him for advice."

"Sure you did, and he took advantage. Tried to steer you in the wrong direction."

"But there's no proof of a connection yet between Burrows and Chuck. It's just speculation."

"Kev, come on. You know that's where this is going."

"But I didn't..."

Bishop sighed. "Of course you didn't. Listen to me, Kev. I'm telling you what's being said so you can be ready for it when it comes up, okay?"

"Shit." Kevin continued to stare out the windshield, his mind whirling.

"Listen to me. I've had my eye on you. Patterson has, too. Believe me, if you were a fuck-up or showed any—and I mean any—signs of being dirty, you would've been out of here a long time ago. Know what I'm saying?"

Kevin said nothing.

"Kev! Hear what I'm saying?"

"I hear you."

"Well, pay attention and get your shit together. You're doing a helluva job as primary. You've got us this far. Don't take your eye off the ball now. We find the truck, and maybe the gun, the phone, and the keys, and whatever else, and we close this thing and you're everybody's fair-haired boy. Nobody's going to listen to Dart's bullshit. Understand?"

"I understand."

"Good. I gotta go; Allore's coming back. Hold your shit together and kick ass, kid."

The line went dead.

Blindsided, Kevin sat for a long time trying to process what Bishop had told him. Of course Dart's dislike of him had been obvious, but when they'd driven to interview Jeanne Clayton and he'd pressed Kevin on his relationship with Chuck and whether or not he'd been offered a job, Kevin had thought Dart was just trying to be as unpleasant as possible. He'd had no idea the man was pursuing an active theory that painted Kevin as a dirty cop involved in a homicide for which he was acting as primary investigator.

Kevin shifted into gear and rolled forward, trying to focus on the ditches on either side of the lane. What could he do?

Something like this would be a stain on his reputation that he'd never outlive. In his jealousy and bitterness, Dart had effectively driven a knife through the heart of Kevin's career.

He drew up to the entrance to another private lane. The gate had been left open and was held in place by a snowdrift several feet high. The lane was wide enough to accommodate a vehicle the size of Hansen's truck, but recent storms and blowing winds had driven snow across its icy surface, obliterating any tracks that might have been there. Eyeing the sizeable drifts, Kevin shut off his engine and got out.

He started walking up the lane, checking the ditches on either side. The lane ran straight ahead through crowding cedar trees, beyond which there was a slight rise that hid the rest of the lane from sight. Crows cawed somewhere nearby.

As he scanned the trees on the far side of the ditch on his right, his eye caught something anomalous. He brought his eyes back to a dead tamarack and there, about eight feet up, sitting on a branch against the trunk of the tree, was a barred owl. Its round, puffy head and pale, vertically-striped body blended almost perfectly against the chipped bark of the dead tree. It stared at him with piercing, dark eyes.

Kevin stopped, staring back. He'd never been this close to an owl before.

It swivelled its head at some sound or movement that drew its attention, then slowly returned its gaze to him. After a moment it lifted a yellow foot and pecked unconcernedly at a talon.

Kevin took a step toward it and it left the branch in a single, silent movement. He watched it glide out of sight beyond the cedars. He marvelled at how large a bird it was and how quietly it moved. In a matter of a few seconds it was gone, as though it had never been there.

He was amazed that it had been sitting there, watching him come up the lane, and that he'd had no idea it was there until he was almost past it. Its coloration was almost perfect camouflage, allowing it to hide in plain sight as it hunted, and its silence was the calm patience of a predator completely adapted to its environment.

He thought of Chuck Waddell then and shuddered. The analogy was almost too apt, and he shook his head, rejecting it. The owl, hunter though it was, was a thing of beauty and wonder. Waddell, Burrows and their ilk were not. End of story.

He became aware of a low droning sound behind him. He turned around. A snowmobile passed his Grand Cherokee and stopped, then turned up the lane toward him. It was Bob Kerr, the sergeant in command of the ERT unit, who was co-ordinating the search.

"You okay?" Kerr asked, shutting off his engine and removing his helmet.

Kevin nodded. "Didn't feel like risking the SUV up here. How's it coming?"

"Nothing so far. Where's your radio?"

Kevin reached into his coat pocket and pulled it out.

"Turn it on, Walker. I was trying to reach you for your ninety-nine." As the commander in charge of the search, Kerr needed to stay in constant communication with all the units for which he was responsible, including Kevin. As a matter of routine, he made constant 10-99 officer status checks, knowing that problems could occur quickly in winter conditions such as these.

"Sorry." Kevin turned on the radio and slid it back into his pocket.

Kerr looked around. "Probably a hunting camp down here somewhere. I saw a lot of deer trails. Keep your eyes open for coyotes; I saw their tracks as well." He put his helmet back on. "I'll run up ahead and check it out. Save you a cold walk."

He started the snowmobile's engine and tooled away. Kevin watched him top the rise between the cedar trees and disappear down the other side.

A crow swirled overhead, riding the current of the cold wind above the trees. It dipped and glided, eyeing Kevin, then pin-wheeled off, disappearing above the forest canopy. The sound of Kerr's snowmobile receded, then stopped.

The silence buzzed in Kevin's ears. He debated walking back to the Grand Cherokee and decided to wait for Kerr to come back.

After a moment the radio in his pocket popped out his name. He pulled it out and answered.

"Come on down," Kerr said. "I'm about two hundred yards from the top of the hill. You're going to want to see this."

"See what?"

"Well, it's snowed in pretty good, but I'd say this truck looks a lot like a black Dodge Ram somebody tried to stash out of sight."

"I'll be right there," Kevin said, unable to suppress a relieved grin.

chapter FORTY-ONE

It was a few minutes past eight o'clock that evening when Ellie walked into the interview room with Carty and sat down in the chair at the little table. "My name's Detective Inspector March," she said, putting down her notebook. "This is Detective Constable Carty."

She opened her notebook as Carty leaned against the wall in the far corner of the tiny room, arms folded across his chest.

Mickey Burrows moved his eyes from Ellie to Carty to a scuff mark on the wall that seemed to catch and hold his interest. The contusion on his cheekbone, a souvenir of his brief scuffle with Kevin, looked a little sore.

"You've been in rooms like this one before," Ellie continued, "so you know how it works. Your lawyer hopefully advised you to co-operate with us and answer our questions truthfully and as completely as possible, Mickey, because the fact is you've violated your parole conditions and you're going back inside. On top of that, the new charges you're looking at, which include the attempted murder of a police officer, could keep you there for the rest of your life. Do you understand what I'm saying to you?"

"Bullshit," Burrows said to the scuff on the wall. "I was just scaring him."

"The doctor removed shotgun pellets from the back of the detective's neck, so you shot him. You figured even if you missed he'd fall through the ice and drown. Isn't that what you were thinking?"

His thick lip curled as he rotated his head to look at her. "I just wanted to see the pig run."

"You wanted to kill him, didn't you?"

"Run, pig. Run."

"You wanted to hurt him."

"Sure. What the hell. Squeal, pig. Squeal."

"So you drove him out onto the ice knowing that even if he was out of range of the shotgun, he'd fall through and drown."

"Only a moron pig would go out on the ice this early."

"So you deliberately drove him out onto the lake, firing the shotgun at him, knowing he would fall through and drown. Didn't you, Mickey?"

"You sound like you know it all."

Ellie waited.

"All right, all right, so what if I did? Who cares? Some moron pig comes to the door and thinks he can arrest me by pretending he doesn't have a fucking clue who I am?" He showed Ellie his large, yellow teeth. "It's a joke. Hilarious. I'll be famous inside. The guy who chased the pig across the lake."

"You figure you'll tell your story to all your Angels friends inside and they'll pat you on the back and tell you what a hard-assed sonofabitch you are."

He lost the smile. "I steer clear of those guys. I got other friends inside I hang with."

Ellie feigned surprise. "I'm sorry, I thought the Red and White was your team. Did I get that wrong?"

Burrows looked alarmed. "I don't have nothing to do with them. Don't go around saying I do, cuz they don't like that."

"How well do you know Steve Barron?"

Burrows glanced at Carty before replying. "Who's that?"

"Are you saying you don't know Steve Barron?"

"I may have heard the name."

"He's connected to an outfit up in Sudbury. I figured he was probably one of the buddies you like to brag to."

"I don't have nothing to do with the guy."

"How about Bill Hansen, the car dealer in the village? Have much to do with him?"

"Not really."

"No?" Ellie pretended to be surprised again. "I've spoken to several witnesses who've seen you with him."

"Maybe I talked to him once or twice."

"What about his wife, Mrs. Hansen? Ever talk to her?"

"What is this? No, I never talked to her."

"Okay. How about Tommy Ratliff?"

"Tommy? Sure, I know him. Works for Chuck, same as me."

"I heard he's affiliated with the Hells Angels."

Burrows laughed. "The Rat? You must be on something. He's scared of his own fucking shadow, that guy. He'd piss his pants if one of them just looked at him."

"So what about Chuck Waddell? He must be the one working with the Big Red Machine."

Burrows lost the smile again and returned his attention to the scuff on the wall. "I don't know nothing about Chuck's business."

"You and he go back quite a ways, though, don't you?"

Burrows shrugged.

"When did you first meet him?"

Silence.

"He arrested you in Kingston on the assault charge, didn't he? Back in '86, when you were twenty. Is that when you first got to know him?"

Burrows shrugged again.

"He kept in touch with you, didn't he? Even after he left the city and came up to Sparrow Lake. You two have a long history together, don't you? He found jobs for you, helped you out, then hired you for his security business and brought you up here."

"So what?"

"What do you do for Waddell in return for all those favours, Mickey? What's your job description?"

"Whatever he tells me to do."

"Did he tell you to pick up Bill Hansen at his car yard last Monday night?"

Burrows frowned at the wall.

Ellie put her elbow on the table and rested her cheekbone against her knuckles, watching him. "We know you were there, Mickey. We can prove it. Why did you go there?"

Burrows didn't respond.

Ellie had a flash of insight. Glancing at Carty, she said, "Did you know Hansen came here that afternoon? To this detachment office? That he was going to talk to one of our detectives about what was going on?"

When Burrows failed to react, Ellie knew she'd guessed correctly. "You were following him, weren't you? I'll bet when we check the surveillance cameras on this building we'll see you behind him when he turned into the parking lot, right out here." She pointed in the general direction of the highway. "You probably hung around to see if he'd get out of the car and come inside." There were no surveillance cameras angled to record traffic passing on the highway in front of the detachment, but Burrows wouldn't know that.

"Go ahead and check."

"Were you following him that day?"

"So what if I was?"

"Did Waddell tell you to, or was that something you came up with all by yourself?"

Burrows sneered.

"Did Waddell tell you to go get Hansen that night, or was that your own little brainstorm, too?"

"I'm not gonna talk about that, bitch."

Carty shifted, but Ellie shook her head. "That's all right, Tom. I understand where Mickey's coming from. He's sitting in here looking at attempted murder of a police officer, but he thinks he's going to get by on the murder of Bill Hansen. He doesn't understand we've got him on that one, too."

"You're full of shit," Burrows said, without conviction.

Ellie opened the file folder in front of her. "I've got

something to show you, Mickey. Pay attention, now." She slid a piece of paper from the file folder and spun it around so that he could read it. "This is a DNA profile report, Mickey. You may remember being compelled to donate a sample of your saliva after your conviction for armed robbery. Well, this is a copy of your DNA profile."

Burrows glanced at it, shrugged, and looked away.

She pulled a glossy photograph out of the folder and slid it across the desk. "This is a photograph taken by our forensics team of a black hair we found on the living room carpet in the Hansen home. We're going to be able to get a complete DNA profile from it. We're confident this'll be an exact match to this," she tapped a finger on his DNA report. "Mrs. Hansen told us you went to see her on Monday night and made a voluntary admission that you'd just killed her husband. Her testimony, combined with this hair and DNA match, will give us a slam dunk case against you, Mickey."

"Bullshit," Burrows said, ignoring the photograph.

She picked up the photo and the report and slid them under the folder. She removed another glossy photograph and put it in front of him. "This is a boot print we found in the field on Church Road where Bill Hansen was killed. It's a size thirteen boot. The prints lead all the way from the road into the field, right up to where the body was found, and then they go back across the field to the road again. The tread marks on this boot are pretty distinctive. One of our identification officers is an expert in this stuff, and he tells me this boot print is an exact match to the boots you were wearing when we arrested you, Mickey. An *exact* match. We can prove you walked into that field with Bill Hansen and walked back out again after you shot him. In fact, he tells me there's blood on your boots where it spattered down when you shot him. It's going to match Hansen's blood, Mickey, and it's going to be further proof you shot him."

Burrows studied the scuff on the wall with an intense frown.

"We searched the property around the lake this afternoon," Ellie went on, returning the photos to her file folder. "We found Hansen's truck where you hid it. Down a laneway about a kilometre from the cottage, in the forest. Waddell owns that property, too, as you no doubt know. Is that where he told you to hide it, or did you decide that one on your own?"

"He never told me nothing."

"So you decided to hide it there yourself."

Burrows shrugged.

"They took the truck to the lab at Smiths Falls. They'll go over it down to the molecular level to prove you were in it, Mickey. One more link in the chain that'll keep you in prison for the rest of your life. You hid the truck there after you killed Hansen, didn't you?"

"They won't find nothing in that truck from me."

"I imagine you wiped it down, Mickey. But you're shedding hairs like a dog in the spring, and I don't expect you had a vacuum cleaner out there. They've probably already lifted half a dozen specimens from the driver's seat already."

Burrows scowled at the wall.

"The point I'm trying to make is that although your fate's already been sealed, your boss, the guy who told you to do all this stuff, is going to walk away scot-free. He's out there laughing at you, Mickey. He won't lift a finger to help you. You'll never have a chance to see the outside again. You'll die in there. And he'll be out here, living it up. Not really fair, is it? Did he order you to shoot Bill Hansen, Mickey?"

As she stared at him, waiting for an answer, she saw him disappear somewhere deep inside himself. Doors closed behind his eyes and the lights went off. He was gone.

She tried for another half hour to coax him out of his silence without success, then finally gathered up her folder and notebook and left the room. With Carty following her, she walked down to the conference room, threw her notebook on the table, and poured herself a cup of coffee.

Everyone who'd been watching the audio-visual feed filed in and stood in a semi-circle around her.

"He confessed to the attack on Detective Constable Dart," said Inspector Fisher, who'd driven down from Smiths Falls to watch the interrogation. "We've got that much in the bag, anyway."

Ellie grunted, gulping down coffee.

"But he wouldn't budge on his boss," Bishop said. "Son of a bitch."

"You'll have to do it yourself," Fisher said to Ellie. "You'll have to get a confession out of Waddell."

"There's no physical evidence on him at all at this point, is there?" Patterson asked.

Ellie shook her head. "Not yet. But he was in that truck. Ident will find something."

"But if they don't," Fisher prodded, "it's going to be up to you. You'll have to bring Waddell in and break him. Get him to confess."

Ellie looked at Kevin, who'd been silent up to this point. "Is he liable to run?"

"I wouldn't think so. He probably thinks he's in the clear."

"We'll bring him in tomorrow morning, then." She stood up. "I'm going to go get some sleep."

"How will you do it?" Fisher asked. "How will you get him to crack?"

Ellie shrugged, still looking at Kevin. "He's a former cop. He'll be glad to help us out, don't you think?"

Looking distinctly unhappy, Kevin didn't reply.

chapter FORTY-TWO

Ellie slept badly that night. She woke up several times and had trouble getting back to sleep. At half past three, she abandoned the bed and sat in the recliner next to the propane stove with a glass of Jack Daniels. She'd discovered a few days ago that the recliner also rocked, and she put it to work now as she sipped the whisky and stared into the darkness.

As a young woman she'd never been prone to experiencing dark nights of the soul at three o'clock in the morning, but now that her fortieth birthday was behind her and her family was gone, she was finding it more and more difficult to sleep all the way through. She was alone in life, and while solitude had its advantages it also meant that she was on her own at times like this. There was no one lying next to her in bed that she could talk to, ask for advice, reach out to for comfort. Sometimes, she thought, you don't choose how to live your life, you just live what's given to you, your best intentions notwithstanding.

She rocked and sipped, rocked and sipped. She was concerned about Craig Dart. It was impossible not to blame herself for what had happened to him. She'd seen very early on that he wasn't a good fit but had balked at the idea of removing him from the team. Because of his father? Even if she was reluctant to admit it, she knew that Cecil's unseen presence had factored into her decision, as had her unwillingness to admit that she might not be able to bring Dart around. She should have made a quick decision on him. Moved him off the team right away and replaced him with someone else, then dealt with whatever fallout resulted from it.

She closed her eyes, feeling the regret burn away inside her like the whisky, hot and rough. She should tell Tony not to bother with her extension. She should stick to what she was good at and not kid herself that she had a stellar future as a case manager. She wasn't the kind of person who brought people together and welded them into a trim fighting team. People like that were good at social interaction. They had outstanding people skills and normal relationships. Peter Whyte, for example, had been married for fourteen years and had three kids. Jack Dawson was on his second marriage, admittedly, but he was the kind of person everyone liked being around—affable, witty, and generous. Tony himself was one of the nicest guys you'd ever want to meet. They'd all found ways to integrate their careers into their personal lives so that the one didn't explode the other into a million pieces. But not her. Not Ellie March. For her it was always career first, personal life second. A distant second. So distant that it was essentially gone.

No life for Ellie. No life, dear. Sorry about that.

She thought about Mickey Burrows, replaying the interrogation in her head, question by question. She'd been too coy. She should have played it differently. She'd been too easy on him.

She thought about Chuck Waddell. She'd instantly disliked the man the moment she'd set eyes on him. And his betrayal of Kevin, pretending to be his friend while playing him for the fool, was unforgivable.

There was something, though, that she was missing. An angle...

She opened her eyes. *What time is it?*

She turned on the table lamp next to the recliner and squinted at the clock on the wall in the kitchen. Twenty minutes before five. She'd fallen asleep out here again.

What the hell. She turned the light off again and closed her eyes. She'd doze just a little more. Half an hour or so. After coffee and her morning routine, she'd go into the village. Because she knew, now, who would tell her what she needed to know about Chuck Waddell.

chapter FORTY-THREE

The only business open at 7:35 on a Sunday morning in Sparrow Lake was, of course, the Silver Kettle. Ellie parked the Crown Vic out front and walked in, pulling off her mittens and digging out her wallet. “Could I get a cup of coffee to go, please?”

Edna stood behind the counter, sorting menus. Skinny Jimmy was nowhere in sight, and his place in the kitchen was occupied by a tall, white-haired man Ellie had never seen before. Two older men sat at a table close to the front window, picking at their breakfast. A middle-aged man at the counter hunched over a mug of coffee and a plate of buttered white toast. It was warm inside the restaurant, a pleasant change from the bitter air outside.

“Good morning, Ellie. You’re up early.”

“I could say the same thing about you. Don’t you ever get a day off?”

“Tomorrow.” Edna poured coffee into a large disposable cup and added a spoonful of honey from a small jar shaped like a bear. “I get Mondays off. Jimmy gets today. This is Terry, Jimmy’s cousin.”

“Hi, Terry,” Ellie said.

“Good morning,” Terry replied, pushing a cloth around on

the grill with the edge of his spatula. "You're the police inspector, aren't you?"

"We saw it on the news last night," Edna said. "You saved that officer's life."

"He saved himself. But yes, I helped."

Terry tossed the cloth into a bucket and put the spatula into a stainless steel pan to soak. "They don't call it Sorrow Lake for nothing. It's a lovely spot, but bad things happen out there."

Ellie paid for her coffee and wrapped her hands around it, glad for the warmth. "I've been meaning to ask you about the second-hand store down the street. Who's the woman who runs it?"

"That's Lois," replied Edna. "Lois Shipman."

"Does she live around here?"

"She lives upstairs, above the store. You're an antique collector?"

"No. I just want to talk to her."

"She's a darling," Terry said, wiping his hands on his apron.

Edna rolled her eyes. "Typical bachelor. He thinks all the girls are darlings. That's why he never married one."

"The best were already taken."

"Put a sock in it." Edna leaned on the counter. "Do you have her phone number?"

Ellie shook her head, sipping the coffee. It was still too hot.

Edna scribbled on the top page of her order booklet and tore it out. "She lives by herself. Her husband was one of the biggest auctioneers around here until he passed away. How long ago was that, Terry?"

"Got to be ten years now, at least. Maybe twelve."

"She sold the house and auction barn they owned just outside of Athens and bought the store here. Brought a lot of their junk in as stock, and she's been buying and selling ever since."

"Thanks." Ellie slipped the number into her pocket and put her mittens back on.

"Say hello to Kevin for me."

"Will do." Back outside, Ellie tried another sip of her coffee as she wandered down the sidewalk to the second-hand store. Still too hot. She looked at the dusty window through which Lois Shipman had peered out at her last Wednesday. It was dark and deserted inside. She casually tried the front door. It was locked.

She strolled back to the Crown Vic and got in. Setting down the coffee, she dug out her cellphone and called the number on the piece of paper.

It rang many times without being answered. Ellie expected it to go to voicemail, but it kept ringing. Finally: "Hello?"

"Is this Mrs. Lois Shipman? The owner of Second Chances in Sparrow Lake?"

"Yes. Who's calling?"

"Mrs. Shipman, my name's Ellie March. I'm with the Ontario Provincial Police. I'm calling from outside your front door right now. Would you mind letting me in? I have a few questions I need to ask you. It won't take long."

"I was asleep."

"I'm very sorry to wake you up. If you could just give me a few minutes, I'd really appreciate it."

Silence.

"I can wait if you need to take a minute to get dressed. I don't mind. I'll just wait right here for you to open the door."

"All right."

Ellie turned on the engine and cranked up the heat, sipping her coffee as she watched the front door of the store. A car pulled up in the angled parking slot next to her, and a guy in a parka and construction boots ran into the Silver Kettle. Ellie sipped her coffee, watching the time crawl past on the dashboard clock. When 7:53 changed to 7:54, the guy in the parka ran back out of the restaurant with a large paper bag and a cardboard tray filled with cups of coffee. He jumped into the car and left in a hurry. Ellie drained the last of her coffee and put the empty cup on the floor behind the passenger seat. The Closed sign in the door of the second-hand shop moved aside and a pale smudge of a face looked out.

Ellie grabbed her notebook from the passenger seat and got

out of the car. The face was gone when she reached the door, the Closed sign rocking gently back and forth on its string. Ellie pounded and waited.

The Closed sign tipped again and Lois Shipman looked out at her. Ellie raised a mitten in greeting.

The face went away, and the door opened a crack. "Who did you say you were, again?"

Ellie had her badge ready. "Detective Inspector Ellie March, ma'am. OPP. May I come in and ask you a few questions about William Hansen?"

"I don't know anything about that."

"Ma'am, please? It's really cold out here. I'll only take a few moments of your time." Ellie didn't need to put on an act to appear cold; it was freezing and she was hating every second of it.

The door swung open. "All right, come in. Just for a minute."

"Thank you, I appreciate it."

The woman looked up and down the street before closing the door. "What do you want?"

The store was filled to capacity with furniture, shelves clogged with books and knick knacks, and boxes of items that had never been unpacked. Narrow aisles ran between the shelves, cupboards, high boys, and hutches to the back. The lights suspended from the high tin ceiling were still turned off.

"Is there somewhere we can sit down for a minute?"

Mrs. Shipman reluctantly led the way to a small office at the back of the store, her slippers scuffing on the cracked linoleum. She offered Ellie a chair next to a desk piled high with stuff. As Ellie unzipped her coat and sat down, notebook on her lap, Mrs. Shipman said, "I'm going to have a cup of tea. Do you want some?"

"That would be nice. Thank you." Ellie disliked tea but accepted anyway, trying to appear friendly and non-threatening.

Mrs. Shipman disappeared through a doorway. Ellie heard her drawing water from a tap. China and silverware clattered.

Mrs. Shipman looked out at her. “How do you take it?”

“Black is fine.”

While the kettle boiled, Mrs. Shipman endured a coughing fit. Ellie listened to her spit several times, then heard the tap run. When Mrs. Shipman came out with two bone china cups on saucers, Ellie’s nostrils caught the tang of alcohol. She accepted her cup and cautiously sipped.

Tea, and nothing else.

Mrs. Shipman swigged and swallowed, eyes closed.

Not just tea.

“Mrs. Shipman, as I said, we’re investigating the murder of Bill Hansen last week.” Ellie found a scrap of free space on the desk and put the teacup down. “It’s my understanding you spoke to officers canvassing the village and told them you knew him slightly, but that was all.”

“Yes. That’s right.”

“That’s not entirely true, though, is it? You knew Mr. Hansen better than that, didn’t you? In fact, he used to come into the store from time to time to talk to you, didn’t he?”

Mrs. Shipman kept her eyes on her teacup. “I suppose so.”

“Look,” Ellie said gently, “I understand you’re afraid. I’m here to help. Bear with me for a few minutes. We’ll get through this together.”

Mrs. Shipman gulped at her tea.

“It might be a good idea just to put your cup down for a minute, Lois. May I call you Lois? I’m Ellie.”

Mrs. Shipman put her teacup down on a stack of magazines and folded her hands together.

“I want to show you a photograph of someone, Lois, and I want you to tell me if you know who he is. All right?”

When Mrs. Shipman nodded, Ellie took out a blown-up mug shot of Mickey Burrows and held it out. The woman looked at it but wouldn’t take it, so Ellie put it down on the desk where she could see it. “Do you know who this man is?”

Mrs. Shipman shuddered, nodding again.

“Do you know his name?”

“No.”

"Has he come around to the store to talk to you?"

"Yes."

"Did Chuck Waddell send him?"

"Yes."

"Did this man tell you he shot Mr. Hansen?"

Tears began to run down her cheeks. She nodded.

"Did he threaten you? Did he say he'd hurt you unless you kept your mouth shut?"

"Yes." She wiped at the tears with the edge of her hand.

Ellie looked around and spotted a box of tissues under an antique box camera on the desk. She held it out to Mrs. Shipman, who took it and pulled out a handful.

"This man's in custody now, Lois. He's being charged with the attempted murder of a police officer, and we're confident he'll also be charged with Mr. Hansen's murder. He's violated his parole conditions and will go back to prison right away. He won't have a chance to threaten you again. Do you understand what I'm saying?"

Mrs. Shipman muttered something into her wad of tissues.

"I beg your pardon, Lois?"

She shook her head, wiping her eyes.

"You still don't feel safe?"

Mrs. Shipman sighed.

"Did Chuck Waddell also threaten you?"

Mrs. Shipman stared at the tissues in her hand.

"On Wednesday," Ellie said, picking up the photograph of Mickey Burrows and putting it back into her notebook, "Kevin Walker and I saw Waddell coming out of your store with a package. He told Kevin the box contained a pair of old ice skates he'd bought from you. How much did he pay for them, Lois?"

Mrs. Shipman pursed her lips.

"They weren't really ice skates, were they?"

She shook her head.

"What was in the package, Lois?"

"Money," she whispered.

"How much money?"

"Ten thousand."

Ellie raised her eyebrows. “That’s a lot of cash, Lois. Where did it come from?”

“Toronto.”

Ellie took out a pen and opened her notebook. “I’m going to write down a few things, Lois. I want you to tell me what you were doing for Chuck Waddell. What was he making you do?”

“He would bring things to me,” she said, watching the pen as Ellie wrote down the date and time on a fresh page in the notebook. I’d send them to someone in Toronto, and they’d send me back money. I gave the money to him. That was all. Am I in trouble?”

“My only interest at the moment is the murder of Bill Hansen. I believe Waddell may have told Mickey Burrows to threaten Hansen, maybe even to kill him, but I need proof. To get proof, I have to understand what was going on. I think he was using Mr. Hansen to do things the same way he was using you. There may even be others in the village he was using as well.”

“There are. Others.”

“Okay. We can talk about them in a minute. Right now, let’s talk about how you got involved with Waddell to begin with.”

“A couple of years after I came here, he came in and was looking through one of my display cabinets. He asked me to show him a pocket watch, a nice Hamilton railroad watch I was asking two fifty for. He opened up the case and showed me where it was engraved with initials. Well, I’d seen the initials before but he told me the watch had been stolen from a collector in Ottawa a couple of months ago. He threatened to arrest me. I’d bought the watch along with a few other things from a man who told me he’d inherited it from his uncle. I realized later it was that man,” she pointed at the photograph of Mickey Burrows that was sticking out from the back of Ellie’s notebook, “but I couldn’t prove it, could I? I didn’t know what to do. He told me to take all the things the man had sold me and ship them by courier to an address in Toronto. I’d receive a package of money back, and he’d come in to get the money. If I did what I was told, he said, I wouldn’t have to go to jail. I went along with it because he was the police, and I didn’t know what else to do. I didn’t want to go to jail."

"Of course you didn't. Was it always antiques that you sent?"

"Yes. Watches, jewellery, coins, snuff boxes, things like that. Small but worth a lot of money."

"Did he ever say where he was getting them?"

She shook her head. "I figured they were all stolen."

"Was it ever drugs?"

"No, thank God."

"How often did you do this for him?"

"About once a month, I guess."

"Did you always send the package to the same address, or were there others?"

"Always the same one." She pulled over a small metal box and opened the lid. She flipped through a set of index cards, pulled one out, and gave it to Ellie.

The name on the card was simply "Mr. Cho," and the address was on Spadina Avenue, in Toronto's Chinatown district. Ellie copied it into her notebook. Handing back the index card, she asked, "Was it always Waddell, or did Burrows come back sometimes?"

"It was Mr. Waddell, but he said if I ever tried to get out of what he called 'our arrangement,' he'd send that other man back to have a talk with me. I knew what that meant, so I always did what he told me to do."

"Mr. Hansen talked to you about this whole mess not long before he died, didn't he?"

Mrs. Shipman stared at her hands for a moment. "He wanted us to go to the police together," she finally said. "He said if we explained everything, they'd go easy on us if we helped them prove what Mr. Waddell was doing. I told him I wouldn't, that I was too frightened. I felt sorry for Bill, though, because he'd been trapped just like me. He said Mr. Waddell started spreading rumours that Bill was selling stolen cars, and when people stopped dealing with him, Mr. Waddell came around and said he could prove Bill had sold a stolen car to a friend of his and that he'd arrest him unless he started sending drugs in his cars to people all over the place. Bill did it for as long as I did, but he wanted to stop. He even told Mr. Waddell he wanted out. Bill said we should do it together, confront Mr. Waddell and tell him we wanted to stop, but I was too afraid to do anything. I told Bill I couldn't."

Ellie thought about Bill Hansen parked outside the OPP detachment building, trying to call Kevin through the general number. In the end, he'd been too afraid to go through with it. Too afraid to get out of the car and walk inside. Too afraid even to complete the call. In the end, he was just as afraid as Lois Shipman had been. But Burrows had been following him, no doubt because Hansen had told Waddell he wanted out, and after hearing that Hansen had made an aborted attempt to contact the police, Waddell must have sent Burrows around to the car yard that evening to bring him in for a little talk.

"Last Wednesday," Ellie said, "when Waddell picked up his money, did he talk to you about Mr. Hansen? About what had happened to him?"

"Yes."

"What did he say?"

"Just how terrible it was. That I should be careful not to let it happen to me, too."

"Did he say anything else about it?"

"No."

Ellie closed her notebook, glancing at her watch. "Lois, our officers have picked up Chuck Waddell and have taken him to our detachment office in Brockville for questioning. I'm going to be the one asking the questions. I appreciate all the help you've given me. It's our job now to see to it that he goes to prison for what he's done. You can help us, though, when you testify in court that Mickey Burrows told you he killed Mr. Hansen, and that Chuck Waddell threatened you. When you do that, it'll help send them to prison and get you free from this horrible situation."

Mrs. Shipman looked away for a moment. A vein pulsed in her temple. Then she straightened and met Ellie's eyes.

"I'll do it," she whispered. "I'll do it for Bill."

chapter FORTY-FOUR

Ellie opened the door of the interview room and closed it quietly behind her. Chuck Waddell sat in the moulded plastic chair at the end of the little desk, sipping a cup of coffee.

"Good morning, Chuck." Ellie sat down, swivelling her chair to face him. "Sorry to keep you waiting."

"No problem." Despite having been alone in the room for over an hour, Waddell looked calm and confident in his black leather jacket, blue plaid shirt, jeans, and black sneakers. "Figured you'd probably get around to asking for my help. Thought I'd be talking to Kev, though. Is he around?"

"We're all pretty busy right now." Ellie crossed her legs and brushed the knee of her trousers with her palm. "Chuck, the reason Detective Constable Carty brought you in this morning is that we've received information that gives us reasonable grounds to believe that you were involved with the murder of William Hansen. As a result—"

"You've got to be kidding me," Waddell snorted, the corner of his mouth lifting.

"As a result," Ellie went on, "I need to remind you that you have the right to retain and instruct counsel without delay. You also have the right to free and immediate legal advice from duty counsel by making free telephone calls to the number we can provide you, and you have the right to apply for legal assistance through the provincial legal aid program. Do you understand, Chuck?"

Waddell shook his head. "You're shitting me. What information?"

"Chuck, come on. You've been in my seat many times. You know what's going on. Please answer the question. Do you understand your Charter rights as I've explained them?"

"Yes, dammit, I understand them. What I *don't* understand is what kind of garbage bullshit you think you're pulling on me, missy."

"Do you want to call a lawyer, Chuck?"

"What the hell for? This is all bullshit."

"I'm reminding you as well that you don't need to say anything. You have nothing to hope from any promise or favour and nothing to fear from any threat whether or not you say anything. Anything you do say may be used as evidence. Do you understand?"

Waddell propped his elbow on the desk and covered his eyes with his hand, shaking his head.

"Chuck, you've been in these rooms yourself countless times, sitting on this side of the desk, so you know this interview is being audio- and video-recorded. Please tell me for the record if you understand your right not to say anything, and that anything you do say may be used as evidence."

Waddell tipped up his hand and looked out from underneath it at her. "I understand. Let's get on with this so I can set you guys straight and get back home in time for lunch. Okay?"

"You've spoken to Kevin before about the case, and to me, you were interviewed when our detectives were completing their canvass of the village last week, and you may also have talked to Detective Constable Carty on the way down this morning. Anything that was said to you previously by me or anyone else should not influence you or make you feel compelled to say anything at this time. Whatever you felt influenced or compelled to say earlier, you are now not obliged to repeat, nor are you obliged to say anything further, but whatever you do say may be given as evidence. Do you understand all this, Chuck?"

"Sure sure sure," Waddell replied, "I get all that. Secondary caution, got it. Move on. Let's get to this bullshit information that's on your mind and get it all cleared up, okay?"

"We may be here for a while, Chuck, so if you want another coffee and a muffin or something to eat, or you need to use the washroom, just let me know."

Waddell rolled his eyes. "I always had that problem with the girls, wanting to leave the room every five minutes to go to the can. You'll probably be hitting the head long before I need to."

Ellie pretended to find this amusing. "I think I'll probably be okay, Chuck. Let's start off with where we are right now in our investigation. Yesterday afternoon we arrested a man who attempted to kill one of our detectives while he was questioning him in connection with Bill Hansen's murder."

"Yeah, I heard about that."

Ellie folded her hands in her lap. "Then you know the man we arrested was Mickey Burrows, who works for you, and that we arrested him at a cottage on Sparrow Lake that you own. Did you know Burrows had violent tendencies when you hired him, Chuck?"

"Yeah, sure I knew. He and I go way back. I was hoping that stuff was all behind him now."

"How do you mean?"

"Isn't it obvious?" Waddell rolled his eyes, as though speaking to an idiot. "I hire ex-cons because I believe in rehabilitation, and guys like him need a second chance to prove they've paid their debt to society and moved on. I mean, it *is* called Corrections Canada, not Punishment Canada. Right?"

As Waddell laughed at his own joke, Ellie leaned forward and put her elbow on the table. "Why did you move him from Kingston up to the cottage, Chuck?"

Waddell looked a little surprised by the question. "Worked better for me. I run the business from home, and I wanted Mickey around to be my gofer, plain and simple. My other guy stays in Kingston and looks after our accounts. You know, all the crap the clients want for maintenance and reports and all that shit."

"Mr. Inside," Ellie said lightly.

Waddell fingered the whiskers on his chin. "Yeah, I suppose you could call him that."

"And Burrows is Mr. Outside."

Waddell said nothing.

"Did Burrows kill Bill Hansen, Chuck?"

"Whoa." Waddell's eyebrows shot up. "Not that I know of. Is that where you're coming from with all this? You think he ran that cop of yours out onto the lake because he offed Hansen?"

"We think we've got a pretty solid case against him. Does that surprise you?"

"Damned right it does."

"Something that confuses me, though, is *why* Burrows would kill him. You're aware that Bill Hansen was involved in distributing drugs?"

"Kev mentioned something about it. Could've knocked me over with a feather."

"Yeah. And you floated the theory to me and Kevin on Wednesday that Hansen must have hooked up with a biker gang in Sudbury, and he was distributing the stuff up to them."

"Sounded logical to me."

"So here's where I'm confused. If Hansen was doing business with an OMG outfit, why would Burrows be involved? We haven't been able to connect him to any biker activity at all. In fact, when I asked him about it, the question upset him. He was afraid word would get back that he was trying to claim some kind of affiliation, and that it would get him into deep shit. Is there something our people are missing? Does Burrows have some kind of gang connection or not?"

Waddell hesitated, as though thinking about it. "Not that I ever heard. Who knows, though. Maybe it happened behind my back. I sure as hell hope not."

"Can you think of any other reason why he'd want to kill Bill Hansen?"

Waddell shook his head. "Nope. I feel bad that the guy worked for me and I had no idea this stuff was going on, but I can't explain why Mickey would do something like that. Are you sure about your facts? What have you got?"

"We can talk about that later. I need to change the subject a bit and ask *you* the standard question, Chuck. Where were you last Monday evening, between five in the afternoon and midnight?"

Waddell smiled condescendingly. "Took you long enough to get around to it."

Ellie waited for his reply.

"I was in Kingston. I went down to look in on my other guy, but the dickhead must've forgotten we had a meeting because he wasn't around. So I stayed down, had dinner, saw a movie, and then drove home. Got home maybe eleven, eleven thirty."

"Can anyone vouch for your whereabouts during this time? You're divorced, correct? You live by yourself?"

"Correct and correct. No wife to alibi me."

"What about your other employee? What's his name?"

Waddell sighed. "Tommy Ratliff. Weren't you listening? I said he wasn't around, so, no, he can't vouch for my whereabouts."

"What about credit card receipts? For the restaurant or the movie theatre or gas?"

"I work in cash almost exclusively, and I don't keep cash register receipts. They have that chemical on them that gives you cancer or whatever the hell it is. Just don't tell Revenue Canada, okay? They'll want to audit me next week, the bastards. So again, no. No receipts."

"All right, that's fine. I prefer to use cash myself whenever I can." Ellie steepled her fingers and pointed at him. "You know what, though. As you can imagine, we've collected a ton of physical evidence on this case. Something that would really help is if you could provide a few samples to help us eliminate you from consideration, Chuck. Would you be willing to do that? This morning?"

Waddell leaned back and crossed his legs. "Sure. Why not? What's a little more work for the Ident boys, right?"

"What about impressions of your shoes?"

"Sure!" Waddell began to reach for his laces.

Ellie held up a hand. “Not right now, Chuck. I’ll get the technicians to come in and do all that stuff. Okay?”

“Bring ‘em on!”

Ellie grabbed her notebook and stood up. “I’ll ask them to come in. And you know what? I’m embarrassed. I have to admit, I need to take that little washroom break after all. Can I get you another coffee?”

Waddell smirked. “Sure. You do that. And make sure it has two sugars, this time, will you?”

“All right, Chuck. No problem.”

chapter FORTY-FIVE

As Dave Martin and Serge Landry took Waddell's fingerprints, swabbed the inside of his mouth to collect a DNA sample, and measured and photographed the soles of his obviously-new black sneakers, Ellie leaned against the door frame and watched on the monitor. Waddell submitted to every request with condescending humour, as if he were indulging young children playing games with him at a Christmas party.

"He's a confident bastard," Todd Fisher said. The detachment commander had driven down from Smiths Falls again to observe the interrogation this morning. Ellie suspected he was doing so at the request of Cecil Dart, but it didn't much matter to her who was watching her work. When she was in the room with a suspect, that was the only end of the AV feed that concerned her.

"He's definitely confident." Ellie folded her arms. "He hasn't heard the case we have against Burrows yet, but he obviously believes that whatever it is, he was too careful to leave anything behind for us to find. He's convinced he can bluff his way out."

"And you're sure," Fisher said, turning on Kevin, "you didn't share information with him that'll put us at a disadvantage now?"

"No, sir," Kevin replied anxiously. "As I already said, apart from telling him we'd found drugs in Hansen's Range Rover scheduled for delivery to Sudbury, I didn't share any other details of the case with him."

Patterson grunted. "You said he came up with the biker gang theory on his own."

"Yes, and he repeated the idea to us on Wednesday." Kevin looked over his shoulder at Ellie. "I probably looked interested in it at the time because Craig was already pushing the same theory."

"And you're positive you didn't specify what kind of drugs?" Fisher asked, although Kevin had already answered the question before.

"No. And since it wasn't in any of the media releases, and the news reports on the Ross raid just said cannabis and cannabis resin—"

"I just hope we don't get into a 'he said, she said' thing with him," Fisher snapped, "because that'll get us absolutely nowhere."

Ellie pushed away from the door frame. On the monitor, Dave Martin was packing up his case and Serge was stowing away his photographic equipment. "We'll just have to see how it plays out."

She looked at Kevin on her way out the door. "Either way, it won't be fun."

chapter FORTY-SIX

"I want to show you something," Ellie said, opening her notebook as Waddell sipped the fresh cup of coffee she'd brought him. A raisin muffin sat on the desk next to his elbow, still in its wax-paper shell. "You asked me earlier whether I was sure your man Burrows is our shooter. I thought I'd run by you what we have, to see what you think."

"Sure. Go for it."

She pulled out Burrows's DNA profile from a file folder and placed it carefully in front of him on the table. "This is from the NDDB," she said, referring to the national DNA database. "It was collected after Burrows's armed robbery conviction." She followed it with the photograph of the hair. "This is a hair we found on the living room carpet in the Hansen home. The root's still there, which, as you know, means we're going to be able to get nuclear DNA from it instead of just mitochondrial DNA from the shaft. We're confident it'll be an exact match to this," she tapped a finger on Burrows's DNA report. "Mrs. Hansen told us Burrows stopped by on Monday night and made a voluntary admission that he'd just killed her husband. Her testimony, combined with this hair and DNA match, will give us a solid case against him."

"If the lab makes the match," Waddell said, staring at the

photograph.

"Mmm." Ellie picked up the photo and the report and replaced them with the photograph of Burrows's boot print. "This comes from the field on Church Road where Hansen was killed. It's a size thirteen boot. The prints went from the road into the field, up to where the body was left, and then they go back to the road again. The treads on this boot are pretty distinctive. Our expert tells me it's an exact match to the boots Burrows was wearing when we arrested him. We can prove he walked into that field with Bill Hansen and walked back out again after he shot him."

"Sounds bad for Mickey."

"It is," Ellie agreed.

Waddell touched his beard. "Boy, somebody should have told that goofball to get rid of those boots. The dumber they are, the harder they fall."

Ellie gathered up the photographs and put them back into the folder. "Where are you from originally, Chuck? Kingston?"

"No, Hamilton."

"Oh!" Ellie pretended to be surprised, as though she hadn't done any background on him beforehand. "Was your dad a steelworker?"

"Union boss. One tough sonofabitch."

"How'd you get into Corrections?"

Waddell shrugged. "Heard they were hiring. Needed a job after high school, and I damn well wasn't going into the mills, and I damn well wasn't going to hang around Hamilton if I could get the hell out. No brainer."

"I see." Ellie put down the pen and leaned on the table, hand cupping her chin. "Not exactly the kind of work most people would go in for."

"My daddy was a bastard, but he didn't raise no wimps."

"Did you only work in Kingston?"

He shook his head. "Started in Drumheller, moved around a bit out west, then came back east to Kingston. Look, who gives a shit? Is there anything else you want to ask me about Mickey, or are we done here?"

"Just interested in your background, Chuck." She pointed

at his untouched muffin. "Don't let it go to waste. How's your coffee?"

"It's fine." Waddell sighed, then picked up the muffin and started to peel off the wax-paper shell.

"The reason I'm interested," Ellie went on, "is that you've shown a willingness to bring other people along. While you were in Kingston you stayed in contact with some of the inmates you'd known or guys like Burrows that you'd arrested. You were concerned about their future, and you did what you could to help them after they got out. Not a lot of people in law enforcement do that sort of thing."

"You make it sound like I'm some kind of bleeding-heart liberal. I just met a few guys who needed a break, and I helped them out."

"It must have been strange coming up to the SLPS after Kingston. Moving from a force of almost two hundred sworn officers to a staff of seven."

"Mm hm." Waddell reached for his coffee, his mouth full of muffin.

"A big fish in a small pond."

Waddell shrugged indifferently.

"They were probably thrilled to get a guy with your expertise, even if it is a pretty quiet place."

"I guess."

"You were their detective for twenty years. After moving around so much in your career, it's surprising you stayed put that long."

Waddell patted his beard with his napkin. "It's a nice place. I like it. Quiet. It was time to settle down, I guess you could say."

"I guess you saw a lot of them come and go in that length of time."

"Yeah." Waddell rolled his eyes. "A lot of kids think it's gonna be all fun and games being a cop, then they find out they're spending their shift with their thumb up their ass or filling out endless paperwork, and it kind of loses its shine pretty fast. Know what I mean?"

"I know what you mean. I suppose you got stuck with a lot of the training and coaching."

"Mostly the deputy chief would do that. I did some, though. Not my favourite thing in the world."

"Oh?" Ellie raised her eyebrows. "I'd have thought you would have really enjoyed it, since you were into mentoring so much."

"It's a waste of my time to stand up there in front of meatheads who'd rather be out driving laps around the lake like mindless idiots. I prefer to pick and choose the guys. You know, the ones really interested in making something of themselves as cops."

"Like Kevin."

"Sure. Smart kid. Always asking questions." Waddell snickered. "Too many questions, sometimes. Could be a pain in the butt when he wanted to. But a good kid, don't get me wrong."

"Very intelligent."

"Yeah. He comes across as naive as hell, but it's mostly an act. He knows what the hell's going on. In fact—"

There was a knock at the door. Carty stuck his head inside. "Detective Inspector March?"

Ellie stood up. "I'm sorry, Chuck. Could you give me a few minutes?"

Waddell rolled his eyes, folding his arms across his chest. "Sure, no problem."

Ellie picked up her notebook and file folder and left the room, closing the door firmly behind her.

chapter FORTY-SEVEN

Twenty minutes later, Ellie walked back into the room, followed by Tom Carty, who put another cup of coffee and muffin on the table in front of Waddell before taking up the same station in the corner that he'd occupied last night during their interrogation of Mickey Burrows. Ellie closed the door and sat down.

"Sorry about the interruption, Chuck. A couple of important phone calls I had to return."

Waddell fell on the muffin this time without hesitation, stripping away the paper and taking a bite. "Can't fool an old fooler," he said while chewing. "Trying to figure out what else to ask me?"

"Oh no, I know what to ask you, don't worry. I think we were talking about Kevin before the interruption. You were about to tell me something about him."

Waddell glanced at Carty while swallowing. "Yeah, I guess. Something about him knowing a hell of a lot more than he lets on. But every cop worth his pay cheque knows how to pull that one. Look, not that I'm not enjoying your hospitality," he took another bite of muffin, "but I really don't see where any of this is going to help your investigation. I really should be getting back."

"On the contrary," Ellie assured him, "you're being very helpful. See, here's something that's been stumping me. We were talking before about whether Mickey Burrows had a connection to biker gangs. We know that on Monday night, Burrows went over to Bill Hansen's car yard and convinced him to leave with him. Burrows drove his Jeep and Hansen drove his own truck. They went somewhere, and at some point Burrows left his own vehicle behind, drove Hansen in Hansen's own truck out to that field on Church Road, and killed him. We also know from the evidence at the scene that there was a second man with Burrows in that truck. He sat in the back seat, he got out when Burrows and Hansen got out, he watched Burrows take Hansen out into that field and shoot him, then he got back into the front passenger seat when Burrows drove Hansen's truck away."

Waddell listened attentively, staring at her over the rim of his coffee cup.

"We figure that Burrows collected Hansen at the car yard in order to take him to a meeting with this second man. The meeting didn't go well, apparently. The second man, who we think was calling all the shots in this whole thing, decided to take Hansen for a ride to scare some sense into him. Maybe the intention wasn't to kill him, just intimidate him into staying with the program. Maybe Burrows acted on impulse and shot Hansen on his own. Or maybe this second guy, who was in charge, told him screw it, go ahead and kill him. Make him an example for everyone else on the string. A powerful lesson in what happens when the others don't do what they're told."

Waddell put down his cup and wiped his beard with his napkin, his eyes still on her.

"The problem is in identifying this second man," Ellie continued. "The one in charge. The one forcing Hansen to distribute illegal drugs in his cars and trucks. The biker gang theory has been unravelling, so we're back to square one with this guy. Do you know of anyone other than yourself that Mickey Burrows would have been spending a lot of time with?"

"Haven't a clue."

Ellie looked puzzled. "How do you keep track of his time?

Do you pay him by the hour, or what? How does that work?"

"Not by the hour. I pay him a flat amount every week."

"So you don't expect him to account for his time? To make sure he's earning what you pay him?"

"No. I give him assignments, he does them, and I don't give a shit about what he does the rest of the time. I'm not his nanny, for Christ's sake."

"So he could be doing stuff for somebody else on the side and you wouldn't know?"

"Sure, I guess so."

Ellie crossed her legs, smoothing her pant leg over her knee. "If you were going to profile this second man, the one in charge, Chuck, how would you describe him?"

"Me? I don't know."

"Come on, Chuck. You put in all that time as a detective. Two decades. Share that expertise of yours with me. Profile the second man."

Waddell looked at Carty, who stared at him without expression. Then he shrugged. "I don't know. We're talking about a guy who's been running a pretty profitable drug operation right under your noses for a long time without getting caught. Which means he's pretty smart."

"Keep going."

"Okay." Waddell leaned forward suddenly. "He's smart, and he takes advantage of his opportunities. He sees an opening and he moves without hesitation. He finds a guy like Bill Hansen, who's got an ideal business going that's ripe to take advantage of, and he puts him into a box where he has to do what this guy tells him to do, or else."

"You mean by using Burrows to threaten him with violence if he doesn't comply? That doesn't sound smart to me, Chuck. It just sounds like some brainless thug."

"No no no, not violence. Nothing crude like that. Not up front, anyway. He gets something on the guy and holds it over his head. Play along, or go to prison."

"How would he get information like that? How would he know Hansen was involved in something that could send him to prison?"

"I don't know. Maybe he's a cop. Maybe you've got a dirty cop on your hands."

Ellie raised her eyebrows again, pretending to consider it for the first time. "A guy who uncovered evidence somewhere along the way, or maybe just fabricated it, and used his authority as a police officer to threaten to have Hansen, and maybe others like him, arrested? Is that what you mean, Chuck?"

"That's the idea. Now you're thinking."

"So, someone smart, someone working the area as a law enforcement officer, someone known to these people already? And with access to current operations so he could stay one step ahead? Is that how you see it?"

"Sure," Waddell said. "Makes perfect sense to me."

"Who would fit this profile, Chuck? Who would it be?"

Waddell suddenly frowned and, fingering his chin whiskers, glanced at Carty before replying. "I don't like where you're going with this."

"Why not, Chuck?"

"You started me off with all the Charter cautions and shit to lead me down the garden path, didn't you? You're not looking at me; you're trying to pin this on the kid."

Ellie pretended to be confused. "Pardon me? Who do you mean, Chuck?"

He glanced at Carty again. "Kev. You're thinking this is Kev, right? A lot smarter than he sometimes pretends to be, knows everybody in the village, has all the inside info anybody would need. Ah, man." He screwed up his face. "Say it ain't so. That's why this guy's here and not Kev, am I right? You shot me that line about having information on me when what you're really doing is getting ready to make your move on the kid, and you want me to fit the noose for him. Is that it?"

Ellie shook her head. "I meant what I said, Chuck. We have information pointing at you. I don't understand why you'd think Kevin should be considered as a suspect."

Waddell shot forward in his chair again and pointed his finger at Ellie.

Carty twitched, but stayed put.

"Think about it!" Waddell exclaimed. "He pulls Hansen over for speeding one day, finds some stuff in his car, and forces him to join his network. Or maybe he just plants the stuff. Or maybe he just spreads rumours around that Hansen's dealing hot cars, kills all his business, and gives him no choice but to play along. Then he does the same with other suckers in the village. Sets himself up as a fence for stolen goods and gets the old woman running the second-hand store to move it all for him. Perfect again. Really smart."

"No one mentioned stolen goods, Chuck. How do you know that Mrs. Shipman was part of this network?"

"Uh, good question. Let me think. Maybe Kev mentioned it to me. Anyway, it makes perfect sense."

Ellie was silent for a long moment, watching him finger his beard, his narrow eyes glittering at her. "Chuck, I interviewed Mrs. Shipman this morning. Before we talk about what she told me, before we go any further with questions about other information I just received when I was out of the room a few minutes ago, I need to remind you that you have the right at any time to speak to an attorney. Do you want to call your lawyer now?"

Waddell's eyes drifted from Carty to the closed door. "No," he said finally. "Like I told you, I don't need a lawyer. You guys are barking up the wrong tree. An experienced detective would see that."

"Mrs. Shipman told me you were the one who coerced her into moving stolen goods to a contact in Toronto. This contact, Mr. Cho, is now in police custody, Chuck, and he's answering questions. Would you like to explain to us where you were getting the stolen jewellery and watches that you forced her to send to this Mr. Cho?"

Waddell shook his head, pushing out his lips in frustration. "Bullshit. Walker must have put her up to it. 'If they question you, say it was Waddell.' He's setting me up. It's a frame. God, you guys are dense."

"We found Bill Hansen's truck on your property yesterday,"

Ellie went on. "It was hidden up a narrow laneway across from your cottage. You own that lot, in addition to the waterfront lot with the cottage. We've been looking for that truck for nearly a week. When you said to me and Kevin on Wednesday in the village that it was 'long gone,' as you put it, did you know it was there all the time?"

Waddell closed his eyes and pinched the bridge of his nose. After a long moment he opened his eyes again and looked at his fingertips. "No."

"Can you explain why Burrows hid it there?"

"Because he's a complete and total fucking idiot?"

"Did you tell him to put it there, Chuck?"

"No, no, no!" Waddell's hands curled into fists. "Didn't I just fucking tell you I didn't know the fucking truck was there? *JESUS FUCKING CHRIST!*"

"Steady," Carty warned.

"What did you tell him to do with the truck?" Ellie asked. "Did you at least have the sense to tell him to get rid of it somewhere farther away than that?"

Waddell pressed his lips together and said nothing. The venom in his eyes was unmistakable.

"Were you the other man who took Bill Hansen for a ride on Monday night, Chuck?"

"No, I was *not*."

"Have you ever been inside Bill Hansen's truck? His black Dodge Ram 1500?"

"No, I have *not* been."

"Our search also turned up Bill Hansen's cellphone," Ellie went on. "It was about five metres from the truck, in the woods. Looks like Burrows took it apart and threw it away. It would have gone farther, I imagine, but it hit a tree and shattered. The keys went a few metres further than that, at least, but he hit a tree with them, too."

Waddell's jaw tightened.

"The gun took a little more work to find. Do you know where he put it, Chuck?"

Waddell said nothing.

"Well, for starters he took it back to the cottage with him. I guess he was a little reluctant to throw it away. Maybe he likes guns and thought about keeping it."

"Jesus H. Christ," Waddell muttered.

"But then common sense took over, Chuck, or what passes for common sense with a guy like him. He went out onto the ice a few metres, cut a hole, and dropped the gun into the water. Unfortunately for him, although the hole had frozen over again, there was no snow covering it. It stood out like a sore thumb once you looked out there for it."

Waddell slowly shook his head. "Okay, so he's stupid. Incredibly *fucking* stupid. Got nothing to do with me, though. Nothing connects any of this shit to me."

Earlier this morning, Ellie had been thinking the same thing. They'd found his boot prints at the crime scene, but while they were the correct size, the treads didn't match the black sneakers he was wearing today, and Ellie was certain that a search of Waddell's home would not produce them, either. He'd obviously followed his own advice and gotten rid of them. The complete lack of physical evidence connecting Waddell to Hansen's murder had been thoroughly discouraging. A quick conversation with Martin, though, had just changed the entire picture.

"Burrows wiped down the truck, inside and out," she said. "No prints on the steering wheel, door handles, dashboard, radio buttons, or window buttons. Zip."

Waddell's jaw relaxed a little.

"He wiped down the seats as well, but he apparently doesn't realize how much his hair's falling out, and he missed a couple. One between the seat and the seat belt sheath, and another between the top of the seat and the head rest. We'll have no trouble putting him in the truck, Chuck."

Waddell's fists slowly unclenched.

"No hairs in the back seat," Ellie said. "No prints, either. Burrows cleaned up back there, too. At least he got that much right, eh?"

Waddell looked at her, the corners of his mouth curling up.

"Except," she said, "he missed something. You'll never guess what."

The muscles in Waddell's face froze, the little smile still in place.

"You're not exactly a young man any more, Chuck, are you? When you got out of the truck, you had to use that overhead grab handle thing. I guess you didn't have your gloves on inside the truck, and Burrows forgot to wipe it down. We found a nice set of prints on the grab handle, and they match yours. You were in that truck, Chuck. You lied to me when I asked you about it a few minutes ago. As you know, that's a serious mistake on your part. So I'm going to ask you again, to give you a chance to tell the truth. Were you present when Mickey Burrows shot and killed Bill Hansen?"

Waddell stared, unable to speak. She watched the smile melt as his head turned away and his chin dropped. His shoulders sagged. He slowly exhaled. It was like watching a punctured inflatable doll lose all its air.

"Were you present when Mickey Burrows shot and killed Bill Hansen?" she repeated.

"Lawyer," he said.

"Did you order Burrows to shoot Hansen, or did he do that on his own?"

"Lawyer."

"Burrows was stupid, but you were supposed to be the smart one, Chuck. Did you order him to kill Hansen or just threaten him?"

"I didn't tell that fucking *idiot* to shoot him, all right? He did that all on his own, the fucking dolt! Jesus Christ, what a fucking waste of space."

"Did you tell him to threaten Hansen because the man had tried to contact the police that day before losing his nerve?"

"I'm not answering any more questions. Let me out of here now."

"Burrows will tell us soon enough, Chuck. We'll put an undercover officer next to him in lock-up, and he'll spill his guts. You should get out in front of this and come clean right now.

Did you tell Burrows to kill Hansen or just to threaten him?"

"I already answered that! I didn't tell him to kill him!"

"You told him just to threaten him?"

"Yes yes yes yes yes!"

"And Burrows lost it and pulled the trigger anyway?"

"Yes yes *YES!*"

Ellie turned to Carty. "Get him out of here."

chapter FORTY-EIGHT

Ten days later, on Christmas Eve, it was snowing. When Willie Bird delivered her dinner at six o'clock, he said the roads were already becoming impassable. Her order was the last one Skinny Jimmy would accept, and as soon as Birdie returned to the Silver Kettle and settled up, the restaurant would close for the next three days.

"You gonna be okay, Ellie?"

"Sure. I stocked up on stuff. I'll get by."

Behind Birdie, the snow was steadily falling in large wet flakes. The windshield wipers on his purple Sunfire kept time above the sound of its idling engine. He thanked her for the generous tip and hurried away.

Even Birdie had family waiting to spend Christmas with him.

Ellie listened to the silence, the cottage door still open. It sounded absolutely wonderful to her. Then the cold air and the smell coming from the bags in her arms prompted her to hurry into the kitchen.

When she'd called in the order this morning and asked for something unusual featuring turkey, Edna had passed the phone over to Skinny Jimmy himself.

"I got lots of turkey, Ellie," he said without preamble. "What do you want?"

"Something for tonight and something else I can reheat for Christmas dinner tomorrow."

"Microwave or conventional oven?"

"Um, oven?" It felt like a test. When he grunted, she figured she'd passed.

"Hot and spicy or mild?"

"How about one of each?"

"Okay." Silence for a moment, while he deliberated. "Spicy, I can do roast turkey breasts with toasted ancho chilies, garlic, and scallions in a butter rub. The other, how about a small turkey with a maple syrup glaze, sage butter, and bacon wraps? Cornbread stuffing. This one I'll package so you can put it in the fridge right away, and I'll send a cup of the drippings for when you put it in the oven to warm up tomorrow. Watch the temperature, Ellie. And I'll send you a couple pans of roasted potatoes and vegetables."

"That sounds wonderful," Ellie said.

"Desserts?"

"No, I think I'm good, thanks."

"Have you got some cabernet down there?"

"Um, yeah, as a matter of fact, I do." Ridge Ballantyne had presented her with two bottles before leaving to spend the holidays with friends back in Scotland. In return, she'd kissed him on the cheek. It seemed to please him immensely.

"Perfect, Ellie. Your Christmas menu's now complete."

As Ellie unpacked the bags on the kitchen counter, she saw that Jimmy had included hand-written explanations and reminders that were taped to each container. As crazy as it must have been the day before the holidays, he'd still taken the time to scribble out these little notes to her, and although they were mostly illegible, she was touched by the gesture.

She ate dinner in front of the TV, washing down the ancho chili turkey breasts and roast vegetables with one of the bottles of wine. She'd finished watching *Die Hard* and was halfway through *Die Hard 2* when she saw car headlights flickering through the bedroom window onto the ceiling above her head.

She frowned when they steadied for a moment and then shut off.

Someone was outside.

She got up, opened the door, and was surprised to see Kevin coming down the slope, carrying two gift bags. He came into the kitchen with a smile on his face and handed the bags to her.

"Merry Christmas. I thought I'd drop by and say hello before the blizzard buries us in."

"That's very sweet of you." Ellie took the bags and set them on the kitchen table. "Come in. Can you stay for a while? I was just watching a movie."

He glanced at the television. "Ah, yes. A Christmas staple. Wait, isn't that a new TV?"

"Yeah, I went shopping."

Kevin looked at the television, a fifty-inch plasma high definition set that she'd connected to the satellite dish on the roof. He noticed a new DVD player, a home theatre system, and a rack filled with movies and music CDs. As Bruce Willis fled on a snowmobile from mercenaries firing very loud semi-automatic rifles loaded with dummy rounds, Ellie reached into one of the bags and brought out a poinsettia plant.

"It's lovely. Thank you."

"They're a native of Mexico," Kevin said. "According to legend, one Christmas a little Mexican girl didn't have enough money to buy Jesus a present, so instead she gathered wild plants along the side of the road and put them in front of the church altar. When the leaves turned blood red, a tradition was born."

"How do you know all this stuff? Never mind, don't tell me." She reached into the other bag and pulled out a four-pack of Beau's beer, from an Ottawa-area microbrewery.

"It's their Mexican spiced ale," he said. "I figured out that you like hot stuff, and I didn't know if you'd tried this yet."

"I haven't. Thank you. Take your coat off and sit down for a minute." She opened the refrigerator and made room for the four-pack between a jug of orange juice and a container of mixed salad.

"I can't stay too long," he said, removing his boots. "The kids are asleep and Janie's online talking to all her cousins on Facebook, but eventually she'll start looking for me."

"Poor you."

He grinned, unzipping his coat. "Yeah."

Ellie grabbed the remote control and muted the sound on the television. "Can I get you something to drink? Coke? Orange juice?"

"No, thanks. I'm fine." He sat down on the sofa and looked around. "I'm really glad you decided to buy this place, Ellie. It's a nice property, and Gerry felt bad that it wasn't being used. He said he's giving you a good deal on it."

"Yeah, he is."

"Good." He crossed his legs and pulled up his white tube socks. "The other reason I stopped by is to tell you I had a meeting with Scott this afternoon. Senior management has decided to accept my 'version of events,' quote unquote, and I'll be allowed to stay with the crime unit if I want to."

"Glad to hear it." Ellie had already spoken to Patterson about it earlier in the day. An informal review of Kevin's performance during the investigation had been conducted by Staff Sergeant Tobin, the regional operations manager. He'd concluded that the young detective constable's performance during the investigation did not warrant disciplinary action. Craig Dart had withdrawn his accusations that Kevin was on Chuck Waddell's payroll, hoping, no doubt, that it would help his request for a transfer out of the detachment. In follow-up questioning, Mickey Burrows had scoffed at the idea, declaring that Waddell was too cheap to pay for what he could get for free simply by picking the unsuspecting kid's brain. Eventually even Waddell himself finally gave up and admitted the truth about Kevin during negotiations on a plea deal. The consensus was that Kevin was clean but naive.

Ellie frowned at him. "You'll stay with the unit, won't you?"

"I said I'd think about it and let him know." Kevin looked away.

"Did you have something else in mind?"

"I don't know. I might ask for a transfer. I talked to Scott about it, but he said the only thing they'd be able to offer me would be something up north, like Dryden or Ear Falls. I've never even heard of Ear Falls."

"He's just trying to scare you. You probably wouldn't have to go any farther north than Upsala."

"It's Janie that scares me. She'll kill me if I put in for a transfer."

Ellie said nothing, feeling particularly unqualified to comment on family considerations when it came to career movement.

"I don't know if I can stay, though," he went on. "I can hardly look these guys in the eye any more."

"The region has given you the green light, Kevin. There's absolutely no reason for you to feel that you should leave."

"I guess you're right."

She studied him for a moment. The light from the propane stove flickered on his round, trusting face. With his lower lip stuck out and his brow furrowed, he looked for all the world like a downcast little boy whose tricycle had just been stolen.

How could you not like this kid?

"The Crown attorney loves the cases we've given her," she said. "She told me she thought you did a very good job as primary. Susan doesn't exactly hand out compliments every day, so you should pat yourself on the back."

"Thanks."

All the key pieces of evidence had fallen into place. Ballistics testing had matched the gun Burrows dropped into the lake with the bullet found in Lackey's field, and a search of Waddell's home had turned up cardboard cartons filled with cash, stolen jewellery, and Waddell's personal stash of weed, compliments of the Ross family. Witnesses prepared to testify against him included Lois Shipman, the pharmacist, and the owner of a local winery. The list of charges was impressive, and Susan Mitchum was confident that Chuck Waddell would end up doing serious time when it was all over, a possible plea bargain notwithstanding.

"I thought you did a good job, too, Kevin. I told Fisher that, and it's all documented and in the case file. You've got a successful homicide investigation under your belt. You need to build on it now, not run from it."

"It wasn't easy listening to all that toxic poison spewing out of Waddell. The sonofabitch tried to implicate me in *his* crimes. On top of that, he was doing all this stuff right under my nose, and I had absolutely no clue. I trusted him. I told him stuff. I talked to him about my work, what I was doing. I asked him for advice. And he played me for a fool. I *was* a fool. I believed every word he ever said to me."

"You were betrayed by someone you thought was your friend. He used you, took advantage of you, then tried to torpedo you when he got boxed into a corner. It happens, Kevin. Deal with it and move on to the next case. That's how this works. That's what we do."

He stared at the propane fire for a long time before looking at her. "Let me ask you a question. Tell me honestly. Do you think I'm too soft to be a good cop?"

"Too soft?" Ellie raised her eyebrows. "Not at all. Why on earth would you think that?"

"I just don't have what it takes to be a hard ass, like Bishop or Carty. I keep thinking I'm too nice. I want people to like me too much. Cops should be able to live with people hating them all the time. I'm not comfortable with that."

"For crying out loud." Ellie got up and walked into the kitchen. She opened the fridge and pulled out a can of Coke and one of the bottles of Mexican spiced ale. Uncapping the beer, she walked back and handed the can of Coke to Kevin. "First of all, you know damned well you can live with it because I know you can name at least a dozen people who've hated you from the moment you first put on a uniform. You've lasted this long, so obviously you can deal with it. Second, don't you think there are more than enough hard-assed cops around here as it is? Think about what your strengths are. You care about people, you have compassion, and you want to separate the bad elements in your jurisdiction from the good ones and help the good ones prosper and grow so they can raise their kids and live happy lives. Can you think of a better description of policing than that? Remember your strengths, Kevin, and use them to your advantage on the job."

Kevin opened the can of Coke and stared at the fire. After a moment he took a long drink and looked at her. "How do you do it? How do you stand all the bullshit? It's even worse for you because you're a woman. Dinosaurs like Fisher refuse to treat you seriously, but it doesn't seem to bother you at all. You just plow ahead and get the job done."

She shrugged. "It bothers me, all right. But you don't let it show. Bottom line."

They listened to the hissing of the propane stove. A clock on the kitchen wall ticked. Kevin leaned over and put the can of Coke down on the side table next to him. Frowning, he picked up a piece of paper. He squinted at it, turned it over, and turned it back. "Hey. This is from Skinny Jimmy."

"Yeah. I ordered food in for tonight and tomorrow. He sent a bunch of notes explaining what was in each container and what I should do."

Kevin blinked at her. "Skinny Jimmy doesn't do that."

"When I talked to him on the phone—"

"You *talked* to him? On the *phone*?" Kevin stared at her, mouth open. "You mean, like a conversation?"

"Sure. What? What's wrong with that?"

"Skinny Jimmy doesn't talk to *anybody*. Ever. I mean, he talks to Edna and the drivers and Peter. Mostly yells at them. But he never, *ever* talks to customers." Kevin read the note again, which listed the herbs and spices he'd added to the roasted diced squash, zucchini, and carrots. "Never mind giving somebody something in writing. He must *really* like you."

Ellie shrugged. "Whatever. The food's outstanding."

Kevin laughed, shaking his head. He put down the note and stood up. "I'd better go. Will you be okay here?"

She walked him to the kitchen door. "Sure, of course. I'm fine. I like it here." She patted him on the arm. "This was a great idea, moving down here to the lake. Thanks for your help."

"You're welcome." He pulled on his boots, straightened, and awkwardly held out his hand. "It was great working with you."

Ellie shook his hand firmly. "Likewise. Always a pleasure to work with a good detective."

She watched him trudge back up the hill to his car, then she closed the door and locked it. She wandered back into the living room, picked up her beer, and took a long swig. The door of the second bedroom was open, and she looked in at the little office she'd set up in there for herself. On the table serving as a makeshift desk was the paperwork extending her in the detective inspector position, pending a competitive process she was determined to ace. Tony Agosta had promised her it would happen this spring. Her advice to Kevin, to build on the successful outcome of this case rather than run from it, had not been gratuitous—she'd decided to do the same thing herself. She'd bought this property, moved her few belongings down from Orillia, and settled in last week. She was already anxious for her next assignment.

It felt right. This is who she was. This is where she wanted to be.

She caught sight of her reflection in the dark sliding doors. Ellie March, embossed on the blackness of Sorrow Lake.

Finally, she thought.

I've finally found a home.

Truly happy for the first time in a very long while, Ellie smiled.

Acknowledgments

The author gratefully acknowledges the assistance of Detective Inspector Randy Millar, Ontario Provincial Police, Retired, who provided guidance and insight into the homicide investigation process as carried out by the OPP, answered endless questions, read the manuscript, and provided feedback. Any errors in fact, procedure, legal practices, or other errors or omissions are entirely the fault of the author or are the result of creative licence.

Thanks go out to Sergeant Terry Goertzen, Ontario Provincial Police, Retired, who shared his experiences and insight into policing in rural Ontario. Thanks as well to Gary Southin for the rental of the cottage at Bass Lake, Lyndhurst, where the idea for this series first began to take shape, and to Rev. Kathleen Petrie for her kind assistance.

The author once more owes a debt of gratitude to editorial reader Margaret Leroux, who read the manuscript and, as always, found errors everyone else overlooked.

Thank you Mary Jane Maffini and Linda Wiken for your unflagging support, and Sylvia McConnell for your praise and encouragement.

Most importantly, thanks once again to Lynn L. Clark, editor, partner, and wife, for your infinite patience and kindness, your editorial skills, and your constant, loving support.

About the Author

Michael J. McCann lives and writes in Oxford Station, Ontario, Canada. A graduate of Trent University in Peterborough, ON, and Queen's University in Kingston, ON, he worked for Carswell Legal Publications (Western) as Production Editor of *Criminal Reports (Third Series)* before spending fifteen years with the Canada Border Services Agency as a training specialist, project officer, and program manager at national headquarters in Ottawa. He's married and has one son.

He's the author of the Donaghue and Stainer Crime Novel series, including *Blood Passage*, *Marcie's Murder*, *The Fregoli Delusion*, and *The Rainy Day Killer*, as well as *The Ghost Man*, a supernatural thriller.

If you enjoyed Michael J. McCann's

Sorrow Lake

you won't want to miss the exciting

DONAGHUE AND STAINER CRIME NOVEL SERIES

Blood Passage
by Michael J. McCann

ISBN: 978-0-9877087-0-0
eBook ISBN: 978-0-9877087-1-7

Would you believe a small boy who claims he was murdered in his previous life? The first Donaghue and Stainer Crime Novel.

Marcie's Murder
by Michael J. McCann

ISBN: 978-0-9877087-2-4
eBook ISBN: 978-0-9877087-3-1

Donaghue's on vacation when he's jailed on suspicion of murder. Can Stainer get him out in time to find the real killer before it's too late?

The Fregoli Delusion
by Michael J. McCann

ISBN: 978-0-9877087-4-8
eBook ISBN: 978-0-9877087-5-5

Their only witness has a rare disorder that renders his testimony useless. Is Stainer wrong to believe he may actually know who the real killer is?

The Rainy Day Killer
by Michael J. McCann

ISBN: 978-0-9877087-8-6
eBook ISBN: 978-0-9877087-9-3

A serial killer preys on unsuspecting women — when it rains. Will Stainer's impending wedding end in murder, or will she survive to say her vows?

CPSIA information can be obtained at www.ICGtesting.com
Printed in the USA
LVOW08s0309230915

455309LV00003B/19/P